NIGHT'S SORCERIES

Azhriaz was at odds with her father, Azhrarn, Prince of Demons, who had besides his own fierce argument with Chuz, the Prince of Madness and Azhriaz's lover.

The Prince of Demons therefore hunted down these lovers, and the wild woods grew wilder. The Eshva, the dreaming envoys of the demons, began to prowl and dance there, and the demon high caste, the Vazdru, rode the paths and glades on their midnight horses. And there came to be many curious ill-meetings, by moonlight and by shadow. . . .

Also in Legend by Tanith Lee

DEATH'S MASTER
DELIRIUM'S MISTRESS
DELUSION'S MASTER
NIGHT'S MASTER
VOLKHAVAAR

NIGHT'S SORCERIES

A Novel of the Flat Earth

Tanith Lee

A Legend Book

Published by Arrow Books Limited
62–65 Chandos Place, London WC2N 4NW

An imprint of Century Hutchinson Limited

London Melbourne Sydney Auckland
Johannesburg and agencies throughout
the world

First published in 1987 by Daw Books, Inc.
Legend edition 1988

Printed and bound in Great Britain by
Anchor Brendon Limited, Tiptree, Essex

ISBN 0 09 958470 0

NIGHT'S SORCERIES

Stories from the Time of Azhriaz

What is any of this to us? Time is endless and ours. Love and death are only the games we play in it.

—*Delirium's Mistress*

FOREWORD

The history of the Prince of Demon's daughter, Azhriaz, (called also Sovaz, and Atmeh) has been recounted elsewhere.*

Yet there are other tales told of that season when she, a being half demon, part mortal, dwelled and wandered among the lands of the Flat Earth. For the shadows and rays of her love, her quarrels and sorceries, her beauty and learning, fell on many lives not her own. . . .

**Delirium's Mistress*

Now when first she lived in the world,
Azhrarn the Demon's daughter was called Sovaz,
and she was the mistress of Chuz, Prince Madness.

For her sake Chuz wore a form that was entirely and most wonderfully handsome, as had not always been his way. But, like her own father, he was a Lord of Darkness.

Quite some while, they say, these two were lovers in the depths of a great wood, which grew enchanted, odd, and perilous, through their nearness.

NIGHT'S DAUGHTER, DAY'S DESIRE

IN THE HEM of the forest a village lay. An old road ran by the spot, on its way to the towns of the south, and in the past this road it was which had given the village importance and prosperity. Since then other thoroughfares had been built, and fewer travelers came and went through the deep woods. A caravan had not been seen in those parts for seven years. The pink stones of which the village was made had softened, and the hearts grown harder. On a hill above, among the trees, stood a temple. Its pillars were ringed by faded gilt and the turquoise tiles had chipped away from its roofs. Nevertheless, the priests lived well, for the villagers had stayed pious. Every night, on the highest point of the temple, a beacon was lit, to remind the gods where the village rested.

It sometimes happened that a decent family of the area, finding it had too many mouths to feed, would offer a younger son to the temple—no women were allowed there—as its servant. Just such a one was Beetle.

At seven years of age he had been left by his nurse, in a shadowy ghost-light before dawn in the temple's outer court-yard. Around his neck was a small flawed ruby on a piece of silk. This was the child's 'gift,' without which he could not expect a place in the fane. Poor Beetle (who at that time had another name) stood and cried in the chilly morning, until at length a priest came waddling out and found him, without much pleasure. "Another brat. Well, it is the tradition. Let me see—ah, what a paltry jewel. Stop sniveling, boy. You are now wrapped in the bounty of the temple." And taking Beetle-not-yet by his scruff, the priest conducted him within.

Here, as the years went by, Beetle (now Beetle) grew up nourished on a religious charity of watered milk, meat gristle, crusts and rinds. And was meanwhile educated by the temple in the intellectual and spiritual arts of sweeping, scrubbing, polishing and picking up. His new name, given him in the first days, was to encourage selfless industry by sympathetic magic. The other servants of the fane had similar names, except for one sleek boy, who was allowed to trim the altar candles and pour the incense, and who sometimes aided the priests at their disrobing and in the holy bath. This one, called Precious, slept always in a separate cubicle and ate at the priests' table. But then, the temple had bought Precious from the last caravan.

Very occasionally, needy travelers might pause for shelter at the fane. Though a fee was required of them, it proved a little cheaper than the costs of the village inn.

One day when Beetle, thin and scrawny and weak-eyed like the rest—saving Precious—was seventeen years of age, a peddler availed himself of the priests' hospitality. The very next evening the Chief Priest summoned Beetle for an interview.

"Dear Beetle," said the Chief Priest, who presided from his couch, a table at his elbow that had on it confectionery, peaches and wine—so Beetle might have dribbled if his mouth had not become so dry—"my son, it has been brought to my attention that you have committed your old fault."

"Father," cried Beetle, throwing himself down, "forgive me for eating the three candles—but I am tortured by such hunger—"

"Alas," said the Chief Priest, sadly toying with a sugar-almond, "you must strive after the virtue of abstinence. Have we taught you nothing in all your time with us? Alas. *Three* candles." (Beetle gibbered, feeling already the thong coming down on his back.) "That, however, is not the matter on which I called you to me. Indeed, since you have made free confession of your sin, perhaps we may overlook it, this once."

Beetle could scarcely believe his ears. Experience informed him that if he was to be let off one punishment, in a moment more something worse was about to be awarded him. Trembling, Beetle could not think what that might be.

"The fault to which I referred, my son, was that of your distressing habitual laziness. The gods are not served by slackness. But you have been leaning on your broom and dreaming, and lying abed until dawn. You are always observed, my son, even when no man is by. The gods are constantly at watch. My impulse was to chastise you, but I have come to believe that your laziness is due, rather than wickedness, to a sluggishness of your blood. For that reason, I propose to send you on an errand which will enliven you, and bring you back to us, we trust, fresher and more zealous."

Beetle gaped.

The Chief Priest nibbled a few candied berries in a reluctant way, so as not to distress them by ignoring them.

Presently he resumed.

"I have learned that a rich lord and his lady have recently made their abode in the forest. They are reclusive and dwell out of the world's eye, which doubtless says much for their modesty. But it seems to me that of the unique comfort the gods give, access to which we may offer them here, they should be reminded. There is reason to suppose they, living so quietly as they do, are unaware of this holy fane a few days' distance from their mansion. I therefore propose that a messenger be sent them, with the news. And for this task I have selected you, dear Beetle. For," the Priest smiled upon him, "though you are often tardy, I believe that your heart is pure."

Beetle groveled. His heart, pure or not, thundered in turmoil. He did not dare question or protest.

"You will be arrayed in some finery," added the Chief Priest, half closing his fat eyes so the pupils of them seemed to glitter on the youth like the points of lances. "You will represent the authority and piety of the temple. Of course, you will not think to abscond, but if fiends of the forest do tempt you from your errand, you must understand that my curse will be upon you. Do you recall the fate of Ant, who, tempted, ran away, carrying with him a small votive offering of silver?"

"Yes, father. He was never seen here again."

"And do you know why this is, my son?"

"Because—so you told us—your curse had found him out."

"Exactly the case. So you realize you must be on your guard, and not stray. For this curse is very terrible and entirely unavoidable, once active. Ant's bones lie in the woods. But you will perform your mission and return to our loving care."

"Oh yes, yes, father."

"Very good. Go away now. One shall come to instruct you more. You leave at sunrise tomorrow."

Beetle crawled from the presence. Outside, in the dusk-dim colonnade, he got up and stood hugging himself with undelight.

Evidently it was the peddler (who had seemed, when he arrived at the temple, unnerved) who had informed the Chief Priest of rich new neighbors in the forest. However, a few peculiar tales had already reached the village, borne in by charcoal-burners, itinerant beggars and the like. Some said a prince and princess had set up house in the woods. Others said, a pair of sorcerers. Surprises went on among the trees. Lights floated, bells rang, and carpets or clouds went flying between the upper boughs.

Beetle, though reckoned a fool and careful not to correct the impression, had already divined the reason for his selection as a bearer of temple greetings. Being superfluous, he could be risked. If the sorcerers killed and ate him, the temple would be no worse off. On the other hand, if the fair quarter of the tales was true, the moneyed couple might be brought into the fold. Or they might, after Beetle's visit, send some splendid token to the fane in the hope it would mind its own business. In which event, Beetle had been risked to charming effect.

As for Ant, presumably now he was at large on the far shores of the forest, spending the votive offering. It was not that Beetle feared the curses of the Chief Priest, only that he had come to the conclusion he had no luck, and all places of the earth would be alike and luckless to him.

Half starved and demoralized as he was, he could not summon the energy to flee from one misery to another.

So he meekly waited, and presently a priest came and told him what he must say, and the direction of the rich lord's (sorcerous) abode—or at least its *supposed* direction (which seemed to alter.) That night Beetle lay awake on his itchy pallet. In the hour before dawn he was come for again, doused in cold water, perfumed from the least lovely of the perfumery vials, clad in a passable robe, and given an elderly mule, a rod of office and a scroll penned by the Chief Priest himself. Lastly, some pale provisions were handed him in a satchel and he was let loose from the temple gate.

Only Precious, from an upper window, bothered to watch Beetle's departure—for motives known only to Precious. The plump form, swathed as ever neck to ankle in a comely drapery, was easily visible. But Beetle did not see it.

He rode away into the morning, not looking back or, particularly, forward.

For several days, Beetle continued to ride through the forest. At first, he did find the change of scene rather pleasant, but he was also greatly daunted by the size and height and depth of the wood, and by the strange sounds and scents it gave off, and the animals that quite legitimately lived there. He had all his days, till then, been restrained inside the temple's narrow confines. To sleep under the trees filled him with terrors. Even by day, the grunting of a badger turning in its slumber put him in mind of demons—of which he knew next to nothing, but all of it bad.

Moreover, the sparse provisions he had been given soon gave out, and the mule frequently fell into a doze in mid-plod. Of human creatures—mundane, wealthy or magical—there was not sight nor sign.

As for the road, on the fifth day it became so overgrown, its paving so displaced, that Beetle was forced to retreat from its surface. Shortly then he was lost.

This achieved, and night coming on, Beetle began to consider the Chief Priest's cursing abilities. Perhaps after all they were efficacious. Meanwhile, the wild beasts of the forest were tuning up their manic howls and trills. Off the road, a lion-cat would be sure to come and devour Beetle and the mule, or a devil-thing would feel free to tear them apart. A feeble rage seized on Beetle. He led the mule into the shelter of a thicket, and hastily made a fire. Chewing his fingernails for supper, Beetle sat and brooded. At last it seemed to him he went to sleep.

But not much later, hearing an eerie noise close by, Beetle awoke again.

In the ferns something crept about. It sounded too small to be the harbinger of horrid death, or maybe it was a venomous serpent. Beetle pranced to his feet, and just then there stole into the firelight a large hare, with a coat like black velvet. Around its neck was a collar of gold, and in each of its long-petaled ears was a tiny silver crescent.

As Beetle was staring, the hare swept the earth with these ears in a polite bow. Turning, it began to move quietly away.

Between fright and curiosity and somewhat thinking he still slept, Beetle felt impelled to press after it.

The hare showed no dismay at this. It kept going at a gentle pace, and soon passed up a sloping glade into a grove of walnut trees, through which the moonlight filtered, turning all the ripening fruit to pearls.

Somewhere among the walnuts, the hare vanished. But by then Beetle had seen faint lamplight shining. He went on, and next, where the grove parted, found himself gazing up at a humble ancient cottage, from whose door and windows the soft glow came spilling out. Here a garden grew, night-sweet with jasmine. Among the vines, a little spring sprang forth like a silver string. Nearby, on a rough table, stood a homely jug, breadcakes, apples and cheese on a wooden dish. These sights filled Beetle with eager hunger. But suddenly he saw, too, the inhabitants of the cottage were resting there, under the wall. Beetle, who had never received obvious kindness from anyone after the age of seven, distrusted humanity. He skulked back, disappointed, behind a cluster of walnut trees.

Just then the moon, less cautious than he, entered the

clearing and blended herself with the lamplight of the old cottage, pearl to citrine.

So Beetle beheld the two cottagers more clearly, and a start of envy went through him. For though they were plainly of the poor, dressed in homespun and adorned solely with vine-leaves, both were young and of an exceptional beauty.

The girl's long hair was black as pitch with the sheen of water. Her eyes, even in shadow, were the blue of the myosotis flower, and made him blink. At her side reclined the young man, and his eyes and hair were more lit than the lamplight. In his hands there was a lyre of crackpot design; incapable it looked of playing, yet from this he coaxed melodious improvisations, and as the girl lay in his arm, all at once he murmured this to her, and Beetle heard it:

In the wasteland, under the tree,
Bread and wine, and you, by me.
And with our song that wasteland shall
Heaven-on-earth become, and be.

After which, the golden young man glanced toward Beetle and it seemed he winked. Beetle was nervously affronted, for he was certain he was well-concealed. No one could detect him. But surely he had been mistaken about the wink, for now the young man said to the young woman, "Let us go in, and leave the night outside to do as it wishes." And at this she, too, seemed to regard Beetle amid the walnuts, but it was impossible she saw him. Both rose up and went into the cottage, and the door shut firm. In a minute more the lamp was doused.

Beetle waited a great while, a century of ravening famine, before he tiptoed up into the garden and took some of the food from the table, and the earthenware jug which seemed full of a dark wine. Most of his real sustenance he had got by thieving from the priests; he had had to do it, and this theft did not bring him to any compunction, for though they were poor, those two, yet they had plenty, and looks and love besides. But after a gulp or ten, he did leave the jug among the roots of the walnut trees, before running away.

Perhaps only by tipsy chance, since he had no luck, Beetle refound his dying fire, and the antique mule snoring beside it. Once there, Beetle swallowed the apples and cheese nearly whole, in case the cottagers came after him. They did not. In the morning they would suppose some wild thing had taken their food, and knocked down the jug—even that black hare Beetle, made mad by hunger, had fancied wore jewelry. . . .

Beetle was dreaming that the sun rose over the forest and the birds were making music like lyres. And there before him was not the decrepit mule, but a silvery horse trapped in saffron and gold, bells on its tasseled bridle, and bulging saddle-bags on either side of its sturdy flanks. In his dream Beetle was, reasonably enough, entranced. And getting to his feet, suffused with well-being and optimism, realized he wore a robe of thick silk embroidered all over, while on his feet were shoes so comfortable he would never have known he wore them, but for the color of their dyes. The rings on his fingers likewise would have blinded him if his eyes had not been, in the dream, so unnaturally strong and clear—

"Well," said Beetle to the morning, "This is a fine dream, but I had better wake up and resume my hopeless search for the mansion."

It then occurred to Beetle that he was quite awake.

Discovering this, he fell down again and hid his head. He was waiting either for the false images to leave him, or the devil-being which had invented them to appear, and tear him in bits.

Presently the noble horse approached Beetle instead, and began mildly nudging him.

"Are you that mule?" Beetle asked the horse.

The horse did not reply, only began to crop the grass. Beetle once more arose. At this another wave of health and vigor bashed him about the body, almost causing him to faint, for it was such an unaccustomed sensation.

Nevertheless, feeling as he now did, Beetle did not find it easy to dally any longer with dread and timidity.

"I will say only this," said Beetle to the forest. "If these gifts last out, I shall resemble the richest man in my village." And at this an abrupt thought sent him to investigate the saddlebags. Sure enough, there within them—along with some appetizing snacks—were a quantity of rubies, huge and unflawed. "It seems to me," said Beetle, "that armed with this, I can return to the temple and tell them I have, after all, called at the mansion. I can render up these rubies as the gift of the lord and lady."

And with this cheerful resolve, Beetle got on the horse.

"If my luck has changed, I shall unerringly and at once discover the road."

Swiftly, riding along at random, Beetle came on the road. It was no longer overgrown.

Beetle rode the horse on to the paving and they trotted in the direction of the village.

"In the wasteland under the trees!" sang Beetle, between eating and drinking, "with wine and bread and figs and cheese, I shall do whatever I please!"

He went on in this way for a day or so, replenishing his stomach at will, making remarks to and cracking jokes at the forest, and singing. When night came and doused the light, Beetle lay out on the ground and was heartily amused by the noises of the animals. "My luck has changed," said Beetle. The fact was he now felt so nourished and fit, he could not keep a pessimistic thought inside his head. And every time one tried to enter there, another wave of vitality would sweep it out again.

Thus Beetle returned along the road. And as the horse went briskly, his homeward journey was more quickly accomplished than had been the other of setting forth.

It was not until the pink stones of the village came distantly in sight, however, that the ultimate decision sprouted in Beetle. "I will give that temple nothing, for these valuables, like the robe and the mount, were meant for me. It would be ungrateful to let go of any of it. And whatever beings made this wonderful spell for me might be rightly angered and turn to punishing me—improbable as that seems. No, I will keep every pleasant thing, and only tell those priests the lord and lady granted me presents. And why should I not," added Beetle, tickled by his wit, "pretend those two simple cottagers were just that lord and his mistress."

And with this final resolve Beetle came in grand style down the road and passed into the village.

You may be sure that on the streets he was much stared at.

"Who is that princely youth?" they exclaimed.

And the good families, fallen on hard times, took down their eldest daughters off the shelves and dusted them.

But the young man, tall and muscular and with the burnish of health on hair and skin and merriment in his large and shining eyes, rode away up the street toward the temple.

"Ho. He is religious," said the villagers, not exact as to how this boded.

While the fane itself, where he had already been noted, flung wide its gates.

As Beetle was riding through into the outer courtyard (where he had been left ten years before, a sobbing child), the Chief Priest himself gushed bustling down.

"My lordly son," cried the Priest, "you are welcome!"

Beetle sat his horse and looked about. His fine eyes flashed with joy and the Chief Priest was greatly encouraged, until the young man spoke aloud.

"Can it be you do not know me, father?"

"Kn-*know* you, my peerless boy?"

"Well, but I am your own Beetle, come home to your loving care."

Now, although an amazing change had been worked in and upon Beetle, the sort of alteration only mighty sorcery could compass, yet Beetle he was still. And after a long gazing silence, there was not a priest in that court who did not begin to see as much, not least the Chief of them, whose obese eyes had pupils like lance-points.

"My son," said he at length, "I perceive that you reached the objective whereto I sent you, in my compassionate wisdom. And that, though I believe you doubted I had your best fortune at heart when I did so, by now you will know that I did."

Beetle grinned.

The Chief Priest picked up his skirts.

"You will follow, my son Beetle, for I will now give you private audience."

"Certainly," said Beetle. "However, I must warn every person present that neither my mount nor its accoutrements or bags are to be tampered with. Those who so rewarded me for my visit are magicians and adepts at cursing—I even venture to think their curses are more effective than those of our own holy father. They have protected their gifts to me with such a bane that I dare not even repeat its ingredients. I only say again—*beware!*"

And this mentioned, Beetle dismounted and swaggered into the inner sanctum after the Chief Priest.

Where: "Speak!" commanded the latter.

At which Beetle told his tale as follows.

After an arduous journey, beset by wood-lions, lethal snakes and starvation, Beetle had reached an enchanted mansion, plainly of sorcerers. Its magnificence was beyond description; he would therefore not attempt to describe it. However, as he was marveling at the gate, an uncanny agent arrived—again, inadequate description should be dispensed with—and conducted Beetle into a delicious garden, where there sat a young prince and princess of peerless attraction.

"Pray what were they like?" said the Chief Priest, rather put out at so far having received so little meat on his bone.

Beetle drew a deep breath. He gestured with the assurance of a popular actor.

"Father, though words are beggared by truth, I will give you my impressions. He was all golden, like the sun, and his eyes were golden—he was like the day at high noon. But she—oh, she—she was the daughter of night itself. Her skin was pale as the moon, her eyes like two blue stars, her hair the darkness. Yes, she was night's child, but the day loved her, as they say the sun is in love with the moon. For he was Day, and there he sat beside her, and from the way he bent his eye on her it was evident she was all his desire. But no woman could have looked at *him* unmoved. Nor did she do so."

Having thus expounded, Beetle continued to inform the Chief Priest of how the young couple had greeted him with courtesy, and wined and dined him with such opulence that to recount it was beyond his limits. When the visit was at an end, they gifted Beetle with a suit of clothes and the horse he had returned upon, and with other hidden treasures he had sworn not to reveal and which, if touched without his authority, would blast the trespasser.

For some minutes the Chief Priest sat pondering, while Beetle helped himself to oranges and sweetmeats from a dish.

At last the Chief Priest said, gently chiding, "But my son, finding such favor with these . . . pious and kindly persons, did you not present to them the holy scroll and extol for them the qualities of this temple, which has been, these many years, home and family to you?"

When the Chief Priest said this to him, Beetle felt a sharp spur of spite in his heart. Heeding it, he said, "But father, why else did you send me? I obeyed you in all things. But the lord and lady, it seems, never leave their house. Instead, they invite you to call on them, if you will."

Hearing that, the Chief Priest's fat eyes bulged almost out of his face, and Beetle must pretend to choke on a nut to cover his laughter. For he pictured to himself the Priest lost in the forest as he had been, and unable to find any such spot as a mansion. And Beetle said to himself, *After all, it is obvious I was successful from the way I have come back. But anyone can lose his way in the wood. I can give him just such directions as he gave to me, and let him have glee in them. As for the magic being which took pity on me, maybe it will pity him, too. But I doubt that.* And once more he had to have a little choking fit, so the Chief Priest came caringly to pat him between the shoulders.

Next morning, an hour after dawn, the Chief Priest rode out into the forest, accompanied by two of his most familiar under-priests, and attended only by the boy Precious, who had been taken with them as a treat.

At no time had any religious of the temple expressed doubt as to the mission. Seeing Beetle in his new magnificence, perhaps they were reminded of a saying of the area: *Does the wasp make honey?* It was no bad thing, when invited, to pay a call on generous eccentrics. For if an idiotic nobody was sent off with such gifts, what should be lavished on an erudite and holy priest?

Beetle had ridden some days, provisioned only from a satchel. The three priests had brought with them an extra mule, laden by bags of this and that deemed necessary for comfort. Precious led this mule.

All the first day then, the procession made its way along the road. They were much plagued by flies, attracted perhaps to the bulging food-bags or the perfume of Precious, but otherwise the time passed without incident.

Then the sun westered and began to set, and a deep bronze burnish intensified the forest.

"We shall camp there, in that glade beside the road," announced the Chief Priest. "Put up the tent."

No sooner had they entered the glade, however, and begun to dismount from their mules, than a strange tremor of music came wafting to them out of the wood.

Be certain, the three priests all cocked their ears at it, while Precious (who, let it be said, had all this while kept some unvoiced reservations concerning the venture) slunk behind a tree.

Next minute, an odd passion overcame the five mules.

First they snorted, then they bucked—so the saddles and bags fell off their backs, and the third dismounting priest, who had not yet reached the ground, did so in a manner unpleasing to him.

Freed of their burdens the mules rushed across the glade, and then standing upright on their hind limbs, began to dance in a ring, often clapping their forehoofs with a neighbor's.

The priests stared at this silly and unnerving sight.

At last the Chief Priest, who usually expected to have some sagacious comment on him for any event, remarked, "The nearness of magic, it is well known, can upset the behavior of the lower animals."

No sooner had he spoken than the mules gave over their dancing, and began instead ramblingly to graze.

The light was now running away fast through the sieve of branches and leaves. Then came a series of spurts of it along the ground—and in the midst of these bounded a black shadow.

The priests made pious signs, and the third of their

number made as if to hurry off—but in another moment they had discerned before them nothing more fearsome than a large black hare, plainly a pet, for it was the gold and silver of its collar and earrings which had fired in the grass.

And now the hare halted and bowed thrice to the priests, so its lovely ears swept the earth.

Then, turning about, it loped along the glade, paused and looked back at them.

"This is most gratifying," said the Chief Priest. "For it would seem our prospective hosts have come out, after all, to meet us. Stupid Beetle, not surprisingly, misunderstood or wrongly imparted their wishes. The hare is their messenger, and we must follow it."

This then they did. Even Precious followed at a distance, equally afraid of being left alone in the forest.

After a few minutes' walk through the darkening avenues of the wood, a great light shone out and presently another glade opened, most extravagantly lit by lamps of colored glass that hung on chains of gold from the trees, or from poles of carved ivory planted where the trees were not. So beautiful and bright it had been made, this place, that all the birds thereabouts, who had just been retiring for the night, had come awake again, supposing the sun had risen early to catch them out, and begun hastily and wildly to sing a hundred twittering tunes. Other melody played about the glade, but this had no source.

In the middle of the glade grew a single walnut tree, but its leaves were silver, and the green husks of the nuts seemed nothing less than emeralds. About the walnut, under canopies of gold, were set divans of crimson silk heaped by crimson cushions of satin.

From one of these there now arose a young man and woman and clearly, from the descriptions of Beetle, these were the lord and his lady, the two magicians.

The young man could not be other than a prince, so handsome and so sumptuously clad he was, in gold for his goldenness, and at his side a modest girl, seventeen years of age, garbed in silver and with sapphires in her cascade of midnight hair, and sapphires, too, in her eyes.

"You are most welcome," exclaimed the young prince.

"Indeed, since our entertainment of your emissary, we have been anxiously awaiting you."

And the modest girl, properly keeping her place, smiled upon the priests, before lowering her adorable lashes.

Soon enough then, the representatives of the temple had been seated on the couches. But when Precious approached, the prince abruptly waxed stern. "Your servant may not sit beside you, reverend father. He must sit over there, out of the light."

The Chief Priest did not argue. He waved Precious away in a lordly manner, and the despised creature sat down where bidden, in the shadow far from the warmth and comforts.

The black hare had vanished, but now out of some mysterious part of the wood there issued a troop of striped marmosets, walking with the utmost decorum. And these came to the priests and washed their hands and feet in perfumed water, while others put out jugs of gold from which drifted the heady fumes of wine on which rose-petals had been sprinkled, and yet others arrived in a stately way bearing jeweled dishes of such worth the eyes of all three priests grew fat and glittered.

A lavish repast was spread. And it was the young prince and princess themselves who now waited on the guests, garlanding their brows with myrtle, filling their golden goblets and heaping their plates—with obvious joy in the service, while they themselves took nothing. (But to Precious they only sent, by the paws of marmosets, a clay bowl of water and a wooden platter of herbs.)

And as the feast went on, the sorcerer prince and princess sat and gazed respectfully at the priests, and the prince entreated the Chief of them for instruction on the nature of the gods, while she, so modest, never presumed to speak at all.

Thus passed a large portion of the night, in eating and drinking, and in the intellectual and aesthetic monologue of the Chief Priest who, finding at long last an audience befitting him, spoke for some hours with hardly a hesitation, needing only now and then to lubricate his throat with wine. And such insights came to him during this talk, such enlightening gems, that he was filled himself by a humble pride and happiness which perhaps never before, since his childhood, had he ever felt. And for the hosts, they hung on every word as beautifully as the lamps hung on the trees about.

Finally, nevertheless, even the Chief Priest's storehouse was exhausted, and he ended his litany. On the adjacent couches, the two other priests might be observed, so overcome by ecstasy at his lecture that they had shut their eyes the better to savor it. At the cessation of his voice they both started, as if coming awake from a wondrous dream or vision, as if, indeed, startled out of a deep sleep.

Then approached the marmosets again, and sweetmeats were served and a wine even more enrapturing than the others. (And even Precious was taken another bowl of water.)

"Reverend father," said the prince then, "it is quite impossible for us to thank you for what you have given us tonight. But since words are inadequate, we hope that a few presents we shall offer you will repay you in kind. For such a mind and heart and spirit as yours demand a special reward. For ourselves, we have a long journey before us and must now, alas, set off. But of such amenities as you find about you we trust you will avail yourselves. In the morning, the gifts will await you. Meanwhile, pray keep for yourselves anything that takes your fancy, for example, the dishes and goblets. And your servant, too," added the prince, "may retain his bowl and cup."

"My son," cried the Chief Priest, and tears bulged in his bulging eyes. "I am overwhelmed. My only sorrow is that perchance I shall not see you again."

"There may come a day when we shall visit you in your temple."

"Ah, my son, what a time of rejoicing that would be."

"Good father, do not flatter me. I cannot believe so."

"Truly, truly, yes!"

And so with mutual protestations, this noon-day prince took his leave of the priests, and she, too, though silently, that girl Beetle had named *Night's Daughter*.

After their departure, however, the jugs still held their wine, and the food kept hot and fragrant, tempting the priests again to stuff themselves.

In a little while they heard a metallic, silky noise, and

glancing up, beheld three lush damsels coming out of the wood toward them, dressed only in bells.

At this the priests looked at each other, but not for long.

To the notes of the unseen music, the belled damsels now began a sinuous and interesting dance. The priests watched them with much attention, and even left their plates untouched.

When the dance came to an end, the dancers separated and moved to the couches of the priests, where they showed every inclination to lie down with them.

Now the rule of the temple was for celibacy, but it was not one which had always been found advisable. As the dancers smiled on them, and stroked and twitched and untied them, with an obvious wish to be helpful and consoling, the Chief Priest issued his last decree of the evening: "It would be a grave and graceless error," said he, "to reject the hospitality of our hosts. Besides, they are magicians, and to insult them is a danger, not to mention an unkindness on our part, seeing they have gone to so much trouble." And after this he found himself too busy to say more on the matter. Though in a space such loud grunts and groans and squeals arose that some of the emeralds were shaken from the walnut tree.

At sunrise, the priests awoke from a refreshing slumber—to find all the means to hand for breaking their fast (though such a brief fast it had been) with the utmost appetite.

Although the luxurious couches and cushions had remained, and the breakfast, there was no sign either of the hosts or any of their attendants. The walnut tree had also disappeared, and the lamps were gone; only sunlight lit the glade. It showed to the priests, however, that they were now gowned in priestly robes of such glory they had become lamps in themselves, while round their necks and on their fingers glowed astonishing jewels, and in the embroidered pouches at their gold-cinched guts lay quantities of emeralds.

Then, what should come trotting through the trees than three silver-gray horses, trapped as if for kings, and of these that one intended for the Chief Priest caparisoned in purple, and with so many clanking tassels of bullion and skeins of pearls, it was a wonder it could take a step without falling down. A fourth horse came laden with coffers inlaid by onyx and gold. On investigating them, they found the jewelry plates and goblets of the feast had been thoughtfully packed for them, also apparel and furnishings, ornaments and appurtenances that caused the forest to ring, once more, with gratification.

Last into the glade then came ambling the flea-ridden mule of Precious, which looked around itself with an affronted air. Precious, clothed only as usual, lay curled asleep under a tree, but at the admonishment of the Chief Priest arose, and after gasping and gaping a moment, averted both eyes and head.

"Take up the clay cup and bowl of wood that were given you by the lord and lady. Do not spurn them—" Precious sullenly stowed the articles on the mule—"It seems to me that in you they noticed some flaw to which I have been blind, and for this reason did not feast or reward you." Precious pulled an exaggerated face. "Do not sulk," said the Chief Priest. "Such a night as that which has been ours cannot but have diminished your worth. Tread warily therefore. Not a word. Get on your mule."

And so Precious got on the mule.

And the priests clambered aloft the elegant horses, and the third priest led diligently the horse laden by treasure.

And in this fashion they set off for the village, discussing as they went how they should be stared at in the streets.

Which was to be as they foretold.

The sun was again setting, as was its habit, when Beetle heard a hubbub in the village below the temple. He had been dwelling, during the Chief Priest's absence, in that gentleman's sanctum, which the rest of the temple had not cared to gainsay him, Beetle being the favored of magicians. Aside from excursions to the priests' own table to dine, and to his new horse, Beetle had spent the hours in counting his rubies and making plans for a future beyond the forest. He had perhaps not expected the Chief Priest to return at all, and decidedly not for some days. But hearing the excited sounds, Beetle's heart all at once sank. *Can it be,* thought Beetle, *that those villains have been gifted, too? Where then is justice?* And he walked up to the high roof where the beacon was lit at night to jog the gods' amnesia. And gazing down, since his eyes were now strong and saw a fair way, he beheld a sight and a half.

Now it had happened that, just as they were turning into the village, the third priest, who led the treasure-horse, had felt a sharp nip in his thigh, and he thought it was one of his mule's fleas at work. But then it came to him that it could not be, for he rode, not the mule, but a splendid horse. The setting sun was in the priest's eyes, and as he turned to his nearest companion, dazzled, he got an extraordinary view of him. For it seemed to the priest that his brother was not clad as the denizen of a king's court, but sat there stark naked but for a few torn creepers and a quantity of mud. The third priest did not express any opinion on his vision, but he did rub his eyes and quickly look at the Chief of his fellowship. "Tut. It is the sun. For there is the father himself, also naked but for several large bird-droppings splashed about him, and at his belt (which seems to be a dead worm) is a gourd in which—no, no. The sun has dazzled me." Lastly, the priest nerved himself to look closer home. And so he noted his own well-fed belly raised all nude and round to the smiling glow of sunset. And just then a flea nipped him again, for he was riding nothing but his old mule, with snail-shells and owl-pellets on its bridle, and a saddle enhanced by nettles under his sore rump.

And thus it happened that the pink-stone village saw its Chief Priest, and two of his holy familiars, come riding their mules through the village street to the temple one evening, garbed in nothing but some sparse coils of arboreal things, and some globs and slops of things botanical, and the liberal anointing of things with wings. And having, too, gourds about them, and piled on one their mules, overflowing with rabbit excreta, desiccated bits of bark, and the leavings of foxes and wild-cats. At which, not amazingly, a hubbub went up, and on seeing which—nor amazingly—Beetle hastened down.

And on the road before the temple gate all met in confusion and the final unmercy of the sun. And, "Why, most pious father," bawled Beetle, "what has befallen you?"

After that came an interval of shouting and bluster, during which the Chief Priest attempted to pelt in through the gate, but Beetle and his own mule would not let him. And after *that* came a dizzied silence, during which up trotted Precious, unchanged and fully clothed, upon an unfestooned mule.

"Let me speak!" screamed Precious then.

So the village, guarding its glance against the Chief Priest's undress, told Precious to do so.

"I will denounce them," shrilled Precious. "I was spared, but they are wicked men, and their sins have found them out—just as the virtuous Beetle was blessed."

And then Precious recounted this: Entering the forest bent on avarice, the priests had met the two sorcerers. These had been able, due to the sinfulness of the priests, entirely to beglamour them. But Precious, who saw through the spell, they left alone.

"Then," said Precious, "these men stretched out on the muddy ground, in the light of the million fireflies that had gathered there, and permitted themselves to be garlanded with stinking weeds and dead ferns. And being offered swampy water, they drank it and washed in it, and being offered rotten eggs and old birds' nests and other horrid things, they devoured them with relish. (Though to me were given wholesome water and herbs.) Then the sorcerers invited the Chief Priest to hold forth on the nature of the gods, and this he did for five or six hours, uttering such blasphemies as I have never heard before, even going by the tavern. Saying the gods had voices like geese and dogs' tails and drooled and made the world out of dung and—preposterous notion—that the earth was round and whirled about in a void. And now and then one of the other two priests would give a loud snore, by which he showed he agreed with it all. When eventually the dreadful recital ended, the two sorcerers took their leave. But next, three monkeys came from the trees and began to dance about, and soon enough these evil priests drew the monkeys down and rolled in the mud with them, and did such things that I could no longer bear to look. At sunrise, the three priests awoke dressed as you see, which they reckoned some advantage, got on their mules and returned here, boasting all the way of their success. I, the only unsullied one, returned also to give witness against them. But all that they did, deluded, was made possible through their unpriestlike greeds for food and strong drink, and their nasty forbidden lusts for flesh and gold."

This said, Precious hid face in hands, which caused several of the villagers to offer comfort. But others cried that a fearsome spell had been cast, and that the righteous priests were innocent of all blame, while especially in the case of the monkeys, Precious, too, had been deceived.

"You think they are above that act?" shrieked Precious. And all at once put both hands to that drapery the sorcerers had not altered, and to certain bindings beneath, and ripped everything from neck to knee. And there stood Precious then, revealed as a plump and comely young woman, blushing with shame and rage, who said, "They bought me as little more than a child and reared me in secret to be the courtesan of that holy father there, and his favorites. To hide the truth they covered me and made me bind my breasts, and threatened me that if I revealed the facts they would put such a curse on me that I would die in agony. And I might have run away, but where was I to go? Besides, I had my own reasons for staying, one of which was a hope the gods would some day strip these beasts as naked as now they are."

Then Precious closed up the drapery and ran away.

But the Chief Priest and his familiars stayed, all shrunken in their fat, and just then a weird calling was heard. Turning toward it, the village beheld three well-groomed monkeys hastening up the road. And these, being let through the crowd, jumped into the priests' reluctant arms, and even into the reluctant arms of the Chief Priest, showering them, each man, with monkey kisses, and all the tokens and indelicate embracings that young brides of the coarser sort would render their husbands.

* * *

Beetle rode out of the village a second time, going in a different direction, to the south, and his heart was high for his luck had changed.

But he had not gone far when a figure came flitting from the trees. It was none other than Precious, in a homespun gown, but wearing flowers in her hair. Beetle had always hated Precious when he had been a petted toadying boy. But as a girl, pretty and put-upon, Precious was another matter.

Behind them in the village the priests were paying many dues, but Precious had not lingered to see. She looked up at Beetle instead, and informed him, "I loved you even before you grew to be so handsome. I left candles where you could find them to steal and eat, and I coated them with mutton gravy beforehand. When they sent you to the forest, I prayed and made offerings to the gods for your safety. I swore one day I should come to you and tell you all this. But now, see, I have brought with me a dowry."

And she showed him a silver plate set with exquisite jewels and a goblet of purest gold.

So then Beetle lifted her up on to the fine horse and kissed her. Which was the sweetest kiss either of them had ever known.

The temple in the village ceased to light its beacon. It trusted gods and sorcerers both would forget it. Beetle and Precious meanwhile lived miles off and in another land. And in another year, they raised together an altar to a summer-day lord and a dark lady they called the Daughter of Night. Precious also worshipped other gods, but Beetle only these. Yet when Beetle—no longer called Beetle, but by his former name—put offerings and incense at the feet of her, Night's Daughter, Fate never told him he was ahead of his time.

But Sovaz-Azhriaz was at odds with her father, Azhrarn, Prince of Demons, and Azhrarn had besides his own fierce argument with Chuz, Sovaz's lover, the Prince of Madness.

The Prince of Demons therefore hunted down these lovers, and the wild woods grew wilder. For the Eshva, the dreaming envoys of the demons, began to prowl and to dance there, and the demon high caste, the Vazdru, rode the paths and glades on their midnight horses. And there came to be many curious ill-meetings, by moonlight and by shadow.

CHILDREN OF THE NIGHT

1 *A Dream*

MARSINEH HAD HAIR the color of red amber, a skin like cream, and love-sick young poets sang sometimes under her window. Her father, moreover, was rich; she dressed in figured silk and put ornaments of gold about her throat and on her wrists and ankles. It was thought that she would marry well. One day a stranger arrived in the town. He was clad like the servant of a king, and attended by his own retinue. He rode to the house of Marsineh's father, and there delivered a message. The mighty Lord Kolchash had been told of the maiden, and regarded her too in a magic glass. She pleased him and he would wed her. The wedding was already fixed; it fell in three months' time, on the eve of the night of a new moon. That was that.

"But," said the father of Marsineh.

"There can be no 'buts,' " replied the costly messenger. "No one gainsays my master, Kolchash. Have you not heard of him?"

"It seems to me," murmured Marsineh's father, "that I have. . . . But rumor is often misleading."

"Since you have no choice but to agree to the bargain," said the messenger, ignoring this inference, "I shall present you at once with the gifts my lord has sent you, in token of his betrothal."

At which slaves—clothed like the slaves of a king—came forward with chests and boxes of such brilliant and glittering things that Marsineh's father stood aghast. He remained so. And in this way, when the messenger and his company rode off, Marsineh's father had not said anything more against the match, and it might be taken that he had agreed.

"You have been greatly favored," said Marsineh's mother presently in an upper chamber.

"An illustrious marriage has been arranged for you," elaborated Marsineh's aunt.

Marsineh blushed like a peach. She was already quite in love, with the son of one of her rich father's rich neighbors.

"Who is it?" she whispered. "Is it Dhur?"

"Dhur?" Mother and aunt laughed scornfully. And Marsineh paled like a lily. "Far better than any such thing as Dhur," they cried. "You are to marry the exalted Lord Kolchash."

Marsineh uttered a faint low scream.

"Now, now," clucked the mother. "Dismiss foolish rumors from your mind. Kolchash, no doubt of it, is a mighty and munificent lord. You can get no better."

"Oh, spare me," said Marsineh.

"It is," said the aunt judiciously, "too late for that."

Who then *was* this Kolchash? In truth, very little was known of him or said of him. In those parts, his reputation rested on two or three supposed facts, and a few vague stories. He was reckoned to be fabulously wealthy, and this assumption at least his gifts to Marsineh's father had verified. He was, while not himself a magician, yet possessed of certain magical artifacts—had not the messenger claimed his master viewed the girl in a sorcerous mirror? In station, Kolchash was a lord or prince, but where his lands lay was quite unsure. That he was old, however, was inevitable, since the incoherent tales of him had themselves existed several decades. These tales amounted to very little. And yet, they were neither domestic or cheerful. It was commonly observed, for example, that Kolchash kept a library of books each of which was bound in supple skin got from the hide of human infants. It was said, rather less often, that it would be impossible to do anything behind the rear side of Kolchash—since, but too literally, he had eyes in the back of his head. There was also a sometime saying of the region, when a cloud covered the evening sun: "Ah, Kolchash has let out his soul for an airing."

Sophisticates of the towns marked such stuff only as nonsense is marked. And as for Marsineh's father, though he himself, in his youth, had been wont to play a childish game known as *'Ware the Claws of Kolchash,* he was convinced that the Kolchash of the rumors could not be the Kolchash of the chests and boxes. One should not get in the way of such ardent and generous love.

Time began to pass swiftly in the house with preparations for the great lord's advent.

Marsineh was caught, as a tender fly in a sticky web, and with as little chance of escaping. As she drifted through her pre-nuptial tasks and duties, listless with anxiety and unhappiness, she could not help but sometimes imagine how differently she would have flown along the path of days and nights toward a marriage with Dhur. (Of that young man nothing at all was said in the town, save that he was handsome and fond of diversion—and that his spurs might have fed a poor family for half a year.)

At first, Marsineh partly believed that Dhur would send some word to her, to convey what she was not certain. When no word came, she thought him as blindly grief-stricken as she was, as hopeless. There was nothing he might do for her, any more than she might do anything to assist herself. Delicately reared and, until now, never seriously at odds with parental decree, she could not envisage any alternative to obedience. Besides, she was surrounded continually by members of the household, by her maids and attendants, by female relations who had come to congratulate her, with bright nervous speculation in their glances. Never was a prisoner more zealously jailed.

But, if Marsineh could not visualize disobeying or evading her parents, neither could she picture her wedding to the peculiar Lord Kolchash, let alone what might follow.

There came then a night, scented by the jasmine that flourished under the young girl's window, when, exhausted and wan, she fell asleep in her bed and experienced this dream:

The marriage had taken place. It was done. She was

borne, with a faint memory of it—of burnished vessels, aromas and spices, fireworks and drums—inside a curtained litter, along an unknown highway. On every side rode or strode a vast company, the servants and soldiers of a lordly household, while a little ahead of her, on a coal-black horse, was *he,* her husband, *Kolchash.*

Now in the dream it seemed to her suddenly that, though wed to him, she had not yet *seen* Kolchash. Somehow, throughout the long ceremony, he had been obscured from her, as she at the beginning had been obscured from him, head to toe, by her beaded and embroidered bride's veil. How this should be she could not guess—for surely, when he had lifted up her veil, if not before, she, too, must have caught a glimpse of him—yet she remembered nothing of it. She could not even have said if he were tall or short, slender, thick, or bowed with age. The black horse alone came to her mind, and that only as if someone had warned her of it.

Accordingly, Marsineh felt compelled to part the curtains of her litter and to look out after him, *after Kolchash.*

It was a night journey, for the marriage itself had not begun until the hour after sunset, when the new moon lifted. By now it would be well past midnight. The procession of her lord moved through the black night world, glimmering like moving water in its materials and metals, for its ranks supported many lamps on ebony poles. They swayed overhead, these lights, rosy moons-at-the-full, and now and then night moths dashed about them and fell away.

But stare as she did through that progressing, nearly silent throng, Marsineh could make out nothing of her husband. Then she did notice another thing, which was that the vast procession was about to enter a forest that had come sweeping in on the road. It had such an appearance, this forest, of smothering darkness and enclosure, that Marsineh, who was already frightened in the dreary enervating fashion to which the months of her betrothal had inured her, now turned cold with a special fear. Unable to prevent anything that might happen, she let go the curtain of the litter.

After a space, the litter's motion stopped.

Marsineh gripped her hands together in dismay. And

sure enough, in another minute, a shadowy figure parted the curtains, bowed to her and said, "Madam, the Lord Kolchash desires that you alight. We are to take rest, for the remainder of the night, in the shelter of this wood."

He assisted her to leave the litter, to do the very thing she wished for least. And there on the lawns of the forest she found herself, in a clearing afloat with the procession's lamps. All around the trees had closed their wall. She had entered, but there was no way out.

"Now, madam," said the shadowy servant, "I will conduct you to your lord's pavilion."

And again Marsineh must do what she wished for least, and over the night grass she went on her dream-feet that felt and seemed as real as feet of flesh—or clay. A great shining tent already stood apart, the far side of a slight running stream with one flat stone at its center. By this they crossed but too easily, and on the farther bank other shadows raised the flap of the pavilion's entrance, and Marsineh passed through.

To be within the tent was to be within a globe of nacre. Its draperies were seamless, and like the wall of trees offered entry but no exit point. The tent was furnished with objects of luxury, while on a gilded perch crouched a bird like a fire, with fountains of flames for crest and tail. But it looked at her with a cold eye like a snake's. Near the back of the tent stood an icon of black and gold. Marsineh's fearful gaze took this for the statue of some foreign god. Then the golden hands quivered on the black robe sewn with golden suns and stars, and the black mask turned a little under the golden diadem. There were eyes in the mask, watching Marsineh as the fiery bird watched her, but she could not tell their shape or shade.

"Now you are my wife," said a low deep voice from out of the mask. "Can you deny this?"

Marsineh faltered, "No, my lord."

"Be seated then. Eat and drink."

Marsineh sat trembling on the cushions. She took up a cup of black jade which stood ready, raised it, but could not bring herself to taste the wine. She crumbled wafers of honey on a plate of the rarest transparency, and cut open a fruit with a silver knife.

"Where is your appetite, my bride?" said Kolchash then, out of his mask. "Can it be you are afraid of me, your own husband? Is it my facial covering which frightens you so? Shall I remove it?"

At these words, Marsineh was seized by a terror worse than any she had ever known.

"No, no, my lord," she protested. "It is not necessary that you reveal yourself to me."

"Yes, yes, dear wife," said he, "for long ago I spied your charms, albeit imperfectly through the mists of a magic glass. In courtesy I will display to you, in turn, my own visage."

Transfixed she sat then, the young bride, in that shining pavilion. She beheld how two gloved hands were put up, two gauntlets of gold to which nails, long as claws and enameled black, had been attached—or else, could it be?—they were the true nails of Kolchash which pierced through. And the blank, black mask wavered and began to shift. It separated away and dropped down upon the carpets— And there: Her husband's face.

Marsineh awakened screaming.

It happened that the foremost among Marsineh's women, a beautiful girl by the name of Yezade, had elected to sleep that night in the antechamber, in order to be near her lady. These two maidens had been brought into the world within a year of each other, and dwelled under the same roof, constant companions all their lives. And although Yezade was not so well-born as her playfellow-mistress, yet she had been daintily raised and educated at Marsineh's side. And as they grew, like a double blossom on one branch, perhaps seated on either side of a harp and sounding it together in the alternating phrases of a tune, or stitching each of them one half of a single flower upon a scarf, so they had sworn often enough that they would never be parted. But next they grew up, and either one turned to her own affairs, although Yezade remained the chief among Marsineh's ladies. Yezade, too, had plainly kept enough in sympathy with Marsineh to see her horror at the proposed wedding-match. And Yezade, while saying nothing of it, had all this time been brooding on Marsineh's plight.

Hearing her mistress shriek, Yezade therefore ran into the bedchamber.

It was the last hour of the old moon (for the evening of the marriage was almost at hand). There in the window lay the lunar scarecrow, over on her back, thin and curved like a sailless boat. Marsineh, whiter and fairer far, was sobbing beneath.

"Dear mistress," cried Yezade.

Marsineh exclaimed:

"Oh, I have had such a fearsome dream—and I believe it to have been not solely a figment of sleep, but a true prophecy of what lies before me."

"Tell it, I beg you."

So then Marsineh, between her sobs, recounted all the dream. And Yezade sat by, her wide eyes fixed on Marsineh, hearing of the procession, the night, the forest, the clearing and the lighted tent, of the masked icon which bade the bride sit, eat and drink, and then asked her if she would see its face, the visage of Kolchash.

"And though I entreated he would not, he raised his golden hands, with the huge long black claws on them, and pulled off the mask—and so I saw—I saw—"

"Oh my dear mistress, *what?*"

"That he had the face of a beast."

And Marsineh hid her own countenance in her hands.

After a brief interval Yezade, perhaps pedantically, inquired, "Of what sort was this beast?"

"Oh, I do not know—cannot tell—it was ghastly, *beastly*. The eyes glared on me and the teeth glittered—I screamed and woke myself up screaming. But there is no safety. This is to be my fate."

Then Marsineh fell on her bed and wept copiously.

Yezade sat by, as if in solemn thought, and seeing her do this, you might have deemed her unusually callous, until at length she spoke again.

"Sister," said she, "you may recall that my mother, before she died, was sometimes called 'the witch.' And it is a fact, she had some skills, whose secrets I have inherited—though never flaunted, for we know, you and I, it is generally more sensible for a woman to pass unnoted. Now you, who have always been kind and loving to me, have also a sweetheart, the young man you had wished, and supposed, you would wed, doubtless-broken-hearted Dhur. But I have no one who would miss me, and indeed, if I am to be parted from you, no one will care for me, and I for no one on the earth. Therefore, let me take your place at this marriage. We are much alike, and of the same height and slenderness, and in the bridal finery and veil, I think wicked Kolchash, who only spied you—as he said in your dream—in a misty magic glass, shall be fooled and never think for an instant I am anyone but yourself. Later, by employing my mother's arts, maybe I can protect myself. Or if I cannot, then I shall encounter whatever trouble was to have been yours. And if he has a beast's face, I say all men are beasts and monsters, whether they look the part or no. I fear him not a jot. And if you, meanwhile, can fly to liberty with your lover, that will be for me sufficient."

Now Marsineh had, throughout their life together, in some ways grown accustomed to taking the advice of Yezade, who was demonstrably the bolder of the two. Marsineh was besides now in the situation of one drowning, and inclined to clutch at any reed or straw in the torrent to save herself. Therefore, although she deplored the idea of her childhood companion undergoing this horrible trial, yet Marsineh could not help thinking that brave and resourceful Yezade could contrive in the ordeal better than she. In fairness, Marsineh imagined, too, that the ruse might be uncovered before the fatal night journey was begun. The resemblance between the two girls was remarkable (nor improbable, for they had had the same father), but surely Kolchash, who had so explicitly demanded one maiden, would be able to tell the difference. Thereafter Yezade would be absolved as her mistress's dupe—Marsineh in the arms of Dhur, and safe.

For all these reasons then, Marsineh was persuaded to the scheme of Yezade, and the rest of the night spent in the polishing of plans.

Dawned the wedding day, the wedding noon and afternoon. And as it wore, the watchmen on the town wall descried a great yellow plume of dust rolling at the horizon. "It is the procession of Marsineh's bridegroom.

Look how he hastens! Yet he is miles off. He will not reach the gate before sunset." And then they touched various amulets they had put on that morning.

The dust-plume rolled slowly nearer as the day shrank into the west. The plume turned to white, to red, to purple, as the sky flushed, until over the road to the town gate poured a host, the substance of the dust, which itself rose against the curtain of sunfall.

On the streets, from the windows and over the garden walls, the town looked a little slantwise, to see Lord Kolchash, the successful wooer. It was a strange thing; his company played no music, as was customary. Stranger still . . . men and horses, litters and carts went by, there were lamps, and the jewelry the lamps set light to—and yet, no one could afterward be exactly sure of the nature of the procession. Of the position of things, the garments, banners. And any who foolhardily gawped after Kolchash himself, they did not pick him out. They murmured that perhaps he had not come, in the end, but delegated his place, as before.

As the last color was bled out of heaven, with a swirl and hiss as of some boiling cloud settling to ground, the host arrived before Marsineh's father's house. And on the door of it fell a loud knocking, one, two, three. "Open!" boomed a voice, "Lord Kolchash is here to claim his promised wife!"

Then the doors were flung wide, and a crowd of the host rode in. Musicians struck up in the house as if in gladness. On the threshold of the inner court, where the marriage was to be, priests made offerings at the household altars, to the gods, who, as always, paid no attention. Maidens crowned with flowers came forward to welcome—what? Some tall swathed creature, crowned itself with a headdress of sheer gold.

In the east, pale and emaciated as if sick, the new moon was rising.

Petals and perfumes and notes of melody—and down the stair came the bride, veiled close under a web of spangles, which concealed all from her amber hair to her painted toes.

And so there were cries of delight and calls of goodwill

and priestly chantings, firecrackers and tabors, bells and harps, birds let out of cages and incenses burning blue.

What a very fine and proper wedding.

2 *The First Night: Lovers' Meeting*

A MESSENGER STOOD before the house of Dhur's father. The messenger was elegantly arrayed, though not mounted, and indeed he seemed but a boy. The porter of the house looked askance upon him.

"My young Lord Dhur is from home. He went off this very morning." The messenger turned pale in the dusk. A harsh master then must have sent him, one who would exact punishment for a message undelivered. "But my young lord will return in three days at the most. He has merely gone to hunt in the woods."

"Oh, heartless," breathed the pretty youth. His eyes, lustrous in any case, had now blossomed with bright tears.

"Is your master impatient?" inquired the porter. "Tut. We servants have a harsh life."

"Either I must impart to the Lord Dhur my most urgent news," whispered the messenger, "or perish."

The porter roused. He supposed Dhur had fallen foul of some debt or irked some vengeful husband, and that this might be a caution from some friend. Having himself a soft spot for Dhur, and not wishing either to expose him to danger or to alert his father in the matter, the porter now took it on himself to save the day—besides, the winsome youth might prove winsomely grateful.

"Now see here," therefore said the porter, "in the stable is a fine riding-ass, of which I am allowed the use, and which no one will miss. This I shall lend you so you may follow Dhur. The way is simple enough. You have only to go out of the town's gate—which is tonight to be kept open in honor of an exiting bridal procession (and a strange one, I hear!). Beyond the town, ride along the highway and enter the woods, but do not stray from the road there. The Lord Dhur and his companions will be at their lodging in the Inn of the Turtle Dove, which lies against the road. It is a journey of only three or four hours."

If the porter hoped for an instantaneous display of appreciation, he was much disappointed. The lovely youth leaned wanly on the gate, approached the ass when it arrived, mounted it inexpertly and, sprawled on its back with a gaze of pain, thanked the porter only in a faint voice, nor offered him either a coin or a kiss.

"And such is the rank ingratitude of the young," grumbled the porter. And too late fell to wondering if the ass would ever be seen by him or his masters again, and if it was not, what excuse he had better proffer.

The winsome youth—Marsineh, disguised—rode through the town, with which she was not greatly familiar, out of the town gate, which she had never done before, and along the unknown highway. The new moon was rising, and she could not but be aware of a wedding about to begin. . . .

At the middle of the afternoon, before the women flocked in, Yezade had gone alone to tend and dress the bride. Thus the bride—Yezade—had dressed herself. She had also dressed Marsineh as a messenger. It is an interesting reflection upon the closeness of this household and parents to their children, that Marsineh and Yezade anticipated the veiled surrogate should be able utterly to convince in the remaining time before the nuptual, while the true victim should find no difficulty in flying the house. Needless to say, both adventures were achieved without a single challenge.

Yet reaching the gate of her lover and learning he had gone hunting, Marsineh's resolve had almost failed her. Then it came to her that he, too, had fled, to muffle his piercing heartache in exercise. Why, he could not even bear to stay in the town where she should be joined to another. So fortified, on to the ass kind skittish fate—and the porter—provided, Marsineh had climbed. And, though she had never ridden in her life, she bore the acute discomfort of it, and urged the animal to an unwilling lollop, which caused her worse anguish than before.

What were four hours to the escaping heart of love? Hours were as nought, when their cessation should see her in her beloved's protecting arms.

Young and blue the night and fierce the stars. This, and her awkward seat on the ass, her hope and fear, prevented her from associating the highway of her dream with the highway by which she now left the town. While, in the later hour, groaning from the ride, when Marsineh entered the outskirts of the woods, she was far removed from making any note that these were no other than the forests of the nightmare, into which dread Kolchash had carried her.

Close on midnight, Dhur sat carousing with a collection of his friends in an upper room of the Turtle Dove Inn. The hunt had been unfruitful that day, for they had started only one mysterious thing in the silver gloaming before sunrise—and this had swiftly vanished. At noon, riding or idling under the pavilions of the trees, a young man or two had mentioned odd tales of the woods, that they were haunted by weird magics. Yet no sorcery came to tantalize them, and no beasts appeared to give them a chase and to fall before their spears and knives. "It is Dhur's sad regret that keeps them away," said one, partly in earnest. But Dhur did not seem regretful, or sad. He had cursed the lack of game, but in the upper room of the inn ate and drank with gusto, and now he reclined on his cushions and eyed the dancing-girl, even as he toyed with the lyre-girl's plaited hair.

"Sing a song of love," said unsad Dhur, merrily, to the singing-girl.

"Oh, handsome sir," said she looking under her gilded lids, "they say it is unwise to do so, here. For many years, so they say," said she, melodiously, "two supernatural lovers have dwelled somewhere in the depths of the forest. And since no mortal love can rival theirs, it is unlucky to sing of any love *but* theirs."

"Sing, then, of theirs," said Dhur. "Who are these paragons?"

"Two demon things," said the lyre-girl, and she hid *her* gilded eyes against Dhur's shoulder.

"He is fair," said the dancing-girl, coming to lie across

Dhur's knee, "all golden, like a summer dawn. "But she—"

"She is black and white, white skin like the white rose, black hair like a cloud of black hyacinth," the singer said, smiling at Dhur but not approaching him.

"Her eyes are so blue," murmured the lyre-girl, "that if she weeps, sapphires fall from them."

"May the gods give me such a wife!" cried one of the young men. "How I should berate and beat her, she should be always in tears."

"This one," said the dancer, "even you, gentle lord, would not dare to beat."

"Well," said Dhur, "but sing the song."

But at that moment, another servant of the inn burst into the room and announced: "My Lord Dhur, you must come down. A messenger has arrived, half dead, babbling he will speak only to you."

Much alarmed, as may be supposed, Dhur sprang to his feet and hastened down the inn stair to the chamber where the arrival had been stored.

Now it must be said at this juncture that it had long seemed to Marsineh that she had regarded Dhur often, and been nearly ceaselessly in his company. And this was because she had dreamed of him almost every night, and daydreamed and thought of him more regularly still. His face and voice were as known to her as her father's and mother's. But in actuality, the two young people had met only on some six occasions, and not at all since the marriage had been arranged.

Therefore, though mostly insensible as she was from the agony of her unpracticed ride, and the enormity of all that had befallen her, when Marsineh lifted her swimming eyes and beheld Dhur entering the chamber, she knew him at once, and the mad glad leap of her heart brought her to her feet. But Dhur, beholding Marsineh, three months unseen and clad as a draggled swooning boy, knew her not at all. The fact was, she was in love with him, and he, though he had liked her well enough, had never been in love with her.

"Speak!" cried Dhur in some desperation, wondering if his father lay dead or the family home in ruins—for what else could such a frantic messenger portend?

And Marsineh, pitiful girl, taking his wild gaze and tone for recognition and reception, flung herself on his breast.

"Ah, you will save me? I am lost without you!" she exclaimed.

"There, there," said Dhur, patting her sternly on the back. "Brace yourself and say what has happened."

"Is it not—" wailed she—"immediately evident?"

"Not at all. Come, speak out!" snapped Dhur, beginning to lose patience. And he held off, as he thought, the importunate fellow.

"Well, I fled," said Marsineh, trembling and teetering. "I had no choice. How could I suffer—*that?*"

"Suffer *what?*" shouted Dhur, beside himself.

"To resign myself to such thralldom—his slave—when I had known the honey of those hopes you had engendered—"

Dhur, his thumbs in his belt, glowered upon the messenger.

"Now," roared Dhur, "cease this wittering, idiot boy, and tell me what has chanced—or I will have it flogged from you."

"But I am not—" began Marsineh. Then her voice faded. In that awful moment, everything came clear before her. Not only that her beloved had stayed deceived, that he believed her to be precisely what she had claimed—a pretty eunuch sent to bear tidings. No, not only that. With love's keen and unbearable instinct she had suddenly become aware of the indifference, the inattention to herself as Marsineh, which alone could bring such a deception about. He might have come before her disguised in any manner he could devise: She would have seen through the cover instantly. But he did not know her—for he had never looked at her with any more than a glancing eye. He had not, as she had done, dreamed and pondered the object of his heart's desire. Oh, now she understood why no word had come from him, why he had gone hunting on the day of her wedding. He had forgotten her.

In that second her heart broke, and with such a loud crack, it woke her from her trance, her swoon, the dream itself, and everything. She saw what she had done, and how she was placed: A runaway, cast on the bosom of the world, quite friendless. For her one true friend, Yezade, was given to a fearful enemy, and only another enemy stood before Marsineh now. And the revelation was so appalling, it steadied her and made her wits dart alive.

Dhur, who did not love Marsineh, would not help her. But since he was now her only means of survival, he must be pleaded with on the terms he offered.

Marsineh dropped to her knees with a cry of mingled pains.

"My lord," she whined, "I am only a poor boy, and I have escaped from a cruel master. You forget, but once you saw me on the street and were kind to me. I beg you to allow me to serve you. Forgive my pretense. I carry no message. But do not refuse me the shelter of your service. Or my former master will kill me."

Dhur was so relieved to find his kith and kin unscathed, rather than grow angrier, he burst into laughter. (Oh, how it splintered the pieces of her already splintered heart.)

"You wretch," said he, "I have a mind to take you on for your impudence. But who is this fiend you have run from?"

"His name is Kolchash," said Marsineh, for a variety of poignant reasons.

"Kolchash? Now, I have heard that name. . . ."

"He is come to the town in order to marry a hapless maiden. The lady must be bemoaned."

"Yes, a wedding—I think I was told of it. One of our neighbor's daughters—the tall thin girl, or she with a nose like a stork's bill." (Marsineh, oh Marsineh!) "But come now, you exaggerate the vices of Kolchash. He is a rich old man, and like all rich old men, is envied. And you are an unproven sauce yourself. But I am in a mild mood. I will accept you for the duration of my sojourn in this forest. You shall attend me at my hunting."

Marsineh prostrated herself as a grateful slave should do—or so they had done in her father's house. Dhur stepped over her and was gone, laughing, back to the top of the inn.

Presently a servant came and shooed her out to the stable.

Here she lay awake all night, from the ache of her bruised limbs and her broken heart. And through a chink in the wall she saw the blooming window high above, where Dhur and his friends drank and sang, until the lamps were put out, and then the window was a dark flower that rustled and breathed, and once a soft cry fell from it to the ground like a ring of gold. Near dawn, the three girls of the inn descended and passed by, the singer, dancer and musician, and they spoke in low voices of Dhur, and his good looks and his generosity.

Then Marsineh wept on the flank of the riding-ass which, thinking her tears only a heavy dew, did not trouble itself with them.

Despite its night of pleasures the hunting party was abroad before the sun rose. Marsineh, exhausted by misery and sleeplessness, crept from the stable at their shouts.

"Now what is that animal there?" inquired Dhur, seeing the riding-ass taking its ease amid the straw. "Surely that is the very beast my father loans our porter."

Marsineh, not wishing to return the porter an ill turn for a good, meekly confessed she had stolen the ass.

"What an imp it is," said Dhur. And with another laugh he gave her a clap on the shoulder that nearly felled her.

"A pale imp, a sickly imp," said the other young men, "not worth its imp's hire. Look at the drooping lily. And how is he to go with us, Dhur?"

"Why, on that very ass," said Dhur.

"I pray you, no,' said Marsineh, so stiff and sore she could have wept afresh.

"How else?" said Dhur blithely. "You are a weakling and certainly cannot run to keep up. Ride along behind us as best you may, and be careful not to lose us, for if you stray in the trees I shall not come searching for you. Do not make a sound either, for the game is already fly enough in these woods."

Presently the hunt set out, fresh as a daisy, eating and drinking as it went. And Marsineh, choking down a little crust, crawled upon the annoyed ass which was as dismayed by this as she.

"Follow, slave!" cried Dhur back to them, "or I shall send you home to Kolchash."

So the hunt rode through the deep reaches of the forest, and Marsineh on the ass went shambling after, it pausing with frequence to enjoy mouthfuls of the turf, she entreating it between moans of agony to make haste.

Beyond the road and the clearing where stood the inn, the trees flowed on like a tide. As the light began to come, the great height of the forest revealed itself, and in the dark green umbra of its upper stories, sun-rays lodged firm as spears, and birds rushed to and fro. On the long enameled boughs the lizards rested upside down, staring with stony eyes, and sometimes a serpent stirred itself to gaze after the riders, such alien amounts of noise and legs, for neither of which faculties a serpent had any use. Among the trunks much lower down, where the young men on their horses passed without a thought and through which the wretched girl was borne willy-nilly, the webs of spiders hung between the broad leaves of the bushes, with the morning dews tinkling upon them. All was elusive and essential in the forest, even by day. And all ways appeared as one. Very soon Marsineh was lost as a traveler in the depths of a lake. And strive as she would with the ass, the party of young men seemed going always farther and farther off. Sometimes she had no sight of them at all, and only heard their voices. And it came to her at last to say, What matter then if I lose Dhur? He is already lost to me. And for myself, I may as well die here, and let the cruel birds and lizards pick clean my bones. For no one cares for me, I can expect no sanctuary. Better I had gone to the evil of Kolchash.

And she halted the ass (which had halted in any case, but in her despair she did not notice), and kissed its face and forgave it the pain it had caused her. Then she disengaged herself from its back and hobbled alone, in a mist of forlorn sadness, away into the vast wood—which still she had not recognized.

So much then, so far, for Marsineh.

But in all this while—a dusk, a night, a dawn—what of Yezade, that beautiful half-sister who had taken the bride's place?

As long ago as three hours past the previous evening's moonrise, the wedding had been concluded, the firecrackers let off, and the feast exposed. But precisely then one had stepped forward, yet another of Lord Kolchash's household retainers, and declared the bridegroom would now depart with his wife.

There were no protests. The marriage gifts had outshone and even outweighed the magnificence of the betrothal items. The bride herself had modestly kept within her veil, and for fear she might be sallow with terror and sobbing, none of her family had insisted she do otherwise. Kolchash, before the altar fires, had raised the veil sufficiently to satisfy himself, presumably, and custom. On his side he had continued his own swathings, and when the shadow of his voluminous headcloth bared a portion of his face, he was seen to be masked in black lacquer. All told, an early start to the honeymoon seemed prudent.

Away into the night then the bridal pair were packed, under a starry sky yet trailed and scored by the pink anemones of fireworks.

The bride rode in a litter; the groom upon a coal-black horse. . . . Yet it was difficult to espy him amid the thronging of his retinue.

Under the town gate, along the highway, the procession went, lit with lamps, but without a note of music or song, and thus reached in an hour or so the forest, which it entered.

After a space, the litter's motion stopped. A shadowy figure parted the curtains: "Madam, the Lord Kolchash desires that you alight."

And the bride (still modestly veiled) was helped to the lawns of the forest and conducted over a slight running stream with one stepping stone, to a pavilion that glowed like nacre. This she entered.

The interior of the tent was furnished luxuriously, and on a silver perch squatted a fiery bird with a tall crest and a long tail. It watched her with a cool pale eye. At the tent's back stood an icon of black and gold, which—if she had not beheld her groom at the marriage—the bride might have taken for a statue. But she had seen the statue move about before, lifting its gold-gloved hands of long black nails to her veil, and directing its masked face this way and that under the heavy diadem. Accordingly she now addressed it: "Good evening, lord husband," and with a bold gesture, threw off at once her own covering.

The mask only turned a little. Eyes glittered behind the eye-holes, in hiding.

"Good evening, my wife," said a rusty voice. "Will you not sit and refresh yourself with wine and food?"

"You are most kind, my lord. But not a morsel of food or a drop of liquid shall pass my lips," said Yezade, "until you yourself have both eaten and drunk."

"Dear wife," said the voice, "I have already supped."

"Then I," said Yezade, "will not dine. For it seems to me," she added, "that I have no appetite to eat or drink when my husband is so displeased with me, he will not show me his face."

At this there was a pause.

Eventually the icon-figure seemed to quiver all over. The voice spoke harshly now.

"Dear wife, can it be you wish to look on that which, out of tasteful concern for you, I have concealed?"

"Dear husband," said Yezade, "since you have wedded me and brought me to your pavilion, I am assured that before the day is born once more, I shall have rendered up to you my virgin state. And that you will, besides, have seen me naked as the moon. Of you, in return, I require only a glimpse of your visage. This is surely not an unreasonable boon to ask of my lord and lover."

A second pause then ensued, lasting longer than the first.

"Dear husband," said Yezade at length, "my mother, before she died, had a gift of foretelling, and this she foretold for me—that if I would gain for myself a great fortune, I must marry another bride's husband. This riddle for many years I did not comprehend, until it came about that my master-father's daughter, whom I much resemble in all but wealth and position, was contracted to a notorious lord, one Kolchash. Yourself. And so, using a charm of my mother's, I sent this silly girl a bad dream of her wedding-eve, and scared her to flight. I therefore took her place at the bridal altar, and here we are. Now you see, I am not the least afraid of you, to inform you of all this. Therefore you may believe I do not fear your looks, and will see them. Unmask!"

There was then a third pause, longer than the preceding two.

Yezade, getting no answer to either confession or demand, rose to her feet and walked without hesitation across the tent. And at that, the fiery bird let out a snicker and turned its back to her, but the figure of Kolchash did not move.

"Now, now," said Yezade. And reaching up, she caught the edge of the black lacquer mask and tore it away.

Yezade let out a cry. She stood staring.

There on the carpet lay the head of Kolchash, which she had pulled right off. For it was the head of a doll, a clockwork thing, and in its sockets the glass eyes rolled, while from the rent neck some strands of wires stuck forth and fizzed with peculiar sparks and energies, that swiftly died.

And as they did so, the light of the tent itself fluttered. It dulled and reddened and went out like a low sigh.

There was then only blackest dark. And Yezade found herself standing on the grass under the trees, not a lamp anywhere, not a tent or a pole, not a man nor a horse, nor any attendant. Alone in the forest and the night.

Until another voice spoke to her, clear and direly melodious.

"You are a fool, Yezade."

And spinning about she found herself after all not alone. For there on a branch perched the fire bird, shining dimly as a distant ocher star.

"What does this mean?" said Yezade, and she strove still to be bold.

"Perhaps it means," said the bird, "that Kolchash, who is no magician, but nevertheless possesses access to certain sorcerous powers, does not like to be cheated in the matter of wives." And then the bird spread wide its wings, and stretched out its neck at her, and there was something so fearsome in this that a great wave of horror splashed over Yezade and in it she submerged, despite her will. And she clutched up her cast veil and turned about and fled. She fled through the spiteful forest, which scratched and bit at her and caught her feet and flung her over, so it came to seem she tried to rush through huge panes and breakers, through the jungle of night itself that came to life and smote her and mocked at her. Until in the end the earth gave way beneath her and she fell, deep down into an abyss, into a nothingness.

And here she swung, and did not see the sunrise, which soon enough took place above her, nor the day which next passed over the forest in a green eyelet that showed high up. Nor this day's ebbing again to a twilight.

Nothing Yezade saw or heard or felt or knew, or even dreamed of. Though perhaps she did dream that the tangled creepers which held her far down in the pit murmured, "Sleep, sleep, while we cradle you so carefully," and the rock, on which she had struck her head in falling, replied, "Sleep? Yes, I saw to it." But in the distance was another voice which said, *"Kolchash does not like to be cheated."*

And then the new night had come, to the forest, to Yezade, and to all other things on the Flat Earth.

3 *The Second Night: Lovers Met and Marred*

WHILE YEZADE HAD been sleeping all day the sleep of ensorcelled and stunned unconsciousness in a hole in the ground, Marsineh had slumbered with exhaustion under a tree.

Unknown to her, during the heat of noon, a spotted lynx and her child had passed by, pausing only to sniff the flower-like scent of Marsineh's hair—for she had flung off the boy's headcloth. And later, as the sun slipped west behind the forest canopy and the golden green of afternoon cooled to a green turquoise, an old stag, whose branched antlers seemed grown out of the wood itself, stayed half a minute to look at her, before he stepped on huge silent feet away.

But Marsineh slept deep in the arms of sorrow and did not wake, though once she cried softly in a dream, and a butterfly like colored paper sipped her tears.

Cooler and darker turned the great wood, for the sun went down. Between the vast pillars of the trees the aisles were hung with dusk.

Marsineh woke. She was chilled, but what did that matter? Somewhere, through the wild lanes of the wood, Dhur would be turning for his pleasurable inn, having forgotten altogether the runaway boy. And elsewhere the riding-ass would be cropping the grass, if no carnivore of the forest had devoured it— And Marsineh wept again, for Dhur's forgetfulness and the imperiled ass. Until, in the midst of her tears, she heard a most beautiful sound—or she smelled a most marvelous perfume—she was unsure which, or even if it might not be something else. . . . In any event, she was compelled to dispense with crying and look about and listen intently.

The forest was by now utterly quiet and completely still, and also entirely black, save for some phantom gossamers of starlight that had somehow come floating down from the tree-tops.

Marsineh did not dare to speak aloud or move, for fear.

Just then, the darkness seemed to gather itself, all in one spot, before her and, detaching itself dark from dark, drew forward. Marsineh caught her breath in frightened wonder.

There, not three feet away, and leaning down to look into her eyes, was a pale and extraordinary face. It was, unmistakably, that of a young man, but so handsome, framed in such black, black hair, and with eyes of its own of such a black and luminous fire—that Marsineh could not bear the gaze. It was as if a piercingly sweet pain shot into every nerve. She recoiled, and perhaps would have taken flight. But in that instant, the fabulous creature reached out a hand, whose pale long fingers touched her cheek more lightly than the earlier butterfly, and yet she felt the touch all through herself, as if her veins ran silk. It healed her, this touch, of all terrible human things, of grief and puzzlement, of fear and decorum. Even, it healed her pains and stiffness. So that when both hands came now and persuaded Marsineh to get up, up she rose and stood before him, so near the slender strength of his whole body, which seemed garbed in shadow, leaves and stars, that she had no choice but to lean on him. And then he stroked her hair, and this was as if a master-musician played upon amber strings, it was music. And then he breathed or sighed, and the incense of his breath, better than and different from any perfume of the world, intoxicated Marsineh. So then she said, in the arms of this stranger, "Oh, you must be a god of the forest, you are so beautiful. Oh, I hear what I say and am amazed by it. But I care nothing now for any human man. I care nothing now for anything. Only for you."

Then the god of the forest touched Marsineh's closed eyes with his lips, and when she opened them, she found she saw the nighttime woods as if by the sheerest brightest moonshine. For everything seemed steeped and soaked in a feral lovely light that was not light at all. The trunks of the trees stood clear, each laminated rib was visible. Above, every leaf glittered as if in dry and diamond rain. The night flowers dashed the grass with spilled sequins. Marsineh raised her hands, and her skin was crystal.

"Come with me now," said the young man, yet he did not speak to her at all.

With him she went.

They moved between the skeins of the forest with the ease of the air itself. Where the starlight poured into the glades, there blazed the sheen of silver mirrors. Black and white badgers gamboled round their feet. A snake glided from a pool to follow and caress them.

There was a bank mattressed with a velvet panther-skin of moss, where briar-roses opened their white cups and filled the night with musk, and primroses had formed a coverlet under the pillared canopy of vines on which the savage grapes clustered like agates. Here he led her, and here drew her down. Here she lay with him, the unmarried bride, her second bridal-night that was her first, in the arms of one whose name she did not know, whose voice she had not heard, learning the joyous deliriums of love, without a protest, without a thought.

* * *

A little before the dawn he left her. She sensed a shrillness in the wood, before ever the light showed itself: It was this he did not care for, unweaving his flesh from hers. But he left her with an unvoiced promise—of continuance, return. He left her dressed in the petals of roses, in vine leaves and in shade, with pale flowers through her hair. She, too, had grown silent, learning from his eloquent muteness. She did not need to cry after him, *Oh how I adore you, my lover and my love.* Indeed, it was not mere love he had brought her—it was Love, the rhythm of the world. He left her, they were not parted. She could not remember her name (let alone any other's), nor who she was. The forest was her home and had entered, too, into her soul. She laughed without a sound to see him vanish like a blade sheathed in the scabbard of the sinking night. She curled herself to slumber among the primroses and the fern.

Yezade had wakened, like her sister Marsineh, as the day fell down asleep. But Yezade's emotions were her own. The curious terror of the nacre pavilion, the headless doll of Kolchash—her frantic spell-bound flight from the cold-eyed bird of fire—but too well she knew she had dreamed none of it, though her head ached from the blow of the rock.

Sorcery there had been, and set against her. Now she lay in the tangled vegetable web and saw the night above, in the eyelet. She resolved she must climb up to it. So, setting her narrow hands and feet into the stony sides of the pit, and gripping the creepers, she did at length, with much difficulty and some hurt, bring herself out again to the open forest.

After the darkness of her prison, the night wood appeared vast and most adequately lit. Yezade lifted her head and snuffed the atmosphere for magic, like an amber fox emerging from its earth. But the night seemed empty now. What she had fallen foul of had lost interest in her. Nevertheless, Yezade muttered a small protective mantra, another of her mother's legacies.

Kolchash had proved himself to be, in his own right, a powerful magician. And it seemed to Yezade that she had been ensorcelled from the start not to have seen the awful mocking game he played with her. For had she not devised and sent the dream to Marsineh which scared her from the marriage, and had not Marsineh retold this dream to Yezade, in all its detail. Finding then this detail exactly repeated—save for a slender disparity here and there, for example that the perch of the uncanny bird, gilded gold in the dream, was silver in the fact—should Yezade not have queried the manner in which life so blatantly imitated her art?

Where was the monstrous Kolchash now? Gone in pursuit of Marsineh, no doubt. That then, was their business. Yezade had no resource to spare any longer for sentiment. Meanwhile, she herself was outcast and desolate, her mother's prophecy had misled her, and had she been any other she would have sobbed, but instead she stamped her foot and frowned her aching brow.

Just then she heard an odd sound rise out of the forest's deeps. It resembled the mad braying of an ass—and in that second Yezade recalled stories that were told of these woods, that elementals haunted them, and devilish things— But she had been frightened enough, and now she only turned her back upon the noise, which swiftly died away. And hearing instead the quiet song of running water she went in that direction, for she was thirsty.

Now, Yezade was no witch, but her mother had been one, and some inheritance had vaguely passed to her of it, along with the several charms, learnt parrot-fashion, which she could wield. And so, as she was going toward the notes of the water, abruptly she checked herself, petrified beside a tree and strove to be one with it. And this, before she knew why she must.

A glade lay beyond, rimmed by grasses high as a child of seven years. And suddenly, between and above the grass, there moved three or four or five flickering and glowing fires, of smokiest azure, most unreal and palest purple. Around and about they danced, mingling and eluding, until all at once they brightened and faded—and there instead were some beautiful and human-like beings, still moving in a graceful flickering dance across the grass.

Their skin was white, like starlight, if starlight were to

become flesh. Their long hair was the black of midnight clouds. They were garbed in a black which was also silver. They came and went in their dance, male and female, young as youth and old as time. In their burning midnight eyes was a mysterious dreaming look. They were those that men sometimes called the Children of Night, afraid to title them otherwise. They were demonkind. Yezade knew them immediately, for her mother had warned her of them, and Yezade remembered, though she had not perfectly believed. Yes, demonkind, and of the wandering, speechless caste of the Underearth, the Eshva, which name, in the Demon Tongue, meant: Those that separately shine.

How brilliantly they shone now in their unearthly darkness. And Yezade stared on them and felt her heart grow scorched and little with a wordless longing, a lust of the spirit, which countless mortals, seeing them, had felt before her.

And then there occurred another happening, more fearful and wonderful still.

Far down the glade there was a noiseless explosion of light, and the ground itself erupted. From the midst of it there came leaping up three horses, black and bright, with manes and tails of blue sparks, and on their backs three lords, alike as brothers of one birth, yet dissimilar as were and are the stars, when closely examined. And they were black and pale as those others, the Eshva, who had been dancing there, yet where the Eshva shone, these blazed. And again the watcher knew them, for they were princes of the Vazdru, the high caste of the demons, and now Yezade was purely terrified.

No sooner were they above ground than they reined in their steeds and looked about arrogantly, while the Eshva, their admiring servants, obeised themselves. Then, one of the Vazdru spoke, and his voice was beauty-and-fear-in-love-with-one-another.

"Our Lord Azhrarn is done hunting, then. He has found her?"

"It seems so," said the second, no less lustrous, no less deadly.

"That pair of lovers has had its season; they are due to be parted," said the third, and he was the same.

But, having said this, they seemed not at ease. They toyed with rings on their fingers, and chided the moon for her childish slenderness.

At last, the first said, "An old quarrel, it is better settled. And there is none can match our lord, Prince of the princes."

"Yet," said the second, "the woods are perfumed by madness."

"And, more fragrantly, by the recreations of demons," said the third.

Then they returned their horses' heads, and as if a fiery wind rose from the earth, they galloped away between the trees. In that moment, too, the Eshva disappeared.

Yezade fell to her knees. She had understood nothing of what had been said. But she had been accorded a frightening recognition. The voice of the third of the Vazdru was known to her, since she had heard it only the night before. It was with this voice, melodious and dire, that the ice-eyed bird had addressed her and sent her into headlong flight. She had thought herself only the enemy of a mighty magician. To find she had engaged the enmity of a Vazdru almost killed this wise girl on the spot.

"My mother," said she reproachfully, "where have you led me?"

And quickly she found a hollow tree and hid herself in it, and there she stayed for the duration of the demoniac night.

Now the dialogue of the Vazdru had referred to those two lovers, Chuz, Delusion's Master, and Azhriaz-Sovaz, the Prince of Demons' daughter. (The very hero and heroine fantastically described at the Turtle Dove Inn.)

Azhrarn had sought and found them out, to punish and cleave them asunder. And all the length of that vast forest away, epic events went on, whose story is related elsewhere. But, as the proximity, however distant, of those two supernaturals had filled the woods with strangeness, so the sorceries increased when the Eshva had entered there and loitered. And the Vazdru also, attending on their Prince, dropped back a fraction from the theater of his wrath, and wrought their own wickedness and mischief in the forest—rather as warriors played chess before a battle. Only the intensity of Azhrarn's thought and mood held them off from doing more. His rage distracted them from their pastimes, as his anguish had done and would do again and again (till they turned and snarled at it like lions under a lash). But the distraction meant that much of what they did in this place was left unfinished, and as well for humankind it was.

Something had already gone on, concerning the wedding of Kolchash, and something else to do with the beauty of Marsineh and an Eshva youth, wandering in the burning dream of night, who had found her sweet to his desire. And something else and other there was still to be, from the fringes of the demon presence that threaded the woods.

Only dawn might balk the demons, daylight was their death. But certain of these antics they set in motion, even the sunrise did not always cancel them. . . .

4 *The Second Day*

DHUR, DRIFTING UP on a tide of sleep, thought himself in the comfortable inn. But if so, the bed had grown grass in the night, the cup of wine turned into dew and spilled, and the curve of the fair singing-girl's hip was unyielding as a boulder.

Dhur opened his eyes, and looked upon the woods with a grievance. "May the gods take note," said he, "that it is my kind heart brought me to this predicament." The gods, of course, did no such thing.

The young man stretched, and taking out a packet of bread and meat and a flask of wine, broke his fast. The green sunlight anointed him and the smell of flowers drifted up from the grass. Nearby a tribe of conies, discounting him, breakfasted on violets, or played. Since boyhood, Dhur had hunted in these woods, and did not fear them or even to be lost in them. If he should meet with an angry wolf or a lynx, he had about him bow and spear and knife. For superstitious tales, he did not credit ghosts, ghouls, sprites or demons. Such were the fodder of poets.

He had begun, during his first day's hunting, to be troubled by a recollection of the town. He had started to consider the bizarre wedding of a neighbor's daughter to the rich old Kolchash. That very evening, after a day of no sport at all, the idiot boy had come to him, escaped from the service of this Kolchash. Dhur had teased the boy and left him to keep up with the hunt. But the boy had been lost, and the ass—the property of Dhur's father—had been lost, and—moreover—the hunt had failed again. Not an animal presented itself. Save once a young doe with her fawn, who seemed to be aware she must not be pursued by men of honor, for she went slowly across their path, seemingly nodding to them as she did so.

As the day waned and they turned back toward the inn—knowing the routes of the forest nearly as well as the streets of their town—Dhur took it on himself to drop aside and seek the lost boy riding the ass. And not to spoil their fun, he had sent his companions away to the Turtle Dove, with instructions each to drink an extra cup and proffer an extra kiss on his behalf, should he not return in time.

(And as he was doing this, it came to him to wonder a little, why he bothered to search for the boy—who doubtless had simply run off again—when he had vowed to the fellow he would do no such thing. And Dhur thought, too, of how he had pretended to the boy, when the subject was broached, that he, Dhur, did not much recall any Kolchash, or any wedding. . . . Now why had that been?)

Being so sure of the forest, not afraid of it, Dhur felt no unease and only a little chagrin when the sun set and night descended. Once he heard an ass braying, and rode in that direction, but search as he would and clearly call as he sometimes did, not a trace did he uncover of the wretched boy. Then Dhur grew melancholy, which was not quite unpleasant. He made a camp among the trees, lit a fire and ate his supper, while his tethered horse cropped the fresh grass. Dhur fell easily now to thinking of a girl he half remembered, a well-born girl who had charmed him, but he had not paid her proper heed and could not now recall who she had been. Some rich man's daughter, it went without saying, for she wore figured silk and had gold on her wrists. But her hair was warm as flame. . . .

Then, in the pleasantly melancholy act of constructing a song to this nameless She, Dhur slept.

Asleep, he dreamed. There he lay under the tree, beside the embers of the fire, when through the arches of the wood came riding three princes on black steeds. They could be nothing less than princes, for they were dressed as such, and their horses were of the best.

And though he slept, Dhur saw upward through his closed lids. He saw the princes pause and glance at him.

"This forest," said one, "is littered with mortals."

"They are everywhere," said another. "They fill up the world. But we taught them love, and there was our mistake."

Then all three laughed, and the third, drawing nearer, looked down into Dhur's sleeping face. "You are fortunate," said this third prince to Dhur, "that you are not ugly, but so comely. For if I had found you irksome, I should have blasted you where you lay." And then this third prince, who was himself of a remarkable handsomeness, leaned over Dhur from his saddle, with a sinuous ease uncommon among men, and kissed him lightly on the forehead. The kiss *burned.* Like cold, or heat, or acid—had he been able to, Dhur would have sprung to his feet, but weights lay on him; he could neither stir nor wake. A powerful drug seemed at work, so that next even the eyes of his dream fell shut.

He heard the three ride away, but the steps of their horses were like tinsel brushing the grass, and only the bells whispered on the caparisons. Then Dhur's own horse gave a neigh, and breaking its tether, bolted after them and was gone. And Dhur, lying drugged by the dream kiss, could not shift himself even to curse.

"But that was only the dream," said Dhur now, in the sunlit morning, and turned to see where his horse was. But it was not. Then Dhur did curse, and so loudly the conies raised their ears and stared at him from the violets.

"How can my dream have enticed away my horse?"

demanded Dhur. None answered, though all the forest might have been said to know. So then Dhur supposed the horse had simply run off out of a humor, and he had incorporated the sounds of this in his dream.

"That damnable boy, if ever found," Dhur promised the conies, "shall be whipped home to Kolchash. He has cost me a night's entertainment and a fine mount."

But there was not much anger in Dhur, he was not a creature for rages, as he was not a creature for deep thought.

Presently he rose from his couch and walked away through the woods, as he believed, in the direction of the inn.

About this hour Yezade was crawling from the hollow tree with mushrooms in her hair, a sorry sight after her adventures.

She had no idea where she should go, but to desert the enchanted forest at least seemed sensible. Having no notion of its scope or paths, however, she could only set out trusting to luck—who so far had been no friend to her. She was also by now tortured by a thirst far worse than hunger, and hearing once more the noise of water, hastened toward it.

Soon she reached the edge of a clearing, and there across it went a slight running stream with one stone in it, and on the further bank was a sort of bothy built of moss and twigs. Something about the spot was unlikable to Yezade, but thirst overruled scruple, the bothy looked too dilapidated to be occupied, and so she hurried to the stream and lay down on the ground to drink from it.

She had drunk less than her fill when suddenly there was movement on either hand. Next instant rough fists had seized hold of her. Yezade screamed.

"It seems human enough," said he that held her right arm.

"I do not trust this wood, even by day," announced he that gripped her left arm.

Both shook her, and Yezade moaned.

"Courteous gentlemen, I am only—"

"Silence, hussy! Our lord shall judge what you are."

"Who is your lord?" inquired Yezade in some anxiety.

"Behold him," said her right-hand captor.

Yezade looked across the stream. There in the entrance to the bothy stood a tall figure in a black robe sewn with golden suns and stars, upon its head a gold diadem, upon its face a black lacquer mask.

"The Lord Kolchash," declared Yezade's left-hand captor.

Yezade swooned.

Noon hunted the forest, shooting bright arrows. Dhur stood among them, looking this way and that way. It had come to him that he had lost his path. This area of the woods was unfamiliar, yet so like all the rest it had deceived him.

The sun then must guide him. Yet the forest at noon, a goblet of dark green quartz, seemed shattered by that sun. All directions were out of their places, all routes were one.

Just then, Dhur heard again the braying of an ass.

"Oh, you boy, you child of iniquity," said Dhur, with a glad scowl, and turned his strides toward the crazy noise.

In a while he caught the flash of a pale hide through the trees. It was the riding-ass for sure, being ridden along before him. Dhur strode after, deeper into the lake-depths of the wood.

Yezade wakened. She recollected everything and also knew herself lost. Her mother had been wrong in two ways. In the prophecy of Yezade's marriage, and in saying that demons did not manifest on earth by day.

For there it sat, the black and golden doll which the demons, by their craft, had made. And yet, the bird of fire and ice, which form the Vazdru had taken, that was absent.

Indeed, everything, for the most part, was absent. There was no luxury in the hut. And Kolchash, doll, demon or whatever, sat on a log of wood. And there his two henchmen stood behind him, and they wore the draggled remnants of finery much as did Yezade herself wear the rags of her bridal dress.

"See now," said Kolchash, if Kolchash it was, "this is

only some poor girl, probably set on as we have been. Ah, maiden, fear nothing, but only tell me your tale of woe."

But Yezade could not bring herself to utter.

"She has lost the power of speech from her terror," pronounced Kolchash. "Or maybe it is my mask which so alarms her. Dear child, shall I remove it?"

"*No!*" shrieked Yezade.

"Yes, it is the rumors which distress her," mourned Kolchash. And putting up his gold gloves with the black claws, began to remove his head.

Hastily, Yezade once more swooned.

The porter's riding-ass, drawn by the glamour of something with which it had once had an association, and which now glowed in the forest's heart like a fallen moon, ambled on and on toward it, pausing only now and then to shave a fern or lick the delicious waters of the wood. Never in its days or nights had the ass enjoyed such liberty. A fat man had ridden it (the porter), next a light but unwieldy boy-girl. Put off to stray, the ass willingly did so. Once, it had smelled the tang of wild cat and kicked up its heels and fled, but this trauma was now forgotten. The forest passed for a safe haven of plenty. A couple of times besides it had heard a divine music shock through the avenues, the hymn of one of its own clan: *Eeh-orrh!*

Even when it began to seem to the ass that some thing came after it, muttering and growling, it had a human scent and sound, and its two-legged crashings boded only captivity and service. The ass did not entirely object to these, nor was it entirely prepared to submit. Thus on it skipped, trotting through brambles where it could so that he that followed must also get through them, and down rocky slides so he that followed must slither and slip, and through streams choked by untame lilies from whose choice chalices rose wasps in droves.

In this way, the afternoon was disposed, the sun turned west and the trees began to spread out their filmy shadows. Just then the ass, discovering its goal, that which had attracted it, clattered out upon the shore of a wide pool. Here the sky was to be seen, in a gilded curving lid above, and with the tops of the forest clustered all about its edge just as the rushes clustered at the water's brim. And the sky reflected in the pool, and both remained so clarified and still, that in that place and those moments, you could not tell if the sky were not the pool above, and the trees that framed it only copies of the actual trees which stood upon a sky resting in the earth below.

The great tranquillity and loveliness of this image stayed even foot-sore, wasp-stung Dhur. He halted to let his eyes drink in the sight. And then he saw the riding-ass meekly sipping at the pool's brink or the sky's brink, and no one on its back.

What Dhur was prone next to do is conjecture. For just as he was about to do it, there came a glimmer out of the trees, as if the evening star were walking there.

Dhur caught his breath. And then he stepped back among the bushes and fixed his gaze earnestly on the shore.

For there, in the warm light, a beautiful maiden took her way, dazzling like whitest ivory, for she was clad only in flowers and vines, and in her tumbling hair as red as amber.

"Now she is like—that very one I recalled," murmured Dhur to himself. "But that other was not so fair as this, for she was mortal. And this is some sylph of the wood—in which I do not believe."

The sylph went into the shallows of the pool, and here she bathed and laved herself with water and light, and though she made no sound, her gestures were like dance. And seeing the riding-ass she went to it and kissed its face, which the animal suffered with apparent good-will. "As well it might," said Dhur, leaning on a tree. "Unworthy thing. If the gods had any compassion, they would grant me the ability to change places with the brute. Then I should feel those hands about my neck and those lips on my face."

But Dhur knew better than to call to the apparition, or approach her. For since the legends of her kind were true, she would be faithful to them, and seeing him, run away or vanish.

So he contained himself with some difficulty, and swore in his heart that this was his fate, to be ensnared by an ethereal being (since the existence of such beings charmed him very much.)

At last, when she had done bathing, having sent her watcher the while half mad, the exquisite maiden left the pool and returned amid the trees. The ass instantly went trotting after her. And Dhur, no less beglamoured, fell in after both of them.

And the three, one by one, climbed up again into the darkening forest.

But Yezade had lain some hours in the bothy, as if dead, and not batted an eyelash, though she was quite aware. She recited the while a mantra to hold her body rigid, and either its potence, or her belief in it, made her into a plank. But despite this, she at length heard Kolchash say, "If only I were half the mage I have put it about I am, I might restore her. Indeed, we should all have kept out of this pickle."

And to that the two henchmen gave hearty assent. After which, saying they would go see if any new provender was to be found, they left the hut.

Presently, Yezade reversed the mantra, opened her eyes a crack, and beheld Kolchash seated still upon his log. Beside him there neatly reposed his head of lacquer face, headcloth and diadem. The loathsomeness of this sight was mitigated, however. For though one head was off, another remained in position on the shoulders of Kolchash. This was the gray-haired skull and countenance of an elderly man of miserable expression.

Yezade sat up, and while the lacquer Kolchash stayed impervious, the elderly and miserable Kolchash peered at her.

"Praise to the gods, the maiden has revived."

"Small thanks to you," snapped Yezade.

"Doubtless," said he, "you are in the right, and I have been properly punished for my pride and folly. Would you wish to hear my story?"

"I would rather be given food and drink," said Yezade, "as I have been two days without them, through your fault."

Kolchash drooped. He said, "My men have gathered these forest fruits, and there is a casket of sweetmeats intended for a wedding. I do not see how I am responsible for two days of your fast, and have nothing else to offer, but you are welcome to those."

Yezade accordingly feasted as best she might, and Kolchash, whether she would or no, launched into his tale.

"Being uncommonly rich, and having in my possession many priceless curios and artifacts, from the beginning of my career," said Kolchash, "I had it put about that I was an evil and fearsome man, and could wield several malign magics. In this way I protected myself from thieves and sycophants alike, and was free to dwell as I would, alone and in peace."

To assist his bad reputation, Kolchash would occasionally ride abroad dressed as Yezade had first seen him, in gold and claws, his entire face and head concealed by an assemblage of cloth, mask and diadem. Stories were told of human skin books, that he had sorcerous eyes to the rear of his cranium, and could detach his soul which he then set on his enemies in the form of a black cloud. Kolchash meanwhile lived a blameless life, performing charitable acts in secret. Only certain of his retainers and guard knew the truth, and being loyal to their master, did not betray it.

One dusk, however, the placid life of Kolchash was upset. He received an unnatural visitor in the form of a ghost, which appeared to him in his study.

"Kolchash," began this ghost, which was that of a female, elegantly dressed in the manner of a waiting-lady of some well-to-do household.

"Madam," interrupted Kolchash in a fuss, "I am no mage, and it is therefore useless for you to evolve before me."

"Of your correct status I am aware," retorted the ghost, "but you must hear me out nevertheless. I have been troubled many years and unable to proceed along my discorporate course because of it. I had, when living, a daughter, and to this girl I made a prophecy, the substance of which I shall not burden you with. Suffice it to say it concerned her future prospects, and that I was in error and misled her, for in the normal way no opportunity would have complemented my riddle. Therefore I intend to create such an opportunity, and so redeem myself as a prophetess in her eyes, and see her besides into a secure situation. In this you will aid me." And then the imperious ghost told Kolchash the name and whereabouts of a particular man, and advised Kolchash that he must send at once to him. "You will say you have seen his daughter in a magic glass, that you will wed her, and in token you will give him such gifts that his avarice will make it impossible for him to refuse you—for he is a selfish wretch, as I learned to my cost when alive."

"Madam—" again interpolated Kolchash.

"More," decreed the ghost. "You will couch your proposal in such a sinister way that all will be alarmed at it, and you will, too, see that all the rumors of your vileness are stirred up, so the prospective bride shall be at her wits' end in fright. My own child," added the ghost, "is quick, and sure to seize her chance, trusting to my former words. You," finished the ghost, "I have chosen for your ill-reputation and your true virtue and wealth, which together will resolve my need."

"And if I deny you?" understandably said Kolchash, somewhat put out. "I am not a man for marriages. I prefer my books."

"If you deny me," said the ghost, with a sulky resolute air, "I shall howl and wail about your dwelling every night, filling the hearts of all who hear me with fear and distress. Being no magician, you cannot yourself dispel me; while if you have recourse to one who can, your reputation will be gone forever. Either way, you will be much the loser."

The ghost (none other, of course, than the dead mother of Yezade) then demonstrated her abilities in the line of howling and wailing. And shortly Kolchash agreed to her terms, and sent at once to Marsineh's father, requiring her hand in a most eerie fashion.

Yezade, the listener, was by now struck dumb with fascination. But she did not need to prompt. Kolchash continued, as generally they do that have a sorry misfortune to relate.

"All then was arranged, and having no choice I was philosophically resigned to the matter, though very grieved to be causing the maiden such dismay. Taking with me a large company and many further gifts, as the ghost had insisted, I set out for the wedding appointment. Everything went well until our travel took us through the outskirts of this forest."

Night having come down, the company prepared its camp among the trees. Kolchash's splendid pavilion was erected, but no sooner had he retired inside it, then he found another there before him.

This other appeared to be, at first glance, only a young man, dark of hair and darkly clad, very pale and disturbingly handsome, who lounged upon the divan cushions and stared Kolchash up and down.

Now Kolchash had once or twice had such an encounter with insolent young men, and resorting to his false personality, soon overwhelmed each challenger. Therefore Kolchash drew himself up and declared: "Do you know me, foolish youth?"

At which the foolish youth gave a laugh so melodious that every item in the tent, from the silk tassels to the alabaster bowls, seemed to melt. And he replied, "Of all the fools there are, there are no better fools than mortals."

And at this, Kolchash (who in fact was not a fool) misgave. So he said, "I perceive I am in the presence of a superior."

"So you are," said the other. "You are a scholar if no mage. And so perhaps have heard of the Vazdru."

At that, a gauze seemed to dissolve from the eyes of Kolchash. He saw a being before him that was partly of flesh and partly of fire, and partly and mostly of the dark. So he took off at once the fakery of the magician's head-piece and bowed low, shaking and shivering.

The demon Vazdru were susceptible to flattery. This one, no exception, smiled and said, "Your foolish mortal good-sense has spared you many torments tonight, Kolchash the Unmagician. But I must warn you. The Prince of princes, Azhrarn the Beautiful, is due to call upon this wood in anger. There must be no marriages, there must be no tender human lovers. Or, if you wish, it is my whim so to interpret the great quarrel between my lord and one or two others."

"It is no use to go against the demon princes," said Kolchash.

"None whatsoever. Be resigned then."

And at these words Kolchash lay down upon the floor. No sooner had he done so, than the tent and everything in it flashed out, and a whirlwind descended on the wood. Kolchash held fast to the earth, though the wind tried to prize him from it. Things fell about his ears—branches, stones, lamp-poles and saddles—and the air was full of neighing and outcry.

When the upheaval ceased, Kolchash found himself bivouacked in the glade with only two of his guard. These were somewhat bemused, saying they had seen men and horses carried away right over the tallest trees and heard them roaring after, but not been able to find them. And of those who had remained and gone seeking, not one had returned.

So the three spent the rest of the night on the ground. And in the morning, Kolchash had permitted the two guards to make a search of the surrounding woods, but always scratching a mark upon the trees as they went, in order to find the way back.

At noon one man returned, saying he had heard others calling and vigorously swearing in the wood, but had not been able to come to them nor they to him. The forest was perhaps sorcerous, or only very tangled.

The second man returned at sunset, and he had stranger news.

"My Lord Kolchash, you may not believe my story, but I vow to you that, about midday, coming on a break in the trees, I looked down and saw a company riding by below. And these seemed your men, about half who rode out with us, indeed fellows that I have known three years and more. And in the midst were the carts with the bridal gifts, and the litter for the bride. And no one led this procession, but on it went as if spelled. And when I shouted, not one man looked or answered. And it seemed to me, though it was daylight, that they moved yet in the night."

"Since when," said Kolchash, "we have kept meekly here in the forest, in order not to annoy the demons. My men built for me this shelter and here, the second night, I had a dream which I think to have been a true one, sent me by the Vazdru prince, either in scorn or irony. For I beheld the procession of my men in a town, and a marriage was going on there. And a veiled girl was wedded to a thing which was exactly the replica of myself when I am dressed in my worst. Now I am a scholar, and I have read how the lower demons of the Underearth can make marvelous clockwork dolls, real as life, and these lower caste demons (who are called the Drin) are even able to work the metal gold, which the higher castes abhor. So now I suppose a demon-doll of a Kolchash has wedded the fair girl betrothed to me. And the gods alone know what has become of her. Or will become of that half of my retainers, doubtless scattered again once the mischief was done. Or, for that, what will become of me—for though I did not properly comprehend the ghost's plan, obviously I must have failed in my part of it, and she will credit none of this. I shall be held responsible and haunted and howled at till my dying hour."

Then Yezade lowered her eyes.

"My lord," said she, "I will inform you now of what befell your rightful and proper bride."

5 *The Third Night*

THE SKY POWDERED her cheeks with rouge, and the forest was mantled in crimson. Then the face of the sky altered, became that of a beautiful black damsel having no wish for rouge, but only for a net of stars and a piece of silver moon to hang on her forehead. And the forest mantled in sable, whispering with waters and the lyres of the grasshopper, and with the turning pages of leaves, and the unheard footsteps of unseen things.

And Dhur, following his sylph from her pool, walked as silently as he could, but in the blackness, lost her. And so he paused, scenting wild honey on the forest's sweet breath—and in that moment another met him, there in the dark.

Perhaps it was his coming to a belief in supernatural beings which made Dhur instantly conscious that here was another such. Or possibly the aura of this other brooked no denial.

Dhur had not seen the marvel of the Vazdru, save in sleep; this was revealed to his open eyes. He was kin to the princes of the dream, this night-born walker, himself less than such a prince, but so much more than any mortal.

So Dhur stood in silence.

And as he did this, or rather did nothing, the Eshva looked back at him, smiling a fraction as at some secret jest. And the night-black eyes of the Eshva—member of that separately-shining sect of dream-burned, wandering children of shade—he read Dhur like some book whose irrelevant meaning can be grasped in one slow heartbeat. All of it, the Eshva saw, the human life of sunlit trivia and—worse—trivia moonlit. The lust of a human man for a beautiful girl he had taken for a sprite—the girl who was in fact this demon's lover. And one other thing the Eshva saw, for to his gaze it showed quite plainly. There on the human's forehead, the invisible kiss of the Vazdru, flaming like a silver rose. And for this the Eshva smiled, in a sensuous jealousy, a surreal contempt, in the prologue to a satin-soft caress of retribution. . . . Only a minute before, the Eshva had come upon the riding-ass, which had lain down at the Eshva's feet. And the Eshva had garlanded the ass with ivy. Now the Eshva read upon the brain of Dhur that memory of an unmeant wish: *Grant me the ability to change places with the brute. Then I should feel those hands about my neck, those lips—*

From your own heart, said the Eshva though he did not speak the words, *this I will give you.*

Dhur flinched away, feeling a curious cold and heat about his head. It was a reflex of his frame, since his mind had not at all caught up with instinct. Nor was it of any use.

The Eshva laughed sharply and with cruel delight—and with his eyes alone—and then he gleamed like one of the turning leaves and went out, was gone.

Dhur, in a sudden onset of outrage, called abruptly into the darkness after him. And from the jaws of Dhur there came a sound that he had heard before, but never from his own lips.

Eeh-orrh! brayed Dhur, so the forest rang at it.
EEEH-orrrh!

Never had Marsineh, who had forgotten that she was Marsineh, been as happy. Her happiness transcended all comfort, and all pleasure. It could not last, for human flesh was not made, then or now, to endure such transports ceaselessly. Only the soul could compass them, and then, differently. And dimly, somewhere within herself, this Marsineh knew quite well. She had already condoned the end of joy. It seemed she trusted her demon paramour to free her from its bitterness. Somewhere in the dance of love, speechless, he must have promised her forgetfulness also of this.

But for that night, her third in the forest, her second in the forest of desire's fulfillment, ecstasy was her familiar.

The demons had invented love. There needs to be said no more.

An hour before the dawn, or maybe in a space of time that was timeless, the Eshva lover of Marsineh murmured, in a language of gesture, hair and eyes, and perhaps of thought, that some great argument had now been resolved elsewhere in the wood. Lovers had been parted at the decree of the lord the Eshva served and worshipped. Now he and she, too, would part. Marsineh wept, and the Eshva wept in the peerless, depthless, heartless lamenting of his kind.

Then he drew her up from her despair, out of the well of it, so she walked as lightly as did he. And there before them were two crouching, simpering creatures, dwarfs, whose ugliness was so unbelievable Marsineh scarcely saw it. And these presented her, at the instruction of the Eshva, with a robe.

The dwarfs were Drin metalsmiths and artificers of the Underearth, and along with the capability to make dolls, they could make almost anything that was surpassingly beautiful. Apparel they laid before the girl which had been spider-spun by many thousands of those furry spinsters, lemans of the Drin. And being what they were, and the denizens of that country under the earth, the fabric of the costume was a film of silver, like stardust, and in it had been trapped a quantity of jewels—the somber jades and yellow and green jaspers found on the shores of an underground lake, the aquamarine pearls and peacock opals fished from the waters of the world's seas. And over all of it the Drin had laid magic that the sun of day should not wither the work, and because of this, here and there, a thread of reddest gold winked in the fabric, from which the Eshva turned his eyes, though it was his parting gift of love to her.

Next he drove the Drin away; they were ogling Marsineh. Then he embraced her and bade her put on the garment. Still in her trance she obeyed him, and clasped her narrow waist with its belt of aqueous gems. She was dazzled then by her own light. And he a little repulsed by it, the gold in it.

Lie down again, he said, *lie down on the velvet moss among the roses.* She did so, in her finery looking like a maiden flung from the stars. *Close your eyes,* he said. *No longer gaze at me.* She did this, too, and the tears spilled on her cheeks. And then he leaned to her, and with some balm or flower of the Underworld, purple in color, he brushed her brow and her eyelids. And at this she fell asleep, and sleeping, his image left her as he must have promised her it would. There she lay upon her bank of vines and eglantine, lovely as loveliness, but no demon lover near her any more.

Close by, two others wandered in the wood, one peacefully grazing and a little out of sorts with a new incompetence it discovered in itself in the matter of eating grass, and one clutching at itself in terror and sometimes hoarsely upbraiding heaven in a voice it did not like to call its own.

As the night's last smokes were stealing between the trees, a tawny lynx came down the byways of the forest, looking for an early breakfast and believing that he smelled it.

There before him, a domestic ass was busy with the grass.

What luck! thought the lynx, in the lynx tongue. And he began to circle round the ass, to freeze it with his olivine eyes.

But as the lynx came round the ass, snarling and purring to himself, the ass turned its head. And it was the lynx that froze, flat to the earth, and his tufted ears flat to his skull, and his whiskers stuck out stiff as the quills of a porcupine, and his tail going *swish-swash* in the fern.

For staring inanely at the lynx from the ass' forequarters was the head and face of a handsome young *man*, with a mouthful of grazing. And though clearly enough the brain within the head had stayed that of a riding-ass, the face was yet that of one who had no fear of lynxes, who indeed had hunted them. And thus, while the mouth chewed inaccurately at the grass, and the fine eyes had a look in them of surprise that chewing grass should be so difficult, there was something all told to the mien which cried to the lynx *Arrow-flight! Spear-flight! Run for your lair or I will wear you on my shoulders!*

And so the lynx bethought himself of an urgent matter he had left undone at home, and with a yowl he turned tail and ran off full pelt to attend to it.

6 *The Wisdom of the Ass*

A HUNT TORE through the morning woods in the sun's first rays. A band of young men, well-dressed and with equipment of the nicest, shouting and hallooing, and whistling, and calling over and over one name.

"Dhur! Dhur!"

"Where can he be? By the gods, we should never have let him linger at sunset alone. I thought it was some girl he meant to meet among the trees, some peasant. Or that he had a fancy for that messenger youth."

"But the weird stories of this forest must be coming true—for our friend has hunted and adventured here since boyhood. How can Dhur be lost?"

"His father will rave."

"His mother will perish of dismay."

"We shall get the blame."

"Dhur! Dhur! Dhur!"

And the hunt careered away, not thinking, as how should it, that the quarry just then was concealing himself inside a hollow tree, his strong long limbs drawn in, and his face, *that* for sure, buried in his arms and all the darkness there was left.

As the day opened out her fan, and only the birds dashed through the forest's upper boughs with the green and scarlet clash of wings, and the sloths hung asleep there like brown fur bags, Dhur came from his hiding place. Beside the path, the dainty tree-rats sat up and gazed at him as he went by; the deer started for the coverts. Wild bees, anxious about a clog of honey high above, came down to stare at Dhur and spin away.

He saw none of them, and nothing. He saw only black horror, which clung about his eyes and mind and heart.

To say he knew what had been done to him is simple. He knew—he could not know. It was impossible, therefore it was not. And yet—it was. So he must fly, he must hide, he must blunder on. And his thoughts were of death, there in the brain of the man behind the head of the beast. And his thoughts came in words, too, though when he tried to bring them out, that terrible sound spasmed forth instead. Then he knew himself mad and reckoned himself dead, and he would run and throw himself on the earth, trying to entreat he knew not what to save him—from *himself.*

In all his life his problems had been few and slender. He was not armed to deal with this enormity. The sun had smiled on him and now there was only winter and he naked in the storm of it. Reason, that traitor, was every moment on the point of deserting him.

Somewhere amid the forest tracks he came, in due course, on a woman's veil. It was rent and muddied, yet still thick with beads—it was the bridal veil which Yezade had inadvertently snatched away with her in her escape of the first night—then heedlessly dropped. Now Dhur took up the veil and wound his nightmare's mask in it, so it should not be seen even by the birds and squirrels, sloths and bees. His eyes, set sideways now, confused them with their views. He did not care that the swathing veil clouded his vision further.

So he stumbled on, a sight that was as fearful and fantastic as before, yet occluded a little.

And as all the travelers in that place, going in a circle,

he came to a glade that had in it the dais of a bank, rich with moss and starred with flowers. And he smelled the wild honey, as before, that the Eshva had stolen from the bees, and the agate grapes and the roses.

There on the bank reclined a maiden whose amber hair was crowned by vines, and who was dressed as an empress, and eating a honeycomb. A noise broke from Dhur's alien jaws before he could prevent it.

Startled, the maiden raised her eyes. She saw—him.

And even as he turned himself to flounder away, she stayed him with a glad cry: "Dhur! My lord!"

Then he could only stand like a stone thing and gawp at her. She was the sylph of his yesterday's day-dream. More, she was a girl of his town. Of his father's neighbor's house. Her name was Marsineh; had she not been wedded to some other? Dhur panted with bewilderment—the ass' muzzle let out a sawing neigh. Dhur forgot all details and questions. He merely stood confronting beauty and wished he had put an end to himself an hour before.

But Marsineh shone for his gloom.

She had wakened remembering nothing, yet with a sense of well-being and delight. And finding herself garbed in silver tissue and jewels had laughed aloud, but not become unnerved, or even dubious. She had learned many lessons, though perhaps the greatest—or least—had been removed from her memory. . . . So she only twined herself a fresh garland, pondering the enchanting dreams she had had and could not recall, and ate the honeycomb and the grapes laid beside her. And then, looking up, saw her true love, Dhur, that she did still know she had followed into the forest in order to avoid wedding another man. She recognized Dhur by his garments, though he was disheveled, by his athletic grace of build—if not presently of movement. By his hands and the rings on them. Her response to the swathing of his face and head was at once sympathetic and intuitive. She had lived awhile with unhuman values. It was not in her any more to say: *Why are you swathed?* Or to say: *What is the matter?* But she felt a stab of pity, realizing some dreadful thing had befallen him. And, having been returned into her love of him, she loved him more for his trouble and the way he lurked there before her, graceless and brutish.

"Dear lord," said Marsineh, "are you hungry? Are you thirsty? This honeycomb is of the best, and the grapes are like wine."

But as she approached him, Dhur pushed himself away. Only his impaired vision prevented his immediate flight.

Next instant her fingers were on his sleeve.

"Do not shun me," she said, and looked up into one of his veiled sideways eyes. "I will help you, if you permit. But if not, let me stay beside you. For I am lost in this forest—" here she laughed again, prettily, for to be lost was no more a worry to her, "and you must protect me."

Then Dhur let out a ghastly bray of anguish. It said: *How can I protect you? I have been destroyed. I am only a husk. Let me go away and die somewhere, for I am mostly dead already of terror and shame.*

And this Marsineh seemed to decipher. But she only took his hand, and led him to the bank of flowers and moss, and he had not the will or heart to resist.

They sat down together, and Dhur hung the head that was no longer his own.

"If you are hungry and desire to eat the fruit and honey," said Marsineh then, "and if you do not wish me to see you eat them, I will go off a little way. And you shall call to me, when I may return."

Dhur groaned in agony. It sounded raucous, *humorous,* in translation.

"My lord," said Marsineh, "I love you dearly, and if it is not modest to tell you so, then you must forgive me. Whatever misfortune has come to you, loving you as I do, I can willingly and eagerly share."

Then the great anger of one who suffers and can only suffer alone, despite all anyone might do for him, burst in Dhur. And he thrust up his hands and ripped and wrenched the veil and shredded it, until it dropped down in bits upon the carpet of the ferns. And there: Her lover's face.

Marsineh gazed at him. She took both his hands and gazed at him still. She said, "It is a terrible burden for you to bear. But believe me, you are visible to me, within the eyes of this poor beast, and I know you are still my own beloved lord, you are Dhur, behind the mask of the ass. And for your sake I love them, too, this long mouth and these round eyes and tall ears. And that voice, though it is not yours, I love that also, for your sake." And she took the garland from her hair and set it on his head and kissed him, the ass forehead and its hairy cheeks. And Dhur would have said to her, "You are the best of women, and I have been blind and stupid for mislaying you, and it is fitting this blind stupid ass' head that now I must wear. If I had ever been wise, I would have valued you from the first. If I were a man again, I would love you." But the ass said to her only *eeh-orrh!* And then tears rolled from its eyes, the tears of Dhur, his shame and despair.

What then was to be done? Neither of these two had access to sorcery. The demons, having attended the vengeance of their lord, Azhrarn, had vacated the dawning forest. Even Kolchash (at this moment canoodling in his bothy with Yezade) was no mage.

Yet a shadow fell just then within that part of the wood. It was not the shadow of Dhur's disgrace. With it came a rummaging and crashing, and the screams of birds that fired themselves away from it, and the clatter of hoofed things that did likewise.

Dhur and Marsineh looked about them, for a moment distracted from their own ills. A cold yet fevered wind seemed to blow into the glade, and something awful charged in its wake, rushing down on them.

Dhur drew his hunting knife. He would defend the girl—as best he could. He wished to instruct her to climb a tree, but words were not accessible to him. So he stood before her, looking with one eye, the better to see what approached.

A silence had doused the forest now. From the void of it the crashing arrival came like a wave on to a shore, and broke, in smashed twigs and leaves and the feathers of birds—exploding into the glade, seeming to fill and crack the air, the trees. Then it stopped still, so the shaken world settled about it like salt in a jar.

Why, it was only a man. Yes, only that. A poor lunatic or hermit of the woods, clothes in tatters, flesh bruised and bloody. Yet round his head an aureole of hair like gold, and in his face, that seemed to lose and twist its shape like wax, two golden eyes.

The eyes fixed on them, the human girl loved by a demon in a dream, the human man transformed by demon malice. And the golden eyes seemed to burn up and smolder down, like light in a lamp.

Two supernatural lovers have dwelled somewhere in the forest, so ran the tale. He is fair, all golden, summer day. She is black and white, white rose, black hyacinth by night. . . . That pair of lovers, said the Vazdru, are due to be parted—

He might have been beautiful, the madman. One might glimpse it through the insane ugliness, the mindless drive that had propelled him here and would shortly whirl him away. Yet did he not have about him the ghost of a damson-colored mantle, and in one hand two jaw-bones—which clacked open suddenly and pointlessly exclaimed: "*Love is love.*"

And at that Dhur felt a pain in his neck as if some enemy had tried to twist it from him like a cork from a bottle, and first a wash of cold water over his head and then a flash of fire. And then he found his mouth was full of grass—which, turning, he spat out, and wiped his lips—and found he had lips, a human mouth and teeth, to do the service for. And flinging his hands over his face, recovered it—*his* face—the bones and skin, flesh and eyes, nose and chin and cheeks, forehead, hair—of Dhur.

(For there had been the luck that one magician, of a kind, yet remained in the woods. His name was once Prince Chuz, Lord Madness. But he was on another errand, now.)

For Dhur, he barely saw his savior depart. He was absorbed, staring in a mirror, which was the countenance of Marsineh.

Presently, ungratefully, if maybe not wrongly, he said to her, "It is your love cured me."

And he took her into his arms, his heart, and, soon enough—though by a devious process of falsehoods and explanations, and the dowry of a remarkable jeweled dress—into the state of wife.

* * *

And, as those two lovers embraced, the whole forest unraveled itself and seemed to fall back into place.

Men of the retinue of Kolchash, scrambling about in a daze, found one another and recollected themselves. It appeared to them a marriage had gone on, and a bridal night, and in a way this was correct. As, discovering their master, they saw the old man—or the evil tyrant, depending on whether or not they were in on his secret—posted by a stream with a succulent girl, whose odd disarray was quickly put to rights out of the wedding chests.

About noon, the procession rode off through the wood, he on his coal-black horse, she in the litter, and passed en route a disappointed hunting party whose quarry was a strange animal they called a *dhur*. The wedding procession, having regretted not seeing such a beast, went on by easy stages homeward to the mansion of Kolchash.

Here there began a new reign, that of the mistress of the house. She was a witch it would seem, a prophetess to equal her own mother—of which mother she constantly boasted.

Her husband, who lost his taste for books at first, anon prudently regained it and left the witch to her own devices. She was an exacting wife, Yezade. And after a reasonable time, odd stories were told of her. That she had ordered a cloak made of the woven hair of deceased young men, that she had teeth not only in her mouth but in another area which it was unwise to mention. And when it rained now and then in the villages they said, " 'Ware! Yezade is emptying her slops on us."

Whether she was happy with her evil repute and her riches and her cowed spouse may only be speculated upon. As the ever after happiness of Dhur and Marsineh is also a thing of supposition.

But one there was who reveled in the result of those three nights and days in the wood. This was the riding-ass.

For it came to be that, even with its proper grass-eating ass head upon its ass body, it somehow kept something of the persona of Dhur the hunter, (though best hasten to add, that was not the case, in reverse, with Dhur).

But the ass, as it frisked about the forest, noted that

the wild-cats and the wolves, meeting its eyes, ran away. And for that reason it lived, the ass, to a great age, its back free of the weight of humanity, its belly full of verdure and flowers, its heart full of the smugness of the manumitted slave. So sometimes it would give vent to philosophical cadences: *Eeh-orrh—EEEH-orrrh!* And the birds scattered and the sloths growled in their sleep and the lynxes cringed, and men, passing on the tracks, said to themselves, "By heaven, what a foul and idiotic noise is that!"

And the ass smiled in its inner person and thought, in the tongue of its kind, "Perhaps even the gods listen to the wisdom of my song." Though the gods, of course, did not.

And after she was parted from Chuz, Sovaz roamed bitterly over the earth.

THE PRODIGAL

1 *Flung to the East*

BABIES ARE BORN knowing how to cry, but not how to laugh. In the world, however, they quickly get the knack of laughter. This is so now, and was so then, in the time of the earth's flatness. And perhaps each of these facts—the instinctive equipment with grief, the swift acceptance of pleasure—says at once very much concerning the school of life.

The rich man for sure, hearing his new-born son howling and lamenting, exclaimed to himself. "*He* will soon change his tune." Thinking of all the good things which would immediately come the boy's way.

And truly, the boy's way they did come. He existed in a mansion where he was waited on by scores of servants. As a child, one entire large chamber was required to house his toys and amusements. As he grew, a great suite of rooms came to belong to him. If he wanted anything, it was instantly fetched. As he inclined to adulthood, white horses awaited him in the stable, and nearby white hounds, and falcons with silver bells. If he hungered for a particular dish or wine or fruit, it was sought and delivered him. To assuage his other hungers, there stole to him in the dusk beautiful women whose hair was scented with cedarwood. He was educated no worse than a prince.

The rich man was not often at home. But as he came and went about his business, he would glance upon the growing boy, whose name was Jyresh, and say to himself, "Well, I have given him the very best of everything." And the father imagined that the son loved him for it and was grateful. Nevertheless, this was not the case. For the boy, lacking for nothing, had begun to have about him an indefinable awareness of bereavement, as if there were some other thing which he could not identify and which was accordingly withheld from him. In this way he grew resentful and indolent, a disappointed creature. His manner was restless, he could not be still. He sensed the magic bird—the unknown real desire of his life—continually flying away from him. In efforts to pursue it, he threw extravagant supper-parties, from which it might take him two days to recover, or he bought up whole libraries of books with which he closeted himself two or three weeks. He bet upon chariot races and horse races and games of dice and did not win. He went hunting after unlikely animals and was gone a month or more. Twice or thrice he fell in love with the wives of other men and seduced them or was himself seduced, and then wearied of such joys and fell in love instead with women of the basest cruelest sort, who bled him of money, just as did his other base and cruel companions, his supper friends and racing acquaintances, the cunning hunters and merchants.

One afternoon, the father of Jyresh called the young man to him.

"My son," said the father, "I have been looking into your affairs and am not much delighted. Do you have anything to say for yourself on the matter?"

At these words Jyresh only stared at him boldly and failed to keep a yawn behind a pale silk glove.

The rich man frowned. He resumed.

"It is plain to me you have been squandering the wealth of this house, making inroads on a fortune which it has taken three generations to accumulate. You must understand, though you spend it freely, not a coin of it is your own, until my demise. Which event, I trust, you do not hanker after."

At this, Jyresh lowered his eyes. His father took the expression as a mark of shame—which in a way it was, since the young man was actually embarrassed to find himself indifferent to his father's death. The rich man continued: "I have decided that your loose living and luxuriousness must be curbed, and have hit on the means, in which my knowledge of old stories and legends has guided me. This is my plan. Your folly springs from my generosity to you. You are quite ignorant of anything but the condition of riches. I therefore propose to send you away to the house of a friend, a business associate of mine. He will accept you into his household as a servant, one who has learned no skill in such work and is thus of the lowest servile ranks. By day you will labor at whatever tasks this man, or his steward, sets you, which may be to sweep the floors or to empty slops. At night you will take your food from the common bowl and sleep on the floor of the kitchens. When dawn breaks you will rise again to resume your duties. After nine months have passed, if you have served him diligently, my friend will pay you a fitting wage and send you home. But if you have failed to please he will, on my orders, have you beaten severely. Thereafter you must serve him another nine months without hope of any wage, and during this time you will sleep on the bare ground and have to eat only what you can beg, or steal from the beasts of the estate."

Having pronounced sentence, the rich man folded his hands upon his stomach. He expected that his softly-reared son, whom he did not know well, would throw himself down and plead for mercy.

Jyresh, however, who could hardly speak for rage, at length got out this: "Sir, if that is your wish, to fling me forth, I only ask *When shall I leave?*"

The rich man was somewhat taken aback. It must be said at this point that he had anticipated any reply but that which he had just received. He had made no plans to send the boy off, but now, roused in turn to fury, announced: "You shall have three days' grace."

"I will not burden you. I will set out tomorrow," cried Jyresh. "Where is the fellow's residence?"

"Directions shall be given you at sunrise," said the rich man. "Together with a donkey on which to make the trek."

"I will travel on foot," declared the son.

"It is a good way off."

"Then," said Jyresh, "I will go tonight."

In something of a flurry therefore did the rich man next sit down with his scribe and compose a letter to a suitable former business partner, who lived some six days distant to the east.

The evening star was only just taking her leave of heaven when Jyresh set out from his father's house. The porter, thinking him off on another junket, saluted him dubiously, seeing the young man had with him neither horse nor attendant. Eastward Jyresh strode, toward the ascending moon. (She looked upon him coldly, for that night she was a perfect round, and full of pride as he.)

Now Jyresh, although he had lived in luxury, was accustomed to exercise—the chariot-racing and the month-long hunt are not to be forgotten. In fact a journey of six days, on foot, did not daunt him. Besides, he had his rage as a heartening companion. There was, too, another thing. As he walked through the countryside by night under the moon, some vague intimation of it came to him, now and then, like strains of muffled music.

The land beside the road was for the most part cultivated, containing fields, orchards and the terraces of vines. On the horizon the moon-gilded hills stretched quietly sleeping. Though he had often passed along the way before, he had been heedless then. Now he smelled the fruit and heard the nightingales. When the moon sank he, too, lay down under a wild fig tree to slumber. Dawn woke him like a kiss. He rose, and bathed in a little pool, and plucked the figs from the tree to eat—for so vexed was he, he had brought no provisions from his father's house.

All that morning he journeyed, only resting in the day's heat by a well. Here others sat, and taking Jyresh for a wanderer like themselves, they spoke to him of the state of trade, the habits of dogs and camels, and the whims of the wenches at the inns. Jyresh, pretending to brotherhood, enjoyed these spurious debates, and spun yarns perhaps only a touch less true. In the afternoon, he walked on, but near sunset a caravan passed him on the road, and from a swaying carriage draped in silks a veiled woman sent her servant back to him. "My mistress asks you what you sell?"

"Tell her: Nothing," replied Jyresh.

The servant returned to his lady, but presently came

back again to Jyresh. "Then, says my generous mistress, take this ring of silver."

Jyresh laughed. How strangely light was his heart as he answered, "Tell your kind lady I am bound to accept no rich gift or token. I have been flung, like an unwanted shoe, to the east, and am on a journey of expiation."

The servant scowled, for he knew his mistress' mind when she was thwarted, but back to her he must go, perforce, with Jyresh's words. The carriage curtains snapped to at once, and soon the caravan went out of sight.

That evening, after the sun had set, Jyresh entered an inn and sold the gold buckle of his belt for a good dinner. The buckle had been a present given him by a woman half a year ago; his father's money had not bought it. Later Jyresh left the inn and went away to sleep on the open ground, among the fragrance of the trees, under the cool sky and the stars.

Another four days this outcast son continued along the roads, going east. He saw sights new to him and sights he had seen before, but even these looked fresh and altered. On the third night, gazing down a sky dyed red with sunfall, he beheld the lamps of a city where he had quite often been to dice and drink and make love, but now, knowing he would not go there, it had a different look. It was mysterious and holy, the pure darkness rising from its heart and, as it seemed, a revel and a feast in all its ruby windows.

Jyresh dined on wild fruits and shared the bread of travelers at the wayside. He drank from the fountains that sprang out of the earth for all men, or he was given milk at a farm, and a cup of wine when he met, one evening, the procession of a happy bridegroom.

On the fifth day Jyresh left the roads and stepped aside into rocky uplands where there were woods. He climbed all day among the hanging garlands of the trees, and bright-colored birds started at his approach, and once a shy doe gazed at him from the thickets. As the sun began to decline, the air turned golden and the silver stars came out, and breaking through the wood, Jyresh saw a track before him which led down into a valley. There, on an eminence, stood a great stone palace among old dark trees. His heart sank at it. Here was journey's end, for this could be nothing but the mansion of his father's friend, some stern and prissy crony of the rich man's turn of mind.

Well, I have had my taste of freedom, thought Jyresh. *Now for my stint as a slave.* And he began to make his way toward the stone pile.

In size and architectural grandeur, the palace dwarfed the house of Jyresh's father, and even the mansions of such lords as Jyresh had seen. Towers tapered up from it and roofs were set one over another. Above a long flight of steps enormous columns upheld the portico. About half a mile from the palace, the track became a paved way, and on either side stood tall marble pillars surmounted by beasts and birds of marble—lions and ibises, cranes and monkeys—which glimmered ghostly in the dying light. Beyond ran gardens of a somber magnificence, plumed with heavy trees, and here and there combed over by waterfalls. These caught the last languid gold of the sunset, but lights also paraded up and down the lawns where golden peacocks walked, flaunting ormolu fans. Yet in the palace itself not a lamp showed.

As Jyresh came out on to the paved way between the pillars, his feelings had already undergone some change. Something in the manner of the spot, the gardens and their perfume, the gold peacocks, the very *silence,* had put a kind of spell on him. In no form was this place like anything of his father's. Just then a figure appeared on the path before Jyresh. It was upright as any of the pillars, though not so tall nor of their shape, and swathed all over in black. It recalled some gigantic bird standing on one leg, and carrying, in the other, a slender staff. It spoke.

"You must announce yourself to me, who you are and what you desire."

Jyresh did so haughtily, not omitting any detail of why he had been sent. (For he presumed he was meant to be humiliated from this point, and refused the state.)

The figure heard him out. Then it made a curious sound that might have been a hoot, perhaps of mirth. Jyresh loftily ignored such effrontery. He understood very well that, as the lowest of the man's servants, whether the rest of his history were known or not, he would be prey to every abuse there was. To seem to mind the torment would only increase it. The figure spoke again.

"If you are intent obediently to serve, go on. There is the house, and in it the one you will therefore wait upon."

Thus Jyresh, as this personage drew aside, strode on up the paved way, and as he did so, he heard the staff strike three times on the ground behind him.

And suddenly every light in the palace was fired, and such a radiance broke from the stones, it was like a sunburst. At every door and every rooftop cressets burned, and in between, three hundred windows.

Jyresh stood in wonder. As he did so, a rush of wings overhead caused him to glance into the sky. A huge bird, rather like a heron, was passing over the garden, and straight in through one of the open bright casements of the palace it went.

The young man continued along the path, took the steps, and himself went in under the portico. The entrance of the house was also open wide, and beyond lay two halls giving on to each other. They were decorated with artful sumptuousness, and Jyresh was beset by doubts and bewilderments. Within a pair of doors wreathed with gold and inset by precious mosaic, lay a third hall whose floor was like a polished coal.

In the room's center a fountain played from a basin of clear green glass, and the columns of the room were clad in living vines, among the flowers of which birds busied themselves. At the room's farther end, a couch rested on a dais, and on the couch lay a being which now lazily upraised itself to look at Jyresh.

Jyresh turned to stone. For a moment he did not know whether to run for his life or if it were better to draw the short blade in his belt, since on the couch sat one of that nation of black leopards, a panther, with eyes of flame.

After a moment, the Panther parted its jaws.

"Come nearer," it said distinctly to Jyresh. "I am not as young as I was, and cannot see you well at such a distance."

Bemused, Jyresh did as he was bid, but only halting again still some yards from the couch.

"Fear nothing," said the Panther. "I have dined. Besides, I believe you to be my guest. It would be uncivil therefore to spring upon and rend you."

At this Jyresh gave way to laughter. The Panther looked on him with evident disapproval.

"Pardon me, sir," said Jyresh. "But never in my life before have I met with any beast that had the power of human speech."

"There I will correct you," said the Panther. "It is possible that you have met with such beasts more than once, but apparently they did not deign to favor you with their conversation."

"Sir, I shall not contradict your wisdom. I laughed only in amazement. Is your master a magician that he has trained you in the mode of talk?"

"Master?" inquired the Panther. "*I* am master here."

Jyresh would have laughed again, and was barely able to subdue himself. "Pray tell me then," he murmured, "if it can be *you* that is my father's friend and associate? For if so, there is more to the old man than I had suspected."

"I will tell you only this," said the Panther, "I have been informed of the wish of your father, that you are to be made the lowest of all the servants, and so learn something to your good. I must add that I am at a loss. In this house everything is seen to by magic, and those that dwell here pass their lives in other ways than service. There is nothing for you to do at present. However, I will give the matter thought. Tomorrow you may have another audience with me, and we will discuss the problem further. Meanwhile, be free of the palace. You have only to ask, and all will be granted you. Save in the area of women, for there are no human females upon the premises. Those females that there are, including my own wives, you must treat with respect."

"My lord, you are too gracious, I will abide by your commandments. May I only ask, aside from your wives, what other females I might chance to encounter, in order to equip myself with the respectfully proper address?"

"Aside from the Pantheresses, there are some Tigresses and feminine Hyaenas and Foxes, a Pythoness, and a harem of Boas. There is also a pious sisterhood of Wolves devoted to the worship of the moon, and innumerable ladies of the winged sort you have already met. Greet all, or not, as you choose. Aside from ordinary courtesy nothing is expected of you. You are ignorant of our ways."

Having said this, the Panther lord lay down again and closed his eyes in dismissal.

Doors at once flew open on a richly-appointed corridor, and Jyresh, like a man in a dream, left the chamber.

By proceeding through those doors which opened before him, Jyresh reached a suite of rooms whose restrained opulence outdid all others he had ever seen or been told of. Here, in a bath of turquoise, Jyresh was laved and anointed with gentleness and precision by unseen minions. And after this, these invisible djinns of the house served him a feast of food on dishes of gold. That night he lay down in a bed of heavenly softness. Above was a canopy on which representations of the stars shone, and over which a simulacrum of the moon passed. When he woke, an image of the sun rose on the awning and in the window, too. Jyresh left the bed, was attended as before, fed on delicacies and arrayed as a prince, and then, returning through a succession of opening doors, was once more in the presence of the Panther.

On this occasion, this lord was not alone. His court was about him.

His Panther wives sat or reclined on their couches in earrings and collars of gems, his councillors stood by, and they were Tigers, Apes, and one old Bull of great sagacity to whom all deferred. Throughout the hall, on all sides, were animals of many kinds, and of an assortment not generally found in harmony. Lions conversed with Lambs, Gazelles strolled up and down with Wolves, while in an alcove a Fox played chess with a Goose.

The giant Heron, who stood below the dais, now rapped with his staff three times on the floor.

Jyresh approached and bowed ceremoniously, gazed on by a multitude of beautiful and bestial eyes.

"Youth," said the Panther to Jyresh, "we have been debating your arrival and your father's wishes. It is in my heart always to provide help where I may. I have consulted the learned Bull there, and decided to send you out to the care of the Pigs who live in the gardens."

"You mean, my lord," said Jyresh, "you wish me to tend a herd of swine?"

The Panther refolded his paws. "That is not my meaning. However, the Pigs are better able than I to explain matters to you, for they are great philosophers. You may go at once. My steward, the Heron, will conduct you to the place."

Audience was plainly at an end. The beasts turned from Jyresh to one another, resuming courtly chat.

Following the Heron (which bounced solemnly along on one foot, carrying its staff of office in the other), Jyresh soon passed outside the palace. Descending through the gardens to the south, they presently entered a wild region. Over-hanging hillsides tumbled down to mossy ravines. Ancient trees bound with creepers closed the ways, and on their ebony trunks might be seen the scoring of huge tusks. Jyresh, who all this time had gone on in a sort of baffled, laughing dream, now began to misgive a little.

"Sir Heron, pause a moment," said he. "These pigs of your master's seem of great size."

"So they are, but you need not be anxious. We are peaceful here and do nothing any harm. Even the meats and fruits of your supper last night, and on which you energized yourself this morning, though highly nutritious, were things of illusion. Our magic is mighty. We have no need of violence. My lord jested ironically when he postulated making a dinner of you. Not a hair of your head is at risk."

Jyresh was not entirely reassured. He was about to put another query to the Heron when there came a loud crashing and thrusting through the undergrowth. Out ran suddenly three milk-white Boars, with eyes like partly-molten gold. Jyresh thought his last seconds had come, and fell to his knees.

"Does he pray?" inquired the third of the Boar. "We will not disturb him till he is done."

"Sir," said Jyresh, "I have only a knife with which to defend myself. But I am outnumbered any way and will not resist. If you intend to kill me, I ask that you do so swiftly. I have only so much courage, and do not wish to show myself up by a display of fear."

The Heron gave one of its hoots. The Boat who had already spoken now went up to Jyresh and gazed into his face. "We offer you no injury."

Jyresh, beside himself, blurted, "But I have hunted and slain your brothers—though I will say they were far smaller than you and did not talk to me."

"It is the way of your kind to kill things, even things which can talk," said the Boar. "But get up now. The pious she-Wolves have brought us the message of our lord the Panther, which the Finches relayed to them. You are to be in our care. Come, then."

So Jyresh got up (bemused and foolishly grinning again), and went with the three white Boars into the overgrown wilderness south of the garden.

All morning Jyresh traveled with the three Boars. At noon they had entered into a deep and elder forest that lay within the estate of the Panther lord, and here lived the herd of Pigs, the Boars and their wives, and all their children, on the banks of a grape-green river. As Jyresh approached he was struck quite abruptly by the uncanny scene. The entire herd was snowy white and golden-eyed, and as the shafts of the noon sun played down on them through the thick arras of the trees, they moved about or rested against one another, couth and clean and shining, and all the while conversed in low, well-modulated voices.

Now surely this is not a dream, thought Jyresh, and his laughter and perplexity, also his fear, left him together. Truth, when it comes so strangely, cannot at last be mistaken.

The Pigs made him welcome when he arrived among them, with very slight commotion. They had chosen a different way than that of the court.

"It seems your father had a preference that you should sleep on the bare ground and live simply," remarked the Boar who had from the first spoken to Jyresh. "There will, however, be no need for you to sweep the floors of the forest, for the wind does that. Nor will you have to carry away any slops, for it is only the races of men, or of beasts men take captive, who require to make such messes. But a simple life indeed will be yours, though you may share what we have, including our portion of magic. Like the court of our lord the Panther, we are magicians, just as we, too, have human speech and some human manners."

And now that Jyresh had got over the barriers of reason, he was next able to sit down among the Pigs—who kindly summoned for him out of the air good homely food and fresh water—and ask them questions. They answered him with perfect composure and willingness. In this way he learned the curious facts of their being.

It transpired, or so they informed him, that the animal kingdoms, as with the kingdoms of men, had gods, but that the gods of animalkind were of necessity sympathetic to their physical creatures. (The gods of the Flat Earth, it is to be recalled, had long ago spurned men. Though Jyresh was ignorant of this, he did not argue the point. He was also young, and the gods of mankind had not yet begun to intrude much on his mind.)

Mostly the beasts of earth were born, existed and died in the natural fashion to which men were accustomed. These animals did not possess each an individual spirit, as in the case of humankind, but were all part of one collective spirit, that of the godhead itself. This sent itself forth a thousand thousand times over, like filaments of some enormous heart-brain—separate from yet psychically attached to the germinating fount. In this way, the animal gods, of whom there were as many as there were animals, and indeed as there were birds, fish, reptiles and insects, experienced at one instant countless earthly lives—and simultaneously the eternal life of the deity.

However, now and again, a beast deity might send out a psychic filament so imbued with the spirit of the fountainhead that it was exceptional. The animal so ensouled would be unlike others of its race. And since the beast-gods were, in their god-state, capable of human understanding, or its equivalent, these higher animals, nearest to the god, would tend to excel in the world in human as well as animal genius. They could talk and intellectually reason, they could become philosophers and artisans, mages and sorcerers. At the same time, all animal ferocity and human-like barbarity fell from them. They led pure if sometimes frivolous and esoteric lives, and for the sake of form would band together in imitation of the mode of men, having an elected lord, systems of justice and society. They might then even dress in human garments, observe human customs or flighty forms of thought or religion—as had happened with the she-Wolves who worshipped the moon—albeit as a white wolf. Or others might turn aside to become hermits, as for example seven owls who individually inhabited the forest and spoke no word, only sitting night after night mapping the imaginary progress of the stars which, this being the era of the earth's flatness, never of course moved.

These experiences, variable and eccentric, were also valuable to the animal gods, although after death the higher-spirit filaments, as with the lower, would be reabsorbed into the maker.

All this the pigs told Jyresh as he sat among them on the banks of the grape-green river, and all this he believed. And, as they spoke to him, the young man perceived in a fleeting second how differently the souls of men went about an education and longed for the savage simplicity of this other. To be a cat, a hound, a horse, or a shining milk-white Boar—

"It is said," added the Boar who always spoke first to him, "that men may sometimes take on, for a short while, the bodies of beasts. Not as the magician or the shape-changer will do it, but after death, to achieve an extra labor or knowledge; in the same way that now and then a dead man will remain as his own ghost, or seem so to do. But there are none among us of this persuasion."

Thus then it came to be that the rich man's prodigal son lived some months with philosopher Pigs in a forest.

The summer, which was dim and green among the trees, turned slowly to the colors of tinder, and the river ran brown as malt, with the burned black and purple irises staring at its edges. The cold came, and mist bloomed through the forest like breath upon a mirror. The Pigs removed into some tall caves that overlooked the water. By their magic they brought Jyresh braziers in which scented logs blazed, and cloaks of fur that was not the fur of any living thing. Frost stood in daggers on the ground, with slender flowers encoffined in them. The Pigs warmed themselves with friendliness, or at the fire of Jyresh. They told weird tales of princes and damsels of their own people, but since their kind did not coerce or corrupt, had no ambition, took love as a matter of fact not fate, and never killed, the tales were unexciting.

One day, the young man thought to himself, *I shall go back to the real world. There I shall love and hate and sin and grieve. But for now, I am content.*

And, as the cold wind drove its flails along the river, he lay to sleep beside his friend the white Boar, his head upon the Boar's flank, and in a calm quiet comfort no human thing had ever given him.

2 *How Sharaq Was Served*

NOW, NEEDLESS TO SAY, the Panther lord was not the former associate to whom the rich man had meant to send his son. A vagueness in directions, some samenesses and changes in the landscape, had misled.

The mounted messenger, better primed and bearing the fatal letter, had gone by another road and soon out-stripped dawdling Jyresh. In four days, the man reached the mansion of Sharaq, a wealthy merchant.

Sharaq, certainly, had once shared business ventures with the father of Jyresh, but for a number of years there had been no correspondence of any sort between them. On getting, therefore, a missive from a lathered messenger, Sharaq racked his brains in alarm, trying to remember. Then, reading the preposterous letter, as may be supposed the merchant was not greatly pleased. Unlike the talking beasts of the Panther's palace (who had learned the stipulations for penance solely from Jyresh's own lips), Sharaq felt himself insulted and put upon.

"Who is this oaf, trading on some slight former dealing of ours, who wants to palm off his pest on me? What a doltish scheme it is—have I no better matter to use up my days? Yet, since I am currently unsure of the old wretch's status, I had best be party to his plan and accept the young wretch. Curses on both of them!"

Accordingly, he left word with his retainers that they were to look out for a stranger, a young man of good family, approaching on foot.

Next day, Sharaq's steward directed his master to a window of the house. There below, on the long path through the vineyard, might be seen a solitary striding figure, clothed in male attire.

The merchant put his crystal spyglass to his eye.

"Why, what an effeminate youth is this," he cried, prepared to find fault and finding it. "See to what length he has grown his hair, it billows out under his headcloth. And the hair is black, which my elderly nurse always used to tell me meant bad blood. His garments conversely are white, and so quite unsuitable for an extended journey. He is barefoot—an affectation. Go down at once," Sharaq added to the steward. "Intercept him and bring him to me. He will need a firm hand."

The steward therefore went down through the house, crossed into the vineyard, and set himself in the road.

"Hold still," declared the steward. "You are expected. You will follow me at once into the presence of my master, the Merchant Sharaq, and there you will obeise yourself in gratitude at his notice."

The sun fell full upon the path and wove there a kind of haze, and in the haze the approaching youth seemed to gleam and glow, to come and go, as if he were not altogether solid.

Then he passed through the haze into the shadow of a vine-stock, and there halted, looking at the steward.

The steward felt a strange unease.

"It will be no good for you, taking that stance, here. You are Jyresh, a wastrel son, and your father has sent you to this house that your prideful ways may be corrected. You see, I know it all. Therefore begin now to be humble, or you will suffer."

"Shall I so?" inquired the youth. And oh, what a voice had he. It was soft as down, as fine as silk, and more dangerous than a viper under a stone.

"Come," said the steward, "follow. Or the dogs shall be put on you."

The youth gave a low malign small laugh that scraped up all the hairs along the steward's skin. Nevertheless, when he turned toward the house, after him the white-clad boy came sidling, lithe and silent as a cat. The steward's spine prickled him like a hedgehog's; he could make nothing of this Jyresh, whose mane was so unlucky black and whose eyes were so blue you could hardly bear to look at them.

When they had gone into the merchant's house and up to the proper chamber, Sharaq lay arranged on cushions, and drank wine, and twitched in his fingers the letter, gazing only at that. For some while he made the visitor wait. And the visitor waited like a post—it was the steward who shifted his feet.

At length, "Here is a pretty thing," said Sharaq. "For the offspring so to distemper its sire. Your disappointed father tells me I am to take you on as the lowest of my unskilled slaves. Your disappointed father says I am to work you hard and, at the end of nine months, beat you, if in turn you disappoint me. What have you to say?"

"I say," said the youth, "you do not know my father."

Now the way in which he said this caused the steward to let go his staff, which clattered on the floor. More, it caused the two birds that sang in a cage by the window to cease singing and hide together behind their water bowl. Not a sound was to be heard there in the room. One might have caught the noise of a wisp of fluff trailing along the floor. Even Sharaq was moved to glance up.

How handsome the boy is, he thought in startlement. *Indeed, he is beautiful. One might take him for a girl, were it not for his clothing, his aggravatingly noble bearing, and the arrogant look in his eyes.*

"It is true I have not seen your father for many years," rejoined Sharaq presently, averting his gaze as if offended. "But here is his letter, and here you are. You are Jyresh the prodigal. You shall not leave this house until a severe lesson has been learned."

"So be it."

And at these words, the two song-birds jumped *into* their water bowl, and the wine cup in Sharaq's hand burst itself, so his elegant robe was stained.

"Go with my steward there!" shouted Sharaq, in dismay. "Away to menial and degrading tasks. Out of my sight."

And so dismissed, in error, Azhriaz-Sovaz, the Prince of Demons' daughter.

After the anguish of her parting from her lover, Sovaz roamed many lands, searching in anger and sorrow, but in bitterness most of all. Yet, too, she was fey, and her moods, though they might resemble those of a woman, were never exactly *like* them. Several tales are told of those wanderings.

She had happened upon the estate of Sharaq by chance, for Fate was a close relation of hers. Her thoughts were elsewhere but there, among the dusty vines. Then, arrested as another, and being what she was, she cast over herself in answer a type of sorcerous veil, which made her seem that much more a young man and a mortal thing. It was her whim, for she was not immune to impulse any more than was her real father—Azhrarn, Prince Wickedness. Which, if you will, says everything that needs to be said. She was Wickedness' child, a demoness, and now she had been told she must serve as a menial in a merchant's house. And that she would be beaten if she failed to please.

The steward, who feared the newcomer, quickly abandoned him in the lower house. Among the hearty murderous cooks, the jealous maids and vicious urchins of the great kitchen and its world, he gave up Jyresh. The denizens of that subterrain pounced upon him. What prey! A handsome boy, a well-born better who had fallen. He seemed impervious to the circling of the clever rabble which lived there, under the rich merchant's home. They were the cogs of its wheels, nothing could move without them. They were the rats who ate its leavings, stole from the very sustenance they had helped create.

"Out, out with the fancy lad!" they cried, much as Sharaq had done over their heads, in paradise, where the good things were enjoyed which they only invented. (Oh, but they spat in the merchant's pies, they murmured banes before dawn as they worked the dough for his bread. And under the star-torn sky of night that Sharaq seemed also to own, they coupled in his vines, and so made him new servants who would hate him as faithfully as did they.)

Laughing in the door, they showed the clean and handsome young man, flung from heaven to their underworld, a yard awash with the blood and muck of recent butchering. "Clean it!" they advised. "Be careful not to get your nice boots dirty."

But the young man walked out into the yard, and all at once a vast silence formed, like a block of liquid glass from the sky. Everything hardened in the silence. Even the butchery blood did so. The yard was paved with red-amber tiles that shone. The slabs were decoratively striped with hard glistening lacquers. And clean, clean, all of it. And there, this Jyresh, in his spotless white, not having raised a finger.

A magician? They came quicker to belief than their master. They slipped away from the alien. And, as in their spite they had laughed and been happy, now they were chill and sly with cautious dread.

"What next?" said Jyresh.

"The *steward* says—"

"The steward *told* us you must—"

"What?"

They pointed, toward the privies. What jewels would he make *there?*

But Jyresh only turned and blinked once, with sapphire eyes, at the noxious spot. A sudden smell of roses was on the air . . . it came from thence.

They scattered before him back into the kitchens. The floors were swept, though no one had picked up a broom. More, the floors were made of colored stones, in marvelous pictures—at which the urchins gawped—and when a pinch of dirt was walked in, or let drip there, the dirt vanished. On the tables, ready for Sharaq's noon repast, reposed a waiting banquet that had not come from the ovens, pans or griddles.

"Take him that," said the magician, cool as you please. "Tell him to eat it. Do not touch it yourselves. You shall have another feast."

Then, as dazzled, squinting servers went by with the

loaded platters, an exquisite perfume passed across every one—it was the magician's breath, he had breathed on them. And they stood transfixed, afraid to drop the dishes. For each now was clean all over, scented deliciously, crowned with flowers, and dressed and jeweled like a prince.

"Blessings on you, master," they wailed, with wild mad eyes, between joy and horror, and in a sort of rage, too, because to be gifted like this was something unnatural to them, an imposition. But—"Blessings, a thousand blessings!" wailed the others, clustering near, begging to be blown on also, like too-hot sauce, and get their share of this ridiculous bounty. And got it in a trice. There they all stood, a collection of grandees, screeching.

Sharaq was prowling the upper chamber, ill-at-ease without yet knowing a reason, when in they burst in a riot. They were drunk on caprice, and on the lovesome breath of a demon. They careered to their work, setting out the food for their merchant master with whoops and gibbers. He stared in astonishment, just recognizing them in the shimmer and scent.

Finally, he bellowed.

"What does this mean?"

"We do not know!" shrieked a glittery boy, who had formerly slouched and cowered with the bread trenchers. And a slut, never noted before away from her pans of sugar, now a princess from an emperor's court, flounced before Sharaq, twirling a diamond: "The wastrel gave us this, and you that, there. *Eat,* master."

At which they all, in insane chorus, barked: "*Eat! Eat!*" and turning, gamboled out of the doors, leaving him to think, but for the spilled petals and gold-dust, that he too had gone mad.

Sharaq sat there, and dumbfounded, knowing nothing better to do, reached out for the wine pitcher—

Ah, horrors! It stank—it was full of rotten ten-year-old grapes and slush. And the bread was collapsing into mildew, and the curds running rancidly—all the beautiful food was erupting. Whole mice burst from the pie as the crust imploded, seeds, husks, and gorged caterpillars dribbled from the fruit bowl, while the roast caught alight.

Hearing their master's outcry the servants, who had

lingered or gathered in the passages, came slinking to see. They peered around the doors and hugged themselves. Tittering, they rushed below, as the steward went running by.

Their own noon meal had been laid for them in the sparkling kitchen of mosaics and marble. They looked askance, but when they tried the food, it was sound. (Above, their master's roars, the steward's commiserations still resounded.) Perhaps the servants' fare would poison them, sorcerous as it must be—too late to stay the teeth and tongue, the gulping throat and growling stomach. Never in their lives had they known such a meal. Worth dying for, as hunger and thieving rarely were.

And as they gnawed and golluped, and burped and sighed, the neglected pots boiled over and cleansed themselves, the spits turned of their own will and the meat did not spoil. In the cubbies and by the hearth, where they had been wont to sleep, were piled mattresses and velvet pillows. The fire would not go out, it would need no fuel. The lamps of silver would trim themselves. It would be light by night and cool in the heat and warm in the cold, in that kitchen. Joints would appear by magic, fruit and oil, wine and cakes. Heaven was in the kitchen now. For how long? Who cared, how long was life? And the reckoning. . . . *That* to that.

As for Sharaq, their dear master, he was busy.

For through the day, the night, the days and nights which came after, they visited him when he summoned them, and spied on him when he did not. And they saw wonderful things happen to Sharaq and the upper house, just as to themselves.

The hangings fell to bits up there, the chairs and the furnishings, the great bed, they collapsed. Out of the frames leapt frogs and toads, lice and mice, rats and weasels, that darted and nipped. The clothes shredded on Sharaq's very body. Moths rose from him in clouds. His metals liquified. He ranted and howled all day and night and took to lying on the bare boards. Sometimes, later, he would wander to the kitchen and stare in. He would demand to be fed and they would hurry extravagantly to tend him. But the viands of heaven would turn to rot and muck in Sharaq's grip. Then he would scream and beat his head on the walls. His servants looked at him in wondrous pity. How they adored to be pitying him.

The steward, having defected to their midst, had not gained cloth-of-gold, nor a single gem, which every other stray servant had acquired simply by passing over the kitchen threshold. Yet the steward was permitted, by the kitchen's sorcery, to eat and drink, providing always he begged on his knees.

"Where is the magician?" he faltered, kneeling to a purple-clad pot-scourer for a morsel of meat.

They were always polite to the steward, and to his incoherent lord, more so than they had ever been—for now they were *gracious*. "We suppose he is gone, sir steward."

"Gone? For sure?"

It must be so, for day after day, night after night, now, Sharaq roared through the house, armed with a rusty sword, thin as a rake and crazed with hunger, and from devouring, perforce, vermin and decay, searching for vengeance and not finding it, while all about him, the last of the tapestries came undone, and the last gold poured to slag. The roofs began to fall inward on Sharaq and his wrath, until he stood squealing one night under that piece of the sky of stars he had once been led to believe he owned.

Where was time? What was it doing? It had all run together. How long had he lived in this way, haunting a ruin in rags, his empty guts clinging to his backbone, and the noise of feasts forever far, far below, unreachable, even if reached?

"A month, no more," said someone. "Does it seem to you, then, longer?"

Sharaq's eyes took fire.

"Where are you, boy?" he coaxed. "Come near, come near."

And there, obligingly, was the beauteous youth, his black hair hanging free, more like a girl than ever. And Sharaq, quite mad, raised his sword—and it shattered in twenty parts and cut him, falling, so that he gave in to tears of fury and despair.

"You will drive me from my house. But who will take

me in? A rich man under such a curse has no friends. No wonder that monster—your father—sent you to me."

"Eight months more I am bound to serve you here," said Jyresh, dimly and gorgeously visible in the lightless corridor. "Then, if I have failed to please, you must beat me." And there came again that terrible small *laugh.*

"Mercy!" exclaimed Sharaq. "Name your price for my reprieve from this."

"Mercy? What is *that*? You yourself pronounced your fate. A severe lesson would be learned, said you."

"Oh, I have learned it," moaned Sharaq, throwing himself on his face.

"You tire me, you bore me with your antics," said the magician-youth. "Doubtless your little trouble has seemed to endure nine years, let alone nine months. Very well. It ends. When the sun rises, it will rinse off your misery."

"Let me kiss the hem of your robe, wise, gentle Jyresh."

But the handsome apparition was gone. Gone in truth, at last, to take up her own journey and her own trouble.

Night-long Sharaq the merchant lay on his face there, praying to the gods that the promise of release would be kept.

The sun rose. Sharaq with the sun, off his face, in the hideous wreck of the upper house.

And behold, a wreck no more. It was a mansion again, of the utmost wealth. The naked day streamed in and embraced the rainbow hangings, the floral carpets; the sun sunned itself upon the gold.

Sharaq, babbling somewhat, rambled from room to room. He fingered the ornaments as if they were another man's; like an outcast, he gazed upon the place, and like a beggar hovered in the entrance of a salon, and eyed the food laid there. Until ravening hunger drove him forward. He sank his teeth in the white bread like a famished dog—and bread it was, and the roast was savory, and the confections mellifluous— All was as it had been. Yes, even to his own person, for as he lay there, half fainting with relaxedness, Sharaq grew aware he was fresh from some bath, clothed in finery, and his rings, that had scalded him as they melted from his fingers, were firmly on his hands once more.

And so, raising one of these sparkling and languid hands, Sharaq took up a little silver bell and rang it. It was the signal at which a certain servant, who had waited always in an ante-chamber, had been used to come running.

Now, only silence came, and absence.

Sharaq lifted his heavy lids. After all the door was opening. There stood the erstwhile slave. He wore crimson, gold at his wrists and ankles, jasmine in his hair. He gazed long at Sharaq, with such hauteur, something in the heart of the merchant shriveled, died. And then the menial bowed, as only a great lord would bow in dreadful mockery.

"Yes, O Master?"

"To your knees, you thing. You shall be beaten."

The servant laughed. He knelt. "We say in the kitchen," he said, as another might remark *We say in my country*, "the rods and whips of this house turn to nosegays when they strike us. Do you know *why?* O Master, paradise is in the kitchen, a spell that enfolds us. Strike me now."

And Sharaq flew at him and struck him. The servant beamed, and spoke of sprays of water and summer grass.

And then Sharaq tried to kill the servant. But all he did—to strangle, to stab—left the boy unharmed. Worse, it left him merry and entranced. At length Sharaq fell back gasping. "Go from my sight," he said.

Bowing yet more low, the servant obeyed him. And presently from beneath in the house, music and song ascended like a level of water at high tide.

"Damned be the magician," said Sharaq. "I am demeaned for ever." And he did not quite know why he was demeaned, or how to be rid of the condition. But when he thought of his servants in their unassailable pleasures and riches, and of their lording it in his mansion, he could think of nothing *but* having been demeaned. Till he thought again of vengeance. *The son I may not have. It is the father is to blame. That villain who has dared to use me so, sending off his devil by inflicting him on me, causing me to enrage him and so ruining my peace, knowing I could not curb him or anything he did.*

And after this, Sharaq grew quiet, and he sat on his couch and did not move.

He called for no more service, no food or drink, nothing. He only sat there, as the shadows shortened, paused, and began again to grow long, so the room lost the light. As if his mind cast out its darkness on the walls and floor.

3 *The Panther's Gift*

BUT IN THE FOREST south of the eastern garden, nine months had passed. They had gone by in a ripeness and down-fall, a frost, a gelid crystallization, in strident winds. After these had come a soundless interval, a wait, during which most things seemed to sleep. Then, living rivulets ran over the ground, stars opened on the bushes. The Pigs rushed from the caves and rubbed themselves on the trunks of the trees. In the river the young ones swam like white amber under thin green jade.

Coming from the river also, Jyresh met the Heron steward, who stood on one leg on the bank, his staff of office in the other, and draped about with wings.

"It is time to leave," said the Heron.

Jyresh exclaimed, "Have I no choice?"

"We observe your father's wishes. None," replied the Heron. "After nine months, if you have pleased, you must be given your wage and dismissed."

"I have not pleased. I am a renegade. Therefore I shall stay with the Pigs."

But the white Boar was at his side.

"For all things, Fate writes his book," said he. "Not a line may be canceled."

Then Jyresh saluted the Boar.

"Back to the world," said Jyresh, "where I shall never rest so well or find such solace again. And if I say, there, a herd of swine sheltered me, how they will laugh."

"Say nothing then. You do not need to speak of it to make it so. It has occurred."

"But I shall think it a dream."

"All life is thus."

Friends do not always part with torrents of words and show.

The Heron preceded Jyresh through the forest. Jyresh walked with his head lowered, sometimes smiling at his own folly, sometimes brooding. It was already as a dreamer that he reentered the court of the Panther lord.

And, "You have served well, and not displeased us," said this lord, looking on Jyresh with the burning eyes in his black velvet mask. "Therefore, take your fitting wage."

He indicated, on a table by the dais, a curious bouquet. It was composed of a thorn-like claw, a tuft of tawny fur, a white dagger of a tooth.

"This?" inquired Jyresh.

"These."

"What may they be, my lord?"

"A key," replied the Panther. He closed his eyes and the court muttered, some of the foxes behind their fans.

"My lord, it does not resemble—a key—of any sort."

"Do you say so?" the Panther purred. He opened one eye a mere slit, closed it.

The Heron drew Jyresh aside.

"Attend now. You must go home. On your road you will come on a fine tomb, which you will know by a blue-black crow seated on its roof, that will speak to you."

"Indeed."

"The hair, claw and tooth are the key to this tomb."

"Why should I desire a key?"

"Much wealth lies therein."

"I," said Jyresh, "am no robber of graves." And his gaze grew dreamier. His heart was harking back to the forest, the days and nights and seasons of needing nothing.

"Nevertheless," said the Heron.

Suddenly it hooted very loudly. It flapped its colossal wings. And all at once the place was in an uproar. Tigers shot from their couches and deer bolted from their games of chess. A bull charged through an apes' stampede. Geese gushed underfoot, birds dived screeching. Hyenas had hysterics. Not a beast that did not make its rightful noise. Snarls and squawks, barks and squeaks and hissings resounded from all sides.

Jyresh staggered there. He cried—"They are animals!

They are birds!" A giant boa rolled over his feet—"And serpents!" And he reached for his knife. But in that instant all was gone, like smoke, like forest mist. All was gone, and there he stood upon a bouldered cliff, under old trees, in a sunset. The dreamer awakened. Though in one hand he held, still, that bunch of claw, hair and tooth. Generally a sleeper brings back only his soul from such depths.

Jyresh the prodigal walked home, westward now, over the rocks and roads, between shorn pastures and bare terraces, with the scintilla of spring bright in the air.

Let it be said, he loitered. He wandered from the track, dallying through fields and woods, and sometimes he met there his fellow men. And Jyresh greeted them with enormous interest and concern, as if they came from some other species of which he was fond.

In this manner, in no hurry, he often missed his path, nor much cared. Then, toward evening, as the sun began to go down, he would set himself again westward.

At the close of the seventh day of Jyresh's thus-lengthened journey, idling in the wine of dusk, he came among some groves and next upon a burial ground.

On the unwatered red light the trees and the various tombs stood up ornately black, and winged bits of the blackness now and then swirled off and flew about the sky.

Jyresh felt at once in the pouch at his belt, after the Panther's gift. With some apprehension, he began to go across under the shut and silent houses of the dead.

Presently he came by a great tomb, of such white stone it gleamed as if wet. On the roof, an indigo crow sat preening, which turned its head and called to him familiarly: "Greetings, my son. Here is the place."

Jyresh eyed the crow, and answered, "I would rather pass by."

"That is not your fate."

"How then am I to get in? Not with a key of fur?"

"The door stands ready unlocked."

"Then others have been before me?"

But the crow took sudden wing and left him there. At the same moment, the sunset ebbed and stars began to rain out on the cooling sky. The white tomb darkened as if it drank its own shadow off the ground.

Well, thought the young man, *if it is my fate, I must essay it.*

And he put his palm on the tomb's iron door, which instantly yielded.

In the tomb was blackness. And every ghostly tale and superstition of childhood, every sensible true warning of the supernatural Flat Earth, came on Jyresh at once. He was afraid, and cast about him for some means to a light. Now it was the custom in that land, as in many others, that the dead be buried with their riches, especially when they had no heirs, and besides this that the mausoleum should have two chambers, the outer of which was dressed as a living room, with all the usual furnishings. Jyresh therefore, advancing with care, soon found a hanging lamp, and this he lit.

Looking up in the radiance of it, he let out a cry.

The chamber had been decorated lavishly, and by the painted walls were tall chests of cedarwood with handles of gold. A curtain of heavy stuff hid the entrance to the inner compartment, where the corpse must lie. And seated before that curtain, in a carved chair, was Death.

There could be no doubt in the mind of Jyresh, for he had heard many stories concerning her. And she was exact, Death, in each particular. She was the color the crow had been, and wrapped in a mantle that seemed fashioned of her own skin. Her hair streamed round her like the blood of amethysts. Yet she was a phantom too, insubstantial—and from this shape of half-transparent gloom, two points of yellow arson glared at him and never moved: her eyes.

After a second or so, Jyresh, trembling in every limb, bowed respectfully.

"Majestic lady," said he, "I was ordered to this destination by another. It was not my wish. Neither to disturb you here."

Death did not shift, not a finger nor a hair. Her eyes glared on.

"Thus, if you do not think it discourteous," said Jyresh, "I will at once withdraw—"

"No," said Death. "You must stay, now you have come in."

Jyresh paled.

"For how long, royal lady?"

Then Queen Death chuckled. It was not a fortuitous sound. She drew her right hand out of her mantle and toyed with a lock of her amethyst hair; the right hand, as in the tales, was a skeleton.

"We shall see," said Queen Death, "how long you must stay. For myself, I am not entirely present, as perhaps you may perceive. I rule in Innerearth. It is my image only that is here. And yet, *I* am here also, in thought and deed. I have come to select treasure by the sorcerous means my queenship and my studies grant me. For there are items in this tomb that I covet. You, it would seem to me, covet them as well."

"I protest," quavered Jyresh. "I will not irk you with all my history, but suffice it to say I have served a magician who, as a wage, gave me a thing he named a key, and sent me to this mausoleum."

Death frowned. "Yes. You reek of magic. Show me then your key."

Jyresh hastily fumbled for the bunch of talon, fur and fang.

No sooner had he brought them into the light, however, than a fearsome noise was heard all through the tomb. It was a colossal snarl, like that of some cat-beast of extraordinary size. And as this happened, and Queen Death opened her glare wider in surprise, a kind of whirlwind tore into the chamber, and catching the Panther's gift out of Jyresh's grasp, cast it on the pavement before him.

And then there was a marvel for sure. Something rose towering up, so the head of it must brush against the roof. It was not to be seen, this entity, yet it was to be *felt,* and its pungent odor, at once carnivorous and bloody, yet also clean as the stars, filled the hollow tomb, and the strength of its being, though invisible, that was everywhere, so Jyresh seemed to himself to be crammed down into a tiny chink in the wall. And even so, the enormity of that animal expression had been itself incredibly compressed to enter here—*it might have filled the earth.*

As for Death, Jyresh could no longer properly see her. She, too, even she, seemed pushed far away, and the ghost-body of her earthly manifest looked wrung out as shrunken washing.

At last then, the Creature spoke—in a human voice, low and deep as distant thunder, weightless as dust, that shook the tomb to its foundations.

"Death," said It, "once you were another. You were a mortal and a woman, and you hunted leopards, and wore the hides of leopards, so you were called for them the Leopard Queen. And still you have their eyes of fire, and still you keep them by you, the great cats, to play at hunting them in the shadow country at the world's core. And this, and that, have made you susceptible to Me. For I am the heart-brain, the soul-cluster, the god of all that kind. From the littlest gray kitten comforting the village-woman's hearth, to the black and golden ones, and the ones who are cinnabar, the ringed and striped and dotted and patched, and those with manes like the sunflower, the stalkers of the dark, whose feet leave the marks of petals in the blood of their kill. And by the power of this, and that, and by that slender talisman which, through one such of Mine I gave the man there, I tell you, Queen Leopard-Death, Death-of-Leopards, you must step aside, this once. You must forego your treasures. They are his. I give them to him. Obey."

Then Death shrugged. And as she did so, her image grew more certain. She rose from the chair and nodded to the Cat soul-source, where it might be. "Few now remember that," she said. "That once I hunted leopard, and was a leopard in my heart. *Death is a leopard,* they say now. But me they do not know." Then she glanced at Jyresh, through the unseen pulsing solidity of what was standing between them. "Take it then, the tomb's wealth."

But Jyresh, prudent and unnerved, stammered to her, "I would not, even so, make an enemy of you, lady."

"I am the Enemy of all," said she. "And a powerful enemy, too. But there, it appears you have also powerful friends. You need not fear me till the end of your life, and then not much." And saying this, her eyes and she went out like lamps.

The whole tomb seemed as if dissolving and pouring off into the air.

Jyresh would have flown out, but he was compelled otherwise. As if a large paw lay on him, he was propelled about the chamber. He was caused to open the chests and to remove from them large bags that clanked and vessels that clinked. He saw, all blurred and wavering, golden coins and rings of gold, and documents in gilded boxes and metal keys on chains of silver, garments and utensils of the best, vials of perfume, precious books, skeins of jewels—and then, at length, he saw the black and glittering sky and the pure night air dappled his face.

Set free, though laden down as he was, Jyresh took to his heels. He ran, like the grave-robber he had named himself, until eventually, in a wood, he fell on the midnight grass, and the bags and boxes with him. And there instantly he slumbered, and dreamed nine black leopards, of the extreme size of months, guarded him through the narrow hours till dawn.

In the morning, Jyresh awoke, and looked about to see if the tomb treasure still adhered to him. It did. With an ill grace, then, he made a huge bundle of it in his cloak and so slung it on his back. Groaning, he set out again, westward through the wood.

"It is a fact," said Jyresh to himself, "that which the ancient philosophers tell us: Wealth is a great *burden*. Besides which I have fallen foul of Lady Death, for all her witticisms, and shall now have to be wary of her at every twist and turn. On the other hand, any vagabond bandit, seeing me with this jingling hill on my back, will suspect the truth, leap on me and cut my throat. I shall be robbed and murdered before another day has gone by. No doubt of that. I therefore think the Panther with profound gratitude for his most generous present."

Having delivered himself of this, Jyresh plodded on, whistling enviously to the unencumbered birds, and admiring the first flowers of the spring. When suddenly, emerging from the wood, he halted with a start.

For there below lay the estate of his own father, and far off, the glimmer of the house roofs of his erstwhile home. By a circuitous route (of geography and mind) the prodigal had returned.

Jyresh, taken aback, paused in thought.

"My father," said Jyresh to a bird on a bough—for he had grown used to birds which understood his chat and replied—"sent me out in high-handed annoyance, which on reflection I can now understand. He expected nothing fortunate should ever come of me, which was perhaps unjust; besides, it troubled him to think so. Therefore, since I am saddled with these goods, let me spruce myself and adorn myself, and go to him and astonish him at how well I have fared."

This notion tickled Jyresh. So he searched out water near by and bathed in it, and then anointed himself with the costly balms from the tomb chests. He dressed in a suit of clothes therefrom, fit for a prince, put boots of white leather on his feet and rings on his hands, and in his ear a fat rosy pearl. After that, he filled an embroidered pouch with money, and hung it at his embroidered belt. The rest of the haul he hid under a tree, and marked the spot with a stone.

"Now if it is also my fate to be stolen from in turn, so be it," said Jyresh to the same bird on the same bough above, which had duly stayed to watch his deeds. "Additionally, I shall soon go back to that mausoleum, and propitiate the gentleman's memory. For though the Panther lord sent me there, it is not right I should plunder a fellow human, even if Death would have done it, had I not arrived. And if it is ever my lot to amass wealth, I must repay him."

At this the bird tweeted, and Jyresh thanked it for its kind wishes. Then he went on his way, and crossed over into his father's lands.

But Jyresh had been absent more than nine months. As he walked along, he saw that much of the cultivated land was lying fallow, or overtaken by tares and weeds; no herds grazed there, and no men or women were to be seen. In the park, the grass stood high as spears, the fruit trees were untended and all their cargo had rotted through the winter on the earth.

The day walked ahead of Jyresh and outstripped him.

But with the sun in his eyes, the land looked no better. Jyresh's heart began to ache with anxiety. As he drew nearer and nearer to the rich man's mansion, a sense of forfeit closed him round. And so it was that, when he stood on the path beneath and the building showed itself before him, he was overwhelmed by horror, but not by amazement. The house was a gutted ruin, black and burned out—but for two or three of the highest roofs, which hung half disembodied there and gleamed in the dying afternoon light: It was their sheen which had misled him earlier.

Jyresh stood still and did not know what he should do. It seemed to him he had woken from a dream to a nightmare. And all at once the most poignant memories of his childhood came sweeping over him. How he had played with his nurses in those charcoal rooms, and climbed the garden trees, and how, knowing that his father was riding home from business, Jyresh the child would run to meet him, and, lifted on to the horse, throw his arms round the man's neck for joy. Until the man became an old man, and the child in turn a man, and so they were severed, and parted in a night, and the stroke of some terrible angel of fire and doom fell between them.

And in a while, the young man wept. And as he did this, the sun sank and the shadows rose from their hiding places in the ground.

These shadows seemed to say to him, *Go, you. This region is* ours *now.*

Jyresh accordingly left the ruin. He walked an hour to the south, to a small town he had, in his extravagances, for years eschewed. He imagined that no one would recall him there, and indeed they did not. They took him for a young traveler, who had a look both worldly and aesthetic. On his side he felt that he must ask questions concerning his father, and the answers would come more easily from stranger to stranger. Yet his heart was full of the shadows which had risen from the ground. His heart needed to ask nothing, nor to be told anything. Nevertheless Jyresh, falling into conversation with two merchants at the inn, declared: "I saw a great burnt house in the distance, some few miles north of this town, and the land all gone to seed." And one of the merchants nodded, and said to him that this was the estate and mansion of a rich man, and named the father of Jyresh, and added, "But a curious tragedy befell that person, and he is dead." And Jyresh felt no pang at all, for he had known the moment he saw the ruin, and for that he had wept.

Thus he called for more wine, and lightly asked the tale, saying all curious things interested him.

Then the merchants told Jyresh the following story.

The rich man had had one son, who was a wastrel and seemed intent on squandering his inheritance. Finding he could do nothing with the boy, the father sent him to an acquaintance of his, with the request that this man, a merchant named Sharaq, should starve and ill-treat the son and give him besides menial and degrading tasks to perform, having him beaten when he failed at them. This Sharaq did, for he was a harsh master, and the boy ended in rags in the pig sty, eating the leavings of the swine. But it chanced that Jyresh—for this was the prodigal's name—then somehow gained some powers of sorcery, and these he abruptly turned upon the merchant Sharaq, causing him untold harm and distress and being very likely to destroy him, and so it might have happened, except that the swine, frightened by the sorcerer's behavior, ran mad, and before he could save himself, trampled Jyresh to death.

Then Sharaq vowed to have vengeance. Leaving the boy's body for the pigs to devour, and taking not a servant with him, Sharaq rode night and day until he reached the rich man's house. Striding into his presence, Sharaq cried—and this was verbatim, for many had heard him at it—"You have inflicted on me the curse of your son's sorcery. But I am not to be demeaned. Listen well. I have killed him, your brat, and fed his remains to beasts. Now I bring *this* for you." And with these words, Sharaq drew a knife from his mantle and cut the rich man down. Then the merchant fled and none had seen him since, but in his house, they said, his servants continued to live, making free of all, like kings.

For the rich man, he lay dying, and so his own people found him. As he perished, he shed great tears, but not for himself. His thoughts were all of his son. "It is my fault he has been slain, my injustice to him it was that brought this horror about. Sharaq is a madman, for my Jyresh had learned no spells, for all the books he read. His death is on my very soul. How shall I rest, knowing it is through me my only child has lost his life? And all he knew of me at the last was my cruelty and my wicked foolishness, and not how dearly I loved him always."

And then the rich man called his scribe and ordered that, as he died without any heir, his servants should take their own prescribed reward, but all the rest of his goods should be sold, and replaced in jewels and coin, in the rarest parchments and volumes, in the most costly furnishings and garments, and this hoard—useless—be buried in the tomb with him, along with the keys to any other caches of wealth that were his. For the house, it should be razed by fire, and the lands let go to waste. "Since I have been so much in the wrong," he said, "in putting these things before human love and compassion, they snall be ruined, or locked in with death, as an example, before gods and men, of their worthlessness. Rather I had been a beggar and kept my son alive," he said, "or rather I had suffered murder seven times that he might live." And so the rich man closed his eyes altogether.

And everything was done as he instructed, the house burned, the land given over to a wilderness, and the hoard secreted in the tomb—the door of which was most securely locked that no robber might ever break in.

When the merchants had finished their tale of the rich man and his prodigal son, they bade their companion refreshing slumbers, and left him, for it was late.

Jyresh himself rose, and went out into the night.

The moon had turned westward. The stars, the flowers of heaven, glowed with a final brilliance.

Leaving the town, Jyresh crossed the fields beyond, and at length climbed a hill, sitting down there lost in conjecture. Such a compendium of fact and fantasy he had heard that his brain would not sift it through. But the phrases that his father had supposedly spoken at the end, these engaged both heart and mind. For just as he, Jyresh, too late had come to remember his childish love, so it seemed the father had remembered love also, and also too late.

As he was sitting in this way, the wheel of this reverie turning slowly and heavily around and around in his mind, Jyresh turned around and around on his fingers those rings he had taken from the white tomb. And it came to him, the nearness of that tomb to his father's lands, and how the hoard tallied with the description the storytellers had given. And he thought suddenly of the sturdy tomb door, which had been ready opened, and the blue-black crow which had said to him, "Greetings, my son."

And when he had thought of it, Jyresh raised his head, and before him on the hill, against the waxing eastern sky, there stood his father.

He was dim as smoke, the dawn star shone through his sleeve; he held fast his cloak against his breast, as if to hide some mark there. But he gazed at Jyresh, and spoke.

"It was I, in the form of the crow, who directed you to enter my tomb and take from there what rightfully is yours. Sharaq lied, and you live. My fortune has come to you. I think you will not squander it, after all."

"Father," said Jyresh, "I cannot tell what I shall do hereafter. But what of you?"

"I," said the ghost, "am free as the air. Only regret has bound my awareness to the world a little longer, and my wish to look one last occasion upon you, as your father."

Then Jyresh would have gone to the ghost and embraced it, but it was incorporeal and could not allow him to get close. Jyresh bowed his head once more. "I do believe," said he, "that your fortune, let alone squandered, will not be spent by me. I have come to like other things—pillows of grass, the world for my house, the brotherhood of beasts and men rather than sour lusts and silly jests. If I live as a poor man and a wanderer, will you forgive me? Will you forgive me, dear Father, after all your care, if I leave your riches in the ground, and go on my journey without them?"

At that the ghost smiled, and now the dawn star had risen high enough it lay on the transparent cheek.

"Jyresh, you see where meddling in your life has brought me. You must choose your path. But I will wish you well on it."

Then the cocks began to crow in the town beneath the hill, and the birds chorused in the fields, and a pale yellow poppy colored the east. Like the dark, the rich man's ghost melted away.

Jyresh watched the sun come up. Then, he took the embroidered pouch of coins from his belt, and hung it on a wild fig tree.

As he walked down the slope, he shed from himself the more cumbersome items of clothing, the rings and mantle, the white boots, the rosy pearl. He left them where they dropped.

Presently, coming to a stream, he kneeled and drank, and the bright water trickled through his fingers as the bright jewels of the rings had done.

And then it half seemed to him that he heard the birds, which twittered in the wayside bushes, singing this:

He squanders garments on the soil,
He squanders every gem and pearl,
And through his hand lets water fall—
He squanders it, he squanders all—
The prodigal! The prodigal!

At last, cheated of love by Wickedness and Fate—so it seemed to her—Sovaz bowed to her father's design.

Then Azhrarn made her the Goddess-on-earth, Azhriaz, who ruled over a third of all the world, in a sky-touching city of miracles and cruelties. Here, at his command, she tutored mankind in the stony indifference of the gods, by her example.

In those years too, some of the Vazdru princes, seeing she was also a demon like themselves (though she could endure the sun, as they could not), went proudly to court her. And she spurned each one, saying she had a prejudice against her own race. Which astonished and irked them, for the demons, in their beauty and arrogance, were unused to any that said No.

DOONIVEH, THE MOON

1 *The Mare's Egg*

NINE OF THE Vazdru wooed her, they said. They said the last of the nine was the Prince Hazrond.

Of all the Vazdru, after Azhrarn, the stories reveal Hazrond to have been, among that fabulous company the most handsome, the most glamorous and rare.

So he stood in the courtyard of his platinum house in Druhim Vanashta, under the earth, knowing as much and musing. Amid the agate-colored trees of the court was a basin of cold green water, and in this Hazrond could conjure images of the lands above. It was a night of full moon up there, and in the way of demons, earthly moonlight inclined Hazrond to inspiration. Presently he left the court and the palatial house, passed through the glories of the demon city, under its towers of crystal, brass and steel, its minarets of silver, its windows of corundum, and expired himself via a volcanic chimney onto the surface of the world.

The courting of Azhriaz, daughter of Azhrarn, Prince of Demons, the Master of Night, had been as inevitable to the Vazdru as was the moonrise to the earth. They must woo her because she had been fashioned and was there. One by one they sought her then, in their pride and splendor, one by one she turned them down. And meanwhile the offerings they had taken her (less to please her than to demonstrate their own worth), incredible jewels and sorcerous toys of Drin-work, these lay abandoned on her doorstep. Or else had been cast aside in Vazdru rage upon the thoroughfares of the goddess' City, where much havoc spread from them. But in this affair of a gift, a seed of perverse reasoning had rooted in the intellect of Hazrond. *They have compared me to her father,* his reasoning said to Hazrond, *therefore, as her sire did, I should create some marvelous hybrid, some exquisite monster—as she is—and give it to her.* For in this way he could both praise and insult her, a dichotomy most appealing to a Vazdru.

The night was young, little more than a girl. She stretched smiling over the sky, gazing down upon Hazrond, holding the silver mirror of the moon in her hand.

"And is she as fair as you?" Harond inquired of the night. "This *Azhriaz?* Or does she not deserve her name?" For he had never seen her, the one he wished to have for a lover.

As he walked over the darkness then, musing still in the inspiration of the moon, he came on a valley deep between high mountains, and here wild horses were grazing. And now and then the stallions gave battle to each other, or they raced along the valley two by two.

If a mortal had approached, they would have shunned him, or perhaps come to attack him, for they were fierce as lions, these herds. But as the Vazdru walked among them, they lifted their heads, clean-carven as the heads of chess pieces, and stared with the pools of their eyes. Some of them stole after him as he went by. And one of these was a beautiful virgin mare, black as the night. Becoming aware of her, Hazrond paused.

Now the horses of the Underearth, themselves black as the blackest night, with dusk-blue manes and tails, were the darlings of their masters. They could run over any sort of terrain below or above, and over water, too. While for beauty of proportion and for fire of spirit, they had no match. And yet, when the glance of Hazrond rested on this earthly horse, he saw at once she was a celebrity of her species, a goddess among mares. So he stretched out his hand, and crooned to her, and she came at once and laid her head on his shoulder.

An Eshva would have crowned her with flowers, leapt on her back and ridden her all night. But a Vazdru must first have called the Drin, and had bridle and saddle and trappings made for the horse—and then he would not deign to ride her himself, but would have given her as a gift to some mortal he fancied.

Hazrond said to the mare, "I have watched you racing, my dear, winged by the night." And the seed of reasoning burgeoned. "Come with me then. I will make you a legend among your kind."

So he passed up the valley away from the herds, and into the boulevards of the mountains. She followed him, over the rocks and among the slender plants that grew there, through the gradations of height and time, until they reached a plateau.

Above, on three sides, the topmost peaks ascended, nearly symmetrical as spires. It was a place for eagles. And Hazrond, speaking or singing certain phrases of the Vazdru High Tongue, that which they used in their sorceries, fashioned a type of impulse, and sent it flying up among the peaks. That done, he waited. And the mare, ensorcelled by his presence, his brief caress, stood on the plateau a hundred paces off, still as a stone.

At length a piece of the night itself lifted from the third, the highest, peak. It circled, looking for the sun, maybe, before dropping down the air, conceding another summons, even less resistible.

The Vazdru wove a charm then, of voice and breath, power and will. It brimmed the plateau and ran over like water into the valleys beneath. The live things there were electrified. Herbs opened their buds, rodents scuttered through their chambered cities in the rock—the spill of magic slipped by, and the birds of the lower levels sang out, and fell silent again in awe. The horse herds, too, were disturbed and sped away over the pastures of the dark. The spillage reached the valley floor, sank into the earth to astonish worms and beetles, and was no more.

But high on the plateau, the magic lake gathered and contained, and through its currents, never breaking free, the black mare wheeled and galloped, and the black eagle stooped upon her—and at a final word of the Vazdru, they were one.

It may have seemed to her, perhaps, the mare, that she mated with the ebony rush of the midnight wind. And to the eagle that he mated, too, with that rushing force which all day long would fill his broad sails and bear him up. But to Hazrond, who looked on at their union, they were a single creature, four-legged black speed upborne under two black flames fanning and beating. The emblem of what should come from this: A horse with wings.

The great plateau was her pen, fenced in with posts and intricate chains the Drin had wrought. The grass grew thick and the creamy clovers sprung for her, and fruit trees let down their fruit, out of season, to tempt her velvet mouth. The Eshva women were her handmaidens, this goddess-princess of the horses. They soothed her and gave her their lawless love; they hung her with purple daisies and, when she allowed it, twined their pets, those love-drunk silver serpents of theirs, between their black manes and hers.

Looking deeply into her, they might see, under the skin, in the pelvic cage, a symbol written as if in starlight on the rose of her womb. She had been mated through sorcery, and by sorcery her body must be trained to retain, to bring to life, the unnatural wonder that now went on there.

Weeks passed. How slowly she moved now, the mare, seemingly irresolute at herself, how she was.

She grew so heavy. She lay on her side under the trees, scenting the approach of pain the tiger, staring this way and that. The afternoon went in a blaze. The sun bled. Twilight staunched the sky, and as the first stars stood out on it, the white stars of the Eshva stood on the plateau. They breathed their perfume into the nostrils of the laboring mare, and over her eyes pressed their leaf-like hands. She slept, and felt no hurt, and soon, easily, carefully, a terrible object came gliding from the labyrinth of her fleshly mechanism. It was a huge oval egg, the shade of polished slate, smooth as marble, hot to the touch as a burning coal.

Two Drin waddled down the plateau, their repulsiveness framed in the sable beauty of their curling hair, and gilded by straps and adornments of unbelievable craftsmanship. They dragged in a sack the uprooted fence.

They carried a harness of black steel set with black diamonds.

The Eshva moved aside. They leaned to each other like frail stems, gazing in each others' eyes to avoid having to see the eyesore of the Drin.

The Drin smacked their lips, no more. All were on the Vazdru business of Hazrond. The two dwarfs grasped the egg and placed it gingerly in the harness, setting it just so, though it burnt their hands. Then they vanished away with it, off the plateau, into the ground. The egg, sorcerous and marked with Hazrond's seal, his property, was able to go with them, through the barriers, soil, psychosm, down and down.

The Eshva stayed to console the sleeping mare, to comb her mane, to heal her with their touches and their presence. When the sun rose they would be gone, and she, rising up at liberty, would shake herself, sprint end to end of the plateau, roll in the fading clover like a foal. After which she would pick a way down to the valleys, and seek the horse tribes. These, in spite of—because of—a quicksilver scent of demons on her, would take her in. She would become again a drop in the ocean of the herds, tidally sweeping in their earthbound flight through endless channels of grass. She would know the weight of stallions, the companionship of her kind, the seasons of weather and age. She would be barren always.

In a platinum pagoda beneath Hazrond's court of agate-colored trees, the mare's egg rested. It lay in the cradle of the harness. Sometimes it rocked a little. It gave off continuous heat, which grew more intense with every timeless second that went by. The vicinity of the egg crackled and shone.

Drin tended it uneasily, if not with terror. They feared what was in it. They feared what might be in it would displease Hazrond. He would come and go, questioning them. He would bring wands of jet and ivory and blue iron, and tap the shell. Once even he brought a wand with a golden point, and when he was done with it, flung it from him in allergic anger.

The Drin watched the egg, coaxed it, reviled each other, and each prepared stories about the negligence of the other attendant Drin, in case the egg should be stillborn.

In the demon city meanwhile, a particular clique of eight princes met in an onyx garden, and discussed Hazrond and his secret scathingly. "He is a fool. He should learn by our example, that beautiful one." "Even Azhrarn the Beautiful," murmured another, "lacks judgment." For at that time there was ill feeling against Azhrarn among the Vazdru, to do with his obsession with mortal ventures. But when the words were said, the onyx bushes cringed flat to the lawns, and the princes drew their mantles round them, parted and strode away.

One morning (at least, it was morning upstairs in the world), the egg fissured—exploded! Shards flew off it in all directions, and the Drin were snagged and snipped by them and dived under the platinum benches squawking.

When the last sounds of falling eggshell ceased, the Drin crawled out again. The Prince Hazrond stood in the doorway. His eyes were wide.

The Drin, with many misgivings, looked where he did.

Despite the eruption, half the eggshell remained entire in the harness, and out of this had just emerged a creature no bigger than a kitten. It was a miniature, the tiniest of baby foals, perfect in all ways—yet with a silver film across its eyes for, like any newborn horse, it was still blind. On its back, resembling the downy stubs of a hatched chick, two wet little wings.

Hazrond smiled. His smile came into the pagoda like moonlight, or music.

The Drin ran and caught up the prodigy on a cushion, and took it to Hazrond. He smoothed it with one finger. The creature shivered, a strange unseen radiance flowed from its body. It was vibrantly warm to the awareness of the demon. Much gratified, through the ranks of fawning Drin, he went away.

As the Drin nursemaids were bathing this infant then, in a silver bowl, twittering over it, too, like proud parents, they heard an eerie scratching behind them from the area of the half eggshell.

"Something lingers inside."

"Can it be there are two? A dual thrill for the princely Hazrond."

They pounded to see.

And saw—this: There in the bottom of the broken shell, partly submerged under shattered bits, struggled an awful little nightmare. She had borne twins, the black horse. They were not alike. The first was that which Hazrond had wished on her. The second, a grisly descant the body of the mare had played upon that wish.

Its blackness was its only claim to beauty. It, too, was an infant, a black beast. A sort of tailless horse, that had four clawed and feathered legs, the legs more of a fowl than of an eagle. But an eagle's head it had and a beak which, opening, let out a bleating tiny neigh—

Affronted, the Drin jumped back. They were ugly enough to find hideousness extremely offensive.

"Shall we kill it, before *he* sees?"

Hazrond was handsome enough to find hideousness almost as offensive as they did.

"Nothing dies here. Impossible."

"Turn it out then. Throw it away down some chasm."

They agreed, and drew lots to see to whom this annoying task should fall. Then there was a fight, as the loser disputed. Eventually one of their number stepped forward and picked up, between finger and thumb, the bleating abomination, shoved it, ignoring its cries, into a pouch, and hurried away to be rid of it.

This was accomplished somewhere outside the city of Druhim Vanashta, in an old quarry where the Drin had sometimes come to hack for diamonds.

In a finished working the horror was tipped, and left mewing and feebly scraping the stone with its beak and claws.

Time went by then, underground, and in the secret yards of Hazrond the winged horse grew. It had no gender, for such as it was—magic, unnatural—it served the function of unreal things, having no requirement to reproduce itself. Yet so sorcerously fair it was that its aura seeped out of the house of Hazrond. And sometimes there would be heard there, out of some invisible cloud, a noise of a thousand feathers high in the skyless sky.

But in the quarry beyond the demon city, the other

beast, the second twin of the egg, dwelled unknown. It ate the stone-dust for its food, and drank the stone's moistures. All that country being enchanted, these nourished it sufficiently. But it did not grow. Its heart had withered and stopped that. It had no social life. Once a glittering insect alighted, but discovering a monster was watching it, hastened off again.

It happened that some of the Drindra came to that place, for what reason is obscure, and perhaps for no reason, for the Drindra, the lowest of the Drin, were generally always unreasonable. Bumbling through the quarry they chanced on the little black beast.

"Why," said the Drindra, lashing their tails and peering from dog's or frog's eyes, "it is of our sort." For they took the form of chimaeric mixtures of this and that animal, not excluding humankind. Accordingly they grabbed the monster—which had tried to run away, afraid of them—and rummaged it over, poking and fondling it until it was almost dead of distress. Then, since they were going aloft to the world to make a nuisance of themselves in the thrall of a magician, they carried their find with them.

Up on to the earth it traveled, in a roar of sorcerous steams—and here, on a hillside, as they were jabbering by, the Drindra dropped it.

It fell among the towering thorns of the world, the mare's second child. The moon smote it like a sword. It lay in a valley of shadow, among huge pebbles. An owl went over the night like the white rim of a wave. The monster hid itself.

The quarter moon was garishly bright and all night the white owls hunted until the moon set. Then the sky became transparent. The sun burned through. Hawks filled heaven.

The stones of the world were not nourishing and the thorns gave only a crabbed drink.

In the end the sky was congested and the light and the hawks went away.

The monster came out from between the thorns. The landscape was so enormous it meant nothing at all, yet a dream of water was on the air. Now the sky was black. Dew dripped into the dry little beak.

An owl hung low, but swung aside, judging the small blundering thing not good enough for its guts. In a thicket, a fox snapped, then averted its muzzle fastidiously: Not tasty enough for supper, this chicken tainted by horses.

It found, the monster, a pond like an ocean. As it put in its beak, a black carp rose to the surface and goggled at it. Along the bank of the pool some grains lay in the mud. The monster ate them.

Lying in a daze, it did not consider contentment or the lack. It had no philosophy.

In the morning, the brown geese trooped down to the pond and stood and looked at the mare's child.

"What kind of duck is that?"

"It is not a duck. It cannot join this worshipful company."

"Peck it! Chase it off!"

Just then the blind girl who owned the geese came with her pannier to feed them.

"Hush! What a squabbling. Are you not ashamed?"

The geese were not ashamed, but they pretended to be, for politeness' sake. By this time they understood a great deal of human speech, having heard it all their days, but they knew very well their blind mistress scarcely grasped a word they uttered. However, she fed them.

"Now what can this be? What have you found?"

And the blind girl kneeled and put her hands around the mare's child before it could get away.

"It is a bird, a *strange* bird—it has no wings. Oh, poor bird."

In fact the blind girl had never seen a bird, nor anything of the world, for she had been born without sight. But her father and mother, before they died, had explained as much as they could to her and she knew a great many things by their description. For example, if she had been allowed to explore an elephant with her hands, she would soon have told you it was an elephant. Because she was blind and not rich and only a plain homely maiden besides, she had not married, but her parents had left her provided with a roof and a bed, with three fruit trees, an herb garden, a goat, and the goose-pond.

"Poor bird. What a strange bird you are," said the blind girl, lifting the monster in her arms and stroking the little body in its coat of felt, and the soft feathery head. The sharp little claws lay meek on her palm and did not scratch her, and the horn beak only parted to let out its silly little neigh. "And *what* a curious song you have!" But she took the mare's child into the house and made it a nest of dry rushes by the hearth, and fed it goose-food in warm milk. "You shall be my house-bird, and guard me," said she, for she was full of fly jokes and affection. "You shall sleep on my pillow, but if you are not mannerly with your claws, we shall have words. And I will call you 'Birdy.' "

So it was arranged between them, and so the mare's monster child became Birdy, and the house-bird, and slept on the blind girl's pillow, and puttered after her about the cot, and followed her when she fed the geese or milked the goat, so it became acceptable, and even the geese said, "There is Birdy," and did not hiss at it any more.

And thus things continued for some months.

The land was turning toward winter by then; the cold winds blew and frost chewed the leaves from the trees. The geese skidded over the frozen pond, landed prow down and bow uppermost, and made out they had meant to do it, until the girl went to break the ice. One morning, as she did this, a man came sneaking up on the cot.

He was an itinerant, but he had got word in those parts of a blind woman who lived alone, and he thought he could make something of this.

In that way, he was already in the cot, taking a look round, when the girl came in again with Birdy at her heels.

"Who is there?" said she.

"Only I," he said.

The girl started. She had before heard only one man's voice in the house, and that was her father's. This man had no sound of him.

"What do you want here?" she asked.

"Well, that depends," he said, "upon what you will give me."

"I have very little, but if you are in need—"

"Yes, so I am. I have already drunk all your milk, I am so needy. But I have kept the cheese and bread in my bag here, against my further need. I do not care for apples and quinces, those you may keep. But best and most of all, I have a need for a nice friendly girl. I know you cannot see, but I am a spry fellow. I have had prettier wenches than you, but you will do me for now."

The frost of the day seemed to fill the girl so her heart stopped beating. But she had no weapon by, not even a pair of eyes to aid her. She knew quite well he could do as he wanted, and that, should she attempt resistance, he might maim or kill her besides. She made a small sound she could not help, and her terror and anger ran all through her with it, so the air about her seemed to singe.

"What is that by your feet?" said he, as he undid his belt, "some black hen? I have a dislike for poultry save on a plate. Send it off. I shall take a goose or two instead, when I leave you. Now, on your bed you get."

"Not on the bed," said she, and her blind eyes shed tears. "My father built it and my mother died in it. If you must, here on the floor, then." And she lay down, and though she did not need to, she turned her head away. It was then she heard a sudden curse, a cry—

She lay, and listened to him, for he was panting and mumbling far off from her.

"What is it?" she said. "If you must rape me, do it now."

But only the gulping and panting went on, and then she smelled a raw hot fiery odor, which seemed to saturate the cot and shake it. And then a loud *clack*, like iron striking the floor. And then— And then she heard such an unearthly raucous screech—like a stallion's trumpeting, the shriek of an embattled eagle—that she flung herself away into the chimney corner and crouched there.

But for the visitor, he was off. Shouting and gibbering by turns, leaving behind his bag, his belt and his breeches, he was tearing over the icy mud, under the fruit trees, scattering the geese without a look, fleeing away and away, his naked yellow buttocks winking.

While the geese, and the goat, these huddled back to the pond, and looked, not in that direction, but up at the house.

Is that Birdy?

For there, framed in the door of the cot which was

now too small for it, stood a great and terrible thing, a black horse some nineteen hands high on the legs of two black giant eagles, and with the head of one giant eagle, set with furnaces for eyes. It glared upon them, and from its beak hung a hank of male hair—the thief's—which now it neatly spat into a puddle.

And then the light and the shade furled over in the door. The fearsome thing was gone. There was only Birdy, trotting across the floor of the cot.

It had found its own sorcery, the mare's second child. Its shriveled heart had bloomed. It could grow, but all in a moment—great, then small again.

It rubbed its little feathered head against the blind girl's hand. She drew it on her lap and wept on its back. It suffered this, though its claws clicked reproachfully on her skirt: Why weep? I saved you.

But, "What can have happened?" she asked Birdy, the room, the world. "Some protection left me by my father? Can it be? Or the compassion of the gods."

Birdy made a nest for itself of the skirt, and tucking its head under one non-existent wing, full of good works, slept.

2 *Go Nowhere On A Horse With Wings*

OVER THE City of the Goddess-on-Earth, the sun was setting. It was, there, a blue sun, the sunset a lilac and not a rose. Then, the seven moons of the City lifted, and began to make their chiming patterns on the ether.

An eighth moon, a silver wheel, had already rolled to its nocturnal place above the tallest tower of the palace of Azhriaz the Goddess. From the wheel hung a tiny figure, which screamed, thinly, over and over. These cries were heard so often, even the citizens had come to mistake them for the lamenting of a night bird.

For Azhriaz, she sat on the tower roof in a chaïr of cut glass, guarded either side by a white stone cat, both of which moved, and one of which was now washing itself.

Adjacent, stood sentinels of the Goddess' guard, members of her court, and fantastic beings that might not be real.

Azhriaz stared up into the curious sky. She was clothed in deep red, and in her beauty. It was enough.

Suddenly a starburst took place a few feet over the roof. After the white flash a black after-shadow was stamped there, which then began to peel open. If any were amazed, Azhriaz did not appear to be. Remember, she had been wooed by the Vazdru eight times already.

Hazrond (very nearly peerlessly handsome, and clad in almost all the magnificence of night) stepped out of the air onto the roof. By a rope of silver he led a marvelous beast. It was a horse of exact proportions, black as black satin, with a pouring black water of mane and tail, plaited through with great round pearls and liquid sapphires. At its withers the satin altered into down. Black feathers spread as it walked forward into a pair of fanning, midnight wings.

Hazrond stood before Azhriaz.

"The whole world speaks of your loveliness," he said, "but does not say enough."

"You are too kind," said she.

"No, I am never kind. But here I am, and there, my gift to you."

Azhriaz considered the creature which poised, in equilibrium, on the night sky.

At last she said, "So you have brought me a bird with the body of a horse."

Hazrond smiled.

"Yes, fairest, nightmost Azhriaz. A bird with the body and head and limbs and hoofs and mane and tail of a horse. Perhaps . . . a horse with wings." And he turned, and untied the leading-rope. "Rise and fly," he said to the mare's first child.

Then the horse pawed the roof with its delicate steely feet. It rose with a leap and a thrust of its wings, as if lifted by invisible chains from above. It veered overhead, rimmed and tipped by the lights of the moons. It whirled under the silver wheel.

("What is that which shrieks there?" inquired Hazrond. "The daughter of he that was king in this land before me," replied Azhriaz.)

The winged horse passed and repassed like a dagger thrust, a south wind. It drifted down like a black feather, to the roof.

"Will you not," said Hazrond to Azhriaz, "mount the horse and ride the sky?"

"When I wish for such a journey, I have other means."

"Azhriaz," said Hazrond caressingly, and he had seated himself at her knee, "whatever means you have, they cannot match this horse. For it is a born thing, though one which I created out of my admiration and desire. It has the best of all states and forms, being both earthly and sorcerous. In glamour, it is your complement. Your darkness and your silver pallor would rest upon this shoal of blackness like black and white lilies on a moonlit river. No one has ridden the horse. Not even I. Take you the virgin ride, and make the creature your own."

Azhriaz got up. Perfumes drifted from her robe and hair. She went to the horse and touched its muzzle. The jewels in its mane swung to lie in her own tresses as it leaned its head too her brow. "My beauty," she murmured, "if you were solely of yourself, then you might be mine. But you are *his*. Therefore, you cannot be mine."

Hazrond also got to his feet. The white stone cats growled softly.

"Madam," said Hazrond, "can it be you spurn my gift."

"It is you I spurn. The rest must follow."

Hazrond folded his cloak about him like an inky wave. In his eyes were things best not told. He had so ringed and laved this hour with power and will, the magical horse smoked with it, the night teemed and vibrated. Yet she said *No* again. His own will, evaded, came back at Hazrond like the edge of a lash.

"You flirt too seriously," he said, "I may believe you."

"Do so."

"How you punish yourself, Azhriaz, to indulge your anger. How you cheat yourself."

"I recall an adage which tends something in this way: Go nowhere on a horse with wings, such schemes will betray you."

Hazrond frowned. (The rooftop was oddly empty, the stone cats crouched and sparks came from their mouths.)

"The saying is not as you have it," said Hazrond.

"Alas, dark lord, is it not?" said Azhriaz, and now she smiled upon him. It was a smile to put a killing frost upon any blossom of love.

And then Azhriaz touched the black lilypetal of the ear of the horse with her lips. "Be *no one's.*"

Mocking the Vazdru prince, Azhriaz—a black swan—rose from the roof on effortless wings and flew away across the sky.

Hazrond spoke a curse and the air shrank and flaming hail crashed out of it.

Hazrond snapped his fingers. Together, he and his gift vanished.

The stone cats sat petrified, all but their stony tails, which they wagged with an abrasive noise.

Up in the sky, the king's daughter on the wheel, self-obsessed, continued thinly to scream.

There was a land at the edge of the Goddessdom of Azhriaz, and as was the habit of such countries, its nearness to her empire had made it strange. A mountain stood there, the center part of which had slimmed to a stalk; it was narrow enough twenty men with their arms linked might have encircled it—yet this stalk ascended many hundreds of feet. At the summit, the stone of the mountain statically spilled into a great granite sunshade, and the shadow, falling on the ground far below, made it a place chary of summer and innocent of high noon.

At the base of the mountain stalk lay a stone town. It had one wide street, dominated by a blue-painted temple of the Goddess. Night after night, choked by the umbra of the mountaintop, a young priest came to meditate upon the temple roof. He stared at the starless sky of stone above him. "So is the overhanging yet indifferent menace of the gods," observed the young priest, Pereban, quoting the temple teachings. Then he would peer out at the horizon, under the mountain's lid: "And thus, the false hope with which men delude themselves," he dutifully concluded.

Pereban, though mortal, was handsome, and his hair

was of the clearest most lunar gold. But in the mental overcast of that town, such things went rigidly unremarked, save through their irrelevance. For life was only a series of pitfalls, not to be enjoyed or celebrated. The gods chastised pleasure just as they ignored suffering.

Finding in himself a profound strain of yearning, Pereban had mistaken it for religion. He entered the temple and dedicated himself to the worship of the Goddess. Thereafter her statue—a roughhewn lump of rock with painted blobs for eyes and black wool for hair—so disappointed him that he kneeled to it, and beat himself regularly, every morning.

But now it was night, and the solitary moon of the earth had just appeared, westering out beyond the mountain's grim parasol.

"The Goddess in the City," went on the young priest, who often talked to himself—who else would listen?—"was not her mother the moon? Or, some child of the moon and the sun. . . . Of course, *she* is more fair than any statue. Perhaps she becomes the moon itself. Perhaps that is her pale face among the stars so far away—Azhriaz in a dark robe, riding the sky on a beast with wings—Ah!" And overcome with contempt at his own intolerable dreams, he flung off his robe and took up a bunch of thorns to beat himself again—when there arrived an interruption.

Hazrond had been passing through some element of interim between the world and the Underearth, when the sharp awareness of his kind overheard, in some psychic way, the words of the priest. They were so apposite and, let it be said, so ironic, they caught Hazrond as if someone had slapped his face. Next second out of interim he pierced. And there he was upon the temple roof under the mountain, like a statue himself but of perfect sculpting, looking upon the speaker of the words with two eyes of brilliant black and baleful fire.

Pereban dropped his flail of thorns, as well he might.

"What did you say?" asked Hazrond, in a voice of the music of murder.

"I—forget—" said the priest, quite truthfully. He sank to his knees and added, "You are one of the gods. You can be nothing else. Doubtless you mean to kill me. I shall die in bliss, having seen you."

For, though taught to be obtuse, Pereban was by nature astute. And besides, it would require more than mental shade to dull the gleam of a Vazdru.

As for Hazrond, he was not, now, displeased. Susceptible to flattery, and to beauty (as any demon), he looked at the reverent young priest, ivory-naked, with only the golden hair and a few silver stripes of old beatings to cover him, and remarked, "Yes, better forget your words. I see you are a Sivesh, or a Simmu.* In your unlearning you do not know these names. Never mind it. You think I am a god. I will tell you," said Hazrond, stroking the golden hair idly, "a she-viper closed her teeth on me just now, and a she-wasp stung me. Are you the medicinal flower to cure these poisoned wounds?" The young priest had closed his eyes at the Vazdru caress. In all his days, religion had never so moved him. But then, "No," said Hazrond, perhaps a trifle regretfully. "You are not enough, earth born, to heal me. Not you. Again, never mind it. You have rendered a moment's distraction from the venom's rage. I shall reward you. What would you have?"

In response to this question, Pereban raised his eyes, lustrous with unqualified emotion, and drowned himself in the gaze of Hazrond. But at that instant the mortal could not speak, could *say* nothing.

"Very well," replied Hazrond. "I will gift you with the thing you most wish for and which you do not know you want, and in doing so, with that of which you exclaimed, thereby attracting my attention. A paradox for sure. The gift is dangerous, but you have earned the risk also."

Then Hazrond stepped aside and only glanced into the dark, and out of it, in a shiver of incandescences, trotted the horse with wings.

"My gift to you," Hazrond repeated, while the young man stared, now at the prince, now at the sorcerous beast.

Hazrond had not heard—or perhaps he had—*her* whisper in the creature's ear: *Be no one's.*

Certainly, Pereban had not.

*Mortal former lovers of Azhrarn, the Prince of Demons.

He rose and went forward in a sort of dream. The horse, glitter-made of ebony and embers, allowed it. The horse was gentle, or rather, it had the same sort of purity written all over it that a tiger has. It was above and beyond sin or righteousness, did not know them.

And Pereban turned then to thank and magnify the god who had blessed him. But Hazrond was gone from there, was already miles off—had Pereban realized—under his very feet, in the byways of ever-radiant Druhim Vanashta.

So the priest must make do with a prayer, and a hasty one at that, for he wished immediately to mount the winged horse. It was a madness on him, partly fired by the touch of the Vazdru, and by long unspecified yearning never till now given its chance. *Freedom.*

As a child, Pereban had sometimes ridden the mules of his father's farm. He imagined that he had the knack, and having petted and wheedled the horse a minute, seized the jeweled mane, set his foot against the satin flank, and bounded on to its back. There was a momentary awkwardness, for the wings of the horse began where properly a rider would sit. The horse, however, starting no argument with him but only standing docilely and helpfully still, Pereban eased himself higher up on the withers. These, due to the big flight muscles which, with the featherdown, extended from this part, were undoubtedly strong enough to support him. He felt them move and slide under his thighs as the wings stirred quietly as two courtly fans.

He roped the neck of the horse with his adoring arms.

"Sweetheart—let us be gone!"

With as little comment as that, finding his unknown want, did Pereban mean to abscond.

The winged horse, catching the ring of truth, obeyed.

Like a bird of black fire, like a spear of lights—up they shot into the air.

Pereban cried out, but he clung on fast to the horse, his fingers knotted in its mane, his legs gripped either side of its neck. But he felt a surge of terror, too, for all he supposed himself the creature's master, since they were already off the ground to the height of several tall towers piled one on another. And soon enough, the mountaintop itself came close overhead, so Pereban could see into it, its veinings and weird crystals, and below, the town was a dolls' dwelling. Then he knew only victory.

The horse was propelled by huge wheeling flaps of its eagle wings, so they sped in a sort of whirlwind of their own making. And presently the mountain passed behind, and then they were in the sky.

How huge that was, that sky. After the cramped confine of the town, it was to Pereban as if he had died and sloughed all heavy fleshly things, and he and the horse were one, and that one his own soul. Not black then, the sky, but transparent indigo, and full of waves and currents as the sea. Clouds went by, moon-shaped gauzes lit by the moon; each had a different smell, some of rain, some of the lands they had risen from, some of energy, and some of stars. The stars themselves seemed to dash along with the horse, sometimes streaming out like diamond cords, or else they kept pace and yet were still, like water beads on the roof of heaven.

The earth below had been quickly lost. It was mysterious now as generally the sky was, hidden by vapors and the dark. Here and there the lamps of cities cast up a sort of pallor-blush. Here and there an amorphous dragon rippled sullen scales—a mighty ocean thrown about by its tides.

"Ride on, dear love," shouted Pereban to the horse, drunk now, fearing nothing. "Brush the stars with your wings."

Obedient, not necessarily compliant, up and up rushed the flying horse, swifter than any beast or bird of the world.

Now they were entering into the portion of heaven over which the moon was then taking her westward path. High above stretched the endless tapestry of the stars, but the moon was nearer the earth than these, and in motion as they were not. She was, too, almost at the full. The disc of her seemed vast, filling a quarter of the upper sky, and burning upon the horse and rider with a white effulgence which also gave off great heat.

Pereban had never thought of the moon as being in any way hot, but cool or cold. In his poetic reverie he had compared her to the delicate face of the Goddess—

now he beheld she was a gargantuan orb, and her glow caused his eyes to swim, and her relentless hot pale ray began to work on him oddly.

For as they coursed beneath, the wings of the horse beating faster and more fast in rhythm with the young man's heart, and the round muscles working in its back and withers and neck under him, another sensation stole upon the rider. And with every heart-wingbeat, as the world fell farther and farther off and the glare of the moon more and more encompassed them, so this sensation swelled. And if he had been in his temple and such had come over him, he would have grasped the flail of thorns, for he had been always strictly chaste. But there was no flail to hand. Only the silken living skin, and the ceaseless fan of the wings—which now and then, soft as a teasing kiss, would light a feathertip upon his shoulders or his spine or side.

So Pereban shifted himself as best he could, and determined he would consider only the wonder of the night and the adventure.

But a Vazdru caress had been set on him, and the moon seared him white and drew the tide of blood in him like the sea, up and down and round and round. And the horse, had he but known it, was so steeped in carnal magics only his naivete, and the unusual nature of events, had so far protected him from it. And no longer.

And it was useless to gaze at the stars or at the formless earth. Try as he would, he could not but be aware of how the engine of the horse pulsed and strove against him, and how the wings coaxed and skimmed. And for sure there was no way of getting down—miles in the air it seemed, and the stars hurtling by—

And next Pereban could do no more than lie upon the horse's neck, his hands clenched in the girl's-hair mane, and sigh and groan and sigh. And soon he trembled and his eyes closed themselves. And not much after that he stretched himself and sang aloud, so the sky might have been astonished.

But in that second the winged horse, bred, never forget by a demon, tigerishly shook itself. It was a fine, a *thorough* shake.

And still stretched oblivious in the fit of joy, Pereban was flung off into space.

And fell—

3 Cold Shore and Shining City

FALLING, HE CRIED OUT in terror now. But the air was thin, he was stifled. Pereban gave up his senses. Then something struck him such a blow it woke him up again.

He lay gasping, bruised, his bones seeming to rattle in his skin from the jolt. But there was a surface beneath him. It supported him. He no longer fell and did not seem to be dead.

Pereban thought, with a pang of unhappiness: It was all a dream. The god. The winged horse and the flight in sky. *And in the dream I sinned.* And now he had rolled from his pallet on to the floor. So he opened his eyes and found the floor was staring white and a glare went up from it and shone in a thick and wandering white mist that was everywhere about, and obscured everything. . . . And the floor was besides hot as an oven-stone. Pereban gathered himself and pulled himself to his feet, so he should only scorch his soles. Could it be? Rather than plummet miles down to be broken in pieces on the hills of earth, he had fallen instead a far shorter distance, to the face of the moon. Which meant he must have fallen *upward,* the moon being therefore in some way magnetic to his flesh or his life.

The young man stood, shifting from one foot to the other to save them, panting from his shock and the inadequate atmosphere, while the ghostly mist drifted continually about him.

Yes, it was the moon and he upon it. He had not perished, but what hope now? Though the disc was after all huge, and permitted him, in discomfort, to remain and bake, surely it was barren of all things? The horse had betrayed him and his formless schemes—doubtless now it cavorted below, due to become some legend of the lands of men. . . . But he had been punished for the fault of carnal delight. He would die, and that slowly, burning, starved, gasping for breath. Better to have been dashed in bits on the bosom of his mother the world.

Nevertheless, since it was impossible to keep still on the cooking-griddle surface, Pereban began to hasten along. He had no marker or idea of direction to guide him, and the mist hid before and behind, and all the outer sky. He might hurry in circles toward his death. And perhaps even some fiend haunted here, some moon-thing that would rise suddenly to tackle him—

Pereban checked and stood still to burn his feet. Before him in the mist had risen a shape. It was half his own height and did not itself move, maybe having condensed itself preparatory to a spring.

"Declare yourself," said Pereban. "I am armed only with hands and feet, but I will use them."

The shape did not answer.

It came to Pereban, now hopping to and fro, that a faint coolth wafted from the substance of the fiend. Pereban resolved to die and marched forward, and next stubbed his toes on the lowest extremity of the fiend, and so learned it was only a hump jutting up from the white surface. In the top of the hump there was set a plate, translucent as porcelain. And from this plate came a breath of chilled air, so he instinctively threw himself upon it. No sooner had he done so than the plate tipped over and tossed him inward and down. The moon herself had gulped him.

And then he discovered himself drifting in a kind of silvery dusk, borne as if on a buoyant river. Some way off a clear fire shone with an unearthly glow, like a winter sun pale as a narcissus. Below stretched a mirror of onyx, patterned with combers of black and white. But Pereban was so cold now he could not bear it, and slowly revolving and sinking in the air, he froze and perished. And now and then he trusted and prayed it *was* a dream, and that he would rouse soon and be free of it.

Yet it was no dream though dreamlike indeed. The air was richer than the outer variety so, but for the cold, the falling adventurer might have breathed without care. Nevertheless, the air had to it this quality of denseness. It allowed him to descend only slowly, also churning him around and turning him over every so often, like a morsel in a stew.

Far away the narcissus of light still shone, but going paler and further off as he went down. The dusk itself had, it seemed to him, a kind of luminescence all its own.

Almost inadvertently in his discomfort and dismay, Pereban took note of these things, and eventually, seeing he was about to fall onto it, of the place below.

Being much closer to it now, he made out what appeared a great sea, moving slowly and as heavy as cream. It had two colors, black as ink, white as milk, that came together and drew apart, but never mixed to gray. Long, moody waves of this ink and milk ran in upon a máss of land that was itself all glowing a smoky white, with smoky black shadows especially cast from a range of mountains.

Pereban was looking at these doubtfully, for they seemed to have been carved and planed, so smooth and polished they were, when a rush exactly beneath caused him to stare that way. And there, lifting from the sea depths, was a pearly sea-beast, with two vast lacy fins or wings that fluttered, and a lacy fan of tail which, as the beast sank again, drove up from the water a spray of drops larger than a man's hand. And they struck Pereban like peculiar soft stones. But in another minute the air had rolled him over again and down—onto a long white shore.

Truly, it was an alien spot. The ground was of a material like the mountains, utterly smooth and only traced here and there with vague runnels where the sea tides, which must come in and go out, had over centuries layered it like worn cameo. For miles this plain extended, to either horizon, the sea on its third side, and the mountains inland on the fourth. The narcissus sun, if such it was, stood now beside them, and lit their crests to a most ethereal pale gold.

Pereban, though, had very little eye for such matters, as he lay freezing on that cold beach. Nor, when more watery stones pummeled him, did he greatly bother that quantities of the whale-beasts were now leaping and diving in the seas of ink and milk, quite close to shore.

But then he heard a long dinning note, in the distance, repeated over and over and growing all the while more loud. And he began to sense a vibration which quickly resolved itself as the beating of several large drums. Pereban dismissed all the sounds as noises in his head due to weakness, or some hallucination of approaching death. And from this notion he passed into a theosophic meditation on whether he might not already be dead and the gods might not have thrust him into this alternate world for punishment. So absorbed was he in his half-fainting debate, that a vast procession, sweeping over the plain toward the shore's edge, was almost on top of him before he considered it. But the dinning trumpets and reverberant drums of which the procession was the source, clashed abruptly to silence. That attracted Pereban's attention. He raised his lids, and saw this:

The land itself seemed to have erupted to form some hundreds of blond warriors in white mail, girded with swords of steel. And to make for them a multitude of low-slung silver chariots drawn by dray packs of albino hounds. It had, too, flown up lengths of ivory to become white banners embroidered with devices of whitest azure and anemic yellow. It had darkened to silver trumpets in the hands of trumpeters turbaned in gray silk with plumes like smolder from their brains. It had lightened again to drums and drummers in ashy dappled skins. And lastly the white landscape had flowered into three gigantic snow-white bears walking on all fours, on the backs of each of which rose a seat of white gold under a parasol like a blue poppy. And three grand personages occupied these seats, the foremost of whom was now alighting by a ladder of steps. Like his bear, he was clad in white furs, and from his crown and chin poured venerable white hair only a tint whiter than that of the blond young warrior captains and the childish pages who assisted him. More certainly the crags of his face betokened he was an old man, and one accustomed to putting himself in the right. On his head was a diadem of bright daffodil gold. (By contrast the other two grandees, upon the second and third bears, were garbed in griseous furs and had on their worthy skulls diadems only of the ubiquitous silver.)

The old man of the gold came over the marble shore until he stood with his shoes in Pereban's ribs. The old man bowed, placing his hands before his face in a ritual manner. Then he leaned nearer and touched lightly the lobes of Pereban's ears, and his lips. "Lord, as predicted, you have fallen from the sun."

Pereban had by now reached a delirious stage of stupidity, and was inclined to find fault.

"Not at all," said he.

"It was observed, lord," sternly corrected the old man. "You were witnessed, like a mote of fire, in your descent. Besides, by your golden hair we know you."

Pereban, wanting to quarrel further, could now only shiver. His teeth chattered so wildly that some of the chariot-dogs apparently imagined he was snarling at them, and began to growl in reply.

"Sun Lord," said the old man, "see how you are, and today it is almost summer here. What are you but a being of the sun?" And he signaled to a pair of pages who ran forward and offered Pereban a robe of fur and golden tissue. When the young man had been helped into it, a moonstone flask of cordial was held to his mouth. He drank. The cordial, though watery to the taste, in a moment revived him extraordinarily, his veins filled with vital heat, and he opened wide his eyes and stared on the assembly in mingled alarm and disbelief.

"My faculties are restored, yet I am dreaming still. It is not a dream."

"It is not. You are here to accord with our prophecies," censoriously yapped the old man.

Velvet footwear was being eased upon the feet of Pereban, and velvet gloves upon his hands.

"Where is my crown?" said Pereban, eyeing the old man's headpiece; such myths as the priest had ever heard had begun to advise him. If he arrived in answer to some portent, he could expect the best.

"Later, you shall be anointed as the king. Will you deign, lord, to share my seat upon the animal?"

Pereban did so, and went aloft onto the bear very

nimbly after another swig of the cordial. The old man creaked up after him.

"How fortunate it is," said Pereban, "that we speak the same language."

"Not at all," said the old man, "that was seen to by magic when I tapped your ears and mouth."

The ladder of steps was removed. The bear grunted and turned with a lolling gait back along the shore. The drums and trumpets began again to sound. In the ocean of ink and milk the whales were going down.

"Where now?" asked Pereban blithely.

"To the Shining City."

"On! On!" cried Pereban waving his arms, smiling about him, annoying the moon-bear, inebriated on moon-wine.

The old man of the gold, whose title was Lord One, proved a great authority on all things, and throughout the journey, which lasted perhaps some earthly hours, on and on he droned. Now and then Lord Two, or Lord Three (the second and third elders on the adjoining bears) would call out some wavering crochety instruction or annecdote. "Pay them no heed," recommended Lord One. "They are both of them senile. I, though older and having reached my thousandth year, am, as you perceive, in my prime."

Pereban did not believe this assertion. Lord One was undoubtedly no more than ninety years of age, and the other dodderers looked scarcely more, probably less.

Meanwhile the procession, the white bears at its head, had passed up a terraced slope that seemed to have been shaped by the same ogre's implements as had quarried and burnished everything else, and so gone into a defile of the mountains.

A wind blew through the defile, sounding it like a pipe, and the upper peaks of the mountains seemed to smoke. Lord One told Pereban that this was a blowing off of the dry frost which gathered there in winter and spring. "In summer comes a great heat," said he, "and as you will notice, at this time of the year we go about almost naked, in one robe of fur alone."

"The outside of the disc, however," said Pereban, who

had contrived for himself perpetual access to the moonstone cordial, "is boiling hot. Why is that?"

"Of what disc are you speaking?"

"The lunar disc, wherein we now are."

"What nonsense," said Lord One. "There can be no *outside.* I see you seek to test me. There is only this land, this sea, and the orb of the sun that was your home before you fell."

"As you desire," said Pereban. For in his term as a priest in the temple, he had learned that it was less wearisome not to contradict cant.

"This land where you have come down, or to where you have been dropped, is the land of Dooniveh. And the sea of Dooniveh encircles it. And presently you shall, having entered through the ring of the mountains of Dooniveh, reach the Shining City of Dooniveh."

"There to be made the king of Dooniveh?" prompted Pereban.

"Provided that you fulfill the condition," said Lord One.

"Which condition?"

"On that I shall, for the moment, remain silent," said Lord One. He continued however to make sounds on all other subjects available. From his vociferousness, Pereban tried to garner facts.

Dooniveh—the world inside the moon—comprised an ocean and a single land mass, that on which they now traveled. In the irridescent gray sky of Dooniveh there presided the one solitary object—its sun. This circled round land and sea in a sideways girdling motion. It never waxed or waned, and never moved across or under the terrain in order to sink or rise, as did the satellites of the Flat Earth. (As did, for that matter, this very moon itself.)

But the moon's sun was a feeble flower, in Pereban's opinion. As it went *by* the land, it would arrive beside the mountaintops and so above the city in their midst, and then they declared summer, the natives doffed all but one thick fur robe and some ten or so undergarments, and praised the benign warmth of the weather.

A year in Dooniveh endured for a month, and each had four seasons.

Summer lasted seven days, days at that without a night. It was preceded by a seven-day spring during which the sun approached over the ocean and drew inland, and was followed by a seven-day autumn, when the sun wandered off again, continuing overland and back out to sea. In winter, which was a period of a little more than seven days, the sun was at its most distant point from the land mass, taking its road over the waste of waters, discernible from shore as a flickering pinprick in darkness. For then there was only night and extreme cold.

It now occurred to Pereban that, although the scale of time was rather different, and the sighting of the effect not exactly similar, these internal passages of a sun accounted for the changing of the moon's shape as regarded from the earth. Dooniveh's summer was full moon, the late days of spring and the early days of autumn—as the sun approached nearer and nearer or drew off farther and farther—must correspond to new, quarter and half moons. The earthly nights of no moon coincided with Dooniveh's winter nadir; the moon-sun was at the far side of the sea, and so at the inner *back* of the lunar disc. (In other words, the moon was yet present in the earth's heaven, but for all purposes lightless.)

Obviously the outer surface of the moon possessed some sorcerous quality, which directed the cool, frail inner light outward on the earth in a glow and heat—

If only the moonlanders had been more aware of their situation, what strange metaphysics and lunargraphics might they not have discussed with the visitor.

For example, a book of Pereban's temple explained how, every worldly morning the moon sank into the ocean of chaos, and rose from it again every worldly night with vigor refreshed. Perhaps the chaos-bath was the very thing which so polished up the outside of the moon. But at the idea of the globe, in which he now was, gliding down the sky of earth, as it now *must* be, and plunging into the abysm, Pereban turned giddy. Allied to which the book had proposed that chaos was inimical to true matter—and so how was the plunge to be survived?

Just then, passing between two conical peaks, the procession emerged from the defile, and there below lay

Dooniveh's Shining City, under its sun, which fortunately distracted Pereban's mind.

The city seemed made of ice, such as Pereban had sometimes beheld atop the parasol mountain of his birthplace. The smooth white terraces and towers were semi-transparent, and pastel hints of color flushed them through. The sunlight caused the city to shine indeed, in a cold and slippery way. Pereban's instinct divined at once that artistry might be found there, but that it would be hard ever to get warm.

Such is the reward of my hot and inartistic sin, thought he, with uneasy complacence.

A chill highway led to the city walls. Trumpeting and drumming, down it they went, casting a reflection as if in a frozen lake, and entered under a grand archway.

From icy balconies along the route, damsels with pale hair looked upon Pereban with opal eyes. They did not tempt him, though they were fair.

The streets of the city were broad, and often there ran by a canal of sluggish black water or white, with strange fish embedded in it, waiting for the fluid to unbind.

As for the buildings of the city, these seemed to be really all one building, cut up into stacks and slices by canals, streets and squares. At length the procession had wound itself into a huge court, where stood some trees like no tree Pereban had seen before, tall and thin and having no branches, yet out of the pole-like trunks stuck clusters of glimmering golden fruit. Beyond stood another slice of the city. Lord One, who all this time had talked on and on, enlarging each subject by philosophic digressions and aphorisms, indicated two blue doors. "The palace. We are arrived."

How silent the city seemed in that moment when the drummers and trumpeters, the marching chariots and beasts—and the Lord One—all ceased making a noise together. Not a sound, but the mountain wind piping, and now and then an odd little *plinck* from the fruit on the trees.

Pereban's sense of adventure, the taste of fear and wine, left him. Full of trepidation, he dismounted from the giant bear and was conducted into the palace.

* * *

They prepared for him a divan of bloodless silk, in a room like an ice cave, warmed by fires of ashen blue. The fashion was, in Dooniveh, to mimic the lush mid-summer cold. Beyond the windows of thin silver, the frost-laden summer wind wailed and meowed like cats fighting.

Pallid, if charming, servitors brought Pereban, on trenchers of nearly invisible glass, watery moon foods, and in likewise cups, likewise moon wines. There was also set before him a dish of moon apricots from the pole-trees outside. The yellow fruit was apparently made of metal, and having attempted to penetrate or peel it, Pereban left it alone, only slipping one fruit into the sash of his robe against the chance there might be some utility in it.

Lords Three, Two and One perched close by.

Pereban, his unsatisfying meal finished and his wine cup full, was brooding again on the proximity of chaos, when Lord One interrupted.

"Pray tell us something of your own country, which is our sun."

Pereban replied: "Do you know nothing of that venue?"

"Nothing whatsoever."

"Then we are united in that."

"How can this be?"

"As I rushed downward," said Pereban deliberately, "I lost all memory of my beginnings and now do not recall anything of my home." (Here, Lords Two and Three glanced furtively at each other.)

Lord One opened his lips to commence another monologue.

But at this point furtive Lords Two and Three broke in with shrill cries.

Lord One held up his hand for quiet.

"They reprimand me," said he, "that I have not yet explained the conditions of kingship. This I am loath to do, as it touches upon my personal honor. And would touch on theirs, too, if their desiccated state had not destroyed all feeling."

At these high words, an altercation resulted. But a moment later the doors of the hall were opened, and seven attendants entered. They were white-clad in garments fringed by gold. The three lords fell instantly silent, and averted their faces.

"Sun Lord;" said the first attendant to Pereban, "you must come with us now."

Pereban drained his cup and rose. Once again, old stories and myths were in his mind. For surely some ordeal would follow, whereby these people would determine his right to the rule of Dooniveh. He did not want it in any case, but having nowhere else to go, went forth consenting.

The latest route led down. The corridors turned to rock, lit by lamps like stabs of ice.

"What a splendid summer day," said Pereban, gyrating with the cold. The attendants paid no heed to his pleasantry.

At length they came to a great door of iron, and here halted. The first attendant bowed, his hands before his face.

"Sun Lord, you must open this door and enter the place that lies behind it. There the queen of this city is sleeping, as she has slept some seven hundred years, guarded by a fearful beast. Overcome the beast, wake the lady, and she will be yours, and with her the Shining City of Dooniveh."

"Just as I thought," murmured Pereban. "And if I had a choice they might make a garland of their doors and beasts and sleeping queen-ladies. But as it is—" said Pereban, "I embrace my fate."

The attendants bowed themselves away.

4 *The Sleeping Heart*

THE DOOR WAS some thirteen feet high and had about it neither a handle nor any visible lock or keyhole. Nevertheless, Pereban advanced, and pushed and heaved at it, and smote it some forceful blows, at which it resounded like a gong. When he had recovered from its booming, he tried to grip the heavy panels and elicit movement, but could get no purchase. After that he stood away, and summoning from his priestly training some esoteric passwords of opening, proclaimed them. The door did not even quiver. Then Pereban kicked it.

"This is a punishment," he said at last. "I did not thrash myself enough with the thorns. I wished to escape the enclosure of the mountain temple, and here I am shut up in a moon."

Then he threw off the fur robe and used the metal apricot, knotted in his sash, to beat himself.

Chastisement comforted him with its habitude. Although he knew the gods were indifferent, yet he had come to believe they still reckoned such practices correct among mortals. Besides, the exercise warmed him more than the robe had done. And, the while, old teachings of the temple entered his mind. One phrase in particular recurred to him, which had been written in an elder book penned before the revelations of the Goddess. This went as follows:

"He that seeks a thing and does not truly desire it, finds it not, though it be put into his hand. Yet he that seeks the most rare thing in the world, truly wanting it, shall discover it, though a hill has covered it over."

(*Well and good,* said Pereban, and beat himself more vigorously.)

"And in this same way, coming to a door, how many shall find it closed. But he that truly would enter there need only knock thereon, and the door shall be opened."

When these sayings had gone through his mind a sufficient number of times, and when he was in a sufficient glow, and his arm tiring, Pereban put on his robe again, tied the sash, stowed the apricot, and turned back to the door.

"And do I truly wish to enter?" inquired Pereban. "Punishment or destiny, I can only proceed. So much I accept." And then he knocked mildly on the door and said, "Open, if you please."

The door opened.

Another might have given a shout of laughter, or curses, but the young priest had by now composed himself. He passed through the portal of iron with a calm tread and looked about him.

The environment beyond was a long chamber tiled by

crystal, in which flickered faint lamps. The illumination seemed unreal and phantasmal, as if the room were filled by water. Nevertheless, Pereban advanced, and soon he came to an avenue of white pillars. At the end of the row lay a basin of inky liquid. The other side of the basin was a couch draped in silver and hung with gold. Did something lie asleep there? Even as he strove to see it, the whole of the floor between the basin and the couch quaked up. And there was a fearful beast, as promised, a colossal white dog larger than a lion, with the horns of a bull, eyes like wheels of fire and teeth like those of a crocodile. And having noticed Pereban, and slavered and growled, it made toward him.

But Pereban, who had nothing with which to defend himself, frowned at the dog, and thought again of his dealings with the door.

"I must go on with the task," said Pereban, as the dog scraped the floor with claws like those of a leopard, "And therefore I must and do truly wish to conquer this animal." The dog came padding on, jaws gaping. Pereban strode forward to meet it. The dog hesitated and Pereban next instant came up with it, and his head was level with its own. He stared into its fulminating eyes. "Whatever your size or accessories," said Pereban to the creature, "you are a dog. Obey me!" The dog seemed undecided. Pereban bethought him of the apricot, and drawing it out again showed it to the dog, which now looked mostly surprised. Then Pereban hurled the apricot away. "Go fetch!" cried Pereban. The dog abruptly reversed itself and went bounding off to search out the fruit, its tail—which Pereban had noted was a serpent—wagging with glee.

Pereban now advanced on the couch. Drawing aside the hangings, he looked down to find some hag-like queen. For though seven hundred years in Dooniveh was nearer sixty of the earth's, it seemed enough to spoil a young woman's initial bloom.

But naturally in this, as with the rest, the priest's adventure stayed faithful to the myths. For her sleep was an enchanted one, and there she lay, the lady of the moon-country, a maiden slender and pale as a stem of the white iris, and with topaz hair. She was robed in purple embroidered with yellow diamonds, and on her brow rested a golden tiara, and between her hands as she slept lay a little casket of dark silver, which seemed oddly to throb with the rise and fall of her breast as she breathed.

Pereban now knew his lesson. He did not touch her, but leaning over her spoke very low. "Awake," said he. And the beautiful queen of Dooniveh, who had slept seven hundred years of the moon, some fifty-eight or sixty of the world, awakened.

Her eyes were the luminous color of Dooniveh's summer sky, and quite as cool, and indeed much emptier. She observed Pereban with no amazement. She said, "You have brought me up out of sleep."

"So I have."

"You are not the first. Others have done so. To our mutual regret."

This did not accord with mythology.

"It is against your will then that I have woken you?"

"Yes," said she, gazing with cool cruel eyes. "For you are not the one who should have done it, as none of them were that one."

"Then I will leave you. You may resume your slumber."

"That is not to be. Not yet. The spell of sleep is torn, and until I have in answer torn your pride and spirit and made a fool of you, I may not raise its magic up again."

And having said these not much consoling words, the queen of Dooniveh left her couch, and going to the basin of black liquid, tipped into it something from her casket. Deep down into the water it went, sending up behind it a kind of tremor. And next the water itself seemed to begin slowly to throb, as if in its turn it breathed.

"What did you throw in there?" asked Pereban, having at that moment nothing better to say.

"My heart," she said. "Since neither you nor I will get any use from it."

Just then the fearful dog came bounding back and placed the apricot daintily at Pereban's feet.

"Wise dog, excellent dog," said Pereban, patting the enormity on its head between the horns. The dog smiled and dribbled and the serpent wagged.

"Ah," said the queen, and now she did seem a little interested. "You are not exactly like those others. They sprung sorcery and potions on this cur and woke me with a kiss."

"I am a priest," said Pereban. He blushed and looked elsewhere than her unkind eyes. "I cannot say I have never sinned, but never with man or woman have I indulged my desire."

"And the door of iron—did you bring a hundred warriors to break it down, or a magical fire to melt it?"

"No. I knocked and asked entry."

The queen folded her white hands. She seated herself at the rim of the basin and turned her eyes on its pulsing water.

"I am named Idune," she said. "I will tell you my short history, for though I have lived long, I have lived most of my years asleep. And my heart, there in the pool, is sleeping yet. For the one of whom the prophecy spoke has never come to wake my heart. It slumbers and dreams, while I am heartless. But you shall hear."

Then she told him her story.

She had ruled her palace-city and her bleak land alone until her one hundred and ninety-second year, at which time she was sixteen. She then consented to wed and provide the world with a king. She had chosen him from her court of princes and soldiers, scholars and mages. He was handsome and noble, all approved the match. And Idune, although she did not love the man, was not averse to him. The fourth nightless day of midsummer arrived, the day of the marriage. But as the royal couple stood hand in hand in the hall where such rites and legalities were seen to, panic-stricken outcry was heard in the streets below. A flaming spark had shot out from the sun and was rushing, on an incendiary trail, even now toward the palace. It struck the ground with a roar and blaze in a court beneath the marriage chamber. And when the crash of its concussion faded, a voice cried out these words: "The Moon Queen may only wed the Sun Lord, the King of Gold, to which her sun-like hair gives the clue. Let her invoke sleep otherwise and so pass the aeons, unless she take him, since in all other liasons she will know sorrow and discontent. Her heart shall break and her husband be disgraced."

The voice was then silent. Putting off the marriage ceremony, Idune summoned her magicians.

For three summer day-and-night days, they labored at divinations. Eventually they came before Idune and her bridegroom and spoke in whispers.

The world of their sun was incomprehensible to the people of Dooniveh, yet so influenced their lives they could hardly ignore its whims. The sun prophecy was valid, all portents endorsed it. The queen of the moon-world must wed the lord of the sun. It would be madness to go against the auguries.

Idune therefore postponed her wedding thirty years (some two and a half of the earth), in order to give the sun lord time to show up.

The city sensed already its queen was doomed. But as government scarcely existed there, and since the people were for the most part unambitious, melancholy and vague, no one took pains over the affair.

When the thirty years were up, and no sun lord had arrived, Idune publicly announced that she would after all wed the fore-chosen, champing Doonish prince.

She did so.

The marriage then lasted a few seasons, at the end of which Idune publicly announced her error in going against the sun's edict. The union was loveless, childless, pointless, and—worst of all—dull. This was naturally ascribed to the jilted wrath of the sun.

Having divorced her king, Idune retired from the world into a chamber under the city. Here, guarded by a magical beast, she contrived to extract her heart—or rather, its intrinsic, nonphysical essence—sealing it in a casket for safety. She had already discerned a chip or two and feared breakages. She then invoked the sorcerous sleep. Her prescribed suiter alone, having descended from the sun, would dare to wake her.

The divorced king meanwhile continued to rule Dooniveh, in whatever fashion he was able and that it would permit him. In respect of title, he was known no longer as the king, but only as lord.

Time thereafter passed, and finally one summer day a young man with golden hair, or at least hair of a more vivid shade of blond than was usual, arrived at the palace saying he had descended from the solar orb, wished to wed the queen and become king of Dooniveh.

It was explained to him that he must first get by an impassable door, subdue a ferocious monster, and then overcome the spell of sleep upon the queen. None of this seemed to startle him, he appeared already aware of the facts, though oddly enough the act of whirling down the sky had deprived him of all memory of the home world, the sun. (And there were even those who said this young man greatly resembled one of the minor princes of the court, who had not been seen in the city for some hundred years, though a camp of bear breeders in the mountains had spotted him occasionally, roaming and muttering.)

Well then, this suitor of the slightly-gilded hair managed to break in the iron door, overcome the beast by tossing a drug in its jaws, and wake Idune by falling upon and ravishing her.

Since he was judged in this way to have fulfilled the stipulations, Idune emerged from seclusion and wedded him. The previous king was ousted, though he was still addressed as "Lord." But the newcomer kinged it in Dooniveh until, after a few seasons, the queen went publicly once more to confess his disgrace.

The marriage was ill-fated, as had been the first marriage. It could not be that he was an impostor, perhaps only not quite of the right solar family.

Idune divorced him. He then presided over Dooniveh as Lord Two, in company with Lord One, the former king before him (this alliance being quite as unhappy as either of the marriages). Idune retired again into enchanted sleep.

Next, of course, came the advent of a third suitor of frailly yellowish hair. He proceeded exactly as Lord Two had done in almost every intent and purpose. And soon, after some sun-amnesia, door-melting, dog-ensorcelling, labial violence, marrying, marital strife and divorcement, ended up also in exactly the same way, under the name of Lord Three.

There then ensued a space of peace, during which Idune the queen slept on, and Lord One established an upper if elderly hand over the Shining City.

It came eventually to be, however, that one summer day-night, watchers beheld another glittering mote falling through the air. The city gathered itself, now somewhat listlessly. Out went a procession and collected the sky-fallen Pereban like a shell from the shore.

What a combination then must have been the feelings of Lord One, let alone of Lords Two and Three. Jealousy and awe, suspicion and superstition, bitterness, dishonored embarrassment and duty.

Pereban, his brain now awash with the tale, gazed on the dejected queen, this ancient girl with razor-steel for eyes.

"Madam," he said, "have no fear of me. Under such circumstances, I would not aspire to be your fourth spouse. I admit freely I did not fall here from your sun, but from another world, whose being I hesitate to describe."

Idune gazed into the pool, where Pereban's reflection nevertheless wavered.

"Yet you are," said she, "uncommonly handsome, and your hair is, this once, of the correct shade. Perhaps you lie. Perhaps you are my true predestined lover, but do not after all like the look of me."

"Your beauty leaves me breathless," said Perban.

"Yet you find the breath to say so. And, you say you will not have me. Possibly Lord One had told you how I bit off the lobe of his ear in a fit of anguish. Or was it Lord Three who has been blabbing how I fed him in his wine medicine to annoy the bladder. Or Lord Two has dragged up again that tiresome episode of the crumbs of glass I shook into his underclothing."

"Madam," said Pereban swiftly, "you are not to blame. You have, as you told me, no heart at present."

"That is so. Which brings it to my mind you cannot be the sun lord, for my heart would wake at his approach, wherever it was. There could be no doubt."

And Idune sighed, so the reflection of Pereban rippled and disappeared from the water.

"What then is to be done?" she asked. "*I* pine, though my heart sleeps on."

"We are taught that the gods do not care for us," said Pereban the priest. "Therefore we must seek for guidance in our own selves."

Idune raised her eyes. In them he recognized for a moment a somber longing long unassuaged.

"Then you must seek this guidance," said the queen. "You have disturbed my rest. I will grant you the seven days of summer to find a solution to the sun's curse. And if you fail I will have you rent apart by the white bears, being presently heartless, as you have observed."

Pereban requested for himself a small uncluttered chamber, and here he paced about, or sat upon the floor, ate frugally, beat himself with the apricot, all the time thinking. Having got through so many eccentric scrapes, he did not now believe he would be proffered again to death. Accordingly some idea must suggest itself to him to solve the plight of the heartless Queen Idune. And being so certain of this, naturally in quite a short while a solution did suggest itself.

Thereafter Pereban paid a second call on the monster dog in the underpalace, and put it to a strenuous but rewarding session of *Go Fetch.*

The last day of summer commenced. Frost sprinkled on the pinnacles of the Shining City and on the floor of Pereban's allotted room—for he had given over coddling himself and gone back to most of the strictures of his temple, which he found a vast relief.

Late in that day, probably about midnight by the reckoning of the earth, Idune came sweeping in through the frost. She was attended by all three lords, several mages and sages, and the chief bearkeeper, who gazed on Pereban in compassionate distress.

"Your answer," demanded Idune without prologue.

"You have been given a fate and a prophecy," said Pereban. "You have misheard and misread both."

"What!" cried Idune. Her court gaped, and the bearkeeper grew less agitated.

"Repeat to me again," said Pereban, "the message the voice delivered on the day before the first marriage was due."

Idune pointed at a sage noted for his memory.

He duly relayed the fatal words:

"The Moon Queen may only wed the Sun Lord, the King of Gold, to which her sun-like hair gives the clue."

(Here all the court then present moaned it was no more than a fact, and how peerless was the queen and how lovely her yellow hair. But Idune glared about her and they were quiet. The sage went on:) "Let her invoke sleep otherwise and so pass the eons, unless she take him, since in all other liasons she will know sorrow and discontent. Her heart shall break, and her husband be disgraced."

"And for this," said Pereban, "you have waited, or you have given yourself to others who could end your sleep if not wake your heart."

"So I have," said Idune in a terrible voice. "Do you tell me that which I already know? Here I am, but he has not come to me. What is new? I hope that the royal bears have had their talons properly sharpened."

Pereban gravely smiled.

"Where in the message then," said he, with cardinal grace, "does it say your sun lord will come to you?"

"It says I may wed him alone. That I must take him or be doomed. How else is any of that to follow unless he intends to claim me?"

"That is not to say he must fall out of the sun to do it."

There was surely silence after that.

At long last, Idune went near to Pereban and stared at him with her winter eyes wide.

"*How* then?"

"You are plainly a sorceress. You must devise a sorcery of ascent. For I believe that, rather than wait here beneath, you must go up to the sun to gain your husband. You were meant to rise to meet him, not to pull him down on this cold rock. Doubtless having invited you, he has awaited your advent in his kingdom as anxiously and disconsolately as you have mooned here below. Hopefully his youth is as enduring as your own, or else you have lost your chance forever."

Idune uttered a wild cry. Rounding on her court, she spoke very ill of it. Pereban recalled her. "Waste not another second. If you are able to effect the journey, do so."

"You will come with me," said she with a look at him, half pleading and half poisonous.

Pereban did not remonstrate.

"Fetch a bear!" exclaimed the queen. The bearkeeper protested. "Not for rending, for riding, O fool!" she screamed.

The bear was brought. Queen Idune and Pereban the young priest mounted it. With no further provision they left the city for the shore in the wake of the wandering sun.

Upon the seashore, in the darkening light of autumn, Idune raised her pale arms free of their purple sleeves, and called the whales of the deep.

Up they came, those strange fantastic creatures, borne on their wing-fins. And as each rose, it blew out the waters of the moon, until these fountains hid the sky in a weave of ink and milk.

Then Idune, who was certainly a sorceress, though of a sort not found upon earth, communed with the whales. She did this in another tongue, like a high thin singing, until Pereban's ears were sore at it, and the white bear rumbled and took itself off along the strand.

"Do not you attempt to leave me," the queen admonished Pereban. "One comes to us to set us on the road you have advised."

But Pereban had only been viewing the weak sun, where it hung now above the shore. Having pronounced, he had wondered if the solar flames would be too fierce after all for an approach. But this did not look likely, so wan seemed the disc. As for Idune, she had made no protestation concerning fire. Though perhaps she was past caring, and preferred to burn after a life of frigid sleep.

The whales were now sinking again down under the water. For a moment all was still, as if no life was in the ocean. But soon came a colossal surge, so strong the waves a mile out stood to the sky, and the nearer waters rushed in along the shore, and went past the queen and Pereban as high as their breast or shoulders—but she had formed some magic barrier, so the thick water could not sweep them away. Then the whole sea appeared to part, and out of it there came up a whale so huge it was like a living mountain made of one gray pearl. And this creature, turning as it leapt, dipped down again in a perfect curve, but, not entirely sinking, and presented to them in the churning maelstrom its back, like an island.

"There is the chariot," said Idune.

And so saying, she stepped out on the sea, which bore her up, and Pereban followed her and found the water also bore him, so buoyant and unnatural it was. In this way they walked out to the whale's back. Coming close, one saw there were runnels and welts on the skin of the beast great as paths and lanes, and up these Idune passaged, and Pereban after her. Thus they reached the top of the whale, and found there a sort of ridge, and to the outcrops of this Idune tied herself with her diamond girdle.

"And you," she said to Pereban, "take hold of my waist and on no account leave go of me, or you will be smothered in the waters or cast off into the air."

"Have you then traveled in this way before?"

"Not I, but a selection of my ancestors have done so, whose histories you do not deserve to hear."

"And did they, these ancestors, thereby visit the sun?"

But Idune did not reply. She whistled to the whale.

And at this signal it plunged straight down into the ocean, and they were taken with it.

What a dive that was. It seemed to last an hour of terror and roaring, while the unmingled black and white boiled by, formlessly yet ceaselessly patterned. Idune's sorcery protected them from it within some cache of atmosphere, and Pereban grasped her so firmly she upbraided him. After the dive—came the leap. The great whale lifted at such velocity the sea became only a blindness, and then they broke out of it again and were shooting up through the sky of Dooniveh like an arrow, all clung round with syrupy boulders of the water.

The sea and the cold land fell away as formerly they had fallen nearer.

The sun drew to meet them at the apex of the whale's gargantuan bound.

Heat filled the air, and gilding, so they became all three beings of gold. And Pereban beheld the streamers of fiery gas which foamed from the face of the sun's disc.

"What of the fire?" he cried to Idune.

But again she gave no answer, and he could only trust

to her magic. For in these moments the radiations did not seem as mild as they had done.

A moment more and a blast like that of a furnace enveloped them.

The whale veered from the gust. Idune seized and snapped her girdle of brilliants, scattering the stones across space.

"Hold tight to me," she instructed, in a shriek, over the wind of the flight and the hiss and crackle of the fiery vapors. Pereban saw fit to comply. And therefore, as Idune flung herself off from the back of the whale, he hurtled with her.

The sea beast was already dropping from them, back toward deep ocean. But they, by sorcery or impulse or solar magnetism, fell upward still, and into the core of the burning sun.

A plunge to the depths, a leap for the sky, a passing through fires—

The heat had grown intense, but Idune resolutely screamed spells. Pereban considered himself toasted but not fried, and found that he could breathe the oven air. They fell rapidly through flamed auras and laval jets, into a hot billow-bath of cloud. And then they were spinning down a sky of orchid yellow.

"We shall die. I, who might have lived a thousand years or more—"

So Idune lamented, striking Pereban as he clung to her and they fell as one.

"To sleep is not to live," corrected Pereban. "Besides, though the air here is more volatile than the airs of Dooniveh, we do not descend at an excessive rate. And besides again, have you no magic to lessen our speed?"

"You might yourself lessen it, were you to remove from your pocket the heavy useless impedimenta I now detect clanking there."

"You are facetious. I will discard nothing."

"Very well. But for magic, I am powerless in this domain."

Pereban did not consent to the logic of this, but Idune was adamant. Meanwhile they continued to fall down.

Suddenly the sky beneath them cleared. There lay

revealed the country of the moon-sun world, like an unrolled carpet dyed with saffron.

It was beautiful and strange, as the moonland itself had been strange but not beautiful.

Pereban and Idune the queen stared beneath them.

No mountains were in sight, but instead undulating rounded hills and valleys. In certain areas lakes of water glinted, as if each were held in a golden spoon. A peach-colored forest sunned itself along the banks of a white-wine river; statelier trees, the buttered shade of crocuses, grouped about some imposing masonry.

"A palace or temple. We shall be shattered on its roof," observed Idune, coldly.

At that moment their fall was arrested. A twanging barrier met them and threw them off again into the air, but on their immediate return, let them lie. A huge net had been suspended between the trees, mysteriously adjoining the area of their descent. They sprawled upon it, safe in everything but dignity.

"Such heat," Idune presently exclaimed, perhaps spontaneously, or in an effort to retain poise.

To Pereban, the climate of the moon's sun seemed like that of an idyllic afternoon of latest spring or earliest summer. He stretched himself in the net, in weak languor, aware of the trilling of birds—unknown it had seemed in Dooniveh—and of other creatural noises in the forest. The sky smiled with a gentle ceaseless light. It must be day in this country for ever. Pereban was swept by poignant regret once more, abruptly thinking of the earth, where there was also night, and cold alternated with warmth. In that moment he heard some high-pitched trumpet notes and the thud of drums.

"A procession is coming," said Pereban to the queen. "Your advent was looked for. This lucky net proves as much."

"But I am in disarray," protested Idune, who was indeed.

Just then, the net began to lower itself and the travelers were let down on the honey lawn, before the architecture they had formerly stared on from above. Nearby, the procession emerged from the forest.

Its participants were clothed, one and all, in black, and

though they might represent warriors, scholars, musicians, and persons of the ruling class, not a single gesture or expression conveyed welcome. Not even those of the large yellow salamanders many were riding.

In the midst of the crowd was a carriage of bronze, shrouded with dark curtains embroidered by skulls.

"Madam—" hazarded Pereban.

"We are too late, as you foresaw."

In her dishevelment she was charming and pitiable, but no sorrow, and now no rage, informed her features.

After a minute, a lordly golden-haired man came toward them, riding one of the lizards.

"Lady," said he without preliminary, "if you are the White Queen of the land below, you must know you have been dilatory. Our king, Kurim, awaited you, prolonging his youth and strength. Your icy barren land is inimical to us, and so he could not go to seek you and was reliant upon his messenger. Getting no word in exchange, he at length assumed you had no interest in the match, although it was fated and any other could bring you no joy. He permitted his life, then, to run its regal span, grew old, and died but thirty hours ago. Now we bear him to his dead rites, in that building which you see."

Idune inclined her head, but that was all.

The lord on the salamander said to her, "Out of deference to your rank, and because of what might have been, we will permit you to follow the death car, and to render your tears with ours."

"There is no point in such an exercise," said Idune. "I have no tears."

The lord regarded her with displeasure. Then, signaling to the procession, he led it away between the crocus trees and into the pillared building.

When the black robes, the lizards, and the drums, had faded from sight and hearing, Idune shot Pereban a look.

"Here am I then, marooned in an alien country, lacking my status, my husband, and all my sorcery. It is your fault I have been brought to this."

Pereban said, "Your injustice to me is my due. Life itself is unjust and cruel. But I will now offer you that which I brought for you, from below—since in your haste you forgot it—thinking you would need it against your wedding." And he drew from the clanking pocket of his robe, of which she had complained, the silver casket that held the heart of the queen, or its essence, asleep. (It was this article the fearsome dog had *fetched* for him from the ink pool during their last game.)

"My heart," said Idune, gazing at the casket. "What use can it be to me now? If I receive it back—for such a spell is tenable even here—I shall suffer a pang of loss, my heart will wake and break and I shall die."

Pereban made to replace the casket. But Idune all at once stretched out her hand. "Give it me. Let me die, then. My life has been wasted."

Pereban handed her the casket, which seemed to dance in his grasp from the uncanny heartbeats. Idune took and opened it. She raised it, and partly turning away, secretively swallowed the contents. That done, she flung the silver from her. She stood like a statue, then gave a low cry. The young priest expected to see her any second drop lifeless on the turf.

Instead she darted round on him with her hair flying and her eyes ablaze.

"My heart—oh, Pereban—my heart is awake and telling me things. It says if I had listened to it at the start events would never have come to this pass. It is an angry heart, Pereban." And here she laughed. "Now it tells me, 'Go into the building of death.' "

Having said which, Idune rushed away through the trees and vanished between two columns. Pereban, agog, pursued her.

5 *Fire Work*

WITHIN THE EDIFICE, the funeral of Kurim the Sun King had entered a massive chamber, and there deployed itself.

The hall was lined by the trunks of enormous trees that had been carved and painted, to a confusion of colors and shapes, but which yet lived, and filled the roof with lacy ivory foliage. On the branches sat slender birds of a brighter yellow, with excessively long tails, and elsewhere grew thick clusters of golden fruit resembling grapes.

Into every space available below, save at the room's very center, crammed the mourners. All wore deepest black. Black-sheathed drummers raised thunder from their black drums. Others engaged in the threnody swung acrobatically across the upper levels under the arboreal ceiling, striking brazen gongs with their feet as they went. Maidens with hair like new-minted money howled softly and shook the sistrum. The courtiers and soldiers of the dead king posed with their heads bowed.

At the center of the room stood the catafalque. Both stage and coffin were of the same painted and carven wood as the pillar-trees, and strewn with flowers, edibles, and vessels of gold. Black-robed officers poured over the pile jars of wine, oil and perfume.

Pereban, who had entered belatedly, was unable to get through the mass of people. With some misgiving as to the act's impiety, he ventured to climb one of the ornate trees, using the shoulders, ears and phalluses of the carvings as foot- or hand-holds. Soon enough he had reached a high bough, begged pardon of its resident bird, and seated himself to look down.

From this vantage, he was well able to stare into the open bier. King Kurim, an elderly man who appeared no less than a hundred earthly years, reclined there, with all his chains of kingship, his rings and armlets and collars on him, and the royal diadem upon his wizened hairless brow.

(The pomp of the proceedings otherwise discomforted Pereban. He had been used to modest and apologetic festivals of death, whereat the gods' forgiveness was asked for the temerity of having lived at all.)

Idune, by dint of great labor, had meanwhile got through the crowd, and just now emerged in the space about the catafalque. She was noticed.

Radiant in her disorder, she waited speechless as the drums concluded and the mourners were silenced. The last gong was struck and its din moaned away. Idune slowly rent her robe so diamonds scattered again. She called melodiously: "Let me mourn with you. I also have lost my lord." And suddenly she wept, a rain of tears of all her months and decades of sleep, the store of grief kept by. So beautiful and passionate, so heartfelt, was her action, the very lord who had been repulsed by her churlishness on the lawn, now came to sustain her, and drew her to one side.

Pereban watched all this in disbelieving acceptance. Until—over the smell of balsam and grapes—there came to him the whiff of fire.

Men and girls stepped from the throng, carrying flaming torches, which they threw against the stage of death. Up it went. Every jot of paint and joist of wood, in its incendiary drench. The coffin became a fireball, and with it the corpse of Kurim the King.

The yellow bird beside Pereban gave a squeak, and the young priest bethought himself of vacating his perch. For surely fire let loose in such a room of wood was tempting providence, if not Lord Fate himself.

Next moment, a concussion occurred in the kernel of the pyre. White-hot shards and showers were sent in all directions.

But before Pereban could accomplish retreat, he was wholly distracted. A wonder was taking place.

Up from the collapsing pyre there rose a shining globe of golden light. Pastel rays beamed from it, and an intoxicating scent like that of a thousand unguents. From the violent discharge nothing else had caught alight—which was in itself supernatural. As the fires of the burning sank and failed, only the golden sun-bulb gave its glow.

Pereban gazed at this unusual light, and his own heart quickened. For a moment it seemed to him that the secrets of the intellect and of the soul were about to reveal themselves. And he forgot where he was, this otherworld to which folly had carried him. That did not matter, since all places were one, were nowhere and everywhere, and perfect truth stood close, hidden only by a veil of faint smoke— But then the golden bulb-bubble burst like a firework. Only magic and a miracle went on, and the high ideal of Pereban's priestly yearning was once again quite lost to him.

Yet there on the smoldering ruin of the pyre, broken from the fire-globe as a butterfly from its winding-sheet:

A young man. He was all clear gold, as the light had been, handsome, a king. He was clad in golden mail and a mantle of gold sewn with hyacinth stones and sunflowers of jasper and chrysoprase. On his breast lay the chains and collars of kingship, and on his fiery hair, the diadem. And Pereban realized this was none other than the ancient corpse of the king which, destroyed in flames, gave birth to itself again as a man in the fullness of youth and pride.

On all sides the courtiers were tearing off their black to reveal bright holiday garments. The musicians smote their instruments, the maidens sang joyously and waved white plumes. The birds in the trees preened, and grapes descended hard as hail.

The golden king stepped from his holocaust. The fire had done its work very well; not a surface of him that was not burnished. It seemed his memory, too, was reborn, unimpaired. He went directly to the spot where Idune was standing, with her topaz hair blown like thistledown and her silver eyes large as an owl's.

"I am honored by your presence at my funeral," said Kurim, the Sun King. Idune did not speak. Kurim took her hand. "You are more lovely even than I had imagined. And though I had been warned you were heartless, I see it was a mistake." Idune blushed like the dawn, a phenomenon unknown either in her country or in his. Kurim the king said, "Will you consent to be my wife and rule beside me? There is neither sadness nor sickness here. And when we grow old, if you wish, we shall enter the fire together, and so shall be reborn, as you have seen happen to me." Idune spoke. She said, "I never ruled in Dooniveh, I slept. It seems to me that never before was I ever awake, until you touched me."

Then the court applauded, the trumpets pealed, the birds twittered and flew about. And Pereban sat on the bough and considered the flawless completion of the mythic tale, as it was enacted below. But then Kurim and Idune embraced. And Pereban turned his glance away, feeling a vast impatience and a deep loneliness consume him.

* * *

The wedding of the Golden King and the White Queen was very lavish, as might be expected. The sunny city of that world resounded to the melodies and firecrackers of celebration. And all the nightless, winterless, untimeable day, which may have lasted three months by an earthly calendar, there was feasting and theater, game and show. But as, in any case, very little of a serious or business nature was seen to in the sun world, though the marriage was much enjoyed, its revels were not greatly out of the ordinary.

For Pereban, entirely forgotten by Idune in her bliss, meandered with the crowds, and soon enough learned he would pass as one of the sunworlders. Indeed, this was quite irksome because, seemingly their own, it was taken for granted that he knew all their customs, besides their history, beliefs, and details of their land and city. Fortunately, the language of the moon's sun was almost exactly that of Dooniveh, to which he had been made privy by Lord One. Nevertheless, Pereban was caused to be uneasy by his ignorance, and the astonishment it now and then elicited. Presently, finding out what was usual, he sought for himself an unoccupied and palatial apartment in the city, and dwelled there in the way of other unattached sunnish gentlemen.

The apartment was composed with many windows of gold-veined crystal. It was furnished with extravagant carpets, beds, and such domestic articles, and also with instruments of music and diversion that he was mostly at a loss to comprehend. Flowers grew within the buildings as without, and birds came and went as a commonplace, singing sweetly and fouling nothing. For food or drink one had only to wend to a public square or hall of the city, where choice dishes and vintages were endlessly set out for any who were inclined to hunger or thirst. The sustenance evolved by sorcery, or so it seemed, for though sometimes certain citizens took a fancy to serve their peers, this was obviously a fashionable fad. In the same way fruit hung constantly on the trees, requiring no attention accept perhaps praise and the casual plucking of the passerby. No rain fell, the weather never altered. The flowers did not wither, even when they had been picked. Tired of her garland, a girl would simply drop it on the earth, where it would take root in half a minute. The people of the sun were also ever young, though not immortal. At a great age they would die, apparently solely of experience. For Pereban beheld a funeral or two of this type, with the fair young corpse lying peacefully on its bier—and thinking the dead had perished untimely, commiserated, only to be stared at. He was then informed of the number of hours the deceased person had lived, which ran of course into intolerable billions, since the sunworlders had no other unit of reckoning *save* the hour. These were therefore measured off by peculiar clockworks in their homes, in groups of one hundred, and the score meticulously kept: Each individual clock was naturally halted upon the owner's demise, and buried with him or her in the grave.

Only the king matured and lived through an old age (for which he was highly respected and revered.) Then, by the power of fire and magery, he returned renewed. In that way there had been no king but Kurim in all recorded time. But there were no complaints on the subject. Inasmuch as a king was required, he fulfilled the post estimably. They had hopes, too, of the queen, no children having been born in the sun world for several lifetimes.

All this static ease and unchallenged idle optimism began to prey on Pereban, so that soon he could not bear it. He was the product of a dangerous and troublesome world, where babies were regularly produced in blood and pain, men and flowers faded and were cut down. As icy Dooniveh had distempered him, the moon's sun unnerved him utterly.

The day was never changing, and all things else.

He took to wandering about the stainless, litterless streets, where the people wafted by like blown kisses. He next went out into the landscape, where the fields and orchards and vines grew of themselves and invisibly harvested themselves. In parts he came on those who had abandoned city life for the pastoral. But their habitat was not much different. They were youthful and fair, childless, long-living, and the food and drink appeared on their tables in a manner baffling to Pereban.

One day of the Day—for the priest measured *his* time

by his periods of sleep—he happened on a crystal cottage in a crocus wood, and there sat two old people on a bench. He saw that they were old from their lassitude, though in looks they were as fresh as he; fresher, not having his cares.

A large salamander stalked the clearing, pulling rosy pears from the trees to eat.

Pereban paused, and greeted the couple.

"Have you," he inquired, "heard tell of the king's wife, the queen of the city?"

"Just so," said they, polite but yawning.

"I, like that woman, am a stranger here."

"Ah, yes."

"I do not understand your world, nor how you live."

"We are regretful."

"How is it," said Pereban, irked to outcry, "that you do nothing, yet are fed and clothed and kept in luxury?"

"So might all men be kept," said the old man, stroking the salamander with unlined hands, "if they wished it."

Pereban stared in anger. He did not know why he was angry. It came to him at last that, unable to regain the true earth, he was furious on behalf of it. Why should mankind toil and suffer, and these ones exist like the never fading lilies in the fields?

The old woman seemed to sense his confusion and his wrath, watching him through her shining, smooth-lidded eyes.

"Stranger," said she, "it is known here that other worlds exist, and plainly you are a being of one of these. I do not presume to help you, but I will reply to your question. Some choose hardship, to acquire lessons from it. All men, even of your world, might live as do we, for matter is mutable, or how do magicians play with it? If your world is harsh, as I believe that it must be, be sure that you and your brethren have in some form chosen its thorny paths, in fact invented them. Here, we are indolent. But do not despise our sloth and happiness. At this time it is what is best for us. Yet we know at length our souls go from us, and maybe are reborn into less certain climes."

Pereban glared on her, and then his fury left him. Tears ran from his eyes. He averted his head. But the salamander came and licked his tears from his face with a gentle tongue aromatic with pears.

"He weeps. In the cold lands below they do this," said the old man. "But I think the cold shore is not his home. Can it be he is of that earth the stories mention, flat as a plate upon a chaos-sea?"

Pereban evaded the lizard's consolation.

"Do you know then of the earth?"

"Without doubt," said the old man. And the old woman said, "Ah, he is sick then of wishing to go back."

Pereban fell at her feet. The gorgeous young old woman caressed his hair.

"Hush. You must seek Kurim the king. He is the magician, for he can grow old and die and return through the fire. He will listen to your plea and discover some means to free you of our land."

An hour following this dialogue, Pereban was running through the woods and over the hills toward the city of the sun.

He had been gone far longer than he knew. Nearing the suburbs, he beheld decorative colored smokes springing up, while bells, bangs and booms shook the ground.

Idune the queen, protected and soothed by sorcery, had borne twin infants, a boy and girl. These offspring of royal love would be fertile, as most of the sunworlders were not. Already petitioners clustered in hundreds about the palace, waiting audience to stake their claim to coition, some incredible amounts of hours in the future. Between whiles they sang and feasted.

Pereban was not able to approach.

In resignation, he joined himself to the rear of the petioners. Hours passed, seventy-seven of them.

"You are welcome. Your name?"

"Pereban, sire."

"Speak then, of your reason for wishing to wed my daughter, and of your qualifications for becoming the father of her children."

"Sire, that is not my purpose."

King Kurim and Queen Idune sat in chairs of gold above a golden pool where floated lotuses of jacinth. In a cradle close by the twin babies slept or dandled their toys. Should they not be concerned that their future marriages hung in the balance? In the land of the sun all was beauty and pleasure; they had no need.

Pereban turned to the queen.

"You do not remember me, Madam?"

Idune observed him sympathetically, for she now had a heart.

"Pardon me, sir, but I do not."

Pereban heaved a deep sigh. He turned again to the king, and related all his adventure, including the mishap with the winged horse, for by now shame had given way to self-experience.

At the end of the recital, Kurim and Idune looked askance at him.

"It seems that I do recall one man came with me on my journey," Idune murmured. "And that to his advice I owe my present glad estate. Forgive me, Pereban, that I mislaid you for a moment."

Pereban bowed, frowning and biting his lip.

Kurim the king said, "I have long credited the substance of such a world as Pereban describes. And that I am a magician he acknowledges. Allow me some hours to review the problem. If it is in my power, sir, you shall be liberated."

He had ridden a winged horse, and an up-diving moon whale. Now it was to be a lizard of gold.

This salamander was not real. It had been made, and in a leaping shape, its pointed face foremost, limbs tucked in and tail outstretched. Upon its back, a fixed seat with great straps of metal. Pereban had been secured within it.

"The sphere, in which our worlds rest enclosed, travels once in each of your time units through your chaos-sea. This idea is not novel to me," had said the king. "Calculations have been advanced. We will send you forth only while this sphere—which to you, you say, is your own world's moon—is above ground, in the air. The salamander will seek one of the vents of the sphere that lie, you explain, above the sky of Dooniveh, and by which you first entered. The salamander will open the vent by use of a sorcerous rune inscribed upon its forehead, here."

Pereban, mad with dreams of home, nodded. Now, strapped to his seat, the crazy flight before him, he doubted all—the calculation to avoid chaos, the opening of the lunar vent. Even so, he was drunk with longing. Let him attempt, or finish.

Far down upon the earth of the sun, fire toiled and flashed. Its heat was mounting. The riding-lizard was no more than an enormous firework. It must be set off. Like a shooting star—unknown here—and rushing upside down, it would cleave the vapors of the sun, the mists of cold Dooniveh, would breach the shell of the moon—or not. Freedom or death.

Pereban the priest flung back his head. He closed his eyes and prayed to no gods at all, but to some element of the universe or of his own self, which might hear and heed. *As you will.*

And then the fire cracked, sizzled. A huge flare corruscated all about him. The golden salamander lurched and launched itself.

Upward.

The sky was yellow, was boiling cloud—it ripped open, scalded, fell away— The sky was gray, blind, it dashed and simultaneously froze. Something dark tumbled upon him. A roof, the moon's ceiling. The lizard tore like a dagger toward some mark. An impact. Machine and man were riven. *I am dead!* Not so.

No, death was not this. There was a vault of coolness and blackness, and sprinkled over it a million diamonds—it was heaven, it was the heaven of the earth, with the stars on its face like loving tears.

Pereban shouted aloud, and the lizard turned over. It pointed its pointed snout toward distant nothing, the unseen land. It plunged.

"So I shall die after all upon the rocks of the earth's breast."

Pereban sobbed and laughed. And fell, slower and more slowly. Until, like a giant dented metal flask, misshapen and spoilt and unrecognizable, the salamander dropped into a wreath of cypress trees beside a river. Caught in their branches, it shivered and was still.

Pereban, smelling the cypresses, the water, the night wind and the starlight, said, "Earth, my beloved, I will not resent whatever stricture you put on me. A tiger may come and devour me, or a serpent bite me, a plague seize me, a man cut my throat, for they are the citizens of my world. I open my arms to all, the fine, the good, the dire, the bad. I am home."

Now they say he went to search thereafter for his own town under the parasol of the mountain. But by then the goddess Azhriaz had received a reprimand from the actual gods, and her City and many of the lands of the City were destroyed, Pereban's birthplace with them. So then he went elsewhere to live his mortal life, and leaves the tale by this gateway, and no more is known or said of him.

But there are others who say most of the tale is anyway a lie. And these sources stress that the moon of the Flat Earth was not as Pereban's narrative suggests, but only a silver disc, changing its shape at the shifting reflected shadow of the world. And they declare that Pereban, having ridden into the sky on the back of a horse with wings which the Vazdru bred, ended that first fall in an earthly gorse bush. The rest of the fantastic yarn, say they, he later invented, to cover his nakedness and his embarrassment. But all storymakers are liars, and the world now is round, and not as it was. Who can tell?

Now after the casting down of her city, Azhriaz fled the rage of the gods (if they were capable of raging). Several were her ventures then. She lived, too, for a while as a child, and then her tutor and guardian was the priestly healer Dathanja.

At last the Demon's daughter renounced her immortality in favor of True Life—the body's death, the soul's continuance. Then she was Atmeh, "Soul-Flame." And having found once more her lover, Chuz, knew a time of unclouded happiness, it is said.

But her father, Azhrarn, Prince of Demons, displeased at the failure of his plans (and by other matters), cast her off, and cast off with her all humanity, saying he was done with it for ill or good.

Yet, being what he was, it may not be supposed he lost all interest in the earth.

BLACK AS A ROSE

THE DESERT SPREAD like a huge lion, sleeping, and by day its hide was the color of powdered turmeric. But by night the moon paled its flanks to ash, the color of dead dreams. Very little grew in the desert, save for the sand, which proliferated constantly. Here and there a well of smudgy water, a tree of thirteen leaves, might entice the infrequent wayfarer. The native creatures were few and stirred mostly after sunfall.

Somewhere in the west of this waste there lay a ship.

How it had come there, in the midst of the sand, even those who had seen it could not decide. The general opinion was the vessel had been stranded millennia ago, when a sea then occupying the region soaked underground by magic. The ship was of an ornate mode, carved and gilded, with a lily prow and a stern like a fish's tail, having two masts and triple banks of oars. And some odd property either of the spell or the ship itself, or of the desert dusts in concert with such things, had totally mummified the hulk, even to its two sails, turning it into a galley of salt.

Below, a long pool of clear water was colonnaded by tall palms, and fringed with thickets of locust trees, fig and lilac.

At this place, several ancient tracks and highways had once converged, but the sands had mostly eroded them. A small shrine to a stone god stood above the oasis. Between the shrine and the ship of salt, sequestered in a garden, was the green-eyed house of Jalasil.

Before her death, the mother of Jalasil, who had been

a sorceress, set on this house many protections, that her only daughter might live there in security. And this Jalasil had done until young womanhood. She was tended by three old servants, who had been her mother's, and seldom saw any other being. Meanwhile she employed herself with the library of books and the life of the garden. Though sometimes she would sit for hours of an evening, gazing through the tourmaline panes, now to the east and now to the west, the north or the south. Green-eyed like her house, Jalasil was neither happy nor unhappy, yet now and then, at her gazing, she would take up her harp and invent brief songs in a minor key.

Across the desert came a band of nomadic young men. In these days the teachings of the priest-magician Dathanja had started a new vogue in certain quarters of the earth. His creed, both cosmic and precise, had a flexible simplicity which, usually, was soon harnessed and complicated by his devotees, or those who had picked up some smattering. The young nomads had, not one of them, ever seen him, or heard his parables first hand. They had come to a grasp of the physical liberty he conveyed and to the wandering and mostly possessionless state he typified. Too, they had some kindness, creativity and healing to impart, and did so, while none of them had ever committed evil, or—more to the point—ever feared evil. Yet their souls were younger than the soul of Dathanja, which had lived in any case two lives in one.

The leader of this group bore the name Zhoreb. Like Dathanja himself, he was dark of hair and brow, a fact Zhoreb had not failed to notice. Beside that he was tawny from the sun, with eyes the shade of some inundating river. He walked with the courage and pride which health and intelligence may bestow, and his comrades followed him gladly, as pleased by his qualities as by their own.

They went where the land itself led them. Finding a hill, they would climb, a valley—descend. Coming on the remnant of a road in the sand, they took it.

By day they strode, resting only at the sharp peak of

noon, where they could in the umbra of a rock or tree, or else merely under their own mantles.

When night closed earth and sky, they made a fire, for they gathered dry plants and husks as they came on them, and sat under the vast arch of desert heaven packed with fruiting stars and a moon near and huge as a cartwheel, but shadowed like a skull. Here they drank hoarded water and ate such eatable stuff as had been found, while the eerie hymns of animals arose for miles about on every side. Then they told each other stories, and mused on the reality (or otherwise) of life and the world. And sometimes, being young and high-spirited, they ran races or performed acrobatic feats, or played at other competitions of skill both physical and cerebral.

At the third dusk in the desert, as they were settling themselves by the decayed road under a tree of only seven leaves, one of the company remarked, "See, Zhoreb, there is a fellow traveler."

Then Zhoreb got to his feet again, and looked away over the ashy dunes. And sure enough, against a rising moon, one came toward them.

"He is clad all in black. Yet," declared the young man who had spoken formerly, "he has no priestly look to him."

"His hair is blacker than the night. Are those the stars themselves caught in his cloak?"

"The cloak beats slowly, like two wings of an eagle."

"Perhaps," said Zhoreb, "a mage."

"And *listen,*" whispered another, "how quiet the desert has grown. As if the wolverines and jackals held their breath to hear—"

"Sir," called Zhoreb boldly, "you are welcome to join us at our fire. We have little to eat, but will gladly share with you what we have."

The figure paused a short distance from the road. The moon now stood behind his head, making his face difficult to discern, but for the somber flash of two black eyes. Black as the eyes of Dathanja they were, and much blacker.

"Since you invite me so courteously," said the stranger, "I will sit down with you. For your food, another feast awaits me where I am going before sunrise. I will not, therefore, trouble yours."

His voice was so thrilling, so melodious, and held such extraordinary power, that even Zhoreb hesitated at it. But one of the band, the youngest of them maybe, broke into a merry laugh. "Why, here is a boaster! Pray tell us, sir, where in all this wilderness and night do you intend to *feast?*"

Just then the stranger moved and stepped onto the road. The fire caught him in a glass of gold. He had the beauty and the presence of a king, or that a king should have. And all the night was his, no wonder it fell silent at his approach, or sought to feast him.

"Where?" he said, and smiled a little on the youngest who had mentioned boasting, so the boy himself grew moon-color. "Why, *under your feet.*"

Then he passed by and sat down among them, across the fire from Zhoreb. And Zhoreb sat in some haste. And after this, for an interval, it was so noiseless there the flames had a sound of breaking bones.

But the stranger, having turned his rings—and magnificent rings they were—upon his lordly hands, the nails of which were very long, squared, and enameled silver, glanced toward the desert and said, coaxingly, "Go on with your music, my children."

And at that such a tempest of nocturnal howls and screechings and whistlings and chirrups burst from the sands, for some thirty or sixty miles in all directions, that every one of the priestly band of Zhoreb jumped in his skin, and almost out of it indeed.

"And now," said the stranger, returning his regard to Zhoreb, "let me delight in your philosophical debate."

"My lord," said Zhoreb, who did not know fear or evil, yet fancied he espied them, "you are, by your appearance and your state, surely the superior in knowledge. How shall we presume? Let us rather, my lord, attend to you. Or keep dumb."

Then the man laughed. (A rill of velvet able to slice steel.)

"You are of the wise, Zhoreb. Is that then through the teaching of your mentor?"

"The teachings of Dathanja are imperfectly known to us. Yet we value his example."

"Do you so? Yet, at his inception, he was a simpleton, and a perpetrator of enormous wrongs. This you will also know, doubtless."

"It combines with the sum of his message."

"Which is?"

"My lord," said Zhoreb, lowering his riverine eyes from the eyes of the stranger, which were not like eyes at all, but like the sky or some space beyond the sky, blacker and more bright. "My lord, I beg to be excused from delivering to you my faulty rendition of the whole and remedial testimony of that man."

"But you have expounded it to others."

Then Zhoreb, caught between his faith and his astuteness, fell. He chose faith. He said, "The basis of the doctrine is purely this: We enchain ourselves. Even in fetters of iron we might be free, but in gossamers, more often than not, we load ourselves, put out our own eyes and break our own backs. For, though he had performed wickedness, Dathanja was able to cast out his own sins, to be free of them, and so to sin no more, being free to do good. And there is none that may not change himself, whatever he has done, or become, or is."

"Thus?" said the stranger. "How you do astonish me."

And again a silence—the length and breadth of the desert as it seemed, as if every creature and every grain of sand had gone to granite.

Then Azhrarn (and not one of them by now, being educated, did not realize but that Azhrarn it was) made a mild gesture to the fire which altered to the starkest white, as if ice leapt and burned there.

Pretending not to heed it, even while the young men drew away, Azhrarn said, "In gratitude for your frank admission of faith, the reckless bravery of which act is to your credit, I will myself offer you a parable.

"Supposing," continued Azhrarn, "a man comes upon a ship in the midst of the desert. Probably he will immediately think to himself, 'Behold, once there was an ocean upon this land which the Sea People, who are sorcerers, dispelled for some mischief. All was destroyed save this one vessel. Stranded here, it has fossilized and remains an object of wonder, a visual tract upon the impermanence of things.'

"But suppose again," murmured Azhrarn, "that in truth the ship had been set in the desert at the notion of some magus, who preserved it there against the sand and the wind, and gave it also the semblance of antiquity. And he did this for no reason of any consequence, except maybe to cause a man, observing his work, to review the evidence and draw a false conclusion."

The fire fluttered, blushed, resumed its proper hue. Across the acres of the dunes, a hawking owl mewed at the moon.

None dared speak after Azhrarn had spoken, but for Zhoreb, though some minutes he did not. Then, sensing the Demon's eyes on him, Zhoreb said this: "Your instruction, my lord, shall be much valued. All the more so since it is yourself who give it."

"And what is your comment upon my instruction, O student of Dathanja the Priest?"

Zhoreb considered. Then he answered, "In the land of my childhood there was a saying, as follows: 'The black rose does not anywhere grow. Therefore let us fondly believe in the blooming of the black rose.' "

Azhrarn was standing some way off. The wings of his cloak beat slowly, and the stars hung in its threads or feathers.

"Where I shall feast presently," said Azhrarn, "black roses are woven in the garlands. Enlighten them therefore in your childhood's land: The black rose blooms. No longer believe in the black rose."

And having told him that, Azhrarn vanished and only a dark and flaming cloud was there, which sank at once into the earth.

Now, at long last, Zhoreb's band started up and ran about in dismay. But Zhoreb sat where he was and fed three twigs into the fire.

"Zhoreb—what shall we do?"

"There is nothing to be done. Demons exist." And then Zhoreb smiled and added under his breath, "Therefore we need not believe in them."

* * *

Jalasil, having gazed long through moonlit tourmaline, lay sleeping in the burning morning.

The elderly woman who was now her body-servant, entered and, beginning to arrange her mistress's toilette, announced, "My little sister, going to get water at the fountain, found a company of young apostles in the oasis."

"They are welcome," said Jalasil, listlessly, for she had experienced strange dreams at sunrise.

"My little sister says they are a fine bevy of young men. They were marveling at the ship of salt and had not even seen this house behind the locust trees."

Jalasil's body-servant was a lady some eighty years of age, and her little sister was just seventy-three.

"Madam," added the elder sister, "may it please you to send food to these worthy lads, or better yet, to permit us to serve a meal for them in the kitchen. They are holy men, and it is a great time since preachers and storytellers visited the place."

"Yes," said Jalasil, under the web of her light hair, fine as frayed silk, which the woman combed with sandalwood, and still under the heavy weight of dreams. "It is three years since any passed this way. And who they were, I forget."

"Only some meager merchant and his poor slaves. And before that, two pot menders who had words with the boy." (The boy was the porter, an adolescent of sixty-nine summers.)

Soon it was arranged over a tray of ornaments—all of which Jalasil declined—that the elder and little sisters, and the boy if so disposed, should invite the travelers to a supper.

Later, Jalasil learned that the social event would go on in the open air, for though they did not spurn the comforts of four walls, the priestly travelers, wherever possible, did without them.

Accordingly, at sunset, down the path to the pool went the two old women, veiled, as was thought proper either in those parts or in their youth, and the boy leaning on his stick.

Jalasil, who had given slight heed to any of the matter, was glad enough they should have what novelty was available.

But, as the evening advanced, the stars broke out of their prisons. Lamplight and fireflies gleamed in the weft of the thickets. She grew restless. At length, donning a veil herself, Jalasil also descended from her house.

The air was still and tinctured with the spices of the desert, and the salad freshness of the oasis and its water. The fireflies flickered in golden strands, just as sometimes they strung themselves among the flowers of Jalasil's garden, inducing in her nostalgias for which she had no name. In the pool, which now came visible between the fig trees, lights of four or five lamps extended.

But under his shrine, amid the crickets' strumming, the faceless stone god was blank, offered no counsel, and the young woman in kind paid no attention to him.

She stole to the darkest edge of the water. She was by nature retiring, and it did not occur to her to flounce among them as the owner of the spot. Instead, where the lilacs grew and a fountain sprang from a rock, composing herself, Jalasil looked on.

The priestly nomads sat with the old people of the house, eating and drinking and exchanging pleasantries, as if they were all of one family. (Which the nomads' teaching would in any event perhaps have said they were.) Now and again one of the young men would tell a story or anecdote, in meaning religious, or not. But as Jalasil stood herself by the fountain, it fell Zhoreb's turn.

Now when he began to speak, Jalasil looked at him with keen attention. The lamplight made him out to be of gold, and the shadows addressed themselves to his hair and eyes and clothing in order that the gold might show to more advantage. It seemed to Jalasil that she had seen Zhoreb on many previous occasions. This unnerved her, for she had not often seen any save her household. And of those strangers who infrequently passed through the oasis, none she had looked on had ever struck her as memorable. So then she could not think how she had ever seen him or heard his voice, which told the story of Dathanja as he himself had been told it as a child. And eventually it came to her that perhaps she had seen him when she slept, that she had chanced on him in her dreams.

Just then, Zhoreb concluded the unusual history of Dathanja, and, glancing about at his hearers, added, "And in the manner of this ideal we strive, though even that not too onerously. For piety itself may be used to make a chain about the soul."

"And does this then indicate that you are free also to enjoy yourself with women or men, as your appetite prompts?" inquired the little sister of seventy-three, who was inclined to be saucy.

But Zhoreb laughed. "Lady," said he, "there is no ban on love."

And when he replied in this way, and looked smiling round, Jalasil's heart seemed to cry out within her—*Ah! I could tell you*—

"For love," said Zhoreb, "is the clue to all life, of the body and the spirit both."

As he said this, his eyes seemed to fathom the lilacs. They seemed to meet the eyes of Jalasil and to fire up, so she saw their color, which was of green like her own, and of a river's brown and silver, too, the colors of that which, brimming, would slake and make flower a desert.

Jalasil was filled by fear. Her heart beat and her limbs were leaden. But quieter than a ghost she went at once away.

Early the next day, at dawn, Jalasil—not having rested a moment of the night—summoned her body-servant.

"Well, and did the traveling men enthrall you?"

"Madam, it was a treat to be sure." And the servant spent some minutes in describing the interest she and her sister and the boy had had, and how it had benefitted them.

"I am rejoiced for you, and only sorry your entertainment lasted but one evening."

"No, madam, there you would be wrong. For these good men have agreed to linger by the pool another day and night, being parched of the sands."

"Then they are not gone," said Jalasil.

Shortly after noon, when three quarters of her household snored, Jalasil began to pace about the chambers. And she said to herself, *I have never seen that man before, he is nothing to me. Let me steal down now, for they will be slumbering under the trees. Probably I shall not be able to tell one young man from another.*

And she felt great uneasiness as she considered this, and was loath to go, so her limbs felt heavier than lead and iron together. Yet she went for all that. Down the path from the house, swathed in her veil, Jalasil crept like a thief.

Most of the nomad fellowship reclined in the shade under the locust trees, but three of their number, of whom Zhoreb was one, had elected to bathe and swim at the pool's lower end. It was a private spot in the normal way, screened round by the trees and bull rushes. Jalasil stole upon it like a lioness. And before she knew what she did, she stared through the screen.

So she saw Zhoreb, to his thighs in the shallows, and naked.

His hair was wet and fell about his face and neck in blackest coils. The drops of the water starred his tawny body like pearls across dark ivory. The gems of his breast were like cinnabar. From his shoulders to his waist he seemed carven, so flawless was the proportion. At his hips he was straight as flesh ruled between two lines, and sheathed in the black hair of his loins the serpent of his manhood lay, blind, innocent, and sleeping. Just then he turned, unaware of any scrutiny, to pluck a pod from a branch above. In his back, the spine and ribs flowed under the skin, like a river under ivory.

Jalasil fled.

"What you have told me concerning these holy men has impressed itself upon me," said Jalasil to the elder servant woman. "He that you say recounted the life of their teacher—send for your sister to fetch him to me here at sundown. I would hear the story, too."

"Why, as you wish, madam," said the woman, puffed to find her praise so influential.

But then her mistress seemed to grow instantly sick. She was pale and trembled. Nevertheless, she bathed and had her hair combed afresh with sandalwood. She put malachite on her eyelids and dipped her nails into rosy lacquer, and, having seen a man in his nakedness, dressed for him in a gown like a butterfly's wing.

* * *

Zhoreb entered a chamber of the green-eyed house. It looked on a garden, where vines and roses grew, and the lilacs of the oasis in more constricted forms. The air was sweet with the flowers, and from other aromatics.

On a couch sat the household's mistress, turned a little from him, seeming to read a book with covers of thin jade.

"Lady," said Zhoreb, "I and my companions thank you for your bounty, the dinners of your kitchens and the freedom of the water. What may I do in return?"

Jalasil set by her book, as if reluctantly—for she kept her eyes only on it. "I would hear something of your philosophy."

So then Zhoreb, seating himself at her invitation on the couch which faced her own, began to speak of all those things his faith entailed. He was most eloquent and besides, in dealing with a woman both arrogant and shy, he exercised tact and mildness. But he wooed her with his words also; he strove to penetrate her heart with the light of the teaching. For, like many who think they have found the one true key to life, he wished it given to all the world.

And as he spoke, he was gladdened to see that Jalasil became responsive. She commenced to look at him, at first doubtfully, and then searchingly, and soon with some intensity. And when he made humorous allusions, she laughed delightedly as a child. And when he discoursed upon the darker aspects, she was anxious. Two or three times her eyes filled with tears. Zhoreb believed he had moved her, which he had, and so helped her—which he had not. Unfortunately, as he urged her so winningly, supposing he led her to consciousness, it seemed to her he exerted himself to such heights because he had discovered something in her which had charmed him. And his clearness and brilliance appeared to sparkle up from the same wild fount by which she was brightened. An interplay of energies wove between them like a fiery net. Then Jalasil was able to meet his eyes, to mingle her eyes with his without fear but with a terrible excitement. And meanwhile, struck by the virtues of his mind and spirit, she saw him to be not merely handsome of person, an object of desire, but admirable, a tutor for her ignorance. In short, she fell deeply in love with him. But as she did so, the morning waned, noon passed overhead, afternoon settled, and Zhoreb, despite a plying with fruit, confections and wine, started to feel rather tired under this relentlessly seeking gaze.

"Well, madam," he said, "I must leave you now. The day is drawing on."

At once Jalasil was flung from her pinnacle to a freezing depth.

"Pray remain and dine with me. I must give adequate return for your kindness and your lessons. For I shall treasure them."

At that Zhoreb, who, it must be remarked, had been flattered by her attention, his success, seemed to hesitate. As if, in the tiled floor, he suddenly beheld a pit concealed under a shawl.

"Alas, madam," said Zhoreb, "it is the custom of my fellowship to take our evening meal always together." This was a lie. He did not like to tell it, and blamed her at once for forcing him to do so.

Jalasil, unaware of her crime but sensing his coolness, averted her eyes again and said, "Perhaps then you would return to the house later in the evening, at an hour which is convenient to you. You will pardon my request, I know. You have divined we are starved here of informed conversation."

Then Zhoreb did see the trap and checked at it. He felt a dim anger, for it seemed he had been sported with, made a gull. It was not life's truth this idle silly woman wanted.

"I will return if you wish," he said very coldly. "But may not then linger. At dawn tomorrow we must be on our road, my brothers and I."

Jalasil's heart started up and fell down. At the same moment she felt the sting of his look she could no longer meet. Her cheeks burned. She thought, *He judges I have propositioned him.* So then she entirely averted her face and said haughtily, "By all means. Do not trouble then. Go as and when you please. Shall I send you money by the servant?"

"We take no money," said Zhoreb in a voice of whips.

"Oh, then it must be given you in kind?" asked Jalasil. "Like the dinners." For now she was hurt enough she must strike back.

But "Madam," said Zhoreb, in a voice of scorpions, "I beg you, have them serve us no food or drink tonight. We have indulged too freely in the shackling greeds of the body. The figs of the trees and the water of the pool will suffice, and they will cost you nothing."

And on such a parting, he left her.

Night covered the world, and in the garden of Jalasil the lilacs and the myrtles were gray, and every petal of the vermilion roses—black.

Wake, said the night to many things of the desert, the phantasmal owls, the wolf-faced foxes. Yet, *Sleep,* the night said to humankind, where it came on them in their sandy shelters, by rocks and wells, or in a silk-hung bed.

"I cannot sleep," said Jalasil. "Night is too restless. It rings with unheard sounds. It speaks in my ear saying words I cannot recall. The moon gapes at me. The shadows are so thick. Under my lids colors surge and fade. I ache. I cannot be still. I can never sleep."

Then she did sleep, and dreamed Zhoreb lay beside her, staring at her with his riverine eyes.

She woke and wept and did not sleep again.

Before sunrise, said the little sister, the young men had vacated the oasis. When she went down to fetch the water from the fountain, all trace of them was gone. Such a pity. They would be journeying *that* way, said the elder sister. Their leader had told her so. A town lay there, ripe for them, no doubt.

"Our lady is behaving oddly," confided the elder sister later to the little sister. "I do not know how to make her out. She will eat nothing, only drink wine and water. She sits with her harp in her arm, but makes no music."

At noon, when the sun was a spike driven from the sky into the earth, three quarters of the house succumbed to snoring. One quarter, Jalasil, with her veil over her head, went out of her gate and took the incoherent track which led toward the days' distant town.

As she walked, the sun smote her and the sand glared up into her eyes. Her feet were scorched, and she shivered.

I must go to him and sue for forgiveness. Surely, surely I have wronged him, and spoken uncouthly to him. That is the fault. Let me put it right.

It happened that there had been some contention, for the very first time, among the young men. Most of them had valued their sojourn at the oasis of the ship, the good food of the green-eyed house. "Fasting and abstinence may also be used to enchain," they quoted at Zhoreb. But he was determined. Supper was avoided, and in the pallor of false dawn they arose and left the place.

Before the heat of the day, however, they took refuge in a gulley by the road, not many miles from the oasis, for arguing had slowed their pace. Here one of the brackish wells contrasted with the memory of the pool's clean water. And they began again to grumble at Zhoreb, at which he finally lost patience.

"Return if you will," said he. "But for myself I shall not."

Then they wished to know why this was.

After some persuasion, he told them.

"The woman there, having nothing better to do, meant to play at love-matching me. It is no vaunt. I was embarrassed at it."

Zhoreb's company looked at him under their lids.

"Well, but," said one, "you have not been immune to women."

It chanced in the way a stone will tumble, or a leaf, that Jalasil at this instant had come upon that stretch of the track. She knew of the gulley and had even tended toward it, thirsting but confused as for what her thirst might be. So she had caught the murmur of their talk, and so she had gone nearer, thinking only to hear the voice of Zhoreb, a drink she craved more than any water.

And thus she spied on him a third time, unseen, and heard this:

"Girls I have had and not regretted, but they were my choice. She guesses me fruit on a tree and reaches out her hand."

"But Zhoreb," cried another of the band, "was she then so uncomely?"

"Not to notice either way. Certainly no beauty to be her excuse. She has two pale green eyes like a cat's, and no other feature of importance. But worst of all, she stares with those eyes like a hungry vampire. You know the kind of woman, who would split one's bones for the marrow." And at that they laughed, and so did he. "Therefore, let us get on when the sun leaves the zenith."

"You shake lest she pursues you?"

"Hush," said Zhoreb, though he laughed yet. "I have said too much."

"Not at all," said Jalasil, although she spoke only to herself. "It is proper you should say such things to cure me."

But she was not cured. She wandered away across the sand until, being clear of the spot, she sat down in the shade of a solitary boulder.

"Zhoreb," she said, "I loved you, I love you still. The one you say you met with was not Jalasil. For if you had met with her, you would not at least have despised her. But you met some other dressed in my skin. And I, some other man dressed in the skin of Zhoreb, who was kinder and more generous than he."

Then the day went on, and she knew the young men would have left the gulley, and she considered returning to the track, and to her house. But she thought, *All regions are now alike, for love and happiness are in none of them.*

She thought: *Even if he had kept himself aloof, yet been a friend to me, this would have contented me.*

But then she thought, *No, it is his love I wanted.*

And soon the sky turned red, and redder, and then the sky turned black and the moon came up.

How cold it is, thought Jalasil. *How the wind whistles and whines through the rock.*

At last she did return along the track, through the darkness. Once a wolverine crossed her path. She smiled upon it sadly. *Why did the gods make me a woman? What does such a beast know of love?*

At her house, Jalasil encountered some outcry, but she put it aside. She went to her bedchamber and lay there, in darkness. She could not bear a lamp, for her eyes had been dazzled by the sun. Even in the black, red petals fell across her vision. And in her ears ceaselessly rang and whined the sounds of the wind through the rock, but now they were inside her head; she could not elude them.

She yearned to die, but had not the courage to accomplish it. She yearned to *live,* and knew this was to be denied her.

My days are to be only this. Before, I did not know it. (For she had come to realize she had cherished some flimsy hope of change all this time.) *He is all the world, and the world goes from me.*

But somewhere in the night, over the restless lights and sounds, the notion came to her that at some hour her love, too, would burn out, and then she would be cold and bitter as the moon. The desert she should be then, sand, ashes.

The days passed, and a month or two they carried away on their backs.

A silence had come on the green-eyed house. It had never been noisy, yet it had been animate. Now the old porter-boy sulked in his lodge, the two old sisters tottered about or sat like two sticks leant on a wall. The youngest thing in the house had begun to warp and wither. They could no longer draw sustenance from a Jalasil warm and resinous, and suitably active at her tasks and recreations. They had found her out to be an unemployed and hollow-eyed and grieving hag, on whose forehead now, abruptly, a single vertical scar appeared between the brows, who walked with no lightness, who had all the ailments of one twice her age—aching and tingling in her joints, cloudy vision, hearing which heard such sounds as did not exist, an insomnia, a quarrelsome appetite—and since they found her to be this, and so could no longer think her a child, it came on them in turn that correspondingly, they, too, had aged. It seemed to have happened in three nights. An evil spell.

"What is to be done?" said the sisters. "If only her mother were here." And then they spoke of Jalasil's mother, which helped them recapture younger years.

They put Jalasil, her sickness and sadness, away in a closet.

Along the garden, the roses shed their blood.

Just before dawn, the old little sister, disgruntled from a dream, went to fetch water early. As she came down through the oasis, she saw a woman standing by the shrine of the stone god.

This woman was tall, and remarkable to look at in some not quite explicable way. For she was clothed only in a coarse robe and her feet were bare. Yet a wave of black hair sprang around her, burnished as the locks of some empress. And the long nails of her hands had been painted with silver.

"Now what are you wanting?" said the little sister, irascibly. "If you have come begging, you must get to our kitchen yard an hour after sunrise. Perhaps we may have some scraps for you."

The woman laughed. The little sister almost dropped her jar in fear.

"So you think me a beggar?"

The little sister frowned, squinted. The black eyes were haughty as a king's. She had none of the modesty or passive decorum of her sex, this female.

"Whatever you are," quavered the little sister, "I have no time to stand gossiping here."

"Nor I, indeed," said the woman. "Do you see that ugly glare in the east?"

The little sister looked. She descried the forecast of dawn.

When she turned about to tell the woman as much, no one stood there at all, save the ancient stone above his altar.

"May the gods preserve me. It was a demon!" exclaimed the clever little sister. And she spat on the earth and rubbed in the spit with her toes, made various signs, and wailed some gibberish she had learned in her infancy.

The manifest of a demon in the oasis provided the sisters—and the porter, who did not credit the tale, and enthusiastically berated them—with a busy and useful day. All about the house went the old women, sprinkling certain herbs and laying occasionally some talisman. Every orifice of the house, doors and tourmaline windows, they dolloped with nasty mixtures. Even the panes of their mistress' chamber were seen to. (Jalasil, seated like the blind and deaf, seemed not to notice.) "A blessing her mother was a witch," they said to each other, "and taught us a thing or two."

"Bah!" shouted the boy and shook his stick.

"Just like a man," said they. "Ignore the brute."

All told, much harmless pleasure that day gave them, and when the sun westered, the sisters huddled in a room above the kitchen, peering from its windows this way and that between vivacious fright and complacence. "It cannot get past the safeguards should it return. It will try to make a bargain. On no account must we speak to it. I recall one story of an elderly person who asked a demon to be made young again. And the demon said, 'That I refuse, but you shall get no older.' And struck her down."

"But I recall the story of a hideous one that the demon transformed to such beauty the whole world ran mad for love at the sight of her," said the little sister. "Even lions and tigers," she added, saucy as ever.

"Less of your squawking," ranted the porter below. He had left the gate and gone in to the kitchen, though he denied this was on account of the demon.

Presently the sun went down. The sky shone like wine in a golden bowl, then became pale like rosy ink in a bowl of platinum. And then the sky was the color of distilled lavender, and a cool breeze ran lightly through the garden as a cat, turning the heads of the flowers as they drooped.

"*Oh!* Oh, look and see!" screamed the little sister.

There, quite *within* the safeguards, in the garden, the black-haired woman stood, the demon, wrapped in a mantle on which the stars were coming out exactly as they did in heaven.

"Open your window," said the demon to the sisters, although perhaps not in words. (They were aware of a wondrous music; noiseless.)

"By no means," said the elder, "open the window."

They opened it, and leaned out chittering.

The woman looked up at them, her white hands and

face seeming to glow and float upon the gathering dark, like the white flowers of the garden.

"Listen well," said she. "You will conduct me at once into the presence of your mistress Jalasil, who lies this very moment drowning in despair upon her couch."

"What do you want with our poor girl?" cheeped the sisters.

"To give her," said this demon, "her heart's desire."

"This is a trick," said the sisters. We must resist these blandishments. We must not stir."

So they scuttled down and the little sister conducted the demoniac being into the house and upstairs to Jalasil's chamber, with the elder sister preceding them to announce an arrival.

Jalasil did lie as predicted, tossing on her divan in a cold fever.

"Madam," said the elder sister, "one has come to comfort you."

The night-haired woman with the kingly eyes entered the room. Where she stood, starlight and moonlight seemed to coalesce in a curtain of crystal.

Go out now. Be gone.

Out went the sisters, gone they were. Down to the kitchen and the porter, to crouch among the pots, muttering and clicking amulets.

The woman stood in her crystal curtain and beckoned to Jalasil across all the hills of oblivion.

"Return to the earth," said Azhrarn. (He might take any form, had taken this one.) "Come here, straying, limping heart. Do not make me impatient, waiting."

Then the essence of Jalasil seemed to fill her like water. It brimmed up to her eyes, and she opened them and saw; her ears, and she heard clearly. She sat up on her couch, staring, not knowing where she had been, where returned, who was there with her, and hardly recollecting, for that matter, who she herself was.

"Jalasil," said Azhrarn, in the woman's voice.

Jalasil recollected everything. Her face became a scarf of pain.

"Yes," said the Demon, musingly, looking at her. "These are the true lessons of love. Desolation, anguish, misery. Have you learnt them well, Green-Eyes?"

Jalasil could not speak. She moaned. A thousand speeches, ten thousand songs, lived in that one note.

"Well, then," said Azhrarn, "what reward do you say you merit, for becoming such a scholar in this school?"

Then she did reply. She wept. "He will never feel love for me, and him only I love, and that forever. He is all I want and all I may not have. The agony of this does not abate. It eats me away. I am poisoned. If only he had loved me!"

"He shall."

Silence.

Then: "Do not mock me," she said. Yet her eyes suddenly burned. Azhrarn was, even in disguise, what he was. She believed him. None, hearing him answer in that beautiful and appalling voice, could have doubted.

"There is some magic in you," Azhrarn said, "the legacy of your mother. I have devised for you a sorcery which, having been performed, will bring you this man, as a dog is brought to a bitch. Loins and heart, mind and flesh—all yours: Zhoreb, upon your leash."

Jalasil only breathed. The last of her strength seemed to leave her in that exhalation. Her head drooped as the heads of flowers before they fall.

"Give me this, if you are able. In return, what? Do you want my soul? It is yours."

"Your soul. Find a way to place it in a handy casket, I will take it with me."

"What, then?"

"To assist you," said Azhrarn, "is payment in itself."

"Yes," said Jalasil. Her condition was so heightened, she saw with more than sight. "It is a wicked deed, to suborn the will of another. And you are Wickedness, are you not?"

The woman made no comment. She said only, "I will tell you the sorcery whereby to gain your heart's desire."

Jalasil waited wearily, pale and stern, to hear.

"Descend to your garden. Search out there the season's final rose. Cut the stem. Cut a finger of your left hand. Give your blood to the rose and let it drink. Say these words: There exists in Zhoreb no love for Jalasil. Therefore believe in the love of Zhoreb for Jalasil."

Again, silence.

"And is that all?" said Jalasil.

"What more would you have? Take the rose to your chamber. Set it on your pillow. You will see a change. In seven days, he will be at your gate."

"Supposing that you lie?"

"You do not think I lie. Repeat the spell. Let us be sure you have it right."

"The final rose from the garden. Cut it and cut myself, the left hand's finger. Give the rose to drink my blood. Say, 'There exists in Zhoreb no love for Jalasil. Therefore believe in the love of Zhoreb for Jalasil.' " The fever had deserted her. She added in a deathly voice, "Yes, you do not lie."

But she was alone in the chamber.

Soon, Jalasil left the room. She descended and sought through her garden like a ghost. The sky was dark now, the moon in a cloud. She detected the rose not by its shape or color, but from its scent. She cut first one thing, then the other. She gave the rose a drink full of the poison of love. She said the words.

She returned to her bed, and let the rose lie on her pillow. She plunged asleep, was buried there, woke at sunrise. And on the pillow lay the rose, not faded, but black as coal.

Where he could, he ran; where the terrain made precipitate speed impossible, he advanced by great strides. As he went, he flung back his head and sang, or whistled the piping tones of the desert wind over. Even by night, while he could, he went on. The animals of the waste fled from him or hid from him. When he stretched himself exhausted on the ash of the sand, he dreamed of her. The dunes became her body, the fine dust silvered through his fingers like her hair. In the wells, he saw, sleeping and waking, her eyes. *Where he could, he ran.*

He had been in a town—some conglomeration of buildings—they had halted there, he and the band of young men. There had been falling out and abrasions. Some slackened, and Zhoreb beheld them as they succumbed to the whiles of the town, to patrons who took them up, fed them and soused them with strong drink, exploiting their abilities as if they were street magicians.

Yet others of the fellowship, too staunch in their views, going against a priesthood there, had been offered stoning and fled. Zhoreb went about his business, as he saw it to be, quietly. He healed, he addressed the crowds in the market. He did not speak against the town temple, which was less corrupt than others he had been shown. He waited out the squabbles, seductions, runnings off. One did not, in the teaching, enforce help. He waited to see if any union of the fellowship might be retrieved. For himself he would not deny, for denial was itself a snare, that he was no longer light, but merely restless. He experienced again and again a curious discomfort, as if he had left unfinished some vital act. Putting his hands upon the shoulders of an old man to ease his rheumatism, Zhoreb glimpsed all at once the fearsomeness of a world all of whose beauties and foulnesses, joys, triumphs and ailments were the creations of untruth. Nothing was real, and for that very reason, illusion had made itself into granite, the better to fake what it was not. To move these granite blocks, such as illness or pain, was simple—but then, the amorphous abyss lay revealed under one's feet. As the cripple straightened his arms, crying out that he felt warmth, then that his hurt had left him, Zhoreb for a second knew all the terror of one adrift in compassless space. *I have been a child at play with fires,* some voice said within him. *Now I see it burns, how can I dare?*

But he remained in the town, at its outskirts, where the hem of the desert was stitched. Sand drifted into his domicile, which was an awning pegged across the end of an alley.

Gradually, some of the nomad band returned to him, along with the poor and the sick, and the children who came daily to sit on the swept sandy earth under the awning. *Quickly, in haste, let us take up again the wandering life.* To be static was never wise. Cobwebs clung to walls which stood. Men must journey, for in motion lay the seed, or at least the symbol of progress.

But then, in the night, the awning's night which had no stars, softly something brushed into his ear. Like a petal—a moth—he started up and felt a golden chain riveted through his very soul with bolts of steel.

And by this, illusion in its turn displayed to him all its

awful and consoling power. The granite was immovable. The abyss, out of which anything might be summoned, vanished from sight.

He was glad. He was made drunken by the relief of it. Powerless, the student of Dathanja, Zhoreb cried aloud a cry that shook the alley.

He went from the town before dawn, telling no one of his purpose, himself barely conscious of it.

Somewhere, as he hastened along, under the burning-glass of the sun, it came to him it was love drove him, dragged him, thrust him. She—that woman in the house with eyes of tourmaline—she, with her transparent satin hair. He could not think what lay beyond the deed, which must be possession. He had seen it in her eyes—not famishment but entreaty, desire—they must have reflected the image in his own. For that very cause he had turned from her, put her from his brain into exile. But uselessly. She had fastened herself under his skull.

Love was the key to all things.

Illusion was granite, an immovable mountain.

Where he could he raced and ran.

On the seventh day the black rose crumbled into soot. There was a loud knocking at the gate. In her chamber, Jalasil, in a gown of colors, her hair combed with sandalwood, malachite paste on her eyelids, sat waiting.

He entered the rooms like a storm, dark flame, male energy, and the old women let him go up alone, as if they knew. They crept to their kitchen, as if they knew it all.

"You are here," she said.

He saw her, how she had been pared by savage need. He loved her for her suffering and her pallor, her green eyes, her hunger.

"Jalasil," said he. He came to her and raised her to her feet. His hands, which had healed many, and soothed many more, and which were not entirely strangers to the limpid skins of women, they clasped her. He drew her in, encircled her. He put back her head upon his arm and kissed her mouth. Her hair glided on his wrists. The touch of her hair, her body against his body, the pulse in her throat, the refreshment of her mouth, broke in the secret doors of a wisdom he had never dreamed of. Having her, he would possess himself. She was the key. The mountain must shatter heaven, they riding on the crest.

He lifted his face, to look at her. Her eyes, too, were pale, and far away. He did not mind it. He spoke all the love-words to her that the poet in him, that was, is, in all human things, knew to utter. They lay upon her bed. Her longing for him, her tortured yearning, palpable as the silk, had remade that couch.

He took her virginity with the gentle care of love, and with love's glorious violence. They rode the air, clove through fire and water, sank in the closeness of earth.

And when it was done, in the death-like honey of after-pleasure, he watched her lean above him.

"Too late," said Jalasil. "My heart had died of the wounds you gave it. If you had wanted me at the start, ah, how it might have been—sun and moon, earth and heaven. Stars would have fallen. But I have dreamed of you so often, I have dreamed you out. You are only a shadow, and even that shadow came to me, not from love of me, but through a filthy sorcery of demonkind, who hate all men, and all women, too. I have suffered and given too much to have you."

And then he saw her eyes as they were, cruel and empty, wanting nothing any more.

"You," she said, "you. You might have brought the best of the world to me, and I, perhaps, some comfort to you. But it is too late, you are a shadow, you are the demon's toy and trick. Zhoreb loves me, Zhoreb desires me. Therefore I no longer believe in Zhoreb's love and desire. Perhaps I am to blame. I made you a god. You are only a man."

And from under the pillow she drew the knife which had cut the rose. And he, like the sacrifice, chained in gold, felt only the granite mountain heaped on him, which there never was, or ever is, any moving.

"In my chamber," said she to the porter, "you will find a dead man with a dagger through his throat."

The porter lowered his gaze, as if he were only sullen.

Jalasil walked down into the oasis. Above, the ship of

salt glittered in the sunlight, and the water of the pool flushed bright below.

Taking off her girdle of green braid, she knotted it into a locust tree, and thereby hanged herself.

And here, through the day, she hung from her bough, and through the glistening noon she hung there. But in the afternoon, the shade came and garbed her round, mantling her whiteness, binding her eyes. In the end each trace of color melted into the ground. And night covered everything, black as a rose.

As a mortal, Atmeh lived long. A seer and healer, she dwelled for many years of her old age in a temple on a mountainside.

Yet she did not end her days there, but in another place.

GAME PLAYERS

WHEN THE WOMAN'S copper pot turned into a frog, she did not believe her eyes.

But there it lurked on her hearth, croaking and burping at her, a great coppery amphibian in which, plainly, it would be no use trying to simmer the broth. So then she came to believe—not her eyes—but the sense of injustice and frustration that swept over her. Had she ever had any luck? No. Therefore, small wonder even the one prize of her home should be ruined.

And "Out with you!" screamed she, taking a broom to it. "Out, you pot-frog!"

And she chased it from the house into the village street.

Save for this incident, it was a quiet evening. In the west, the sky still burned and smoked a little, but on the hilltops the stars stood in small groups, as if awaiting someone.

The frog capered off up the street. "Perhaps I dreamed it." But on glancing over her shoulder, she saw the hearthstone was empty. "Then, again, can I have offended the gods?" She had come to the conclusion that either the gods hated her especially, or, since she deemed herself unworthy of such attention, they were asleep. Married in her fifteenth year, her first husband had perished a month after, mauled by a lion in the hills. Her son, born dead, had in some way injured her and left her barren, and thus, when she wed again a man she did not like so well, he cast her off after three years as a wastrel of his seed. The last of her kindred, an aunt, had taken her in. Presently the aunt fell sick. At her death, the two-roomed house became the property of the niece. But she herself was by then in middle life, had lost her looks, and besides was reckoned unfavorable, under some curse. For nothing she did or had ever prospered—even her cows died, and the herbs in her garden were sour. The men of the village shunned her, and the women, who would sometimes give her the time of day, still called her *Unluck* and pulled their children aside at her advent, lest her passing shadow infect them.

On the hills, a couple of herders' fires had blossomed. (Unluck observed them a moment; once young herdsmen had admired her.) She turned back to her house, to search out the other battered pot which spoilt the taste of the food.

She was scouring it when the second thing happened. The second thing was heralded by a faint noise, like the sounding of one string on a harp, and when she raised her head at it, she saw a flower had sprung among the stones around the hearth. Perhaps a seed had lodged there and the fire now quickened it, yet how swiftly. It was a lotus, and even as she watched, the petals unfolded to form a goblet of the thinnest flower-skin, through which the firelight shone as if through alabaster.

The third event followed instantly on the second.

Unluck heard barks and angry rumblings in the street.

She got up at once and went to her door. "That pot-frog has caused some annoyance. They will suspect it is mine, accuse me of witchcraft and fine me." (Something similar had already taken place a year before, when someone's goat, having eaten an apple stolen from Unluck, had given three days of bad milk.)

However, on looking out of the door again, Unluck perceived she was not the author of this disturbance.

Several of the villagers were standing on the street. Lamplight from windows and doorways showed two figures set aside by the well, under the cinnamon tree.

"Yes, they will be beggars," said Unluck to herself. The village pushed all itinerants off, unless they could prove their worth. "How young they are, a young man and a girl. So slender she is, and so weary—look how she leans on him and he supports her." And then Unluck felt an inner qualm of pain and envy and other less translatable things. *So I might have leaned, had life been other. But who is there for my tiredness now?* But she put the quavering from her, pushed it down. She thought, *If I go after them when they are clear of the village, I suppose no one need know what I give them. I can spare a loaf, and a handful of dates, and the curds—I must warn them the gift may be unlucky, but in the past when I did this, I do not reckon I worked much harm.*

So then Unluck went back into her house again and started to busy herself assembling the food. While she was doing it, the altercation in the street finished, and the dogs felt their masters' feet and prudently grew reticent until presently it was easy for the woman to hear a soft scratch upon her open door, and in that way she heard it.

She had something of a shock then. For there under her lintel stood the two beggars. And they were not a youth and maiden, but an old, old man, thin and bowed as a winter branch, and she that leaned on him, she seemed older even than he, by a century or more.

A spasm of pity clenched Unluck's heart. She took up the bundle of food, and some other items besides, and went forward.

"Here, take these provisions. They say I am cursed, so it may be best to speak a blessing before you eat. But I think to have my unlucky bread will do you more good than to go luckily without."

Then the old man smiled at her. The smile seemed to smite out of his ragged cloak, his ragged face, and hit her a great blow so she nearly reeled. And as this went on, the ancient crone he held against him, she opened her eyes.

And oh, her eyes, her eyes. They were the sky at spring and noon, and summer midnight, they were the seas that were kingdoms, they were sapphires and the sapphire flowers of vines and mountains, and the color of mountains also at a vast distance, and the whole earth as the bird in flight might see it—so blue, so *blue* they were, they put out the light.

"Madam," said the woman, "lord—"

"Let us come in," said he. "The village shall not punish you for it."

"Fly blowings on the village, and may it be damned. Are they so stupid? Yes, and I always guessed as much, the clods. Enter and be welcome. I have nothing worthy of you, but since you are here perhaps it will do." And she stepped smartly aside, kneeled down on the floor and bowed her head.

The elderly couple passed into the room. With them came a muted, pleasing scent, such as would not generally be associated with antique and starving bodies. . . .

When Unluck looked again, they had seated themselves on her wide chair before the hearth. They were so gnarled and slight, so crumpled in, both fitted there.

Then Unluck approached on her knees and offered them milk and honey, and began to set the food on a low table.

"How tiresome that must be for the knees," said the old man. "Would you not prefer to stand up?"

"I know you do not ask me to kneel," said Unluck, "nor am I fawning. But I take solace in it."

When the table was ready she brought it close and added to the array a crock of beer.

"There is no harm can come to you through my paltry curse," she said.

The old woman spoke.

"But we require nothing. Only I—to rest, and that you have given me."

Her voice was frail.

Unluck stared at her and for the first time seemed puzzled. The eyes, the manner of Unluck asked: How can it be that you need *anything*, being what you are?

"Do not be afraid," said the old woman. "I am near death."

Unluck gasped. She blurted: "But can the gods die?"

Then the old woman gave a frail laugh.

"I am not a god. No, I am a mortal, as you are. And as with you, death will be nothing to me. For you and I, our kind, have souls, and so live forever."

Unluck gaped at her. Then dropped her gaze. This one existence of Unluck's had been sufficiently unhappy she had lost all hope, and perhaps all wish, for everlasting life.

Then the old man spoke again.

"My companion has been a priestess many years, aloof on a mountain. But she has an uncle—older I may say than she is—and he came to visit her, to bring her certain news. And so she undertook this last journey."

"I am a mortal," the old woman repeated in a sleepy whisper, like a child's. "It is fitting that I die where mortals are." And then she directed her wonderful blue look upon Unluck again. "I am called Atmeh."

"Lady—I have no name but what they call me. *Unluck.* I beg you, do not you use that name for me."

"I shall not," said Atmeh. She closed her eyes. She seemed peaceful, leaning on the old man, who held her so supportingly, so strongly, in his own fragility.

"No, we will call her *Frog,*" said he. "For she has lost her best cooking pot."

And then Unluck—or Frog—burst into mirth.

"Why, lord—was that *your* doing?"

"Mine," said he modestly. "Some call *me* Oloru. But I have another name. It is the other name makes frogs of pots."

"Well," said Unluck-or-Frog, "since it was your making, it is welcome, and the frog shall be welcome, if he cares to return."

And then it came about quite suddenly that there was no more restraint and no more suspicion of gods in that room. There was respect and concord. And the food was eaten, and the beer hastened between the old man and the hostess, and it had a taste of superior grapes, and in the same way the plates were never empty and the jars stayed full. And the fire did not need attention, or the lamp, which gave enough light for nine. And once or twice, when she glanced about, Unluck or Frog seemed to see a rare polish and gleam on her possessions and that there were more of them than she recalled having, and she felt such a weightlessness in herself and such a sparkle that finally she said, "It comes to my mind that once I was known by the name Flaxen. For I had in my girlhood the prettiest hair."

"Flaxen, my heart," said old Oloru, "pass the beer-crock."

But later yet, the lamp and the fire grew rosy and russet, and from the warm safe stillness of the house, Flaxen heard a nightingale singing in the very thatch of her roof. The beauty of it let tears into her eyes, but no pain put its claws into her heart.

From his cloak, old Oloru drew a kind of lyre, a botched and creaky implement, on which he began to thread music of gold and silver. The nightingale, enchanted, alighted on the sill of a window to serenade the lyre.

Then the nightingale flew into the house. A plain little brown dab, it perched upon the wooden chair, and chimed and chirred and rang, and filled the room with bells and stars.

"Long, long ago," said old Oloru, "when the gods were half awake and made things, they fashioned many animals and other creatures. Last of all they made a bird so exquisitely beautiful that the other birds, the peacocks and canaries, the ibises and swans and doves, went into a pet from jealousy. (For the gods' inventions are notorious by their errors.) Everywhere this bird was shunned or set on. It came to hide by day and to live by night, alone. After a while the moon, however, spied the outcast, and cried, 'Oh, how fair you are!' 'Hush,' implored the bird. 'Do not betray me. I wish you would burn my splendor up with your cold white rays.' 'That is not possible,' replied the moon. 'Beauty can never be destroyed, merely transposed.' And in that moment all the painted feathers vanished from the bird, he was drab and small upon his bough. But when he opened his beak to thank the moon, out burst a spill of melody at which the earth caught her breath. And does so yet."

And when the fire was red as a king's scarlet, the nightingale slept upon the chair's back, and the moon did come in person to the window. Then Oloru sang softly this, to the ancient priestess, and Flaxen heard it.

My love, my constant moon, within your light
I see that changeable other scale the height
Of sky, and know we shall be long-lost to her sight
In those far futures of the moonlit night.

And then the old woman murmured, "Beloved, that is not true of you. Do not forget, this is just a foolish form you took, to complement my own. It is not true of you."

"Of all things, beloved. And maybe even of the moon. Passing over the mirror of some lake, she may one night look for her own self in vain."

But after a few minutes, Atmeh said, so very low Flaxen scarcely made out the words, "It will be soon. Let us be going. I must not darken this kind house."

Then Flaxen resolutely said, "Lady, if it is a fact your final hour is on you, do you think I would turn you out upon the hill to die?"

Through the rose and scarlet, the sapphire distances of those eyes were casting their last look on a mortal face.

"I know you would not. But one will come to meet me on the road. He must not enter here, believe me."

And at these words, Flaxen felt coldness creep all over her. Without knowing why, she acquiesced.

The old man got to his feet. He leaned and lifted the old woman in his arms. You could not make out how he could do it, nor with such ease. But her little skull in its worn hood rested on his shoulder, her worn webby hair lay over his breast, and bending his head he kissed her. And then he looked back at Flaxen with a wicked fox's grin.

"I sense a madness in you, Flax-Hair. A madness to see what is to be seen. Follow us, then. But for your own sanity's sake—since the baskets overflow—do not come *near.*"

And in that way they went from her house, and along the silent village street. Not a single lamp shone there. Above, the herders' fires were out, and overhead the stars and the moon masked themselves.

Flaxen Unluck stood hesitating in her door. But then even her compassion grew skittish, for this night was like no other. And keeping back as he had told her, still she followed the old man with the old woman in his arms.

After about a mile, the goat-track came on to the brow of a hill and up against a tree. Here a figure stepped from the night. He, too, was garbed like a beggar, in odd yellowish tatters apparent even in darkness. His head had been shaved and he leant on a rotting staff.

"Greeting, un-relative," said he to the old man. "Is that my un-niece you bear? It is time then."

"Be wary," said the old man, "one patters behind me who has had such a life she will spit in your eye, should she fathom your name."

"But you have been busy since at your games, you two. Come morning, I imagine she will praise me instead."

And this bizarre exchange concluded, they went on together, and over the hill and down into a black hollow beneath. Here they stopped, and Flaxen, alert to old Oloru's warning, lay along the rise to watch from afar.

Shortly her skin was clammy, she was agitated and became afraid, although she could discover no reason. Then, as if broken by an earthquake, the ground itself, there in the hollow, was flung open like a colossal door.

Out from the dark into the dark came a night-black man clad in a moon-white robe.

Flaxen hid her face in the turf. If she had supposed the gods ever listened, she would have prayed. For she knew exactly who stood now not seventy paces from her. It was King Death.

Nothing was to be heard, save for the wind which blew sometimes over the hill. The company in the hollow did not speak, or else some wall had come between their voices and her mind. Curiosity forced Flaxen to look again.

And, as she did so, the moon also uncovered her face to see.

It was Death who held her now, that frail stick of a mortal old woman. He held her, and she had put one arm about his neck, as if in love and certainly in utter trust. To her lips he held a cup. It was of bone. She drank from it.

Flaxen gazed. The strangest picture filled her brain, so vivid that for a moment it blotted out the uncanny tableau. She saw a young man lying on this same hillside. A lion had mauled him as he guarded the flocks. The villagers were calling for him over the slopes, but he, in his agony, did not hear. Then there leaned above him a man, a man who was Death, and the husband of Flaxen caught at Death's mantle. Death said, "It is sure, you cannot live long enough to see her again." And then he lifted the dying man and gave him a sip from a cup of bone, and the agony left her husband's face. He said, wistfully, "Why, you have given me a drink of the beer she brews. How can this—?" But then he sank back as if he slept. And so the villagers found him, sleeping in death, alone on the hill.

"Death the comforter," said Flaxen.

"And unkind Fate," said the shaven beggar in yellow who had come up on her and now stood at her side.

Flaxen glanced at him, then back into the hollow. The moonlight once more was fading. There was a glimpse of a sleeping girl couched on a veil of midnight hair. A young man, all gold in the silver light, sat by her in silence. Death was gone. The earth was shut. And then the moon closed itself again away.

"I will see you to your door," said the beggar in yellow. "You know you know me, though we have never met. But do not spit on me. Tomorrow you will become my most fervent disciple."

Thus they walked back together to the village, the beggar-king, Fate, and Flaxen. She barely noted him. She felt all empty, not as if she had been robbed of anything, but rather as if she had been rinsed clean. If you had asked her who she was, she would have been hard put to it to say. And reaching her house, she only knew it because a nightingale was sleeping on the chair and a lotus grew in the hearth.

Fate, having seen her in, sauntered off up the street. Reaching the cinnamon tree, he dissolved, and was gone.

Flaxen lay down on her bed. She dreamed of an old woman who died and became young. Perhaps an hour before sunrise, she also dreamed that a chariot thundered over the sky above her roof. A man clad all in black and black-eyed as the dark, cracked a diamond whip above blue dragons. Something told her, even in her dream, it was not sensible to stare at him, and so she turned her face into her pillow. For all that, she heard the daggers on the chariot-wheels mincing the air to bits.

* * *

The dawn promised fine, and Flaxen opened first her window to emit the visiting nightingale, and next her door to see how the world went.

Then she sat in her doorway to comb her jasmine-pale tresses. Only fifteen years of age, and having property—the well-appointed house of a deceased aunt—and being besides a virgin and something of a beauty, Flaxen did not object to the admiring eyes and polite words of the young men wending up to the pasture, or coming down in turn from the hills.

She was popular and thought lucky, was Flaxen. Nothing she did ever went awry. Her cows were proud and full of cream, her herb garden put the rest to shame.

Basking there in the sunshine, not a member of that village knew that every memory had been changed in the night, or that Flaxen had herself been changed entirely. Yesterday was only yesterday, and last night nothing much had happened.

This morning, though, there was to be an event. Up the village street bounced a huge fat frog.

"Fate defend me," cried Flaxen, giggling, for she knew Fate would.

But nevertheless the coppery frog bounced right on and past her and plumped itself *splat* on her hearthstone. Where, in the blink of an eye, it altered to a round copper pot.

Flaxen clapped her hands with pleasure. But not surprise. Life had been so good to her that a domestic miracle of this nature was only to be expected.

But the mortal soul of Atmeh was deathless; nor was it done with earthly life.

THE DAUGHTER OF THE MAGICIAN

1 *The Butterfly Trap*

LORD RATHAK'S new bride wore satin and sorrow. The young girl had been vowed to a temple, which prospect she infinitely preferred to the demands of matrimony. But her father had then thrown a banquet and it chanced he had, at the peak of the drinking, allowed two or three choice guests to peek through the screens into the women's court. And one of these chosen, the magician Rathak, had espied there herself. "Who is that one?" said he. "She is easily the fairest."

"That is my youngest daughter, Shemsin. A dreamy girl. I am persuaded to give her to the Temple of the Three Goddesses. It is no daft thing to keep the priesthood sweet."

At this, Rathak had remarked, "By all means cut your blossom, but do not then cast it into a pit. Give the Goddesses some other. *I* will have that one."

Such was the power and influence of the magician, far greater than anything the temple could muster, that Shemsin's father quickly agreed. Thereafter, all former plans were thrown to the winds. A fortune was lavished on the betrothed maiden. She, having learnt early the futility of protest, resigned herself to wretchedness for, though murmurs of men entered the court of the woman, only the worst things were said of Rathak, from whose dark brain black deeds took their being. He was the familiar of fiends and had trafficked even with demons. His temporal sway sprang from the fear the king of the city had for him. Those who were his friends, and obedient, prospered. But whole graveyards had been stocked with his enemies. *It is my own grave I go to,* thought Shemsin. They dressed her and crowned her with jewels, and the bridal procession bore her away to the house of the groom.

It stood on a rocky promontory some miles outside the city walls. Though the surrounding lands were lush, this area inclined to barren stones. Below the promontory, however, on three sides, there lay an uncharted swamp, perpetually smouldering with vapors like some great cauldron. So enringed by quag and rocks, the magician's mansion was not easy to come at, though it might be seen far off from all directions. An imposing home it was, with domes of red bronze and black-green enamel, having to the north side a looming, bulging tower of brass.

The procession arrived and wound its way up a rocky road to the brazen doors. These flew open by magic.

Within there yawned a courtyard of black marble with a window-roof of blood and emerald.

Here Shemsin was wedded, with all legal forms, to Rathak Black-Wits, and glancing in stupefaction and awe into his face, Shemsin's bones turned to water. For no one had warned her that, as well as being a bad man he was also a handsome one, with hair as red as the roof glass and eyes as dark as the marble.

When dusk bloomed over the mansion's heights, uncanny spangles began to flirt over the swamp. Shemsin, led to a chamber in the brass tower, saw across the parapets the stony descent into the night and the ghostly luminants at their dancing. She no longer knew what she felt. She had begun to make allowance for the appurtenances of the house, since they were his . . . the curious screeching of unknown things in the mansion vaults, the line of horned skulls along a battlement. . . . He was her husband. She must not prejudge.

In a seven-sided chamber of spicery and musics, Rathak received her.

He kissed her mouth. "Dear wife," said he, "you must know I loved you at sight."

He gave her a green floweret to smell, its scent intoxicated her. He gave her black wine to drink, she sank against him.

"I have hoped, but not believed that one such as you existed, my Shemsin. You see, dearest girl, there is an ambition I have. And you shall help me to it."

He carried her to a bed red as poppies, rubies, fires. It stood within an unfinished circle marked with powders and strange gems, which, now within, he closed by the exhalation of a vial that steamed and flamed.

Shemsin lay naked on the bed, burning white into its redness, for her hair was very pale, her skin like snow.

Rathak caressed her, with his hands and lips, but firstly with a wand of basalt.

Acres below, the monsters howled in his cellars; spans away the phosphorus pranced in the swamp. Shemsin was lost. She raised her arms to implore him.

"Wait, my swan. Soon I shall be with you."

Then she beheld, drifting in the air, a glassy bubble. She did not know what it was, or care what it was. She cared only that he should embrace her. She cared only that he should invade her, deliver her—

"Presently, my swan, my moon-girl."

And then she saw the air was full of butterflies. They flew here and there, everywhere. They were transparent as silk against a lamp.

Rathak spoke the words of a spell. He drew himself upon her. He moved upon her like the sea upon a shore. She was the beach and he the ocean. She was crushed, she was torn. The waves ran through her. She leapt and cried to touch the sky and touched the sky and fell back, dead.

"No, Shemsin. You are not dead. You are alive. You are *doubly* alive."

"Do not send me away," she moaned. But it seemed to her the bed went drifting down. It came to rest far under the ground. She heard the monsters scream and turned upon her face and slept.

Sleeping, she saw inside herself a bubble of glass that now held captive a butterfly. The wings flicker-tapped on the glass until they grew weary. A chrysalis formed about the butterfly, confining it, so the wings could not move.

"Forgive me," whispered Shemsin to the butterfly trapped in the glass.

But in the tower of brass, Rathak Dark-Brain was planted now on a great plate of gold inside many new circles of symbols, powders and talismans. He was not quite as Shemsin had seen him, but for all that he intoned the words of an invocation and smote about with wands.

Beyond the protective circle and the golden plate, the floor cracked. Up heaved a hideous dwarf with a head of black hair for which many a woman (or a man for the matter of that) would have done murder. He was clothed solely in a metal kilt of exquisite smithwork, from which arose three enormous phalluses of silver, sprouting jade leaves and coiled by zircons. A Drin.

"Master," said the Drin, with a smirk that told you the title was not wholly sincere.

"Loutish little one," replied Rathak with adequate disdain. "I may say, it is accomplished."

"Is it?" asked the Drin. He jigged from foot to foot, then raised the left of these to nibble a toenail. He peered at Rathak. "Then you are on your path. Where is my share of your happiness?"

"A moment. I have employed your advice. But you were to have performed your own part, and are due to prove its value. That first."

The Drin pouted, lowered his foot.

"*Master,* you are ever cautious and erudite. Let me remind you that my caste has no truck with such matters. Therefore I must apply to others of demonkind, bribing them with bewitching presents from my own forge. (For that you are in debt to me.) It then chanced a mighty prince I serve heard of your needs. He took it on himself, much to my astoundment, to make sure your way. It is no trouble to the Vazdru to enter that *place.* And now," added the Drin, squirming with vainglory at the quality of his demonic associate, "this mighty lord stands in the psychic anteroom. He will, if you have sufficient courage, enter here and confirm your success."

Rathak might well have trembled, but he controlled and concealed his nervousness if so. "Does such a lord," said he, "require my invitation?"

At this, the air folded aside like a curtain. Into the chamber there stepped a dark, tall and slender man of such impossible handsomeness the false beauty which Rathak had donned for his wedding, was made, beside it, a figure of fun.

"*Azhrarn?*" murmured Rathak, dropping to his knees (with a swift glance as he did so to verify the circle was intact).

"His shadow," answered the Prince Hazrond. "I am sometimes taken for him, though never by those who have seen his manifestation for themselves."

"Excellent prince," said Rathak. He paused obsequiously. He continued: "Am I to believe that one, there, when he tells me *you* have concerned yourself in my business?"

"Believe it."

"Then—it is as good as done."

"Not quite, magician. You share in a common human mistake. The soul does not enter a woman's womb at its quickening. It comes later, when the child is grown, to fill and wake it and so send it forth."

"Then—?"

"In the foggy mire beyond the earth, I met your quarry. Being ready to return it was a simple affair to stay it in its incorporeal thickets, this butterfly."

"And it is *she?*"

"Neither he nor she, nor anything at present. But it was hers. It has all the proper marks. The soul that once inhabited the form of ebony, milk-crystal and sapphire that was Azhriaz, Night's Daughter."

Rathak shut his eyes. He was, as he knelt there, a monument to avarice. Then, he said, "But—I do not anger—*him?*"

Hazrond, smiling like the dawn of dark: "No. What does he care? He made the flesh she *was*. The spirit *she* made herself. It is only a soul, one of billions, of which, mage, even *you* possess an example, if somewhat soiled and uncombed."

Rathak's mouth twisted. He said hastily, "I am glad my small wickedness pleases you, lord. But tell me, if you graciously will, if the magic I performed did as it was supposed to."

"Your swan-white wife is with child. The seed within her, at your magic and connivance, has sent out a thread of inexplicable substance and unapparent light. This, at its farther end, enters the place beyond the world, the thickets of that border country, and has netted there your butterfly. At the elected time that one soul must come to the body of the infant you have created."

At these words, Rathak lost some of his control. He let loose a bestial cry.

Hazrond turned his head and spat. The spit burned with a marvelous violet flame. The Drin darted forward and vented some spell upon it, trying to keep the essence intact, in order to make a jewel of it, no doubt—but the incendiary saliva of the Vazdru vanished. The Drin stamped his foot and glared upon Rathak. Of Hazrond, also, no trace remained.

"Give me now what you promised me," rasped the Drin.

Rathak rose. "It is yours, and welcome."

He gestured. A narrow door opened into the chamber. Through it came gliding a girl of the magician's harem. She was young and fair, and quite ensorcelled. With glazed eyes she beheld the demon-dwarf, evidently saw some other, and beckoned to him ardently. Glad to oblige, the Drin bounded forward.

From his safe circle, Rathak watched their liason, but they did not, with their unusual acrobatics, much claim his attention. For his was to be the rape of ultimate knowledge, of powers to rival the knack of the gods. The trapped butterfly was due to reveal to him all its former learning, and thereafter it would be his vessel and weapon, a beautiful girl under his supreme authority, a goddess reborn—as formerly, through a white-haired mother—into his grip. What might he not do with and through her? All Azhrarn had failed to do. Not to anger the gods, but to overthrow all the petty empires of men—that would be enough, for Rathak.

And such ideas moved his mind from the erotic and athletic enterprises the Drin (whose race had no female counterpart) tried with the slave-girl. Indeed Rathak was not sorry when, scenting the approach of sunrise, the demon wormed away through the floor again, leaving his leman lying, a discarded rag upon the carpets.

She dreamed of walking in a mist. She thought she had lost her way in the quag beneath the mansion, but this was not any such domain. It was a region Shemsin half-remembered, though she could not guess from what era of her young life. Yet, it seemed only yesterday. . . . As she strayed there, searching, others rushed by her. And as those shadows passed, they cried to her in slender voices: "On, on—follow us on this great and terrible journey." "Where are you going?" cried she. "To be born!" they cried in return. "To the tomb of flesh." "I am already in that grave," said Shemsin sadly, "and this is but my dream."

Then she saw that she had about her waist a silken wire; the end of it was so long it trailed upon the ground and led away out of sight. Shemsin pursued the wire into the mist . . . and came at last upon a burning bush. Not that, in fact, the phenomenon was either bush or burning, yet in this manner it suggested itself to her. And what caused the burning of the bush was the element which lay tangled there. It had no true shape, or at any rate none mortal Shemsin recognized. However, it glimmered and made the non-bush seem to burn. The silken wire of Shemsin's girdle ran in and out and all around, and had formed a cage.

"Why, you are a butterfly," said Shemsin. "Poor thing, my girdle has caught your wings."

And she leant forward to try to free the shining creature.

But as she stretched out her arms, she saw another, another flaming thing, black and blazing, guarding the bush. The image seemed to have snakes for hair, black snakes bound by restless silver, and in its uplifted hand, a sword.

Shemsin drew back. She put her fingers instead to the girdle at her waist, to break it. A fearful pain shot through her.

She opened her eyes to discover herself upon her bed in a private chamber of the magician's house. The two chief midwives of Rathak's harem bowed low to her.

"Lady, you are with child."

"He will be gratified, lady. To get you planted at one couching."

Shemsin waxed heavy, a flower burdened with a bud.

She lay wan beside a fountain, in an upper courtyard with a window-roof that was turquoise-green. She was kept from the other women of the house, though sometimes she saw them parading below her, on an enclosed avenue that was fenced with orange trees. Their fans winged to and fro, and she thought of butterflies. Occasionally, at night, her sleeplessness was disturbed by a rustling on the inner stair, the *chink-chink* of an anklet. One of Rathak's wives had been summoned to his bedchamber. (In the dawn the same sound awaked Shemsin, returning.)

"He spoke to me of loving me. He valued me so much, he said. Yet never does he send for me."

The darker midwife—both had come always veiled to her—answered this reverie. "There is an antique law. Once you are filled, you are holy. He may not touch you again."

"No. It is only he is tired of me," said the girl. "While I, seeing him, became his forever." She had no one else to confide in. Harmonious sights were always about her. Food fit for a queen was served to her by unseen servants. She entered the chamber to find the meal laid out but no one there, and half supposed it was done by magic. If she wished for music, too, musicians played for her, or others read to her, or acted scenes to amuse her behind a high thin wall of porphyry.

In this way, the young girl grew to think more and more of the darker midwife, who in any event now tended her alone. It was this woman, of course, who tutored and steadied her in the maze of pregnancy, ministering to her alarms and the upsets and small ills that lent themselves to the condition. The woman's voice was also dark, and pleasing, and her narrow hands never rough. Shemsin began to request the woman's company, not only by day, but in the hours of night.

One evening, "You come always veiled before me," said Shemsin. "I would dearly like to see the face of my friend."

"It is the Lord Rathak's decree which keeps me veiled." Then she added, in a whisper, "Better you had seen through the veil of the magician."

Shemsin was surprised.

"But I have looked upon his face. I have seen his handsomeness. It is that very sight which now breaks my heart at his neglect."

"My innocent," said the woman. "Know that once I was of a rank which equaled your own. I also was wife to him you speak of, Rathak Black-Brain. I learnt many of his secrets in this way. Then, when he wearied of me, he enslaved me by his spells, and for my knowledge, which was considerable, put me to this task. I can never leave his service, nor betray what I know. I must tend the bitches of his kennel."

"Alas," said Shemsin, "you are after all my foe."

"Strangely, not," replied the woman. "For you are only a child, not having any viciousness in you either. I bear you no malice. It is *him* I hate."

"If you are enslaved as you say, how do you dare to speak of it?"

"I may not leave him, I cannot give his foulness over to justice. But liberty elsewhere he allows. It diverts him, my hate. Therefore seldom do I indulge in the treat. I utter now only in order to advise you."

"But of what?"

Then the dark woman sat gazing some while upon her charge, so that even through the heavy veiling, Shemsin could detect the glowing ferocity of her eyes. Eventually she spoke again.

"You are enamored, he has seen to that. Let it be. Think of the child within you. In another month you must hold it in your arms."

But Shemsin said, "If I stand upon the brink of a precipice, better I should see the drop beneath my feet."

The midwife nodded. She rose.

"Three hours after midnight, expect me again. I know the hidden way into the tower of brass. If you have the strength of mind and body, I will show you your beloved husband in his sleep, drunk with wine and wickedness. Tonight is a time of the calendar he lies alone after his spell-making."

Shemsin shuddered.

"So be it."

For already her heart, which somehow always kept its doubts, had gone over to the midwife.

Midnight then came and went and the first hour dragged behind it, but the second hour hastened and the third arrived on running feet. A tap upon the door. Shemsin, laden with her unborn baby, moved out into the walk beyond. There stood the dark one, muffled faceless, not even a lamp in her hand. "Follow. Say no word, ask no question, make no slightest sound, whatever you may hear or see. Or both of us will die."

They progressed along this corridor, and others, and ascended and descended in the mansion's gloom, lit only here and there by the influx of the stars. Shemsin trod with difficulty and dread. Eventually they reached a door no wider than a boy's shoulders. The dark woman waited a moment, her hand lifted in admonition. Then, partly raising her veil, she breathed upon the door. It opened.

Within lay not a stairway but a stony ramp. It was visible by the rays of phosphors, each burning in a lamp that was a human skull of abnormal proportions, either gigantic or curiously tiny.

The woman went floating up the ramp in the skull-light as if she moved on wheels. Shemsin labored after.

No sooner had they got a quarter of the way up the incline than a weird noise began to toll and buzz from every area of the enclosure. Shemsin was in fear lest it alert the magician, but since she had agreed to total and unquestioning silence, and since her friend yet climbed ahead of her, she did not hang back or cry aloud. Presently the atmosphere became full not only of the buzzing and ringing, but of peculiar gleaming flakes and motes that flitted against her and sometimes briefly stuck on her clothing or skin, so she was in a torment of fright. But still she stayed speechless, and went on.

At the top of the ramp, again the midwife paused. The lights whirled all about her, but she gave them not a glance. She beckoned to Shemsin and when the girl was close, leaned nearer.

"We are now within the tower of brass. Here is the

hardest part. Whatever occurs, do not shrink, do not murmur, or both are lost."

Then she glided on and Shemsin toiled to follow.

They seemed to go over a floor of black glass into which the light motes fell and expired, hissing. Then a profound new blackness drenched Shemsin's vision. She stumbled and found that now the air itself, or some covering of the floor, bore her upward. Such was her terror that her leaden body felt weightless.

As she traveled, beings evolved above, beside, below her, and whimpered in her ears, and sometimes struck at or caressed her. Once or twice a nightmare face swelled from the black like sudden luminous smoke. Shemsin bit her tongue not to scream. She did not dare to hide her eyes for fear she be separated from her guide who—even then—was faintly perceptible to her, skimming upward as did she.

The surge ended at a platform that seemed to rest in space. Another door was visible at the platform's center. It glowed with a hot and deadly glare. Across the threshold lay a beast of restless coils, with soulless eyes that glared as the door did. And seeing them with these eyes, this thing roused itself.

Shemsin was by now oblivious to whether she dreamed or woke, lived or had died. When her companion continued to advance, Shemsin followed still, stupefied.

The guardian of the door writhed up its great neck into a fountain from which several other heads started to unfold and pour over. The eyes of each slowly opened, every pair a twinship of malevolence. The many jaws separated and gaped, and again half-lifting her veil, the midwife spat straight into each of them—*spah! spah! spah!* There were lightnings. The guardian became a mosaic of fires, sparks, embers, which shattered apart like a breaking plate and went out entirely—but all this without a sound.

The woman caught the fainting girl and shook her. "*Not yet.* Now you must claim your reward."

The door melted away and Shemsin beheld, as if it swam in water, the seven-sided chamber where she had lain that first night with her lord.

The bed of rubies and poppies was no more. This bed

was of brass and sable, with curtains deep drawn, though torches blared at the room's every seventh point.

"Come," said the midwife loudly, "We have defeated his safeguards. He will not wake."

And seizing a torch, she pulled Shemsin to the bed. The woman thrust the curtain aside, and held high her light.

"Gaze now on him you adore, and that you have suffered so much to see."

And Shemsin saw Rathak lying there, her husband and her love.

He was, to look on, as obscenely grotesque as some ninety years of wrong-doing could make him, for this was the length of his existence, bolstered by his arts. No blood-red hair of silk had he, but withered rusty grass. His eyes, wide even as he sightlessly slept, were colorless and tarnished membranes. A bag of bones, with the belly of a full-fed dragon, he spilled upon his sheets. He smiled as he slept, too, with rotted teeth that sorcery kept drugged and sharp. He smiled, he slumbered, perhaps he even gladly dreamed, not knowing any in the world could breach his lair and see him so. For he had his little vanities, Rathak.

Shemsin shrieked, as she had not at the horrors of the journey. But just then Agony the empress came up behind her, threw her skinny arms about Shemsin's heart and womb, and shut her mouth.

The baby, a female, was born after a long and tremendous labor. It was deformed. Yet it lived.

And since without a soul mortal life could not have been admissible to it, undeniably the trap had been sprung. The butterfly was *caught.*

2 *Prisoners*

RATHAK RAGED. His scheme was amiss. The child, a vessel of the soul of the sorceress-goddess Azhriaz, was crippled and repulsive. Somehow the mother had connived a way into his sanctum. She had seen him, as he *was,* and the sight had so dismayed her in her idiocy that she had wrecked his careful creation. He had found the girl lying alone at the foot of a stairway in the tower of brass. Here she must have fled and fallen after her shrieks cracked the sphere of his sleep. How she had overcome the safeguards of his stronghold he could not fathom, nor did she seem to remember anything of it, delirious with pain and panic as she was then.

He did not punish her at once. He required the child. But she had spoiled the child—ah! How she had spoiled it. The premature eviction into the world might have resulted in still-birth had not the soul been sorcerously linked to the flesh (and by a better steel than even Rathak could manufacture). And so the spiritual essence was hauled in with the body by the relentless hand of life. The dualism lay before him now within the circle of powers and powders, humped, askew, and mewling. In the crushed blob of its face, the sickly eyes slid senselessly after flutters of the light.

"Yes, little horror, I can do nothing with you. Even my arts could not undo such mess; they are geared to make and not to mend. For a mask of beauty . . . I need that fount for another, myself. It transpires therefore I may not use you as I had dearly hoped. Nevertheless, you will give me all you can."

Then Rathak spoke terrifying words, made gestures of force, so the chamber reverberated as if at unheard thunder.

The lamps failed down to an overcast, the air went icy cold.

"I command you, spirit," said Rathak, "spirit fresh from Nothingness. The memories of your former life are with you yet, though you may draw no help from them. The mutilated fleshly case of a baby holds you, yet you are, at the core, still *Azhriaz.* I command you, Azhriaz, by the sign of *this,* and *this.* You must answer."

Then the formless mouth of the child parted. Out came a voice nearly human, but of no gender, very beautiful, and, too, disembodied; also metallic, fluid, ethereal, while even as it filled the room, eons off.

Yes, I answer, magician. But I am not she you name. I am only I.

"Do not play at theosophy with me. She you were you *dwelled* with."

A thousand mortal years ago, or an afternoon, I did.

"And I have bound you. Do you know yourself bound?"

I know myself bound.

"And that I am your master."

Of the flesh which contains me master you may be. But of this I am, which now speaks to you, master you are not.

"Yet you must obey me."

You are in error.

Rathak said, "I will have from you all the knowledge of which you were possessed, which you will remember, and though some particles are gone from you in translation, it shall amount to a tolerable volume. Either obey in that, or I will torture at leisure, and with intent precision, the cage of skin and bone and blood that, until death, you may not now escape. Shall it gladden you?"

It will injure me, both body and spirit. I, too, shall suffer, as you know. But know, too, that Azhriaz, when she I was, incurred some debts. I will submit to the suffering, and offer it to my inner self as payment for past wrongs of hers. In that manner, each cruelty of yours will ultimately assist me. Shall that gladden you?

"Soul," said Rathak, "I do not bother myself with your ambitions. I have those serve me that will get much joy from your anguish. I will call them now. Let us gladden *them*."

Because she heard her child shrilly crying, Shemsin came to herself and said, searching about her in confusion, "Where is my daughter?"

But the crying had faded away and instead she heard a stranger sound, which she did not know at all.

So then she murmured, "What noise is that?"

"Madam," said one at her side, "if it might be kept from you, willingly I would do it. But seeing you must learn at last, I will tell you at once. It is the noise of Black-Brain's masons, who even now wall us up alive within this room."

Shemsin started from her pillows. Immediately she heard the sounds for what they were, the setting in of giant slabs to mortar.

And she saw the daylight had already shrunk from the chamber to a miniscule dot which now, as soon as she had looked at it, went out.

Peculiarly then, details of her surrounding came to her, such as they were. For the room was bare, save for a guttering candle, and the divan on which she had been lying, while upon the floor rested a jar of water and a loaf of bread.

"Provisions have been left to prolong rather than to alleviate our suffering," said the voice quietly.

Shemsin turned to find, seated beside her, her companion the midwife, still in her veil, and seeming calm as a stone.

"You—why are you here?"

"I am to be chastized, too. We allowed the offspring of Lord Rathak to emerge weakly and deformed."

"My baby," said Shemsin.

The veiled woman hesitated. She appeared to decide her course. "Madam, it did not long survive. Which is as well for now you could not, as you are, save the child."

Shemsin wept. But through her tears, her mind wildly scurrying, she said, "Nevertheless, we are not to die through that, you and I. But for entering the forbidden room. For looking on the deceiver in his disgusting state."

The veiled woman started violently in turn.

"Did you so?"

Shemsin's voice rose to a scream.

"You know it well, since you were with me! Oh, how you beguiled me, killing my child in my body by the rigors of that way, delivering me to this fate. Yet," her voice sank low, "mine was the greater evil, to love an abomination. The Goddesses know, most probably the child came out malformed from his sowing and is better dead. As am I."

In that chamber, the candle also was near death. Outside, all sounds of any sort had ended. Silence and the dark laid hands upon the room.

"Shemsin," said her veiled companion presently, "we are to finish soon, and thus you will believe I have no reason to invent. If you entered the tower of the magician, I was not with you. Though, if you had asked it of me, out of my regard for you, perhaps I should have ventured the exploit."

"Then I am mad," said Shemsin dully. "For I remember how it was you persuaded me. And in that place you were my guide, opening its immovable doors, subduing by sorcery its fiends and supernatural guardians."

"Not I. How could I perform such miracles?"

Shemsin, there in the dark, discerned as if by a lightning flash.

"It is true. It cannot have been yourself who came to me that evening, for she had neither your walk nor your accustomed ways, and none of your kindness. She was proud, hard as a woman of iron."

"As I was going to you in the dusk," said the other, "one met me on the stair beneath your court and turned me back. She, too, was veiled—Oh lady, this house is infected with abnormal things, with flits, haunts and, I have heard, by demons. Such will make purposeless mischief for the mere happiness of causing harm."

(In this, the young midwife was not quite correct. The Prince Hazrond, when he had adopted her guise to lure Shemsin into danger, had had a distinctive purpose, which, be sure, was now achieved—the physical demolition of the child. Old scores settled?)

But Shemsin said, "Let us speak no more of these awful things. Soon it will be night, for us." Then she added, "Yet, before the candle dies, let me see your face, for comfort's sake. Or is it not permitted you?"

"At any time."

And the midwife drew the veil up from her head and shoulders and let it fall on the floor. Revealed, she was a maiden of Shemsin's age or a very little older, and darkly fair as the iris by the lily.

"Shemsin," she repeated, "we are soon to finish."

"So you have said, and so I understand."

"Then let me tell you why I never put aside my veil. It was out of fear because, from the moment that I saw you, I loved you."

Shemsin answered, "And so said Rathak at our couching."

"But *he* lied."

And at that instant, the candle's flame went out.

The women flung their arms about each other. In blackness, on the sea of death, they clung. Each thought in her heart: *At least I am not alone.*

He had learnt nothing.

The soul had refused to render him another sentence. It had not cried aloud, as the child did. The air was choked by the stinking vapors and louring excrescences of Rathak's minions. After some hours, he foresaw the infant must die of its treatment, despite the spells of retention he had cast to secure it. Its death was not his aim. Dead, the soul evaded him once more and might, besides, seek some vengeance on him. Such were the great mage's notions of astral business: He saw all worlds by his own light.

Thus, he left off his labors.

The ventings of his frustration and anger were then accommodated in a number of ways.

And thereafter, in the emptiness of that sorcery-scorched and psychically-abused tower-high moral basement, Rathak shed like a blistering curse a charm of healing on his daughter.

But, despite his magecraft, not much healing was in Rathak. He had spent his days in nurturing poison. Though the formula thrust off death, it did little to encourage life.

When he had seen to it, he called one up to him, from the vaults of the mansion.

The creature came with a slow shuffling of its limbs and hung its heavy skull so its thick tongue poured upon the flagstones. It was like nothing on earth—or like such a patchwork of earthly somethings—that to describe it would be needlessly pedantic, and perhaps impossible. However, there it was, and with two or three bulbous, gleamless eyes it viewed the magician, its master.

"Slave," said he, "do you see the infant there?"

By some means or other, the creature affirmed that it did.

"I have a use for it, the child, which I cannot now effect. Maybe I never shall effect that use. But meanwhile, the brat must be my captive. And, most definitely, it must survive. Assure me of your grasp of these words."

By some means or other, the creature did assure him.

"To your charge, slave, I give the wardership. Take the child below into your own place, and there feed it with the nutrients of your own trough. Guard it equally from misadventure, escape, and the release of death. It will with time grow larger, and may begin to make sounds. Only then should you alert me by uttering that whistling note I taught you. Otherwise, the task is solely yours."

The creature nodded or made some corresponding gesture of compliance.

"In return for your vigilance and care, you shall receive from me payment, under the code of such sorcerous bargains. Your wage is this: For three minutes of every day, you will experience an untold bliss of all the senses, such as I can devise. To gain a repetitive ecstasy of comparable magnitude many humans would undertake far greater toil. Is the fee acceptable?"

The creature drooled. It evinced agreement.

Rathak snapped his fingers.

The creature crawled to the unknit circle, and pulled out the baby. It carried her, by some unusual route, to itself quite mundane, down into the foundations of the magician's house.

Sunset came to the mansion, and reflected on the brazen doors, so they shone red. After the sun had gone, came the melancholy dusk, and lingered awhile. Then night ascended the rock—but dusk was still standing there, in the portico. Dusk was a man in a purple mantle.

Raising his gloved hand, he knocked upon the doors.

High up, on the left side, the fossilized braincase of a dragon had been fixed. Now its jaws creaked wide. It spoke.

"Who is there?"

"Darkness," was the answer, "one fifth part of it."

"Who is it that you seek?"

"He that nailed you to your post."

"You may not enter," said the dragon's cranium.

"I am, it seems to me, already within. Shall I take off my gloves?"

The cranium hissed. The left-hand leaf of the door opened two or three inches.

The man in purple had vanished from the portico. Inside the courtyard of black, blood and emerald he stood now, gazing about. Faint phosphorus from the swamp had gone in with him; it glittered sharp as glass. He seemed handsome, though he kept the left side of his face well hidden in his hood.

"Rathak, Rathak, Rathak," whispered he.

The court took up the sound and bellowed it.

Rathak appeared suddenly in a cloud of light. He gazed at the visitor, then evolved from the air a scarf of vapor. In this Rathak swathed his eyes. Then, he bowed very low.

"You know me," said the visitor.

"I believe I do, imperial lord."

"But not all my legends."

"If I have offended in some form your royal person, I will give due recompense."

"Name me," said the one in purple.

"Lord, excuse me from doing so."

"*Name* me."

"You are," said Rathak, "a Lord of Darkness and a Prince."

"More."

"You are Chuz, Delusion's Master."

"More."

"You are Madness."

Chuz smiled, with the handsome portion of his face that was visible, and shook a lock of blond hair from his long-lashed, downcast eye.

"You have nothing to fear," said Chuz, "your wickedness has so infested you, you are already a mindless madman, Rathak. And yet, one day you will look into your own mirror, and see me there. You will see what you are. And *then*. You will dance and sing the song."

Rathak mimed with his lips a word of averting.

Chuz smiled again. "It is not to be avoided. I do not hunt you. You are out hunting yourself. You are hot on your own heels, Rathak Dark-Wits. Do you hear yourself baying?"

Rathak shook, but such was his control that it was not

to be seen. Even Chuz, Prince Madness, did not see. Only Rathak himself knew that he had shaken. And for an instant he heard a distant baying in his ears, as of hounds upon a scent.

When he thrust off the notion, Chuz was no longer before him.

So then Rathak ascended again into his sorcerous tower of brass, and there he ringed himself with such bastions of power, the air of those chambers turned as sluggish as treacle, while in the sky above the tower no stars or moon were visible, and when the sun should rise again, it would look shrunken from that spot, like an aborted pomegranate.

But even inside his overloaded honeycomb of protection, Rathak stayed aware of Chuz, who seemed creeping all over the walls and roofs, all up the pillars and over the ceilings, like a purple insect.

"He is scratching on a windowpane," said Rathak. "He is tapping on the stones." Rathak struck sparks of music from the atmosphere. Through the music, he thought he heard Chuz, still on his insectile progress. "Who else is scratching on the stones? Who is tapping on the windows?"

"Who?" breathed the pale girl to the dark girl, "who is that, tapping and scratching on the stones?"

"Hush, my dearest. It is only our fancy. It is a dream of hunger and despair. Or perhaps it is gentle Lord Death, who has come quickly to free us from prison."

Just then, the slabs of the walling-up dissolved.

Chuz, in his mantle, half hidden and half beautiful, smiled graciously with gloved hands and lowered eyes.

"Pretty ladies, leave this dismal cell."

Bemused, they got to their feet and felt themselves wafted to the vanished barrier. Outside, the evening, very silent and occluded. Some length below, the domes of the mansion, and here a huge carpet woven of velvet, midnight black and midnight blue, magenta, violet and gold.

And handsome, hidden Chuz, beckoning and cajoling. So the next thing they knew they had stepped upon the wondrous carpet, and all three were sailing away across the star-embroidered night.

"Here is wine and here is milk," said courteous Chuz. "There are meats and fruits and cakes. Here are transparent lilies for you, and dusky irises for you."

He beamed on them and told them stories. He hymned their loveliness in a voice they would never forget or remember.

"It is a hallucination of death," the maidens said to one another. But weakness deserted them, health seized them. They laughed and ate and drank, and even jested with Prince Madness.

"You are dear to me," said Chuz. "Once, I was another, who loved another, who is now another, but this latter other you have both recently known."

Then, with half the moon-crescent of his smiling mouth, he kissed them asleep.

The carpet had passed above an ocean like a storm of silk, and over a diadem of mountains, and now, in a land of rivers and green corn, he brought it down and left them. Left them sleeping, with the velvet vehicle for their coverlet and the flowers and the feast at their side.

But on the bed of a stream, in letters of gold (where at sunrise, astonished and rejoicing, they found it), he wrote:

AZHRIAZ

"But who is Azhriaz?" said Shemsin softly.

"I do not know."

They turned to each other, among the sea-green corn. The writing soon faded in sunlight.

3 *An Ill-Earned Fee*

DEEP IN THE cellarage of the house, the creature of the magician performed its duties. Twice a day, it dragged the small scarred bundle of the infant to an obsidian trough which, sorcerously at those times filled with pap, tasteless and somewhat disgusting, though nutritious. And thereafter to the waterspout the creature went, its charge in tow. The baby, at the onset no more than a month in age, should normally have perished long since, let alone been able to digest the viands of an unhuman brute. But the spells of Rathak, while doing the child no good, had staved off all current ability to die or to sicken. Nourished she was, at the trough and the spout. And sleeping day and night otherwise, among the filthy straw of weeds, things which rooted there in the dark and which the creature-slave hacked for a couch, lightly she existed and imperceptibly took the upward path to life and growth.

The creature-slave however received, once in every diurnal unit, its three-minute wage. During those three minutes it lay oblivious of all else. The phase would also come on it at different hours, without warning, and once even it had fallen in the trough, so extraordinary was its bliss, only emerging at pleasure's termination in a cloak of pap on which it subsequently dined. (On that occasion the feeding of the child was neglected, but by then she had learned sufficiently to stumble at last to the trough and feed herself.)

In the subterranean gloom of the cellar, not much was visible, but the least brilliant of glows emanated from the bedding plants, while erratic breaths of the quag issued in between the stones, and then phosphorus limned every surface, including the misshapes of the slave and the child.

She was a poor little thing, all humped and buckled, with a head poked forward like that of a tortoise. Her stick-like legs were of unequal length, her skinny arms hung askew. The scars had sewn together in strange ribs and laminations, so her flesh resembled some shell or slate marked for years by the sea.

Though her soul, or some element of it, had spoken at Rathak's interrogation, now that soul was folded up at her core, and she had no more memory of it than she had of the events of yesterday, in that dayless, nightless hole. If one had come to her and said *Azhriaz,* like her mother she, too, would have stared.

Life and the world were the dark underground, the fungoid straw. Eventfulness was the trough, the spout, the occasions of phosphorus, or the movements of her fellow inmate, the creature. (She did not know fear or liking for the brute, for it had given her cause for neither.) Asleep—and sleeping was her only recreation—

abstract dreamings might have lessoned her in other forms and conditions. But having no reference for them, not even any language, her starved, unbudded brain forgot them instantly.

In this fashion then, the child spent her early months, her initial garnering of years. And although she grew and sometimes even thoughtlessly exercised herself by crawling and stretching, scrabbling at the weeds, swinging from the waterspout, she perceived no urgency for speech, for sounds of any complexity, and made none.

The creature, in fact, came to be able to ignore its charge, to concentrate only upon its own needs, and to await hungrily the trio of ecstatic minutes, to enjoy them, and then once more to anticipate their return.

What actual amount of time proceeded is unsure. It may have been as much as five years.

Unknown to all the underdwellers of those cavernous vaults, their master the magician had turned somewhat dubious and fraught. The isolate nature of his home had become more than ever that of a hermitage. A forest of thorns now guarded the rock, so the road disappeared, and only the topmost domes of the house pierced through. Their bricks and stones had been reinforced by the densest magics. None of the windows or doors would give save at the recitation of a particular vernacular rhomb. For the mortal accessories of the mansion, the slavegirls and servants, and the harem of wives, they had been dismissed—or slaughtered, it was said. He dwelled alone now, Rathak, the rumor went, with just his zoo of phantoms, flits and fiends for company.

Perhaps he had mislaid the idea of the child. The plan had gone so wrong, it was doubtless better put down to experience.

Yet the warder-creature's fee, the three delicious minutes, that continued. Once active, only Rathak's wish could halt the blessing.

One morning, at dawn, the merest of earth tremors slipped under the rock. It disturbed not much. In the manse a pane or two of stained glass was cracked, and being ensorcelled immediately de-cracked itself. A tile fell from a ceiling. An amulet in the tower of brass turned upside down.

In the vaults below, the foundations shifted, and settled. In one area, where the stone abutted on a cave-like tunnel under the swamp, a piece of the wall parted. It was an aperture no bigger than the girth of an undergrown child five years of age.

Perhaps it was the smell of the cave which drew her, for the bedding weeds flourished out there and her couch was due for renewal. Or maybe some intimation of openness hung beyond the stink of the cellar and within the stench of the swamp.

And it happened that, in the moment of the wall's parting, the child's approach, random investigation and half-involuntary exit, its three minutes of ecstasy claimed the creature who was to have been her jailor.

When it regained awareness, the break in the foundation was already sorcerously sealing. For some further minutes, the slave, languid in after-bliss, did not notice it. Much later it did so, and then it sought the child. The lair afforded few enough opportunities for concealment, but these the creature ransacked over and over. The cloven wall had meanwhile entirely closed.

The slave knew a mighty terror then. For surely the magician would learn of his ward's escape. The warder would be reprimanded, and at the expectation the brute was convulsed in anxiety.

Nevertheless, no summons, no reprimand arrived.

Indeed, the next day, even as the creature lay upon its straw in dread, its dose of bliss crashed upon it and in contrast almost slew it with delight.

Could it be Rathak was in ignorance?

As day succeeded day, each one with a period of joy, the creature again became sanguine. It, too, forgot. The fee it accepted as the reward for services past.

And truly, Rathak had by then no space for errant souls or children. Or the curtailment of others' pleasure.

Having walled himself in against some inchoate enemy, horror fastened on him at the chinks the earthquake started. Though every slightest crack had healed itself, Rathak guessed his fortress breached. And when he saw the tile on the floor he reckoned it had been flung at him in threat, and when he saw the amulet reversed, he supposed it an omen of destruction.

And in the midst of his shouting and panting to and fro, he caught a sudden sight in a mirror of bronze.

It was of an ancient man befouled by crimes, with rusty hair on end, and with mad eyes and a mad panting mouth of bad teeth.

Then he heard the noise of hounds in his head and felt their hot breath on his bones.

"Chuz!" howled Rathak. And he recognized himself and believed his enemy had hold of him and he was lost.

And, since he believed it, so it came to be, and so he was.

But the house stood many more decades inside its fence of thorns, avoided by all, virtuous and corrupt alike.

4 *The Changeling*

DURING THE DAY, she lingered in the cave, where the shadows hurt her eyes with their brightness. At some point she sought to go back into the creature's vault, but that, of course, was gone. And then she was afraid, felt a vague gnawing in her breast which could only have been nostalgia, a sickness for home. But it was so muddled and so flimsily founded, it could not last. And then night came outside, and wandering around in the tunnel, she missed her direction and came up instead onto the surface of the quag.

The garment of mist was down. In it burned far off eyes of dull silver, so she imagined that the creature was up there after all, peering at her, with others of its kind. But these filmy lights were just the stars in the mist.

When the phosphorus emerged it was familiar and comforting, though so broadcast it would have seemed, to an observer, the tiny hunched figure of the child straggled through a whole sea of milky liquid. Sometimes clouds rose from the surface like ghostly gigantic moths and fled slowly away into the upper air. Sometimes phosphor stars, fiery as the sky stars did not appear to be, dived through the fog. The child, not fearing them, turned wondering looks after their passage. She did not follow them. And most curiously a kind of animal instinct kept her always from the sinks of the swamp, guiding her small twisted feet aside. She was nearly weightless, also, as the vapors. The quag would have needed its most strenuous tugs to suck and gulp her down.

And as she went, to one who observed, another odd thing became apparent. For though deformed, scarred, dehumanized, there had been thrown over her a veil of purest silk, which the roaming lamps lit to a selection of elusive colors, though it would need the rise of a sun to uncover its warmth: Poor little child, she had the most beautiful hair.

"See, see!" sibilated one observer to another.

"I *see*. I *see!*" the other sibilated back.

For she had her audience, the lost girl.

Two flits of the quag, free spirits the magician had never inveigled, hung in the mist and stared with their chill mercurial eyes.

"*So scintillant* a lining for our *sweet nest*," sizzled the first.

"*So soft*, our *sisters* will *sleep* their *best*," sizzled the second.

"Yes! Yes!"

"Yes! Yes!"

And that decided, they swooped upon the child like wasps. And like wasps they stuck into her the glinting stings under their nails. She was only a degree bigger than they, yet they stung her soundly, and no sooner had her gaze of wonder gone to a thin wail of pain, than she dropped in a daze from the venom.

Then they attracted others of their tribe, by vocal sigmatics. Presently some thirteen or so hovered there on chitinous wings.

They were willowy and hollow-boned, these flits, being most like females, but not essentially like either sex, their bodies characterized by omissions. Hands and feet had fingers and toes all of a length, all equipped with indigenous darts. They were clad in wisps of gauze, metal and mist, were themselves hairless, and in their noseless, earless faces, nearly flat as discs of pared white nacre, each had her little pursed mouth and two huge eyes.

"Let *us* take it to our *sweet nest.*"

"Let *us snip* and *scatter* the *silky stuff.*"

"How *soft* we *shall sleep.*"

"But the *rest* of it? *Its* frame and *skin?*"

"*Cast* it forth. Let the *swamp swimmers feast.*"

"The *goddess must speak.*"

"*Yes,* let the *goddess* mete out *justice.*"

Next, picking up the child between them with kissing sounds of flit curses, they sculled their wings and made off with her to their burrow.

The *goddess* was lying well inside, on a divan of mosses and bog-lotus, with pillows of toadhide under her shoulders, to ease her wings. Every flit burrow had some elected deity, as every wasp hive possesses a queen. She was, for a flit, fat and cumbersome, and bowed besides under the heavy royal jewels her court continually brought her, for they were dedicated scavengers. These included such items as the burnished kidney-stone of a dead ox that had foundered in the swamp, a lizard's nicest teeth, a chip of quartz, a pip of glass, some mummified beetle carapaces of burning mulberry-green, tinsel wire from the lobes and nostrils of travelers who had met ends not unlike that of the ox, rings, pins, and dagger-hilts, ditto, and the whole skeleton of a rat.

The patrolling flits, entering with the conscious but paralyzed child, dropped her at the feet of the *goddess.* The burrow had proved only just wide enough to admit the catch, and some damage had happened at the entrance.

The *goddess* looked on, impassive.

"*See, see, Serene* One!"

They lifted and flapped about the hair of the child, showing the *goddess.* They explained how well the material should line the sleeping nest.

The *goddess* indicated a slender primal worm with teeth, tethered to her divan. The flits used it vigorously, causing it to bite through the strands of hair, until the child had been completely cropped.

Much of the hair was then borne into the inner chambers of the burrow. But some was woven in garlands and loaded on to the *goddess'* neck, and there secured with a knob of vitreus got earlier.

The child began to tremble as the venom dissipated from her system. Several flits were close by, ready to sting her again.

"*Shall she* go out, *goddess?*"

The *goddess* cogitated. It was difficult and tiring for her to make any movement. Finally she spoke.

"*She shall stay. She shall* be my *servitor. She shall* fetch *substances* and *assist* me to lie down and to *sit* up again. Bind her, *so she shall* never *escape.*"

This was done, the child being tied to the end of the divan opposite to the tethering point of the worm.

The *goddess* subsided.

The remainder of the flits hastened into the nest chamber whence soon issued whooshes of revelry, terminating in this song:

Sleep, sleep, Serene One,
See, she is so.
Sloth—Ah! Solace so,
Silken sleep.

But overexhausted by adornment, the *goddess* did not slumber for many hours, nor the stung child either.

Accordingly, the magician's daughter served. She was a curiosity of the burrow, which boasted of owning her elsewhere. She was known, in the flit tongue, as "Child," an invented, derogatory term, for flits hatched directly from larva to adult, and reckoned any interim a stupidity. Child was taught something of the flit language, too, for convenience's sake, and that they might insult her better. For, though they boasted of owning her, they were jealous of her attachment by the *goddess,* and tried constantly to put hardship in her path. Also they would constantly sting Child, as if through carelessness, but it was malice.

Yet Child was a durable being, hardy in her malformed fragility, graceful in her ugliness. Most of all, her total inexperience of everything had granted her the priceless gift of acceptance. She neither flinched nor strove.

She did not lament, and was never the victim of worry, or hope.

In the early morning and the late dusk, the flits would go about the swamp, gathering dews and the plants of the quag, and such reptiles and insects, stung stiff with toxins, as they liked to eat. Their treasure seeking was additionally eternal. In the heat of the day they lounged about the margins of moss-clogged pools, under the shade of broad weeds. At night they might go to dance with the phosphors of the quag, or roister in the burrow, drinking fermented juices and refurbishing their own ornaments of wire and seeds. They were savage, and sometimes went hunting fanged fishes through the shallows, or fought with enormous hornets and winged beetles as large as sparrows. After these forays, one or another of the sisterhood might not return. Then the others held a death-watch, shrieking and writhing under the moon all night, but not in sorrow—more in anger. When dawn broke and the moon and the mist seeped down, the dead one was forgotten.

But the *goddess* never stirred from her divan, except to achieve the purposes of nature, which had themselves become dilatory and uncommon.

Properly, certain of the flits always guarded the entrance of the burrow, but often they were sidetracked and deserted. The rest arrowed in and out ceaselessly with booty. However, to Child, the *goddess*' maid, now fell all the intimate services. These were to bathe the *goddess* by means of mosses steeped in dews, to assist her in sitting and reclining—and to the holy dungheap, should it be necessary. Child must also tend the cushions of her lady's couch, correct the balance of her jewels when so instructed, anoint her wings with herbal oils, and endlessly pulp and grind up, on little shards of stone, newly brought eatables. The feeding of the *goddess*, as her decoration, was ceaseless. Her obesity and flesh were the honor of the burrow. (No *goddess* lived long. At her demise, a replacement deity was selected, the burrow abandoned, and all the architecture of flit life built up again from scratch.)

Child, though, knew nothing of that, or of how things had been before. She only did as she was told, and sometimes, when it was demanded, answered in the sounds of the flit tongue. The upsets and stingings she bore with equanimity. The boredom of her task, and of the *goddess* herself, likewise. Nor did Child remonstrate if the *goddess*, when they were alone together, wished that this or that ornament should be removed from her, or even hidden, or thrown away, though the flits sometimes noticed an absence and Child was berated. Nor did Child take umbrage that often the *goddess* did not eat, or spat out mouthfuls, or ordered that Child devour whole dishes—her ordained share was slight—or else bury them in the dungpile.

Now and then, the *goddess* sang in a toneless warbling. Her vast eyes gazed myopically into nothing.

One morning, when a pinkish dawn haze still drifted in the burrow, the *goddess* spoke to Child.

"*Listen. Something has* come to me. *Yes.*"

Then she indicated some globules of black silver that were wreathed over her arms and ankles.

"Off. *Yourself shall dress* in *these.*"

So Child removed from the *goddess* the globules and put them on herself.

"It *is* well. Now *this this this.*"

So Child removed from the *goddess* some seed-pods and carapaces and a large bone. And clad herself in them.

"It *is* well. *Yes,* how well it *is. Thus, this.*"

And so it went on for quite an hour, interrupted only by the entry of other flits, who as ever were in such excited hurry they seemed to note nothing unusual.

Finally, the *goddess* was bare, but for her wisps of gauze, and so lightened, that she was able to tumble off her couch without aid.

"*Rise* up now. *Stretch yourself* where I have *sat. Slide* the *skull* of the rat lower, and the *tinsels, so. See!* Bow your *face. Use* only *eyes.* Do not *shift.* Or if you *must* make dung, *seek* the holy heap. Eat all *substances sent.* If any *ask* where *is* Child? *Say* them *this: She is busy steeping mosses.* Or *she is searching sweets* for me."

And the *goddess*, wheezing and rolling in her fat, expelled herself from the burrow, falling down with an audible *plop* into some bog-flowers below.

Child remained on the divan. She was so smothered in the royal jewels that it was true, not much of her was visible. And even though her hair had begun to grow quite lavishly, it did not undeceive, as the flit *goddess* had long since requested and received a cap woven of Child's worm-cut tresses.

The flits, buzzing in and out, continued to leave food and to hang ornaments over the mass on the divan, not hesitating.

Child prepared the food in the old way, but did not eat much of it. Eventually, the flits began to question her: "Why have you not *consumed, Serene* One? Where *is* Child?"

"*Steeping mosses,*" said Child in the flit tongue.

"How *sunken* your *voice is, Serene* One. You are *starved!*"

And vowing to sting Child purposely, they crammed food into Child's mouth, still supposing her their deity.

The fact was, the symbol was all that mattered to them. A sufficiently large toad would have done, providing it ate, could be decorated, and answered approximately in the right way.

Days and nights without number passed in this comedy.

Once or twice, Child beheld the lawful *goddess* flitting by the burrow. At first she had been heavy and unwieldy and kept mostly from view, but swiftly she shrank and slimmed, and became active, chasing hornets and moths with her sisters, returning with them into the burrow in the dark. Not one of the flits seemed ever to have suspected or challenged her. She herself gave no sign she was any more than a sister of the sisterhood. Presently she was indistinguishable. If Child had wished, she would have been unable to sort the *goddess* from her subjects. (Although into the mind of Child, of course, such an idea could never have come.)

On the other hand Child, in the natural way, had grown a little, and nourished on an ever running stream of fairy-food, a fresh bloom of health was added to her oblique graces. There she sat, a mound of ornaments, the most shining credit to the burrow. Nowhere in the world (the quag) was there such a *goddess*.

The human thing, the monster they had kept for shearing like a sheep, that they soon unremembered, as was their proclivity. Until one morning, a touch before noon, three flits came home with the most gaudy of all the treasures they had ever found, and brought about deception's undoing.

The treasure was a great brazen rattle, so polished—before its castoff in the mud—that it glowed like old gold. When shaken, it made a wild clincketing noise as of many fragments of something or other whirled together. Its stem had been tangled by a strand of mauve lotuses. The whole compendium was conducted to the *goddess*-who-was-not, and swung over her head, the three flits fizzing with satisfaction.

But, in going on, the rattle and the strand somehow dislodged some pivot of the adornments. Down they started to slither, to skitter and plonk, in a rain—the rat's bones and the lizard's teeth, the seeds and pods and beads and bobbles, the wires and pins and beetle bits—and crashed about the divan.

The handmaidens sibilantly exclaimed in aggravation. Months of artistic labor were to do again. One hastened to the burrow opening to recall her entire sisterhood to toil.

The remaining pair bent nearer to their lady.

"What *is this?*"

"*Surely* it *is* that *snout some* call a *nose!*"

"And *these?*"

"*Nostrils! Brows! Ears!*"

"And *see! See!* Only five *fingers,* of unequal *size!*"

"Our *goddess is diseased!*"

"It *is* not our *goddess.*"

"It *is some species* of *beastliness.*"

"It *is* Child!"

An explosive uproar then broke out in the burrow, increasing as the residue of the sisterhood returned there.

Like a colony of wasps disturbed, in and out and round and about, now rushing from the burrow entry effervescing and whirring, now zooming into it again so the whole bank should palpitate.

Each flit was hysterical. Even the original *goddess,* having herself forgotten her own antics, had hysterics like the rest.

In the center of the whirlpool sat the revealed child.

If she was made afraid, she did not demonstrate. Perhaps, being accustomed to the excesses of the burrow, she did not completely relate the drama to herself.

But in the end, as the afternoon spread its awning on the swamp (usually the time of ease), the flits flew out of the burrow and swarmed upon a raft of oily lily pads. Here they vibrated like fired arrows, in sudden almost-silence, and took some inner council. The nest must be abandoned, a new *goddess* created, all redone, starting from scratch. But indeed, the *scratch* came first.

Like a spearhead they drove back into their dishonoured house, and fell upon Child to sting her to death.

Shortly before sunset, a caravan was crossing one edge of the quag. A causeway ran here. Nevertheless, the travelers had desired to quit the region before nightfall. They were already familiar with tales of the swamp, and did not care for it. The house of the magician had previously been pointed out in the far distance, ringed by darkness and with weird sheens upon its domes of enamel and bronze, and superstitious signs were resorted to. The phosphors of the swamp, which would emerge with the dusk, were accredited with awful talents.

The wagon master of the caravan was, nevertheless, a steadfast man. Seeing they should not be free of the place at sundown, he gave orders for lamps and torches to be lit. "Since we fear to sleep in such a spot, we will make on, keeping the while sensible watch."

Now there were among the travelers some religious persons, and these privately decided on an additional precaution. Which was, to prepare an offering to the elementals of the quag, and leave it by the causeway. They therefore put together a roast that was to have supplied their supper, some wine and figs and confectionery, six copper coins and one of gold, and a prayer of goodwill inscribed on parchment. The collection was then done up in a bleached sack, its pallor selected the better to apprise resident frights of its position. Slipping aside from the caravan they deposited the bribe among the mud and mosses below the path. The sun was just parting from the sky, and in that darkening light, the offerers pondered the shape of their sacrifice. "It has," said one, marking himself with a protection, "the look of a dead infant." "Tush!" said a second. "Hush," said a third. "They are lighting lanterns, let us not drop behind," gabbled a fourth.

Day died, and all color left the land. The torchlit caravan lumbered forward like a huge animal hung with blazing eyes. Out on the swamp a hundred other phantom caravans, eyed by silver lamps, commenced wiggling back and forth.

As it chanced, several of the religious persons had by then progressed up the line on their mules. They intended to fall in with the wagon master and perchance comfort him at supper, their own being gone.

They had scarcely exchanged polite greetings, however, when the first man let out a cry.

"In the name of all gods, wagon master, halt the caravan!"

The wagon master regarded him impassively. "Why so?"

"Because I and my friends made an offering to the evil spirits here, miles back and an hour ago—and see where said offering lies *ahead* of us, at the roadside! They have flung it in our teeth. Heaven knows what will follow."

Then the caravan was halted, and some altercation occurred. At length the wagon master, armed with stave and torch, but unaccompanied, strode to investigate the pale, sack-like huddle.

He leaned down, straightened up.

"Poor thing. Not a fool's sacrifice, but a dead child." And raising his voice, he informed the caravan.

"Worse and worse," said the religious ones, shaking in their boots. "Fiends have changed our wholesome votive into an immature corpse."

But the waggon master only called for spades to cover the sad remnant over.

It was as the spades began their labor that the dead child moved, and by rotating itself, showed them its revolting scars and deformities, its innocence, its great eyes—and veil of lovely hair.

Though the flits had attacked her thoroughly, she was by now, through all the repeated stingings of earlier times, and the eating of stung lizards, immune to flittish bane. It had drugged but not curtailed her. Yet, singlemindedly thinking her execution seen to, the sisterhood had carried her to the world's edge (the outer limits of the quag) and thrown her away there by the foulest object they could see, a causeway built by men. Having much of their own then to do, they had hurried off at once.

"Child," breathed the wagon master with horror and tenderness, but he spoke in the tongue of humankind. She could not understand.

5 Ezail and Chavir

THEY MIGHT HAVE named her for her hair, which in the sunlight was the color of marigolds. Her hair was the dower she brought to her new life, but she had been received without thought of transaction. Later, she herself offered the bounty, explaining eloquently, if with very few words, that the vast billowings of that silken veil hung heavy on her, that it suited her to have them lopped, every third month, to her shoulders—for, from her seventh year, if left to itself, the hair went on growing, to her knees, to her feet, and farther, till it lay along the ground. Besides its pigment, its marvelous softness, luxuriousness and luster, it exuded a faint radiant perfume. These glories lasted indefinitely in the shorn locks as with the growing ones. Indeed there was, in a box of the wagon master's, a tress from the child's second year with him, and it was as perfect on her seventeenth birthday as at the minute of its cutting. Tractable, too, the hair could be woven into braid, or gummed for fringework. Sold, it went for the enhancement of wealthy garments or the caparisons of costly steeds. Those who bought it did not know its source, yet often it was called *Angels' Fleece,* or *Ethereal Threads*. By her hair one knew, unknowingly, what she might have been. But not only by that.

The wagon master, who accepted her, unreferenced, from the swamp, shortly carried her to the town which was his home. To those who inquired, both in the journeying and the town, as to what he meant by it, he said only, "She came in my road. The gods put blossoms at the wayside. We may pluck them, if we desire." "But," said general opinion, "*that* is no blossom. It is an accursed misbegetting, doubtless exposed by aggrieved parents." "My house lacks any feminine being," said the wagon master. "You cannot mean to breed up *that* for such use—" "I shall neither breed nor use. She must grow and be of and for herself. But she shall do it under the shelter of my roof."

The fact was, the two wives of the wagon master, both of whom he had loved dearly, were a decade dead of the plague. His unborn offspring had gone with them. At that time he had felt much bereft, and taken to the caravan trade, leaving his house where it stood. When he was in it, after, he would hire only male servants, and for his solace, he came to value boys. While in the line of business he met merchants and drovers, and priests and lordlings. It was as if he feared the plague might cling about him yet, to harm that other sex he liked the best and knew the least.

But the child changed all that.

Seeing she was so tiny and so young, he straight away engaged a nurse for her, and later on he purchased an infantile slave girl and freed her, to be the child's companion.

All who had to do with the child at first proximity turned gray with loathing. In seven minutes that had gone to pity. An hour more and they were appeased, or intrigued, or only dumb. In seven days they were playful and full of brightness. They were hers.

You could not say exactly how this happened. Something in her eyes. Something in her manner. She was a hunch-backed little dwarf thing, who moved like a seawave, like the bird in flight. She was malformed and disfigured and perhaps mentally mostly a simpleton—who had the scent of white flowers about her, who had an infrequent voice with the chime of pale gold. Her fool's gazes were full of some wisdom intelligence would obliterate. As he had said she should, the wagon master, she came to be. She *was*. She did not fret or strive. No one had ever seen her discontented, testy, seen her afraid, ardent, bewildered, eager, weeping. She would smile, but only in the way a leaf turns to the sun.

She was, she grew. She grew up. The household grew with her. She learned the habits of human society, and if she did not copy, respected them. She learned the language human society spoke in those parts, and occasionally uttered it.

The first time she cut her own hair, she took it to the wagon master. It was the evening she was nine years old, for he reckoned her birthdays from the night of her finding, and he had brought her as he always did a gift, a necklace of amethyst beads. She set the wonderful hair before him like a coil of gilded rope. She smiled. She said, "Too heavy. Sell it, could you not?" Then she sat down to play with the beads, smoothing and sometimes kissing them, or holding them up to catch the pulsing clarity of dusk. Patently, living in his house, she had heard of commerce. But what a plan! (Going to look again upon the perfect tress of her second year, the plan's value began to nag at him.) He recounted the tale to partners of his.

The canny one said, "Do it. I never saw such stuff. It is magic and will pave the paths with money." The other said, "You had best obey her. She is so beautiful, you can hardly refuse." "*Beautiful!*" cried the wagon master, shocked and shamed to hear another air his own thought. "Yes," said the partner, "this strong wine of yours has loosened my tongue. But I will stand by my choice of description. Beautiful." And then this man quaffed more of the wine and looked up at the starry sky, (for they lay out at their dinner on the summer roof of the house, and it was midnight). "I will suppose that all humankind have souls, a condition which, when sober, I do not hold. And the soul of that one you found beside the causeway shines through her skin like flame through a broken lamp. Can I see the lamp then, its flaws and ill-making, with such light in my eyes?"

"But the hair of her head," added the canny one, "*there* you see the flame burning *free* of the lamp."

He thought of her, the wagon master, when he was hundreds of miles off upon the routes of the caravans, in the courtyards and camps, in the dust and havoc, when robbers threatened, tolls were officious, animals or men fractious, when he was tired, when he recalled the ghosts of his wives. He thought of her burning in his house like a lamp in a window. He was past his prime, or he would have wed her—not to lie with her or possess her in any sort, but to secure her, to draw her further into his heart. But it was unnecessary. Some instinct kept him from it. Though love her he did.

And then, when she was about thirteen, it began to be that he would take her with him as he journeyed, and the companion-girl and the nurse also, and it fell out that after all he had a wagon full of women on the roads; and soon enough other women were allowed among the travelers, merchant's wives and concubines, priestesses, goatmaids and ladies. These sometimes drew him aside.

"Who is that dwarf-girl? Such a gentle smile she gave me. And her hair is fit for a goddess."

"That is my daughter."

"And what is her name—for I should like to speak a word with her."

"We name her Ezail."

Ezail: Soul.

It happened that on a certain night of a certain journey, when Ezail was fifteen years of age, the wagon master had a curious dream.

The caravan had wended all day across a great bare plain, but come near sundown to a haven of groves and villages. Here a lake floated in the earth like a glimmering spell, and cream-colored oxen drank there under the cedar trees. Ezail had not gone with the wagon master on that journey, for he had reckoned it would be rough venturing, all of it like the plain, and rougher caravanserai by night. Seeing otherwise when the twilight flowered upon the water, and the oxen drinking in the shadow of the cedars' reflection, he was sorry. "I will tell her how it was," he said. But when he slept, someone stood before his tent. The wagon master got up and went out to him. It was a young man wrapped in a magenta cloak. His chisled profile was such that the wagon master took him for a prince, and stared at his moon-yellow hair and the gilt lashes of his downcast eye.

"Sir, how may I be of help?"

The handsome prince did not reply. Only, he drew the hood of his cloak about his face, so its left side was invisible.

"If it is your wish, my lord, to join this caravan, I vouchsafe we can accommodate you."

Then the prince laughed. For a moment it was the most offensive row the wagon master had ever heard—next it was the most charming sound of his experience, more a melody than amusement. But as he laughed, the young man's teeth sparkled very oddly.

The wagon master stepped back a pace. In his dream he thought, *I must be wary.*

"Not essentially," said the prince. "I am at *your* mercy. For I have come to ask of you your daughter's hand."

The wagon master was so flurried he said at once: "I have no daughter."

"Yes, but you do have a daughter. Soul-flame Ezail."

Then the wagon master did not know what he felt. He felt too much. And disgust and sorrow, jealousy and irony, contempt and flattery and fury were not unmixed in it.

"You cannot," said he at length, "mean what you say. For she is—she is not made for the forms of marriage."

"You say," murmured the prince, "she is not made for love."

"Indeed . . . I will say that."

"For death, then."

The wagon master's feelings rushed and froze into one. He was terrified.

"Do not curse her, she has borne enough. Curse me, if you must."

And then he caught the glint of an eye. A horrid eye, tinted all wrong.

"You mistake me," said the eye's owner, turning away from him a fraction more. "Love and death are the games we play, while we live."

The wagon master burst out, much to his uneasy surprise:

"But you, lord, live for ever. Death can be nothing to you. Let alone love."

In that instant, the moon winged up over the cedar

groves. It cast the lake in white mirror. It smoked through the figure of the princely one, through his hood and his hair and his body and his gorgeous cloak on which were sewn, in splinters of glass, the constellations.

"I insist I am a mortal," said the transparency, "as are you. But is this my dream, or is the dream yours? Do I dream you? Do you dream me? Ah, now, before one of us awakes, pledge me Ezail. I care nothing for her physical deformities. I, too, am deformed. This left side of mine, hidden in my mangle, oh, it is a sight to make you run howling mad, I do assure you."

"Then do not dare imagine I would let you have her."

"You could not keep her from me," said the prince, or the fiend, or whatever he was, "if she willed it so." But the moon, streaming through him, was washing him away. He spoke only once more, in a vocal noise like thin gravel sifting through a sieve of brass. "I do not care for this dream. Waken, you, and let me waken. I have three more years to grow to man's estate. I am a king's son by one of the lesser wives. I have no birthright. My destiny is to roam and rave beyond the walls of my father's house, to make of myself a sort of hero. Trust me, I have no margin for madmen's dreams."

At which he vanished. But where he went, for a moment the wagon master thought he saw another country in the night, a walled palace on a high hill, the lattice of a window and a chamber beyond where someone lay tossing and groaning in a dream.

But that, too, faded away, and the wagon master also turned away, and found himself upon his mattress in the tent. Where, like any sensible man, he blamed the date wine and the bare plain, the oxen drinking in the twilight, the aroma of cedarwood, and fell asleep once more. And rising at dawn, the dream was only like a healing bruise. He had rubbed it better by noon.

Chavir commenced in the king's High House, where he was the king's thirty-third son, which did not augur well for him. His hair was raven black and his eyes the blue of turquoise. But in that, too, he had somewhat erred, for black hair was considered unlucky in those lands, while blue eyes were hardly known there.

The mother of Chavir had believed herself barren, for though a lesser wife, at one season she had been a favorite of the king's leisure. Often called to his bed, her womb chose to ignore his efforts. Thus she had recourse to an old wise woman who now and then visited the women's courts. The witch probed the king's lesser wife, asked pertinent and impertinent questions, and finally removed from her robe a casket.

"Since you are willing to add your mite to the ninety-seven others, of both genders, already or about to be making clamorous the king's palace, put in this cask your right hand, and draw therefrom, without one glance, the first object your fingers shall encounter."

Then the lesser queen, with a thrill of nervousness, did as she was told. What came into her grasp was a small square thing, hard and cool as a river stone.

"Dice?" queried the beldame in apparent interest. "I have never seen a die plucked out before. Are you sure you did not put it there yourself?"

"What would be the point in that?" retorted the lesser queen irritably.

"What is the point of anything?" unhelpfully returned the witch. "Flesh is dust, life unreal, an illusion, a play we are at."

The queen tapped her foot and frowned.

"Shall I then summon my slave and contrive for you the illusion that you are being struck upon your dust by an unreal rod?"

"You must please yourself," said the witch with an air of indifference. "Do not, however, in such a case anticipate my advice."

"There shall be no rods, real or unreal. But two cups of honey beer and a ring of gold."

"Then you may take the die, reduce it to granules, drop these in liquid, and drink the brew when next you are sent for to attend your husband."

This the queen did, having the die, which seemed not unlike amber but was more friable, crushed in a mortar. The grains she kept to hand and swallowed at the appropriate hour. Her subsequent rapture in the arms of the king was unduly extreme, and soon enough she found herself with child.

It then turned out the king lost his appetite for her entirely, and in due course the baby was born, a son, to no special effect. And even the pleasure of the mother faded. The child, though handsome, was blue-eyed, black of hair, and sufficiently elusive in his behavior some said he was touched in the mind. He had the tendencies of a cat, liking much slumber and contrary exercise. Before her son was five, the lesser queen gave up on him, and took lovers. Being come on with one of these by the king's steward, she was gone before her son was seven.

A disgraced satellite of the court, the boy continued life's journey, rather impeded by the cosseting and niggling, tutelage and tantrums, amorous overtures and pranks of an idle harem, several educating scholars, and most of the soldiers of the king's High House.

By fourteen years he could or would neither read nor write, nor fight, nor fornicate. He would nevertheless insult anyone within an inch of murder, sing birds from branches, speak poetry to pigs, and offer smiling verbal poison to his superiors. He could also climb trees to a height unmentionable. He could dream such dreams that waking was an interruption. Such was his strength and presence, additionally, he could seem in repose a grown man, and a sagacious one. And could appear, when in vitality, to be a warrior, the proper heir of kings, and possibly a sorcerer. But he was not exactly any of these. If anything, he was a cultured lynx in human form.

What is he doing here? said all the house, meaning, why ever had he got himself born there, to annoy them.

"You must mend your ways," said pedants to Chavir, as he lay along the dappled boughs above them.

"I have no ways," answered Chavir, diving into a rock pool.

"Conceivably he is infected by a devil. Or a multiplicity of devils," muttered some. "Does he perhaps change into a were-creature at the ripeness of the moon?"

But Chavir did not do so, save in those dreams of his.

"Eat with me, get drunk with me, plot with me, quarrel with me, lie with me," said the court.

"Go elsewhere," said Chavir.

More than thrice, enemies—rejected suitors, incensed others—sent agents. The fleet-footed assassins tripped and fell from roofs. The cobras were found nestled in the bosom of unbitten Chavir.

"Who is that boy?" said the king, when Chavir stalked by him, unbowing, unnoticing, as the crowd fell loyally prostrate.

"The thirty-third son, majesty."

"Award him," said the king, "thirty-three lashes."

"That must undoubtedly kill him," said the king's steward, with optimism.

Having been given the slip, they did not find the boy again before dawn, for he was in a spot they had not thought of—his own bedchamber. There he lay as the sun stared in on him, tossing in a golden nightmare. He sang in his sleep, in the grip of the dream. He sang he was a mantis balanced on a lake. He sang he was a lord and lay in a bag of dice. He sang he loved the girl child of a magician or a wagon master or a prince whose eyes were night. He sang of one he called Night's Daughter.

His voice was so musical they paused to listen. Then they shook themselves and woke him up.

"Come to the yards, Chavir."

"Come and be whipped, Chavir."

"Thirty-three strokes. You have outshone yourself before the king."

"Thirty-three?" said Chavir. "Madness. I did not get myself born to die. I have better things to do."

And leaping from them, like poreless lightning searing through their hands, he broke the metal lattice of the window, sprang from its sill, entered a tree—blazed there, outshining the sun, this time—and was gone."

At the king's command, Chavir was hunted for some months about the hill country. And not found.

A bunch of days after Ezail's seventeenth birthday, as her guardian sat contemplating that lock of her unwithering hair, a stranger came seeking him.

"Wagon master, I will be frank with you. I and mine desire to make a pilgrimage to the holy city Jhardamorjh. It is a long way off, and no other will take our custom. We mean to arrive during the festival month of the Exaltation, whose obscure rites we would study. Here is gold. We shall pay generously. What do you say?"

"I have heard of Jhardamorjh, but thought it a legend. Are you precise that it exists?" The pilgrim protested that it did. "Then it has great wonders, does it not? Animals of stone that speak, a mystical fountain that cures all ills?"

"So it is said."

After some further exchanges, the wagon master agreed to the enterprise. In his heart he had beheld Ezail, rising from a magic basin in that unknown city, straight and fair. He rebuked himself for the fantasy, for miracles were nowadays in short supply. "Nevertheless, she shall ride with me. For if it is true the statues talk or chant, as I remember being told when a brat, we had better witness it before I am too old. Besides the road lies northward, this fellow says, a trek of nearly half a year. I would not be parted from her so long."

The road north passed among high plains and tunneled through vast forests. Winter met them on the way. Pillars of rain stood from earth to heaven where the trees did not. They came to a yellow river, storming in the wet. A bridge of black granite went over it that it took an hour to cross. But four months had gone already.

Then they rode into a country of valleys, a land of spring. Other caravans were on the paths. As men hailed one another, all spoke now of going to Jhardamorjh. And in the encampments there came to be dancings and fairs, barter and selling and unbridled tales. Many lovely girls were traveling in carts, or in litters borne by strong slaves, chariots pulled by snowy asses.

"It is for the Festival," said the pilgrims, who gossiped with all and sundry. "The month of the Exaltation falls once only in every seven years."

But the rites were merely alluded to, not discussed openly. The glamorous girls looked proudly between their beaded curtains and under their pearly veils.

The pilgrims gleaned this much: One maiden would be chosen for a nameless honor. All wanted it, and glared upon the rest with daggers for eyes. The same with their families and kin who accompanied them. And as they drew nearer the city there were sometimes hot words or blows, and once a poisoning, it was said. And once, as they traveled, the wagon master espied a girl seated at the wayside sobbing. Drawing rein, he called to her, but she would not answer, hid her face.

Now Ezail's nurse had grown elderly and had not come on the trek, but the girl companion of Ezail, who had bright sharp eyes and neat sharp ears, she announced to the wagonmaster, "Last night I saw that one standing by her father's cart and weeping. *She* said, 'I will not,' and *he* said, 'Then go home on your own.' And there she is, about to do it."

"But what would she not do?"

"It is something concerning the choosing, the Exaltation. You know I have been about, looking, at the fairs among the caravans, and I have taken note. *She* is not as pretty as others I have seen, and doubtless dreaded to be publicly dismissed."

They came down to Jhardamorjh, the holy city, in the morning. The sun rose on its left hand. They flashed with rainbows and gold, the tops of Jhardamorjh, and around it there passed three rings of mighty walls, the innermost wall the highest, and the outermost the lowest of the three, being, that one, just the height of seventy tall men, sixty-nine of them standing on another's shoulders. The lowest wall had towers plated with copper, the middle wall had towers plated with bronze. The topmost wall had no towers, but a wide walk where gardens grew. At sunrise every day during the Festival, a thousand blue birds were released into the sky. At sunset a thousand red birds were sent after them. The highway which led to the city was lined by icons and obelisks of crimson and black basalt, and beyond lay flowering fields watered by countless canals.

The lowest of the three walls was pierced, where the road came against it, by a gateway having three doors. Separating the doors, and on either side of them, were four huge beasts of coal-black basalt. As each hour of the day gave place to another, these beasts would, by clockwork or magic or both, lift one foot after another, turn their heads as if to look about, and finally emit a long, bell-like note, which could be heard all over the city, and also over all the surrounding country for miles.

It happened that the wagon master's caravan was drawing near the gateway, in company with many others, when there occurred the displacement of the first morning hour.

Stiffly the black beasts unlocked their limbs, rotated their necks, parted their beaked heads, and vented the peerless note.

Several horses, asses and mules began to buck and rear, the wagon master's among them. From the carts men and women cried aloud, or, sinking on their knees, made esoteric genuflections.

But, imperturbable stone as they were, the great creatures of the gate, their duty finished, only resettled their feet, returned southward their heads (which had the visages of eagles), and were still.

On reaching the gatemouth, every traveler stared upon these wonders. They were, all four, each as big as an elephant. Their carven bodies were those of horses, but their legs were the legs of giant fowl. They had collars of gold, gold on their claws and beaks, and in their eyes black mirrors.

Ezail's guardian had, in the event, been troubled that the girl might be distressed; her companion had screamed with honest fright. But Ezail showed no fear, nor any amazement. She gazed interestedly on the beasts of basalt, as she had gazed on more ordinary things.

"Clearly," said the leader of the pilgrims, "it is for those creatures the city is named. For in the ritual tongue of the Festival, which is the antique language of this land, that is the meaning of *jhardamorjh*—a hybrid prodigy, a horse having an eagle's feet and head."

A while it took to get through the gate, so full with pilgrims and other visitors it was. And now and then, as they waited, they heard a sound like breaking pots.

Presently the way was open, and there came a man to the wagon master.

"Prosper in our home, stranger. Are any women with you?"

"As you see, there are," replied the wagon master, for though Ezail had withdrawn herself from view, the companion was peeking forth.

"And this, or these, being maidens, unwed?"

"To my knowledge."

"Do you accept for them, then, tablets of the Exaltation?"

The wagon master felt a compunction.

"Is it the tradition?"

"At this time, no unmarried girl between fifteen and twenty-three years may be within or enter into the city, but that she accepts a clay tablet, broken, one half of it being given her and the other half marked for her name and origins, and cast in with the general lot. By that means, when the hour of choosing arrives, no unfairness is likely."

"I have heard of a choosing," said the wagon master, "and seen how the beauties of all regions flock to it. But before I accept any token for my girls, who are of a more homely sort, I would have further information. If it is a choosing among women, why is the choice to be made?"

"We do not speak of it," said the officer of the gate with a face of adamant. "It is nevertheless understood."

"I am an alien in your land, and do *not* understand it."

"Regardless, I may say nothing more. Either accept the tablets, or leave your women outside the gate."

"I will not accept. They, and I, will remain outside. These pilgrims I and my servants have escorted, let them go in, for it is they who wish to do so."

Then he drew his wagon aside, and his men gathered around it. With expressions of flummox, the pilgrim band parted from them and hastened into the city. The rest of the crowd went after, several girls and young women of unusual attraction hurrying with them.

Since he spurned the city, it happened the wagon master, after coming such a distance, never saw it. But, as he had contracted to conduct the pilgrims homeward, when the Festival was done, he made a camp for his own wagons and people close to a village in the flowering fields. The village itself was almost deserted, its inhabitants having gone into Jhardamorjh.

There stood the city then, about three miles off, its towered walls gleaming under the sun and under the moon. At dawn a blue cloud of birds winged up from them, at dusk a feathered scarlet thunder. All day the note of the gate beasts sounded out the hours, though between sunset and sunrise they were silent.

The wagon master kicked his heels, waiting on the pilgrims. He began to wish he might see inside the walls of Jhardamorjh. Yet also he did not wish it. Besides, the disappointment of the companion of Ezail weighed on him. "Could I not disguise myself as a boy and so slink into their city of sights?" The wagon master would not comply. "Something in this rite of theirs is unsavory. They will not tell it. You must not risk yourself, must not enter. Nor shall I."

But for his men, he saw no reason to forbid them any more.

"Go in," said he, "and when you have had your fill, come back to me and tell me what you have seen and learned."

Therefore the wagoners went off into Jhardamorjh that evening, and stayed there some while. But after two or three days and nights had passed, the oldest man returned.

"Sir," he said to Ezail's guardian, "never in all my born years did I behold such a place. I have heard a story that once a goddess ruled on earth, and her vast metropolis cannot have been more grand than this.

"The main streets are paved with colored stones, and the buildings are of milk-white marble and black marble, trimmed with gold, and with dragon-green tiles or rose-red tiles to crown them. Everywhere are fountains which pour from spouts of bronze into basins of porphyry. All of these are said to be magical, and I have drunk from nearly all, so no doubt I have had benefit! Besides there are parks and gardens of diverse plants, and design peculiar, some making patterns that are to be seen only when looking down from the upper windows and walks round about, or having only a single series of shapes, or one color, such as a garden of white magnolias and hyacinths, the grass of which was also white as the purest sugar, and even a white palm grew there with a trunk like a bone and fronds of vellum, but some green butterflies played about it that the gardener tried without success to chase away.

"Near the center of the city there are many towers of

basalt, on whose high roofs, gold-railed, gardens also grow, and enormous prisms stand there to entrance the sun.

"During the Festival, a visitor has only to proclaim himself to be given food and drink of the best quality, though they do not invite him into their homes, for it is a sacred time and that, it seems, would be a profanity. As for taverns, and houses of delight, I did not chance upon any, although yet again there are many beautiful women in the city, of twenty-four years or a little more, who, having missed being chosen when of age in previous Exaltations, now live only for sensual sport. And to lie out in the sumptuous parks is no hardship in spring weather.

"At the very midst of the city there is a sort of hill, and if it is man-fashioned or a natural thing I could not tell, nor would any of them enlighten me. For if you say to a native of Jhardamorjh, 'Explain the rites to me,' she will say, 'Pray have another apple.' Or if you say, 'What is that hill?' She will say, 'Oh, kiss me again! Here is a rise more appealing.' But the hill is there, and it ascends in vast steps or terraces, and a wood seems to clothe it, in which golden columns catch the sun or moon, and out of which sprinkling waters go glittering. It ends above in a bright something. But if you say to her, 'What is that which shines there?' She replies, 'Are you feeble that you cannot embrace me three times?'

"But there is this: In the intervals of the night I have heard tabors beating and the sistrum clinking, and like phantoms the lovely virgins of Jhardamorjh dance through the avenues and under the white and blue and the rosy and the dragon-green palms. They dance with ribbons in their hair, and their eyes are wide and wild, like the eyes of mad dreamers. There is surely something they drink or eat here, the women, from the age of fourteen or fifteen upward, and in the outer lands they take it, too, I suppose, and the female visitors get to have it. Or maybe it is only what they are taught to believe rather than what they are trained to swallow.

"In the event, I have had enough. Tomorrow is that choosing they mention—and then will not speak of again—

but which fills the air like dust. And I did not want to see it.

"Yet, I can tell you one thing. There is a girl I saw dancing at midnight by a magical fountain, and she wore a dress of gold fringed with scintillant marigold fringes, the hair of your ward, sir. Your ward's companion, it must be admitted, has been braiding and gumming, and selling the product on the sly, at the camp markets along our way, and for this girl who danced some Ethereal Threads must have been purchased, to adorn her garment. And as she danced, on her white feet under the fountain, beating the tabor with her narrow hands, I heard her murmur over and over: 'I have put witchcraft on my tablet, they will pick it out. I shall be among the chosen. And am I not fair enough that of those chosen I shall be chosen again, shall be chosen over all, shall become the Exalted?' Exactly then the woman I had been with, some twenty-five years old (she thinking I slept as I pretended), crept up to the dancing girl and perused her with envious hatred. 'Hear me,' she said, 'even if they choose you, they may break the rule like the tablet, if they can discover one fairer than you that they did not take from the lot. It is so. For, seven years back, my tablet was among those plucked, and of the damsels thus assembled they judged me the best. But then my sister, whose tablet had been missed, she stood forth before them with her skin and hair and breasts and face, and those who were to judge found her more beautiful than I. And so they broke the rule, and took her in my stead. Since when I languish here and lie with foreign men to ease me of my memory.' And at that," said the wagon master's man, "I pretended to wake up, and both of them ran away, but I had learned all I might, and now I teach it to you."

"In the name of life, what is it, what is it that they do?" exclaimed the wagon master, Ezail's guardian.

"They have in their city neither a king nor a priest that I noticed, nor any king's palace, nor any temple," declared this man. "I believe their wealth and ways spring from some powerful being or idea, which is evidenced upon that central hill. And for this the women are chosen, to go to it. And the honor and blessing is frantically coveted. To be just whoever judges must first choose at hazard from a tub of broken tablets, and then choose again from the certain number of maidens so drawn. And this chosen Exalted One, she goes to the hill, and never returns from the hill. And seven years later, it is done again. And so it has been for some two hundred years or longer. And I will add only these words. That if I were a man here with sisters or daughters between fifteen and twenty-three summers, though it is a fine city, I would take those girls by night, however much they lamented, and be gone with them to another distant country."

The gate beasts sang for the last hour of the day, the sun declined, the sunset birds fled over the sky. In the golden chalice of the afterglow, before the gates should close, one more traveler entered Jhardamorjh. It was a handsome man in the splendor of his youth, his hair a black mane couthly combed to silk. To come on him from any side was to be struck by his looks. On his tall and slender body was belted a robe of rich magenta, on his feet were blanched leather shoes. But no sword was at his hip, and though his blue eyes sometimes blazed like the edges of knives, they could turn also smoky, dulcet.

Out of the dusk the women of the city swam to him on tides of perfume, veils and voices. He put them away with a gentle hand like a whiplash.

He was offered wine. He poured it on the paved streets. "A libation to your gods. Who are they, here?"

The women smiled secretively, some glanced toward a high hill of terraces, woods, columns, on the west of which an ebbing flicker of the sun yet played, like one golden star.

When hungry, he took fruit from the trees of the parks. The gardeners, who also watched there by night, remonstrated. It did not charm them to find a beautiful young man lying in the carefully tended boughs absorbing their decorations. But the foreigner vanished like a snake through the branches.

In Jhardamorjh, every seven years, there was elected a new council to judge the Exaltation. Word came to these fellows. On the very eve of the choosing, a stranger was within the walls who did not go on as the stranger should. Soldiers of the city went with torches to seek him. The tramp of their feet was harsh on the avenues, for no one was abroad that night. Even the visitors, drugged by attentions, slept in the depths of gardens. The wild dancers, the girls between fifteen and twenty-three years, lay upon their backs, sleepless, conning the future.

The soldiers found Chavir seated on the steps of a fountain. This was at the center of the city, up against the mysterious hill. Coming to the hill's base, Chavir had seen it, too, was ringed by a great wall, more than seventy feet high. In this, though he had prowled about it, no gate was visible. There was no sound in that spot save for the evening breeze upon the trees of the height, the whisper of its waters, and the louder plashing of the fountain on the ground nearby.

Then presently came the soldiers' clank and the sputter of torch grease, and the question:

"What, O youth, is your errand in this city?"

Chavir lowered his eyes, his look was clandestine.

"To rest from my adventures."

"You vaunt yourself. What adventures were these? We hear you will not even show courtesy to parched ladies. You do not carry the steel or iron of a warrior."

"I have never," said Chavir, raising eyes of smoke, "lain with a woman, nor fought with a man." He smiled. "Nor, for that matter, fought a woman, or lain with a man. There are other deeds. I fled the wrath of a king to whom I would not bow, and ever since, for a year or so, have gone through many lands as nimbly as daylight. But here and there some loved me or took against me, or a lord's dogs followed me from fascination, or a cutthroat attempted my life and something in my manner caused him to rush, screaming, away. Or I have tamed panthers, or answered riddles through which other men, not answering, were put to death. And I have found an odd knack for this thing, or that. I have seen temples built or towns burning, or mountains that roar or seas that change in the cold to glass. None of these things can compare, however, with the curious dreams that come when I sleep. I shall not recount them to you. Suffice it to say, in some form I do not comprehend—nor am I disturbed that I do not—my dreams have brought me to your city."

The soldiers stood and stared.

Their captain said, "Tomorrow is a sacred day. You must not take it hard, but I think it best you should have your ease in jail, until tomorrow's sun has set."

"As you please," said Chavir. "Do you desire to bind me? I warn you, there is sorcery I have acquired, or have always owned, by which I am inclined to undo bindings."

The soldiers scoffed and made a din in the street. Three strode upon Chavir, took him between them and put on his wrists fetters of steel. Chavir lifted his arms and the fetters uncoiled and plopped to the paving with a clatter.

"It seems I am a breaker of chains," said he. "But nevertheless I will go with you to prison, and remain there until tomorrow's sunset."

The soldiers had fallen back in outrage and dismay. The captain stood alone and faced out Chavir.

"It is a madness to trust you, yet there is no choice. We march now to the jail. Follow us if you will."

Then they turned about and marched, and Chavir followed them on his blanched leather soles, looking with eyes of harmless knives.

Before the dawn, in an hour of amethyst, the girl who had danced with a tabor left her bed and put on her dress of gold. How it shone, and how its scented fringes rippled. They were themselves magical. This maiden's doting aunt, journeying to Jhardamorjh for the Exaltation, had bought them from a sharp female among the caravans. "Made from the hair of angels!" declared the female and consequently the aunt. "Long ago," the aunt alone had added, "I missed my chance at the choosing. For, as you know, niece, I was born half the world away, and we were ignorant there. But who knows, your beauty may win *you* the ecstasy and the honor, and your kin the glory."

All across the city, the maiden knew, other maidens rose and bathed and were anointed and clad themselves like queens. The golden girl flung open her casement. "*Let it be me,*" said she to the city and the sky. But all over Jhardamorjh a thousand windows, balconies, featured maidens who said just the same.

Then the sun flung open *his* window, and from a thousand doors and tent flaps, and other exits, issued a thousand varieties of human flower, each attended by her servants and her family, each grasping firm one part of a broken clay tablet.

There was a spacious square among the towers of basalt; here the choosing was to be. A fountain plashed close by under the flank of a mighty wall, seventy feet or more in height, that encircled a wooded hill. (On the steps of the fountain lay two broken fetters and the pit of a damson, but no one noticed these.)

The crowd in the square was packed close, while elsewhere men and women filled the upper stories and the rooftops. And from the press, as if from fields of grass, the tall slender flowers were raising heads of gilt and honey and auburn and henna and chrysanthemum. . . .

The council of judges mounted a platform at the middle of the square. Then a long tub of bronze was lugged up there. It was closed by a plate of lead, with several iron locks and some twenty or thirty seals of wax, which must all be undone—and they could have employed for that, to save them time, a handsome young man reposing that morning in the prison, with all *its* locks off the doors and lying on the flag-stones. But they had no recourse to Chavir. They opened the seals and locks laboriously and elaborately in the sight of the crowd. Total silence prevailed throughout.

The plate when off revealed heaps of clay half-tablets. They were daintily stirred by blindfolded slaves.

Then a man came through the crowd leading a black stallion yearling, and a second man with a wicker cage in which there stared and stamped a tabby eaglet.

The first judge of the council addressed animal and bird in this manner:

"Say—how many tablets shall be drawn?"

Then the yearling tossed its head three times, and the eaglet flared its stubby wings once, twice.

"The number is, for every man, five."

Then each of the council rolled up his priceless sleeves and, a hood having been cast on his head and over his eyes, every man was led to the tub, thrust in his arms like a washerwoman, up to the elbows, and clawed and scrabbled, till he had pulled out, every one, five broken tablets.

And since the number of the council itself that year amounted to ten persons, at length fifty of these tablets lay out on the platform.

Horns and drums sounded. Then the names of the chosen fifty were exclaimed.

At every name shrieks arose and bodies fell down fainting. Then immediately there was a swirl and eddy through the crowd. The maiden came forth alone. She came forth as if dazed and dazzled, and drifted like a sleepwalker to the platform, and mounted it.

When all fifty maidens had been named and their tablet portions verified, a noise of misery swelled over the square from the throats of those who were missed. The youngest, who knew that in seven more years another chance would be offered them, did not take it quite so ill. But those late in the seventeenth year or more were beside themselves. Some tore their garments and hair. Some forced their way from the crowd and threw themselves out before the judges, exhibiting their claims to beauty without any particular restraint.

But it was a fact, the fifty already selected were in themselves such matchless articles, they could not it seemed be transcended.

Eventually outcry subsided. Heavy lacquer screens were erected on the platform. Noble women came and examined, behind these screens, the chosen maidens.

The sun meanwhile, perhaps himself desirous to pry, lifted above the screens and dropped his inflammatory light down on the examining couches. It was noon.

The screens were removed. Every maiden had been certified as flawless.

There they waited then, fifty young jewels of the earth, each clamouring in her thundering heart to desert that earth and to go instead—to what?

Here is the truth. Not one of them could have said. The stepped hill which was always there, the rites which were always behind or before them, the sacred ambience which was ceaselessly referred to, mooted, and murmured of, none was ever explained, not by any, for no one knew. None inquired after it, either, save for strangers, who were fobbed off. It was a Wonder. It was a Holiness. It was eternally present in the life of Jhardamorjh. But it was *unknown*. And in this way, many had come to believe, in inner chambers of the brain, that they had been granted knowledge. That it was this thing or that thing. And now and then a secret cult had sprung up in the city, implying access to the answer. But such were quickly suppressed as heresy. To the maidens of the city it came to represent what might be expected, given the era, their youth, female station and female tuition.

The maiden in the fringed dress of gold, therefore, she stood upon the platform among the chosen fifty, secure in the certainty that the witchcraft on her own tablet had ensured its picking up, spinning every second fresh witchery on her own self, like a spider in a web: *Now choose me again.*

For it seemed to her she did know what lay under the rite. Exaltation was a marriage to a god. The god of the city, who dwelled upon the hill. The hill passed through, by some fabulous means, into an otherworld, a kingdom of heaven. And there he was, the divine husband. The quality of their union and its condition were supreme enough that only seven years of human life could endure the onslaught. But what did that matter? In seven years her gloss would have faded in the world, she would be a hag of twenty-three, and past the chance of choice. Besides, if he loved her, would not the god give her immortality in the upper lands? She would become a goddess after her mortal death, forever young, forever fair—and, if he had *truly* loved her, for ever his?

Now choose me again. From so many dreaming spirits and shouting minds.

The three mystics of the council, who had fasted, spent the night in deep thought, inhaled incense for breakfast, now approached and went wobbling up and down the line of maidens. Sometimes the hands of these men twitched, or their brows. Sometimes they might halt and gaze upon one girl with dilated pupils, and she would turn paler than pale and clench her fists.

The third mystic came to the girl in gold, the girl who had danced, and who had marigold fringes on her dress.

He came to her and having done so, did not move away. He stood before her like a swain smitten with love. And the golden girl met his gaze. Her eyes branded *choose me* into his skull.

At last, he left her, he went to his chair on the platform and leaned on the arm of another man for support, but did not sit.

The crowd marked this, and made noises of approbation and disapproval.

And, perhaps swayed a little by the decided action of the third mystic, the first and second mystics gravitated toward the girl in gold, and presently they also turned from the line without another glance, and went to their chairs.

Already tears like drops of glass, tinted by the kohl and paint upon their petal lids, were sliding from forty-nine pairs of eyes. Already forty-nine flowers were wilting. But one flower was straighter on a stem of steel, with steely fire, not water, in her eyes.

And then the first and second mystics, as the custom was, got up again and pointed to the girl they had chosen, the golden, steely girl. And going back to her, took her hands and led her forward. And in that instant she, too, wept in transport as forty-nine others moaned and toppled and showered downpours of despair.

And the third mystic, who should now go to the Exalted, and proclaim her, flung out his arms and cried in an insane voice:

"No! Not she! Not she! It is the other who is there, where *she* is. The *other* is the chosen! The other one!"

At this, a further silence crashed upon the scene. It was so quiet, you might have heard a hundred tears drop.

The council and the brother mystics pressed toward the dissenting third.

"What are you saying?"

"What can you mean?"

The third mystic composed himself with some hardship.

"I do not have any idea of what I mean, or what I say. I know only this. As I stood by that girl, I saw another girl. She was tall and pale as a white lotus. Her eyes were like the light itself. She was mantled in hair the color of tawny golden flowers, and from it exuded a scent that dizzied me. *She* is the Exalted. None, seeing her, could doubt it. Even if her tablet had not been plucked, if she had come before us we must have chosen her. But when I looked again and saw her led out, there was only a lovely girl like all the rest. Not she I had seen."

The council was nonplussed. The crowd, recovering itself, began to create a great effect.

"Come, we must have order," insisted one of the council. "Let us abide by the choosing. The girl in gold is the Exalted."

And many agreed with this.

But the third mystic, who it seems was genuine among his calling, cried again: "No, not she! You fools," he said, looking upon the whole throng with contempt, "can you not perceive a vision was given me. Can you not understand—*another than I has made this choice.*"

And at this monumental pronouncement, silence stole yet again over platform and crowd, and over the high roofs, into the sky.

All looked upon the golden girl, not as they had looked formerly. She fell on her knees, weeping now in fright. So unbridled was her distress that even some of her vanquished rivals were moved to go to her, to offer comfort. They saw besides she, too, like them, had missed her chance.

The third mystic also went back to her and observed her gravely with his unfocused eyes.

"Damsel, I am sorry to have wounded you. But I cannot go against Fate, or truth. Tell me, do you know who it can have been I saw in place of you? Have you some sister maybe, sick or hidden in your house? Or in another land? For if so, we must send for her." The girl only wept. The silver rain of it lay in the golden fringes of her clothes. "See," said the mystic, slowly, "the fringe upon your garment—that is the very hair in which *she* was mantled. How can that be?"

At these sentences, which carried by the acoustics of Fate or truth all over the square, the doting aunt of the golden girl gave a dreadful screech. She could not help it. Nor, when some hundreds of persons turned upon her to ask her reason, could she contain it.

"Among the markets of the caravans I found an impish maid, who sold me these fringes, calling them *Angels' Fleece.* But another told me they were the hairs of the maid's own mistress, which were so excellent they often sold them in this way. And though the mistress had never been seen by my informant, yet he showed me her wagon. And it lies now outside the city, near the village of the Crooked Street, for they would not come in to the choosing."

When the wagon master heard the rumbling, he took it for thunder.

"But a moment ago the sky was clear."

And he went out of his tent to see.

And he saw the thunder was not in heaven but along the ground.

It was all Jhardamorjh, running toward him through the fields.

He cursed, and called the men he had about him to his wagon. There, with stares and drawn blades, they waited.

The crowd began to arrive. At its forefront, the council came, guarded by its soldiers. But the ocean of faces was not hostile, the gestures were open and bemused. The wagon master found himself gazed on. He did not care for it. "What is it you are wanting," he said, "that your whole city needs to come ask for it?"

Then humbly and kindly, congratulating and praising him, the council told him what was wanted, but they spoke in the antique tongue of the rite. He grew angry, and they checked themselves, and humbly, kindly, congratulatory and praising, said it all again. And the crowd garnished the request with applause.

"You are mad," decided the wagon master. He stood across the entrance to the wagon. "My girls are not beauties. The one you talk of is—" and here he stammered, for it went against his heart to speak it—"is . . . crippled, and hunched. And if you tell of her hair, that is her only finery. She is a dwarf, and like a child—and dear to me as life."

The council staggered, smitten. They turned to each other.

"Let us see," said one who had a mystic's face.

The wagon master raised his cudgel, and his men their blades and staves, even those who had roistered in Jhardamorjh.

The third mystic stepped forward. He said, "She has been chosen . . . not by us . . . but by that of which we never speak. *That* has chosen her. And if, to that, she is beautiful, then beautiful she is. Let us see."

Above the head and behind the back of her guardian, Ezail parted the hide flaps of the wagon. There she stood. She was so little and humped, that mostly the crowd could not make her out, yet they detected the gleam of sun upon her hair, and called and cheered. Nearer, men's jaws slackened. The council gaped as if in terror. And the wagon master, looking round at her, had the countenance of terror, too, but his was fear for her.

The third mystic alone looked on Ezail with eyes that seemed to see, and it was indeed into his eyes that she looked in return.

"It is the moon before sunrise," said the third mystic, in his carrying tone, and in the antique tongue of the rite. "It is the dragonfly within the chrysalis and the rose under the ice. It is beauty enclosed—Oh, such beauty that only such a shape could keep it in. This is the one. The chosen. The Exalted. This."

And it was so strange that it took hold of them. They saw Ezail, and they saw *Ezail,* for there she was, the light in the lamp, the rose under the ice. They saw her and acclaimed her. Even the wagon master in a sudden weakness, between horror and tenderness (as at the very first when he had seen her on the causeway), even he knew that destiny had staked its claim, that they were in the net, and to struggle was no use. For Ezail, surely, she did not seem much to mind. She kissed her guardian, and the wheyfaced maid. She allowed the council and the citizens to take her away, toward the holy city. She did not once look over her distorted shoulder. Not a word of pleading or doubt was spoken. Not a word of farewell.

You could not find a gate in the wall because there was none. Every seven years artisans came and broke in the wall at a location decreed by horse head tosses and eagle flaps and similar omened things. When a hole of sufficient size had been achieved, the Exalted went into it and through it, to the foot of the wooded terraces of the hill. And swiftly then, as if in abject alarm, the artisans walled up the way again with bricks and stones and ready-mixed mortar, and the sweat bursting from them and their eyes on stalks. For after all, did the barrier not enclose a spot which, at some point, must stab through into another world? But one did not speak of that. One only shut the wall again as fast as could be, and came away from there with an easy heart, to rejoice another seven years.

Ezail, walled in, did not linger at the foot of the hill. Perhaps some sorcery of habit had been created there, by countless maidens who could not wait, for whoever entered now must quickly begin to climb, up and up, toward . . . the summit.

Myriad paths twined about the hill. All snaked toward its top. No sooner did you take one than the thick groves of the hill closed on you their curtains. Climbing upward, though the city was sometimes discernible as it sank away below, the views were distorted by patterns of foliage, by the spray of fountains, by a kind of glowing haze that may only have lain in the eyes of the beholder.

The afternoon sun had also come up upon the hill. He was not to be kept out of anywhere so pleasant. Once, he had had a garden of his own on the earth, had he not? But that was millennia ago.

The little hunched dwarf-maiden climbed steadily, with a strength she had always had, and with her accustomed delicacy, scarcely disturbing the grass and plants beside the path.

Perhaps she noticed that no birds sang in the trees, that no insects were busy there. Not a frog or lizard basked among the basins of the fountains. The only snakes were the paths.

On a turning, a bright pavilion sprang into sight. It had columns of white gold ringed with red gold, and a yellow gold roof, and it shone as if about to catch fire. It was a shrine, but to whom?

Not troubling, Ezail went on. And not long after, she

came upon another such shrine, also of gold in many forms, and burning bright.

The terraces of the hill had blurred with the years, and with the undergrowth, but old steps of stone were still to be found in them at junctures, to facilitate the ascent. Ezail's path now brought her to one such stair. A streamlet ran down beside it, and on the green moss under the heavy trees, a strange object was standing.

Had Ezail ever seen such a thing before, to know now what it was? Probably, for she was well-traveled. But in such a stance, such a condition; that was doubtful.

One hand was raised to the head, the other cast outward as if to seek balance. Moss had grown over the feet, and here and there, in the strands of a garment whose metal sequins had preserved it against total eradication by time and weather, ivy now mingled. On the head a tiara of dim pearls, all lopsided, but caught there some colorless stuff that flowed in the breeze. It was the skeleton of a girl. Some fluke had struck it there, upright and hard and fixed as a thin brown tree.

Another, taking this path, coming on this thing, what would that other have thought or done? Would she have credited, even, the marks of death and misfortune on this upland of sanctity?

Or, if she had taken a different path, would she have seen nothing untoward, and continued her exalting journey without qualms?

It must be said that, on any path the ascending maiden had selected, she was very likely to come on such relics, for the hill was littered, and this Ezail discovered, climbing on, looking only in her tranquil way, barely hesitating.

Each image was like the first, not in its mannerisms, not even all of them upright, for some were down headlong, with asphodel making vases of their eye-sockets. But they were, all of them, *rigid.* It was this rigidity which, when they became what now they were in a standing posture, had kept them standing, for a great many decades. And though, in death, the normal process had worn off their flesh, the bones stayed locked as at death's initial instant, bones like stones, as if the bones had *turned* to stone.

To have gone about over the hill and counted them,

would have been to tally all the maidens of the Exaltation, from its inception two centuries or more in the past.

But Ezail only climbed onward, upward, between the shrines and the fountains and the skeletons of young girls.

A million miles away, the city now. The world well lost?

The sun was westering in a brazen cloud when the trees opened on the slope of the highest terrace.

The path which Ezail had taken ended with the trees. Ahead lay a smooth lawn, cropped as if by a multitude of sheep. In the lawn was a pool in a bank of marble. It was an old pool, stagnant and muddy, black for the cut glass of the falling waters lower on the hill. But on the marble rim of the muddy pond were the perfect effigies of a flock of geese, all in gold. And just beyond, a golden goat leaned its head to a golden flower. Higher up the slope, three fruit trees, overblown and bowed to the earth with age, and barren, held in their branches fruits of silver. Was it not bizarre?

But to Ezail, gifted with acceptance, it was only another facet of the riotous marvel of the earth. For all was marvelous there, was and is still, but humanity becomes innured to repetitive amazements—that the sun may rise, that a tiny seed may become a tree or a man, that life, coming from nowhere, sets us to moving like clockwork, and going out again leaves us to sleep. Or else, as then, takes us away with it, who knows? But we are used to it all, dawn and growth, living and dying. It takes a dragon on the houseroof to wake us up now—and then, too. But to Ezail, all was wonder and no single item more than another: Dawns and dragons were one.

Above the lawn with the golden goat, the golden goose pond and the trees of silver fruit, there rose a building. Its roof had tiles of crystal, and rested on white pillars ringed round and round with the yellow gold, like the arms of a princess, but every bangle was as great as a mill grindstone. In the polished walls were huge golden doors. The slanting sunlight tinctured them with red, and showed that they stood partly ajar.

The shadows were lengthening, too, from the effigies of the geese, the goat, the old bowed trees. And from three thin figures of bone which were transfixed at various distances over the slope.

From the vast house, if such it was, the shadow poured east like a black liquid. And the red of sunset ran down the golden doors.

Ezail went over the lawn, and up the hill toward the golden house and the shadow.

Presently it seemed that she detected how, although the last sun lay on the doors, it could not get between them. Something impenetrable and black was there, far blacker than the shadow, or the shade of coming night. And then, high up between the parted doors, there was a blink of light, once, and again once.

Then the doors, with a faint groaning, began to open outward, and between them there came all the black core of all-shadow, tall as those doors, nearly as wide as they, black as black, with eyes of fire, with a bending of a fearsome head, and a rake of colossal talons shaking the roots of the hill—

And so Ezail beheld that which was the essence of the choosing, the Exalting, and the mystery, the jhardamorjh itself, for which the city was named.

Briskly Chavir walked from prison.

"I have done what you wanted," said he. "Until sunset I have inhabited the dungeon, and taught the pretty rats a new song or two."

A soldier barred his way.

"Where now? You are still intent on mischief."

"How true, dear pig."

The soldier shied away: "Would you transform me to a swine?"

"My name is Chavir; I am not numbered among the magicians. Besides, there is quite a resemblance already, what further transformation is needed?"

The captain alone dared to put out his hand to stay their guest.

"But where *next*, Chavir?"

"I have a great yearning to admire once more that wooded hill beyond that gateless wall."

The captain felt the touch of Fate upon his shoulder.

He replied, "Well, go then. The wall is gateless again, as you say."

In the ruby sky a crescent moon was riding. On earth, the darkness, and the moods of night.

Chavir walked among the basalt peaks, to the square with the fountain of steps. (Tonight the square was frilled with leavings—husks and broken flowers, spangles, the tines of fans, indecipherable marks of tears and anxiety. Over this space the golden girl-who-danced-with-a-tabor had run, in a madness of spoilt hope. To Chavir, in some unintelligible way, the imprint of her running feet shone clear as fire on the paving.)

In the wall, the signs of recent bricklaying were visible enough to any who might look for them.

Chavir did so.

Then he looked up the height of the wall, up to the somber bestial shoulder of the hill. All now was dusk. Even sound had darkened there; not a hint of leaves or water.

Chavir put his foot against the wall, at a foolish angle, the sole flat on the stonework and the bricks.

Then he put the second foot there.

First one foot, then the other foot, in their shoes of blanched leather.

To see him, it appeared so simple, you would quite believe it. His robe hung back, his hyacinthine hair, that, too. He moved in an exact horizontal. He held his arms straightly to his sides. Like a fly, Chavir walked up the wall.

(If any *did* see, they closed their shutters and their eyes.)

The maidens who had gone on to the hill expecting all manner of unusual delights had died, every one, of terror. They had been petrified with fear, so their muscles turned to stone, their bones to rock, their blood to rain, and their hearts were stopped.

The jhardamorjh came like nightfall at sunset or in the yellow hour of noon. It was so black, so huge, so terrible. It had the body of a giant horse, four legs that were the struts of giant eagles, it had gigantically an eagle's head, with a beak of basalt. Its hide was like pitch and its feathers like pitchy wire, its eyes molten. Cruel and mindless, it towered there, and the shadows fled from it and left it a composite of shadows and blackness, without equal.

The sacrifices did not cry out *Where is the glorious and beautiful reward? Where is fulfillment, where delight?* They only died. Which said it all.

But Ezail, the last sacrifice, stood and gazed up at the living tower of the beast. Perhaps without knowing why she did say something. She said this:

"You were meant for me. *You are mine.*"

It was no less than a fact.

Those centuries ago when the demon Prince Hazrond had wooed the daughter of Azhrarn, Azhriaz the Goddess—what had he done, Hazrond? He had mated a mare to an eagle, and from the mare's egg bred up the mare's first child, a horse with wings, to tempt the lady to his suit. But that gift Azhriaz had refused, for she refused Hazrond. The second being in the egg, however, the mare's second child, the little horse with the eagle's legs and head, cast out on the world above, became the pet of a blind girl, her house-bird, set to guard her. And guard her it had, and found thereby the means to swell itself into such a creature that men fled in fear.

But the blind girl grew old. She became an old blind woman, and at length she died.

By then, there were stories of her, and of her guardian beast. So humankind came and made offerings. And over the years they built her a tomb of marble with golden doors, and planted groves and quarried waters and put up golden effigies and shrines, and hid there offerings also. But the beast which roamed the hill, that they avoided. "It is a god, and she was its priestess. We must appease them." In time, though the beast was never seen below the hill; they walled it in, for gods are best kept behind some fence, an altar, or the sky, or bars. In time, too, a city spread from the hill's foot, for it was reckoned a place of power. But the tradition of some mighty thing, which must be honored and which must be avoided—that remained. And at length, in the fashion of myth, they gave the god every seventh year a bride. They dedicated all their women to the dream of this, and their whole city to the forgotten truth. The entire area became a votive offering. Living there about the hill, they worshipped by every deed and word, since by every deed and word the hill was invoked—through *not* being looked at, through *not* being spoken of. And since they prospered, and since the marvels of the city were renowned, they knew they had done well. While all day long, the black beasts of stone at the city gates made their hourly hymn, heard far and wide. And the visitors said, "What is that hill?" Or they said, "What is the Exaltation?"

But the maidens given to the god, seeing the jhardamorjh, they petrified and their hearts stopped. Therefore what would have become of them otherwise goes unknown. Or what the beast itself thought when it came on them, and witnessed their extremity. For was the beast not still the pet of the little blind girl, none other than "Birdy," the mare's second child, who had stayed to guard the house?

Do you spurn my gift? had said Hazrond. *It is you I spurn,* said Azhriaz. But now the soul of Azhriaz resided in the body of the dwarf girl, Ezail, and Ezail said to the forgotten second portion of the gift: I accept you. *You are mine.*

And Birdy lowered that benighted head of wiry bitumen feathers, and sighed a burning sigh. It beat back the leaves upon the trees, and ruffled up the goose pond where once real geese had sipped and pecked.

Then Ezail seated herself on the lawn, and taking off her necklace of amethysts began to play with it.

A colossal shadow, the jhardamorjh approached her. It stood at her side and bent its head to see. Ezail raised the beads and rubbed them on the hard beak, gently. Ezail leaned on one of the great legs, with the splayed talons about her, while the beast mouthed the beads carefully, letting each one fall back into her hand.

This was how Chavir found them, when he came walking up through the groves in the night, with the rising moon on his shoulder like a lyre.

"Now," said Chavir, "in the stories, the hero must slay the monster and rescue from death the maiden." Chavir frowned. "But I have neither sword nor dagger." He plucked a branch from the ancient trees. "This must do."

And going to the jhardamorjh, Chavir touched it lightly with the branch at the throat and on the side. (The eyes of the jhardamorjh only smoldered. It did nothing, but let the last bead from its beak into Ezail's palm.) "That seen to," said Chavir, seating himself close to the dwarf girl, and leaning on another leg of the jhardamorjh, "it comes to me I have my own story to tell."

Yet some while they only sat there, he and she, with the beast at their backs, and the three looked up into the sky where all the stars hung on the vine of night.

Then Chavir did tell her.

"It seems that once I was some other, but in order that this moment might be, I allowed myself to go down into the womb of a woman, and to wake there the unborn rose of her child. And in that rose of flesh I was carried out into the world of men, and there I grew and was Chavir, who wears your colors of blue and black, as you wear mine, my marigold girl."

Then Ezail answered Chavir, and she did not speak by any means as ever she had spoken before.

"But, dear friend, you have not slain the beast. And should the maiden perhaps be beauteous?"

"Oh, you are beauteous," said he. "As a crone you were beautiful to me, and I, in the old double guise, the two-faced foul one, was to you a handsome lover. Is that not so?"

"No doubt. But it was my will to live as I have lived, to be as I am. And also to exist without your love, for I am due this deprivation, after the other."

"Beloved," said he, "grant me a boon."

"No."

"Grant me that you will allow me to free you, for this one life only. To be with me."

"No," she said again.

"We shall be mortals. We must die. What harm? Our days are short."

"Beloved," said she, "do not distract me from my course."

"There is all time," said he. "All time to work out your plan. But on this occasion, play again with me the game of love. And the game of death will end it all too soon."

"Now," said Ezail, "should I give in with such slight protest?"

"It is you yourself called me Breaker of Chains."

Above, the stars blazed motionless, the moon flew slowly upward. The vast world of the Flat Earth lay between its mountains and its seas, robed in panther black, and jeweled with the lights of mankind. And from however many thousands of towers did the dreamers and the scholars scan heaven for a trace of gods and fortune, and in how many millions of hearts did the forgotten knowledge of all things seethe and sleep. While in the forests the animals of the night went to and fro, and lipped the streams and hunted and danced, and in the cities animal man went on at his feasts and lusts. While in the tombyards lay the dusts of all greeds and sorrows, and under the white lilies of the woods and fields, the white bones, and in the secret dark of how many men waited the seed of beginning and in how many a folded calyx of a woman's womb the phantom of new life. While over all blazed the motionless stars and the slow moon flew upward.

Presently, there came down a wooded hill, and out of a high wall that burst asunder with no sound, a giant beast, both horse and eagle, black as jet, treading soft as an autumn wind. And before the beast, leading it by a rope of grass, walked a handsome young man, blue of eye and black of hair, in shoes of blanched leather and a garment of purplish dye. But up on the beast's remote back rode a slender lovely girl, tall and pale like a lotus, clad in white, with hair the color of marigolds.

Through the city of Jhardamorjh then, they took their silent path, over the paved streets, between the houses and the parks. At the gate, if nowhere else, possibly they were seen, or possibly not, being too extraordinary to notice. Nevertheless, the city gates were opened, and out onto the road they passed, where the obelisks and icons led away towards the south.

But the sorcerous clockwork beasts of the gate, they made no sign, and gave no cry, for it was night still, and not the hour for it.

Of the rest, nothing further is said, save that lovers love and live and, in due season, as all men must, they also die. And so with Ezail and Chavir who had been Sovaz and Oloru, Azhriaz and Chuz. For such was and is mortal life, mortal death. But for love, who can predict or measure, plot, ascribe, or declare an end. Love is one of the immortals.